ICE MECHANIC

LUCKY STRIKERS BOOK ONE

LIA BEVANS

COPYRIGHT

This is a work of fiction. Similarities to real people, places or events are entirely coincidental.

ICE MECHANIC
Copyright © 2024 Lia Bevans
Written by Lia Bevans
Edited by Jalulu Editing
Cover by Nisa Sanchez

CHAPTER ONE

CHANCE

My veins buzz the moment I step into the rundown stadium. One-by-one, the lights thud on. Some of them flicker a few times in silent protest, reluctant to shine on me.

That's a metaphor for my life if I've ever seen one.

I take a big sniff, the scents both foreign and familiar. Nothing beats the dry, crisp air in the stadium. The perfect circumference of the rink. The way the lights bounce against the ice. The way the seats smell like varnish and W-D40...

I wrinkle my nose.

Actually, that smell is new.

"Ack!" A thin black man wearing a jumper streaked in oil explodes into my line of vision. Sharp brown eyes land on me, narrow slightly and then widen. "Well I'll be."

"Hey." I slip right into my people-greeting persona, tucking away my fidget spinner and reaching out for a handshake.

"Oh, I..." He swipes his hands on the sides of his pants and then hesitates. "I'm Bobby Hewitt. I'm a huge fan and I really want to shake that hand, but you mind saving it for later?"

"I'll save it with interest."

His smile widens a tad. "Wow." His eyes gleam. "Chance McLanely. The Clairvoyant in the flesh."

I rub the back of my neck. "The Clairvoyant. Haven't heard that name in a while."

Bobby laughs and mimics the movement of a skater on the ice. "Man, you knew where the puck was going ten years before it got there. You were on a roll before the…" His eyes shift away. "Uh, before everything."

Something sharp pierces my heart.

Before you got suspended…

Before…

It's agony to know that my plummet from the top is the marker of my life.

Before the league.

After the league.

But my chapter isn't done. I'll walk through hot stones in flowing lava to reclaim what's mine.

Joining The Lucky Strikers is my first lava-soaked step.

"Uh," Bobby's eyes dart to the ground and he chuckles awkwardly, "Look at me yapping. You must be here to see Max."

I nod and notice his oil-stained hands. "Were you fixing something?"

"No, no. Well, kinda. I'm the Zamboni driver, but the stupid machine's been breaking down left and right and the mechanics haven't been able to find the problem so I'm here reading up on engines like I know anything about, oh… here I go talking too much again. Let me show you to the office."

"I know where it is," I assure him.

His eyebrows hike. "Then why'd you come this way?"

I glance at the rink.

"Ah." He lifts an oil-stained finger. "Gotta make your introduction to the lady."

I chuckle. "I'll see you around, Bobby."

He waves and goes back to his Zamboni-fixing research. I continue to the admin area.

You got this, Chance. Go get 'em.

Despite the self-talk, my nerves attack me like those defensemen at last year's Halloween charity game.

Heart? Palpitating.

Lips? Trembling.

Fingers? Fidget-spinning.

After one more tug, I shove the fidget spinner back into my pocket, paste on my don't-care smile and blow open the door marked 'TEAM MANAGER'.

"McLanely!" A man twice the size of a defenseman in the Canadian league lights up at the sight of me.

"Max." I smirk.

Max Mahoney springs out of his chair so fast, it spins like a top before careening into the glass window facing the arena. He launches at me, grabs my arm and pulls me in for a bear hug.

I'm 6'4" and used to towering over people, so it's an odd sensation to be looking up at anyone but I do have to tilt my chin up to grin at Max.

"I thought you got lost in traffic!" Max bellows.

"What traffic? I didn't even see a single traffic light driving down here."

"We have a traffic light," Max says haughtily, like it's some kind of flex. "It's over on Howard and Green." He pats me on the back. "Have you settled in yet?"

"Yeah, man. Don't worry about me."

"Worrying about you is kinda my job." He smirks. "By the way, where are you staying?"

"Somewhere with an elevator and housekeeping."

"Long term, that's going to get old. If you haven't found any rentals yet, you can always room with me."

"Once in this lifetime was more than enough, buddy."

"Door's always open as they say." He laughs. "I know you

didn't have much time to prepare for the season, but I have all confidence in your skills."

"Is that my official welcome?"

"Wasn't good enough?" Max coughs and then spreads his hands wide. "We're over-the-moon that you chose to join the Lucky Strikers, Chance."

"He didn't *choose* us. He had nowhere else to go," someone mumbles.

The smile freezes on my face, and I glance over my shoulder. I was told I'd only be meeting the manager today, but I'm not surprised to see a few guys from the team lined up and waiting for me. Their faces are tense, frowns hard as the puck that makes or breaks our game.

Max coughs, "Chance, meet the, uh, the Welcoming Committee."

I hope this Welcoming Committee also serves death penalty inmates their last meal. They'd do a bang-up job.

Facing my teammates fully, I tip my chin up in greeting.

No one returns it.

Max points to a man wearing multiple gold chains and a gold ring on his finger. "That's Cooper Theilan. The guy in the Hello Kitty Crocs beside him is Viking Renthrow. They're our two best forwards."

I'd have guessed by their confident stance. Charging in to retake possession of the puck takes a certain level of daring. You can't be afraid of making mistakes or second guess yourself on the ice. From their haircuts to their style choices, it's clear Theilan and Renthrow are daring both inside and outside of the stadium.

"Ren Watson, our goalie," Max continues, nodding to two bulky men wearing gym clothes. "And that's Gunner Kinsey."

"Center," I say before Max can explain.

"Yeah." Max blinks in surprise.

I'd have known Gunner was the center even if I hadn't studied every game the Lucky Strikers played last season. Out of all my new teammates, he's the one staring at me like he wants me to fall into an open manhole walking down Main Street.

"Hey." My wave encompasses them all. "I'm Chance McLanely, your new captain."

Theilan, the guy dripping in gold, snorts.

Renthrow, Mr. Hello Kitty, rolls his eyes.

Watson, the goalie, folds his arms over his chest, showing enough muscle to prove he doesn't skimp on the protein shakes.

Gunner sneers. "A reject from the league gets team captain just by showing up?"

"Well…" Max begins.

"If the former team captain had done a better job, it wouldn't have been so easy to take the position."

Max coughs. "Ch-Chance, why don't you—"

"You want to take this outside, McLanely?" Gunner stalks toward me, his face reddening.

"No, there will be no fighting." Max waves his tree-trunk arms.

I flick my fingers at the window overlooking the arena. "We can talk on the ice."

"One on one, I'm going to chew you up and spit you out," Gunner hisses.

"No, no, no." I point to the others. "You need at least three of you guys if you want to do that."

Max smacks his forehead.

The other men get very tense.

Gunner scoffs. "You sure that big mouth of yours can survive outside the penalty box, McLanely?"

I stiffen.

Watson snorts out a laugh.

Renthrow and Theilan smirk.

Fingers fisting, I lunge forward. Max tries to wedge himself in front of me, but I sidestep him so I'm facing off with Gunner.

"You wanna know why I'm captain, Kinsey? Your center is putting up more of a fight here than on the ice." I point to

Theilan. "Your right winger is your only defense." To Renthrow. "Your left winger is right-handed and his back hand is insanely weak. So like I said, it'll take all three of you—"

"Alright, that's enough on the introductions for now. I need to speak with Chance privately."

No one moves because they're all too busy glaring a hole into my skull. Thankfully, eyeballs can't turn into jackhammers or my skull would be shattered on the floor.

"Ehem, gentlemen?" Max's voice turns firm. "You're dismissed."

Gunner stares me down. "See you on the ice."

"Looking forward to it."

The rest of the guys file out after Gunner.

The door clicks shut, and the silence that falls is so thick, it's suffocating.

"Make friends, I said." Max sinks into his chair and covers his face with his hands. "Be nice, I said. Why'd I waste my breath?"

"Putting it all out in the open is better for everyone. At least now we know where we stand."

"Did you *have* to antagonize the wingers too?"

I shrug. "You called me here to stir the pot, didn't you?"

"I didn't ask you to turn the pot over and dance on the chicken bones."

That's a vivid image.

"Gunner's got a grip on this team and you know it. You're in as shaky a position as I am."

"Oh, no, McLanely. After all that," he gestures to the door where my new teammates stormed out, "you're in a much, *much* worse place than me."

Maybe so.

But the thing is, I'm not here to make friends. I'm here to claw my way back to the league and nothing in this Podunk town of Lucky Falls, USA can stop me.

CHAPTER TWO

APRIL

THE RICKETY SOUND OF AN ENGINE TURNING OVER AND STALLING fills the air. I grin maniacally at the scans on the computer, reading the lines like my sister with the latest social media gossip.

"I hate having to pull off B-pillar panels just to get to a wire."

"In English please," screams an exasperated voice. "You can't expect regular people to understand that gibberish."

"It's not gibberish. It's science. Mechanical engineering, to be exact." I tuck away a rebellious curl that fell out of my ponytail. "A car is an intricate ecosystem that requires knowledge of chemistry, physics—"

"Blah, blah, blah." My sister pops an exaggerated yawn and shuts her phone off. "April, I can't film like this. Seriously. I love you, but this is not what the people want."

"The 'people' want us in bras and shorts bending over their cars at a car wash, not fixing their engines." The voice that echoes across our garage is followed by the *click, clack* of stilettos marching in a familiar rhythm.

I smile when a slim, perfectly gym-toned arm hooks around my neck and squeezes. At the end of that arm, a plastic bag dangles from perfectly manicured fingers.

"Rebel, you *angel*," I mutter as I grab the bag filled with my lifeblood.

"Yes, yes, sing my praises." She trades the bag of donuts for the OCB scanner.

"I'll take that," May says, stealing the donuts in a classic younger sister move.

Hands free, I hurry to the giant sink against the wall. Pushing up the sleeves of my oversized jumper, I grab the lavender scented, industry-grade soap that Rebel special orders for us and lather my hands.

When I return, the donut box is already open and May is staring, slack-jawed at it.

"Are those chocolate covered, jelly-filled donuts?"

"Mm-hm," Rebel answers distractedly, her eyes glued to the OCB screen.

"But they sell out by, like, six every morning! There's even a line…" May holds up a precious donut in wonder. "How did you do this?" When Rebel doesn't immediately answer, my sister turns to me, her brown hair bouncing as she demands, "How?"

"*Doof muf tig*," I mumble, my mouth crammed with delicious baked goodness.

"What?" May scrunches her nose.

I wave my hand in front of Rebel's nose. Swallowing before I speak again, I urge her, "Do the thing."

"Oh." Rebel startles. "Hold this." She shoves the scanner at my sister who takes it and watches expectantly.

Batting her baby blues, Rebel moves her long, voluminous blonde hair from one side of her head to the other. Glancing up from beneath thick lashes, she smiles and holds my sister's gaze. Coquettishly, she bites down on her bottom lip and giggles before cooing, "Please."

"Ew," May says.

As if a switch went off, Rebel drops the act. She takes possession of the device again and refocuses on the scan. "It doesn't work on girls."

"But it worked on Phil," I sing-song.

"Wait. T-that's it? That's how you got the donuts?" May's jaw drops.

"Isn't it the best?" I say excitedly, pulling out another donut. They're so bad for me, but they taste *so* good. "I've been trying to charm Phil for years, that old geezer. I even offered to do free oil changes in exchange for these donut. As soon as Rebel did the thing, we've had zero problems."

My sister's eyes gleam with an idea and she holds her phone up toward my business partner and co-mechanic. "Hey, Rebel. Why aren't you the face of our social media page? I think you're exactly what our demographic is looking for."

Rebel pushes the phone down. "I don't do social media. Ever. Besides, our demographic is everyone who has a car problem that no one else can solve."

"Exactly." I grab a relatively clean rag—which isn't saying much given all our rags, even Rebel's pink ones, are oil streaked—and wipe the chocolate off my hands.

May rolls her eyes. "Forget it. No filming today."

My smile plummets. "But you said promoting our store would be good for your résumé."

"It will, but I need to find another angle to promote the shop." She mumbles under her breath, "You'd think two female mechanics would be interesting enough, but you two…"

"Are special?" Rebel jumps in, showing off her picture-ready smile.

"Are really smart?" I supply.

"Are boring," May says.

"Hey!" I protest.

Just then, my phone rings.

I brighten. "Maybe it's a customer."

"It's probably spam or that creep who keeps calling and

hanging up," Rebel says with a shrug. "I'll change off so we can test those spark plugs."

While Rebel scampers off and May pilfers another donut, I answer the call. "Hello, this is The Pink Garage. How can I help you?"

"Hi, April. This is Bobby from King Stadium."

"Oh, hi, Bobby." I walk a few paces away. "How are you? How's your car been running since that hiccup on the 1-24?"

"Great. Great. You ladies did a bang-up job. You did so well, that, uh… I'd like to ask you for some more help. You see, the Zamboni's gone in—"

"Again?"

"Yes, again. The new owner of the stadium has it on the list to buy a new one, but he's trying to get the team ready for the season and it could be a while. You know how that goes. Anyway, I can't do my job well if I don't have a working machine and the athletes can't practice on choppy ice, can they?"

"No, absolutely not," I agree.

"So, I was hoping you could maybe pop on by and help me service the thing."

"Of course. I could come over right now."

"Well, see, the thing is…"

Unease spreads through me. "Yes?"

"You know Gunner's uncle, Stewart Kinsey?"

I bristle.

"He's who we usually work with. It's nothing personal. It's just that I don't want to step on Gunner's toes, the team being one family and all…"

Unpleasant memories roar up in my head, bringing the taste of bile. I actually *do* know how territorial the Kinsey family can be.

"Are you asking me to fix it on the down low, Bobby?" I ask quietly.

"If it's no imposition, I'd mighty appreciate that."

Something about the request rubs me the wrong way. I don't

relish feeling like a thief sneaking through the back door for a job, but it's so difficult saying no to Bobby. He's such a sweet soul. Besides, we need the money.

"Alright. Text me when the coast is clear and I'll come by."

"Neat. Thanks, April. You're the best."

Rebel's voice sounds behind me, "Who was that?"

"Just another timid customer who doesn't want the Kinseys to know they're calling us." I turn and shake my head at my best friend.

She scowls. "You'd think the Kinseys own this town the way everyone's scared to get on their bad side."

"On the bright side, everyone loves an underdog," May says. Tapping her bicycle, she grins mischievously. "Are you heading out now? Want a ride?"

"No, thanks. I've still got some stuff to do around here." I pinch her cheek. "Ride safe, squirt."

"Stop calling me squirt. I'm twenty-one."

"Still a squirt."

"Squirts can't legally drink."

"Legal squirts can." I wink.

She groans and mounts her bike. "See you at home, you doof. Later, Rebel!"

Rebel grunts, focused as she is on the car.

For the next few hours, we work together to diagnose the problem. We're making great strides so when Bobby texts me the last thing I want to do is leave.

Rebel offers to go in my place, but I reject it. First of all, she doesn't want to leave in the middle of a diagnosis any more than I do. Second, I don't want her knowing about Bobby's request or she'll throw an absolute fit.

"Be back soon," I say, waving and grabbing the keys for my personal truck.

"Aren't you going to take the company car?" Rebel asks.

I freeze halfway to the door. My eyes fly to the bright pink car that we invested most of our savings into re-painting. Rebel was convinced it could act as a mobile advertisement but she's the only one brave enough to ride around in that ostentatious Pepto Bismol on wheels.

"Uh…" Pretending my phone is ringing, I put the device to my ear and yell loudly, "Hello? Yes, this is April. Would I be interested in learning more about alien abduction insurance? Why yes I would."

"You're such a bad liar, April!" Rebel yells at my back as I dive into my car and speed down the road.

I'm not just a bad liar.

I'm also a pushover.

But hey, no one's ever died from either of those things… I think.

The ride across town doesn't take long and before I've belted my lungs out to two Whitney Houston classics, I'm already pulling into the stadium's parking lot.

Inside, the arena is dark except for the rink which has the spotlights on. I'm surprised to see a player skating back and forth this late at night.

For some reason, my body can't turn away from the skater. The way he moves on the ice is mesmerizing. Someone as tall as a giraffe should be all gangly knees and discoordination, especially when he's pushing around a stick half his size. Instead, he's graceful, skilled, and totally in control of his body.

The skater successfully pushes the puck around the last cone and skates to the other side of the rink. He leans against the rail and takes off his helmet.

I have a mini heart attack at the sight of an out-of-this-world, hewn to perfection, *David* sculpture of a face. The mini heart attack turns into a full-on 911 emergency when he throws his head back. The harsh fluorescent light glitters against the spray of sweat from his hair. Little dots of light fall around him like stars that flash brilliantly before disappearing.

I'm suddenly reminded of that scene in *The Little Mermaid*

when Ariel surfaces to croon about wanting to be a part of the human world.

Except this guy is no slim, red-headed mer-gal.

He's every bit a Prince Eric with his black hair and ginormous height. I watch as he skates to pick up the cones and set them behind the divider. Even in the bulky hockey uniform, I can tell his shoulders are about the size of two bus engines...

"April."

"Gah!" I shriek.

My voice reverberates around the stadium and I panic when I see the hockey player look up in my direction.

Mayday, mayday! My brain cells fly the coop, and I do what every empty-headed woman would when faced with flight or fight.

I go with option c.

"April?" Bobby whispers, staring at the top of my head which is all he can see since I cannon-balled right into the ground and hunkered beneath the benches.

"Where's the Zamboni?" I whisper back, fighting back a blush that's so hot, it'll probably melt a few cartilages in my nose.

"This way," Bobby says.

Thankfully, he leads me *away* from the rink.

Away from the new hockey player who's a little too hot to be playing on frozen water.

Away is good.

Because something tells me *Prince Eric On Ice* is a show I would pay to watch, but in real life, it'd be way too much drama for me.

CHAPTER
THREE

CHANCE

MOST ATHLETES HAVE A QUIRK, SOMETHING COMPLETELY INANE THAT they have to do before or after the game to ward off negativity.

My quirk has become a lifestyle.

Every time I do something new, I mark it with time in the rink.

The first time I rode a bike, I went skating immediately after and fell a hundred times more than I did on my bike.

The tradition started then and it didn't stop.

The skating, not the falling.

Tonight, I've put in my time to mark my first day in the Lucky Strikers. As I sit on the bench and swap my skates for sneakers, I feel that familiar buzz. So I sit there and just... bask in it.

For a while after getting kicked out of the league, I had the thought that my time as a professional hockey player was over.

Even if this town isn't where I want to be, even if none of my teammates want me here, I still feel immensely grateful to have a chance at getting my toe back in the door.

My phone buzzes.

Mom.

I stiffen. My thumb hovers over the answer button but, in the end, I send the call to voicemail. I love my mom, but I already know what she has to say and it's not a discussion I want to have right now.

Slinging my skates over my shoulder, I head straight for the showers.

Man, this exhaustion is the best kind. No thoughts in your head, no worries, no anxiety. Just the bone-deep contentment of getting in a good workout.

No, it's more than just a workout.

It's what the ice does to me. I love everything about hockey. The balance of skating and skill. The plays. The teamwork. The speed of the puck. The juxtaposition of being in the ring. Of fire and ice. Of hot and cold. Of sweat on chilled skin.

It's like coffee hitting my veins. If I wasn't so tired, I'd crawl back on the ice for one more sip, but my aching muscles warn me not to do anything that idiotic.

After grabbing a towel, I strip off my hockey gear and whip my shirt off. Passing by the mirror, I notice all the nicks and scars from my years of ice time. Hockey took its chunk of my flesh. I'm still waiting for it to take a few teeth too. It can take all of them if it wants to. I'll play with dentures.

After the shower, I towel off and change into a simple T-shirt and basketball shorts.

My stomach growls. The steak I spotted in the hotel's room service booklet is calling my *name.*

A chirp sounds again.

Mom.

I decide to answer because if I don't, she's going to keep calling. Then she'll send a team out here to check on me and I don't want that.

"Hey, ma."

"Darling," her impatient voice fills my ears, "are you coming to the Children's Foundation Gala next month? You haven't sent in your RSVP."

I sigh heavily and walk outside to my car. "Mom, I'm not available for any social events. I'm focusing on hockey."

"Chance, do you really need to dedicate all your time to a little rag-tag team in the minors? They're so far behind, they drafted you in the off season."

It's a fair assessment, but it still makes me defensive. "They're a solid team. With a few tweaks, they could be a real force. And either way, I'm only here temporarily."

"Oh, honey. I thought the league never lets you back in after they kick you out?"

I cringe because that stings. Hard.

"Don't worry. I'll figure it out on my own."

"But you don't have to." I hear the scolding behind her words. "You should come home so we can figure it out together."

Correction, I should come home so mom and dad can convince me to trade my skates for a suit and tie.

The Lambo dad gifted me unlocks with a chirp and I slip inside. "Fine. As soon as things slow down around here, I'll pop in for a visit."

"I'll see you at the charity gala then?"

Rats. I fell into her trap. Mom is the daughter of an heiress, but that alone didn't turn her trust fund into the money-printing machine that it is today. She's diabolically smart.

"I didn't say that…" I hedge.

"How long will you be on this little hockey team anyway?"

"Mom…"

"Darling, you really should have taken your father's offer and joined the company. The CFO position was wide open. He had the corner office cleaned and everything. It would have solved all your problems. Those nasty tabloids can't say anything about a powerful CFO, can they?"

I massage the bridge of my nose. "There are plenty more qualified, experienced people than me who should be the CFO."

"But they're not family." Mom tsks. "Do you know why we're doing all this? It's for you and your sister. You're the ones who'll be running the company when we're gone."

Oh, I hope not. I'd rather run into Gunner and the rest of the welcoming committee in a dark alley in a post apocalyptic earth than spend the rest of my life scribbling my signature on documents for a living.

"Mom, I have to run. I'll call you later."

"I'll see you at the gala. Remember you need to bring a plus one. And not one of those little fan girls who can't carry a proper conversation either. Someone nice. So... someone you don't normally date."

Oof, mom's on a roll tonight.

"Noted, ma."

"Love you honey, buh-bye." She hangs up.

Feeling ten times more exhausted than I did after my training, I start my car and wait for that beautiful purr.

Instead, there's a sad cough, like the sound of someone holding on to life and losing that battle fast.

"Oh, honey, what's wrong?" I rub the dashboard. "You're not feeling well?"

Another attempt at a start.

It chokes again.

I climb out of my car and open the hood, but the cavern is strangely empty. Tired, hungry and getting crankier by the second, I call Max.

He answers on the first ring. "'Sup, Captain."

"Max, do you know a mechanic I can call? My car won't start."

"Oh no. Do you need a ride? I'm at the Tipsy Tuna with a few business people, but I should be done soon."

"No, I don't want to put you out. I just need a mechanic."

"Gunner's folks run a mechanic shop. I can call them over—"

"Nope. I'd rather not mess with anyone related to Kinsey right now. Isn't there another mechanic in town?" I reach for my fidget spinner and give it a whirl, but my nerves keep getting tangled inside.

"Hold on a second. I think Bobby mentioned someone had just opened…" I hear papers shuffling. "Let me see if I can get in touch with them and I'll call you back."

"Thanks." I huff out a breath and grip the elevated hood again, wishing I knew how to fix a car.

"Need some help?" A soft, feminine voice sounds behind me.

A glance over my shoulder reveals a petite woman with a curly brown ponytail pulled through the back of a baseball cap. She's wearing a flannel shirt opened on top of a tank top and baggy jeans.

The brim of the cap hides her face but, when she lifts her chin, I crash headfirst into sea-foam green eyes set above a faint sprinkle of freckles that follow right across an adorable nose. When I get enough of counting those freckles, I glance down at her mouth and am totally blown away.

She's got the face of a fairy with those emerald eyes and delicate cheekbones, and those lips are definitely my wish come true. They're pink, plump and perfect.

Well, almost perfect. Their only flaw is that they're not tipped up in a smile.

"Hello?" She plants her hands on her hips. "I asked if you need help."

I realize I'd been too busy drooling over her face and respond, "No thanks."

"It looks like your car won't start."

I lean against the side of the car. Even if it's broken, it's still a luxury car and that usually greases the wheels of every conversation with the opposite gender.

"Don't worry your pretty little head about it." I flash her a smile that's been known to cause a swoon or two.

"You're not from around here, are you?" Her tone has a hint of suspicion.

"Yeah, I'm new. Just rolled in today. Still don't know my way around."

She makes a noncommittal sound in her throat.

"Maybe when my car is up and running, you can take me on a tour? Show me around? By the way, my name is—"

"Are you sure you don't need my help? Last offer."

I blink unsteadily.

"Suit yourself." Without another word, she turns sharply and stalks off.

So… that went well.

As I watch her get into her pickup truck, my phone rings.

"Hey, Max," I mumble distractedly. "Did you get that mechanic?"

"Yeah," Max says cheerfully.

My eyes lock on the truck that's currently speeding toward the exit like the driver wants to run me over, but she'll settle for the pottery on either side of the ticket booth.

"Like you requested, I got the only other mechanic in town. Well, I asked Bobby to call them. He should be contacting them right about now."

"Ah, I see."

The pickup at the gate suddenly stops.

"What's going on?" I mutter, straightening up and paying close attention.

"Huh?" Max says.

"Nothing." Perplexed, I notice her brake lights blinking to life.

And then she reverses back to me.

"Later, bro." I hang up, feeling genuinely excited to see her again and not entirely sure why.

Her window winds down and she peers at me, eyes narrowed and lips pursed as if contemplating whether she should spare the potted plant and return to me as her original target.

"Finally ready to exchange names?" I ask, flashing another, encouraging grin.

"I'll go first," she says stiffly.

"Of course. Ladies first."

She parks the car, shoves her door open and slams to the ground with a huff. "First name—'your'. Last name 'mechanic'."

CHAPTER FOUR

APRIL

"You're a mechanic?" Prince Eric says with an emphasis on the 'you'.

Although I've gotten this very reaction a million times, it's still annoying.

"Could you step back... please?" I throw out the 'please' through gritted teeth.

"You?"

The flabbergasted look on his face is, frankly, off-putting.

Rather than answer, I use the rear wheel of my pickup to mount myself up. Wiggling my sneakers forward for balance, I fold back the tarp. The loud rustling sound is like a crack of thunder in the empty parking lot.

Sticking my hand in the bed, I push away the boxes of clothes I've been meaning to drop off at our local Goodwill and grab my toolbox. The moment I swing it over my shoulder and prepare to launch to the ground, Prince Eric appears beneath me.

"Whoa. Let me help you with that," he says, muscular arms reaching for the kit.

"I've got it," I mutter. "Just get out of the way."

Despite my words, Prince Ursula stops right where I'm catapulting myself and my heavy toolbox from the bed of the truck.

I'm already mid-jump, so all I can do is let out a loud, goat-like *blaaah!* as my toolbox makes a very clear and axe-saw-murdering arc toward the side of Prince Eric's head.

Thankfully, his athleticism kicks in before I can end up on the nightly news for bludgeoning our newest Lucky Striker outside the stadium.

He leaps back, missing my tool box by a hair.

Unfortunately, he doesn't account for the fact that *I'm* attached to the toolbox.

There's no time for a course correct. Our bodies collide in a mash of arms, legs, and more embarrassing goat noises.

"Are you okay?" he asks, his arm secure around my waist and his eyes intent on me. They're a dark, swirling blue. Like the ocean right before nightfall.

I massage my temple, feeling a dull ache in my head. I'm pretty sure ramming headfirst into a brick wall would have had the same effect. What's this guy made of? Steel?

"How many fingers am I holding up?" He waves a peace sign under my nose.

"I'm fine," I say, scrambling up to prove the point.

He sits up more slowly. "Are you sure?"

"Just hand me your keys."

He climbs to his feet and takes out the keys, but he hesitates when I move to take them.

"What?" I huff, letting my impatience seep in.

I never should have listened to Bobby when he called for another favor. *'Can you please help us out, April. My friend is new to the team and new to town. He doesn't know anyone yet and now his car's broken down. If anyone can get it running again it's you.'*

I really need to stop letting Bobby pull on my heartstrings.

"I just…" He slips a hand into his pocket, "have you worked on a car like this before?"

"Seriously?"

"I just got it a week ago and it's really expensive..."

I'm not one to jump on soapboxes. I find people ten times more complex than cars and I'd rather stick to four wheels and an engine over having an argument about feminism any day.

However...

And that's a big however...

He's a real-life Prince Eric, so it's disappointing that he had to open his mouth and ruin the kind, princely-pro-women-in-STEM fantasy I didn't even know I had about Ariel's human husband.

Throwing my hands up, I step back. "I'm sorry. I can't help you. Why don't you call the Kinseys? They have a mechanic shop and a twenty-four-hour tow service..."

"No, no. Wait. Here." He hands over the keys with his eyes squeezed shut like he's giving away the code to the family vault.

I let out a frustrated breath. Everything in me wants to storm away, but it's not every day I get *this* close to the engine of a 1966 Miura. I *have* to take a peek. I just *have* to.

It's difficult to stay professional and I'd say I'm about thirty percent fan-girl by the time I walk over and uncover the mid-engine. An absolutely *glorious* system unravels before me and my muscles tense in appreciation.

"What's that?" Prince Eric walks beside me and then freezes. His eyes skitter to me and back to the car. "Is that the engine?"

I nod, too dazzled to speak.

"Then... what's that." He points to the front hood that he'd been leaning against when I first saw him outside.

"They call it a frunk," I explain. "It's the trunk, but it's at the front."

"That explains why I didn't see an engine. I thought I'd been sabotaged."

I can't help it. I giggle. "You thought someone carried away an entire *engine?*"

"Go ahead. Laugh at me. I deserve it." His lips tremble as if he's seeing the humor in it too. "I was stupid. And not only about the frunk." He turns fully to me. "I'm sorry. About earlier. I've never met a female mechanic."

I shrug. In the presence of a '66 Miura, it's hard to stay angry. "At this point, I'm used to it."

"I feel like an idiot," he says with a sheepish grin. There's something much more genuine about his smile this time. The way it lights up his eyes. The way it forms laugh lines around his mouth.

This is a completely different guy than the one asking me to take him on a tour of the town. And somehow, I like this version more.

"I've met worse." I shine my flashlight on the engine. "Actually, earlier, there was this guy in the parking lot whose car broke down and he rejected my help. Now that guy… that guy was a tool."

He smothers his smile, trying to look contrite, but it only makes him look mischievous.

"Guilty." He holds up both hands.

I return the smile—it's really hard not to—and turn my attention back to diagnosing the problem.

A car says a lot about a man, so the fact that he owns a Lamborghini definitely hints at deep pockets. I'm talking *Journey To The Center of the Earth* deep. However, the fact that it's a 1966 Miura tells me that his kind of rich is also old and cultured. He has no need for the latest, flashiest vehicle to prove his net worth.

I wonder how much a hockey player makes. Whatever it is, I bet it's enough to cover my entire business loan and mortgage for the garage.

Thinking about my debts makes me turn off my fan-girl side completely and focus on solving the problem. Leaving the engine behind, I open the front door and check the dash.

"I know what's going on," I say.

"That was quick." His voice is closer than I expect so I twist around, only to come inches away from his face.

Prince Eric stares at me with frank, expressive eyes and I back up immediately, flustered for reasons that I don't want to interpret. Unfazed, he blinks naturally long lashes that I know for a *fact* Rebel pays a girl in the city $300 to install.

"There's nothing wrong with your engine," I say, clearing my throat.

"Don't tell me… was I really sabotaged?" His eyes narrow slightly and I can tell he has a few suspects on his list already. I wonder what he did to gain enemies after less than twenty-four hours in town.

"No, your immobilizer key is the issue. The key is malfunctioning." I press it a couple times to show him.

"But the car started." His eyebrows knit in confusion. "I pressed the button and it did what it usually does, and then it died seconds later. Are you sure?"

"A bad immobilizer doesn't mean the car won't start. It will, but the computer shuts down because of a corrupted signal from the immobilizer."

He tilts his head and I can imagine this is the expression my high school Calculus teacher saw on every face in class.

"See that?" I widen the door so he can peek in and view the dashboard. "That light that's flashing? That's telling you that your key fob has malfunctioned."

"So what's the solution?"

"Do you have another one?"

"It's at the hotel."

"You'll need to get it." I hand him the dud key. "Did you drop your key or have it around a very strong magnet?"

"I think I might have dropped it on the ice earlier."

My head bobs in understanding. "Yep. That's what got it. Come back with the other key fob, and you should be good as gold."

"Thank you." He pulls out his phone. "I don't have cash on me, but if you give me your bank number I can wire it—"

"It's okay. I didn't do anything."

"Are you kidding? If it weren't for you, I would have filed a report for a missing engine." He points to the frunk.

I laugh again. "Officer Derek would probably ask around for eye witnesses too. There aren't too many cars like yours around here." As I speak, I give the Miura a loving look.

"Really? It's all I've ever known. Collecting is kind of a family hobby."

My initial assessment was right. He does come from old wealth.

"I've got a bunch of these in storage back home. If any of them have a problem, I promise I'll drive them over to you."

He's just being nice, but the thought of working on more exotic cars fills me with a dopamine rush.

And maybe that's why, against my better judgement, I turn to Prince Eric and say, "Get in."

"In…?" He points to my car.

I walk around to the driver's side. "I'll take you to get that key fob."

CHAPTER FIVE

CHANCE

I messed up. Big time.

In my defense, fans have impersonated janitors and hotel employees to get access to me. I had one fan steal her father's police badge to sneak into the lockers.

If I'd seen the female mechanic wearing a jumpsuit or if I'd spotted a logo of a garage on her car, I *might* have been able to tell who she was.

Heavy on the *might*.

But I don't know many guys who would have seen a pretty woman in an unmarked vehicle and instantly assumed she knew her way around a Lamborghini engine.

No matter my excuses, I've learned my lesson: *keep this big mouth of mine shut.*

I don't speak a word as we drive into the heart of town. The stillness is awkward, but at least I don't have another chance to put my foot in my mouth.

I don't much like the taste of socks anyway.

She seems happy with the quiet and doesn't even turn on the

radio. Which is unfortunate. Because when my belly suddenly decides it wants to practice a yodel for the good of mankind, there's nothing to cover the noise.

Forest-green eyes shoot over to my reddening face and then down at my stomach. Her pretty mouth tightens at the corners, but she politely turns away without comment.

Shut up. I give my stomach the eyeball of doom, a skill I saw from my mother growing up when my sister and I were being particularly rowdy in church. But maybe I need more practice because my rebellious intestines change from a yodeler to a sperm whale that just. Won't. Shut up.

The pretty mechanic tightens her fingers around the steering wheel and shifts in her seat.

Since it would be impolite not to say anything now, I explain, "Uh… I haven't eaten since this morning."

"You were skating on an empty stomach?" Her shocked tone is louder than my stomach's next whale call.

"Did you see me training earlier?"

"No," she says quickly. Too quickly. A blush forms over her cheeks and makes her freckles stand out in the dim lighting of the dusk.

I wonder why she's lying. Is it possible her first impression of me *wasn't* as a clueless buffoon? Did she see me on the ice before then?

Something tells me she did.

And that blush tells me she was intrigued.

Or at least, reluctantly intrigued.

I lean forward but before I can ask more, she blurts, "There's a burger joint two streets down. The burgers are good and the price is reasonable."

I could very well tell her that a 'reasonable price' doesn't swing me one way or the other since I'd planned on dining at the hotel's restaurant with very little thought to what the cost would be.

I also don't tell her I can't eat greasy food when I'm training.

My stomach, appeased by the promise of sustenance, calms down and we make it to the burger joint in record time.

The burger joint looks like every diner across America, almost as if one guy shared a blueprint with his diner-owning buddies and no one bothered to change anything.

From the neon sign outside, to the red booths, to the glass window with the sprayed-on 'Bob's Burgers' logo, it strikes a chord of nostalgia.

My college teammates and I used to drive to the nearest truck stop after every away game, rewarding ourselves with milkshakes, burgers and questionably large servings of French fries.

"I'll wait out here," Tinkerbell says, pulling out her phone.

Yep, until I know her name, she's Tinkerbell—the fairy I had a somewhat questionable attraction to for an embarrassing number of years.

"Do you want anything? My treat." I offer.

She scrunches her nose and, at first, I think she'll turn me down. But then she shrugs and says, "My sister might be hungry since we had a light lunch. I'll come with you, but I'm paying for my own burger."

I grin because I have zero intentions of letting that happen. However, admitting that might send her skittering back to the truck, so I don't argue.

The moment I open the door of the diner, there's a stir. Gasps ripple like a wave with every step I take toward the counter.

"*Is that Chance McLanely.*"

"*Quick take a picture!*"

"*Is it really him?*"

I'm used to the whispers and walk confidently forward but soon realize I'm walking alone. I glance over my shoulder and see Tinkerbell hunkering back.

I tap her on the shoulder. "Everything okay?"

"Yeah, yeah. By the way, is your name Chance McLanely? Because if it is, I think you forgot to mention that you're *famous*."

"Not a hockey fan, I see." I chuckle. If she was, she'd have recognized me on sight.

"Not a sports fan in general. Especially if there's violence and fighting in the middle of a game."

I cringe. Given her view on violence in sports, her not recognizing me is a blessing. If she'd known about me, about… everything, she probably wouldn't have bothered to help me with my car.

Eyes alert, she huffs past me and flings herself at the counter.

"I'll have a double cheeseburger with onions, chopped not sliced. And no mayo please."

After tossing her order like a star pitcher in a losing game, Tinkerbell ducks her head.

Hissing at me, she demands, "Order and let's get out of here. I think people are taking our pictures without permission."

I smirk at her aggrieved tone and look around. She's right. Everyone has their phones up, recording us.

I walk to the counter and give my order. Sadly, the clerk isn't writing anything down because she's too busy staring at me.

"Did you get that?" I ask with a patient smile.

"Sorry. I just… I can't believe you're here in Lucky Falls, the town where *nothing* ever happens." She bounces on the tips of her toes. "So the rumors are true? You're playing with the Lucky Strikers this season?"

I smile, not admitting it outright. Max wants to have a big press conference and make a splash of it.

Not that it'll do him much good, but all publicity is good publicity, I guess.

Stars in her eyes, the cashier shoves a pen and the corner of her work apron at me. "Can you sign this?"

"Sure." I scribble my name shakily. It's been a while since a fan has come at me with anything but disdain.

Is it small town hospitality? Or is it that I've been so focused on my losses, I hadn't seen the support that still remained?

She leans in and whispers, "I don't care what anyone says. You were the best part of every game and they robbed you of that cup. I can't wait until I see you in the league again."

My heart warms. "I appreciate that."

"Let me get your order." She taps it in when I repeat it and then personally comes around the counter. "I'll show you to your table. Wait here. I'll bring your order to you when it's finished."

"Thanks," I peek at her tag, "Shaina."

She blushes.

I start to walk after Shaina when, once again, I realize I'm missing a pint-sized fairy by my side.

Tinkerbell is still standing in place, looking dumbfounded.

"Tink," I gesture to her, "over here."

She blinks a couple times and follows me to the table.

I pluck some napkins from the dispenser because I'm a messy eater and there are never enough napkins. Tinkerbell slides into the booth across from me. People are still staring so she lifts the side of her flannel and ducks behind it.

"They'll stare even more if you act like that."

Her tongue darts out to swipe across her lips. Slowly, she drops her flannel and sits straighter. "What did you call me back there?"

"Back where?" I check my phone.

Still no call back from my agent.

Let's see. I called about six hours ago, so I'll try him again in another hour. If I keep calling, someone's gotta pick up, right?

"At the counter. What was it?" she demands.

"Oh. Tink? Short for Tinkerbell."

"My name isn't Tink."

"What is it then?" I set the phone down.

"It's April."

April. The end of hockey season. The season of balmy blue skies, fresh blooms and grass that's as green as her eyes.

"I'm Chance." I lean back, studying her.

"I gathered," she mumbles, eyes darting around.

I gesture to the onlookers. "You get used to it."

"Used to what? Being on display?"

I chuckle.

"Here's your order, Chance." The clerk from earlier sets our bags and drinks before us. "I added a little dessert. On the house."

"You didn't have to do that."

"I did." She lifts both fists in a 'cheer up' gesture. "You got this."

I smile and leave her a generous tip.

When I look up, I'm not surprised that April is already booking it for the car. A glance out the window shows her flannel shirt flapping like wings.

It's cute seeing her like this. She was so confident when inspecting my car that, somehow, she grew to ten feet tall. Now, she looks every bit of her petite frame.

With a nod at all the folks snapping pictures, I crash through the front door of the diner.

"Hey, April, wait up!" I jog toward her.

My calls are in vain because she's already come to a standstill.

And it's not because of me.

A scrawny guy has her by the wrist and is leaning way too close to her face.

The moment I see his hand on her, lightning strikes behind my eyes and thunder claps from somewhere in the distance.

I'm moving before I can really think it through.

One minute, I'm standing a distance away. The next, I'm holding April's wrist and dragging her behind me, going toe-to-toe with the guy in a mechanic jumpsuit.

"Who the h—" The guy's eyes widen when he sees my face. "Chance McLanely?"

"April," I say, turning to her. "You okay?"

She nods and slips her hand out of mine, massaging it lightly. The guy sidesteps me and approaches her again. "April, come on. Don't be like this."

"I said not now, Evan."

"How much longer are you going to ignore my calls?"

"Back off, man. She clearly doesn't want to talk to you." I shove his shoulder.

Eyes on the ground and voice a quiet croak, April says, "It's okay, Chance."

I passed third grade. I know the definition of 'okay'. And it's as clear as day that this isn't okay at all.

"Huge fan, McLanely. But give me and my girlfriend some space," Evan says.

My fingers curl at my sides because I instinctively dislike this guy. His beady eyes travel to my fists and he smirks.

"There's no sin bin in town, McLanely. Put your hand on me again and you're spending the night behind bars."

I grit my teeth, ready to grab his collar and show him how I *really* earn a penalty.

But before I can, small, warm fingers clamp around my T-shirt and tug.

"He's not worth it," April says quietly. "Let's just go."

She's only touching fabric. Not an inch of her is on my actual skin, and yet I drop my hands immediately like she sucker punched me to the gut.

April releases my shirt, loops an arm around her waist and hurries to her car. I go after her, hoping she's not crying. I've never been a guy who knows how to comfort a woman when she cries.

"I'll call you later, April!" Evan the Bozo yells behind us. "And McLanely!"

I stop and face the jerk.

"This doesn't mean I hate you." He smirks. "Next time, I'll have a jersey for you to sign."

My adrenaline pulses, but I force myself to keep following

April. Whoever that guy is, he *better* not see me again. Because the next time, even if April tugs sweetly on my shirt, it might not be enough to hold me back.

CHAPTER SIX

APRIL

My palms are so sweaty that they keep slipping over my leather steering wheel cover. I know Chance has questions about what happened with Evan, but he's not sharing them and that makes me even more embarrassed.

It's funny how quickly our roles have changed.

When I didn't know his name, things felt much simpler.

He needed a mechanic, and I was the powerful technician who saved the day.

Now, I'm just the clueless woman who got cheated on by her ex for a *whole year* and he's Chance McLanely. *The* Chance McLanely.

Talk about a power imbalance.

The only hockey game I ever saw was the one Evan forced me to sit and watch for his birthday. It was Chance's team in the finals.

I had no idea which player was Chance at the time. Everyone was speeding too fast for me to recognize a face. However, I heard the word 'McLanely' mentioned often enough that I asked Evan about it.

"Who's McLanely?"

"He's the center. Guy knows where the puck is going almost like he put a tracker on it. But when you're that strong, the other team sets a target on your back and the guy always falls for it. Ends up in the penalty box so often, there's a joke that he's got a microwave, a bed, and Netflix in there."

I can totally see why Chance would get sent to the penalty box. Remembering how he flew right into Evan's face, jerking me behind him and shielding me in the process, he definitely wouldn't be able to handle players intentionally baiting him on the ice.

"I'm sorry," Chance says without prompting.

I glance at him, my eyes wide. "Huh?"

"If I hurt you when I grabbed your hand." Brows knitted, he stares a hole into my arm and I notice there's a slight, reddish bruise forming there.

"Oh, you didn't. This was from…" My voice trails.

"Evan?" He prompts.

He's pitying me and I guess, in a way, I gave him something to pity me for. Any woman who willingly dated Evan Kinsey for three years probably has a few screws loose.

"Did Evan… used to hurt you?" Chance asks hesitantly.

I shake my head so hard my ponytail whips my cheek. "No, no. It was nothing like that. Even if he tried, I know how to use a wrench."

Chance blows out a breath. "That's good."

I bark out a nervous little laugh that sounds a couple degrees better than my goat scream. Silence creeps in between us because I don't know what to say.

"I, uh, actually thought you were apologizing for something else," I mumble.

"I already apologized for not recognizing you as a mechanic." He scratches his chin. "Did I do something else to offend you?"

"You didn't offend me, per se."

"Then?"

"I thought you were apologizing for stepping in."

"Oh." His shoulders relax. "Why would I apologize when I'm not sorry?"

His words are so frank and matter-of-fact that I slam too hard on the brakes when approaching a crosswalk and we both jolt forward. Instinctively, Chance's arm comes up to protect me.

I clear my throat. "Well then, *I'm* sorry."

"Sorry for what?"

"This is a small town. Everyone is going to be talking about what happened. It's probably all over the nursing home group chat now."

"The fact that some jerk grabbed you or the fact that I stopped him?"

"Both."

"You shouldn't be sorry." He raises his chin. "None of this is your fault. If it's anybody's fault, it's mine."

"So you admit it's your fault?"

He stares straight ahead, choosing his words carefully. "If you expect me to apologize for intervening…" He shakes his head. "I won't. I only apologize for things I'm actually sorry for."

"Noted." I crank up the air conditioner because, for some reason, my face is getting hot.

He taps his fingers on his knee. "So… you and Evan…"

I groan. "You were doing so well."

"I have to ask."

"'Have to' is relative."

"What's the deal with him?"

"We dated. He cheated. We broke up. Case closed."

Chance scrunches his nose. "He cheated, and he's still demanding you answer his calls?"

I shrug.

He looks genuinely outraged. "You shouldn't have stopped me from punching him."

"Please don't pick a fight with Evan. He meant it when he said he'd have you thrown in jail. The Kinseys pretty much own this town. His cousin, Gunner, is the captain of our hockey team and Gunner's dad is the sheriff."

"Which means Evan is the nephew of the sheriff?" He scrunches his nose. "So Lucky Falls is a kingdom then, not a democracy."

"Sounds about right," I concede. "You'll get the hang of it if you stick around long enough."

"I don't plan on doing that."

He takes out his phone and checks the screen. I briefly wonder if he's hoping for a call from his girlfriend. Or maybe his many girlfriends. With a face like that, he doesn't scream '*my dream is a wife, a white picket fence, and two and a half kids*'.

I know the deal with athletes. Our hockey team is popular around here and I've seen how girls throw themselves at Gunner and the rest of the players. Athletes, at every level, are never in want of company, attention and adoration. Since Chance has been at the very top, he's probably reaped the benefits of that.

Why do you care who he dates, April?

I shake my head to clear the thoughts. Seeing Evan threw me for a loop and now not even my thoughts are making sense.

Speeding a little faster to the hotel, I drive my truck right up to the front doors and let Chance out.

I'm glad our time together is over. In this state, my emotional defenses are down. I'll start talking about the cheating incident or the incident that hurt me even worse afterwards. And that'll be beyond embarrassing.

"Thanks for the ride," Chance says. "And for the help with my car."

"Thanks for the burger. And… with Evan…" I say stiffly.

"You're welcome." He unleashes a soft smile that would

probably have me falling flat in my chair if I wasn't already seated.

I bet women always go weak at the knees in front of Chance. The man should walk around with a warning.

May cause kneecaps to suddenly burst into Jello.

First impressions aside, Chance has a way of disarming me and I don't like it.

When he hops out of the car, a flyer from the overstuffed glove compartment sails out and lands at his feet.

"What's this?" He arches a brow. "The Pink Garage? Is that your place?"

I hesitate before nodding.

"Competing with the Kinseys?" He tips the paper to his head in a salute. "You've got my vote."

"I'll need more than a vote to keep the lights on, but that's appreciated." I stare straight ahead.

He chuckles and shuts the door. "Hey, maybe next week, I can take you out for a proper dinner as a thank you and we can discuss how to take down the Kinseys together."

Oh-ho, no.

No way.

Time to nip this sucker in the bud.

"No need for a thank you."

"At the very least, I can leave you tickets to our first game. Max said they're selling fast."

"I'm not much of a sports fan." I pause and then tack on stiffly. "I doubt we'll be seeing much of each other."

"Oh." He blinks, taken aback by the distance in my tone. He recovers quickly, his smile only a tad unsure. "But it's a small town, right? I'm sure we'll run into each other now and then."

"Probably not. You'll be busy competing and I'll be busy working."

The smile finally disappears and a part of me wishes I could say something to reverse the movement. *Sure, let's be friends. Let's exchange numbers and get coffee and I can geek about cars while you geek about hockey.*

Pffft. After Evan, I don't want any male companionship, friendly or otherwise. Someone like Chance can probably be just-friends with someone like me, but I know for a fact that I can't handle too much of him. He's one hundred percent handsome, one hundred percent charming and I am one hundred percent delusional.

It wouldn't take long for me to catch feelings. And then, not only would I be opening myself up to getting hurt again, but it'd be with an athlete who has—not only the people in town to cheat on me with—but a bunch of away games, fancy photoshoots with models, and international business meetings that provide plenty of enticing, non-monogamous entertainment.

Am I overthinking?

Maybe.

Probably.

I said I was delusional.

But it's this very delusion that made me believe I'd be marrying Evan this year instead of finding his tongue searching for treasure in the caverns of my hairdresser's throat.

The reminder of my ex-boyfriend's duplicity gives me strength.

"Can you close my door please," I snap, noticing the way he's lingering.

"Oh, right." Chance sheepishly shoves the door closed.

Without a word, I slam on the gas pedal and speed away.

As I'm telling myself that I made the right choice, my phone rings. Since I rigged up my old pickup with a new, touchscreen dashboard, I can see that it's May calling without touching my cell.

I tap the button on the dashboard and say, "Hey, May. I bought burgers for—"

"April, how do you know Chance Mclanely?" My sister shrieks.

I blink a few times. "I don't."

One misunderstanding, a conversation, a car ride, and a little knight-in-shining-armor-ing doesn't count as really *knowing* a guy.

"Really? Because you two are all over social media."

I jerk the truck to the side of the road, yank my phone from the cradle and set it to my ear. "May, say that again?"

"Our page is *blowing up*! This is crazy!" Her footsteps thud in the background. I can imagine my sister running back and forth in our worn living room, leaping and whooping loudly.

"May, you're not making sense. Why would people care about our page just because our pictures got shared in the local group chat?"

"Local group—did you not hear me? I said you're all over social media."

"Sure. The town's social media page." Lucky Falls has its own social media branding manager, so it's no surprise that they posted sightings of a famous hockey player.

"No, April. You don't understand. You. Are. *Blowing up.* On. The. Internet."

"Me?"

"Everyone wants to know who Chance Mclanely is dating."

I choke. "D-did you just say *dating?*"

"Oh, this is great! I need to draft up a new social media calendar. The shop *has* to bank on the Chance momentum before it totally dies out. They say it's not your fifteen minutes of fame, it's what you do with them that counts."

I am one hundred percent sure no one says that.

"I'll see you at home," May squeals. "Oh, and thanks for the burgers."

As soon as May hangs up, I type in Chance's name in the internet search bar.

There are millions of hits.

The top stories are:

Up-and-Coming Hockey Player Voted Sexiest Athlete Alive

Chance Mclanely Out of Chances

The Downfall of Chance Mclanely: How One Man Lost Everything

And right there underneath all the big headlines is an article that popped up literally minutes ago.

It's a zoomed in picture of me, possibly at the worst angle that a camera could capture a face. My face looks splotchy, my hair looks like a giant ball of frizz and worst of all, Chance looks absolutely dashing in comparison.

The header simply reads *'Chance McLanely, New Town and New Girlfriend. Who Is Mystery Girl?'*

"New... girlfriend?"

My cellphone feels like it weighs a ton and my hand drops limply to the seat.

The internet thinks *I'm* dating Chance McLanely.

And they couldn't be more wrong.

CHAPTER
SEVEN

CHANCE

I'M FACE-DEEP IN A TOWER OF CHEESY ONION RINGS WHEN MY PHONE buzzes. Popping out my wireless earphones, I pause the Lucky Striker's playoff video and mindlessly tap on the screen.

"Hello?"

"Chance, my man!"

My eyes widen and I whip my gaze down to the phone.

Derek - Agent

"Derek, I've been trying to reach you." I look around for a napkin. When I find none, I stick my ketchup-stained thumb into my mouth, wipe the vestiges of salt from the rings on my T-shirt and scoop the phone up.

"Sorry, Chance. Been super busy. You know how it is."

I'm sure he's been busy...

Busy ghosting me.

Busy taking down my pictures from the company walls.

Busy scouting the next kid who'll catapult him toward his next paycheck and the in-door pool he wanted to build.

My agent has always come across as more oily salesman than

genuine friend. However, it never bothered me. Growing up with money means I've met a hundred Dereks in my lifetime. What made Derek different was that he saw me as his money ticket *because* of hockey. Not because of my mother's trust fund or my family's connections.

I know exactly what gets Derek up in the morning.

Which is why his sudden call is so left field.

"I heard you signed with your college buddy. Max Mahoney, was it? Word on the street is he's getting a local team off the ground. Plans to parade them around in the minors. How's that working out for you?"

"We'll see when the season starts, but actually, Derek, now that I have you on the line, I wanted to discuss—"

"Negotiating with the league for a shortened suspension?"

I brighten. "Sounds like you already have a plan?"

"No, I don't. And I'd give up on that dream if I were you."

I reach for my fidget spinner which is dangling on the edge of the coffee table and give it a flick.

"Look, Chance, even high school students serve their full detention. What kind of havoc would it wreak if every athlete tried to negotiate out of an official ruling? Especially players with a reputation as awful as yours?"

I bristle immediately. "Who's the one who encouraged me to take a stand on the ice? Who said it would be good for my 'aggressively, masculine brand'?"

"Sure, sure. I might have encouraged you to play hard, but that was just for the ice. I'm not the one who took it off ice and started a brawl with the opposing team?"

"I didn't start that fight…" I clear my throat. "I just… finished it."

"To the tune of getting a suspension, losing all your brand deals and handing out millions in settlements. If it weren't for your family's money, you'd be done."

I'm flicking so hard the fidget spinner sounds like helicopter blades. "I bear full responsibility for the mess I'm in. I'm assuming you didn't call just to rub salt in the wound?"

"The opposite, actually. I've got good news."

"If it's not a shortened suspension, then it's not good enough."

"Your name's trending."

I groan. "What now? Is it Sethburg? Trying to lie to the press again?"

The other player who'd gotten suspended along with me, Sethburg, has been on an apology tour. Honestly, he should just give up on hockey and go right into acting. The guy's single-handedly responsible for the rise in eye drop stocks. I'm sure he bought a ton of them to help him produce so many tears on camera.

Derek chuckles. "Don't blame Sethburg for playing the game. I offered to take you on a media tour. You're the one who wanted to settle with money."

I lean back in the sofa, my legs spreading wide. "You know I can't apologize for things I'm not sorry for."

I'm suddenly reminded of April and how she reacted when I told her the very same thing. Her eyes had widened slightly and a blush spread over her face. Watching the red seep into her freckled cheeks had my chest tightening strangely…

No, not just strange.

Scary.

I'd never felt like that before.

I need to keep my distance from that woman because I can see myself becoming addicted to making her blush.

"…I agree. She's a looker that one."

I sway forward, planting both feet flat on the ground. There's no way Derek read my thoughts about April, did he?

"…the flannel shirt and no makeup schtick is cute…"

That definitely sounds like April. Although her flannel shirt is mostly for the comfort of working on cars and not a 'shtick'.

"I personally prefer the glamorous types, but I can work with this. I'd brand her as the girl-next-door, fresh-faced, Farmer Jill..."

Farmer Jill? *What?*

"... It's not a bad angle, Chance. All those glamorous, social media stars look the same now anyway. Fake this. Fake that. This woman stands out because she's the opposite of all that. And more importantly, your fans are responding to seeing you with uh, a more down-to-earth woman—"

"Derek, you mind backing all the way up there? I think I missed a big chunk of this conversation."

"I was saying I could do a Farmer Jill brand—"

"Before the Farmer Jill thing." I wave my hand.

"Oh, your new girlfriend is trending."

"My what is *what?*" I explode from the sofa.

"Your girl. Your lady. Your woman."

"*Woman?*"

"Why are you yelling?" He gasps. "Farmer Jill *is* a woman, right? Not that I'm judging. I mean, it would explain the flannel—"

"Yes, she's a woman, but she's not *my* woman. April is..." I stop short of saying 'a friend'. We didn't exactly have the best interaction when we parted outside the hotel.

From the way she turned down all my invitations and tore out of the hotel's driveway leaving skid marks behind, she's not gung ho about seeing me again.

"If she's not your girlfriend, why did you fight over her with some guy?" Derek sounds genuinely baffled. "Why'd you take her out to eat in front of everybody? Why'd you let so many people film it? You're usually so careful about who you're seen with, so I thought... with her... weren't you trying to make a statement?"

I lean my head back and groan.

In the height of my popularity, I jumped through hoops to make sure the paparazzi never took pictures of me and my dates. Being the source of tabloid gossip was a hassle. The paparazzi hunted me like a rabbit with a hound dog and it felt like my life was under a microscope.

Dating became a rather unpleasant business, so I did less and less of it as I got older, choosing to focus on hockey alone.

"She's a mechanic," I say in exasperation. "We stopped to get something to eat on our way to grab my keys. We ran into her ex-boyfriend—"

"I don't need the play-by-play."

"I should clarify for her sake," I insist.

April must be horrified. She was nervous about being the topic of a neighborhood group chat. I can't imagine how she's feeling knowing *the world* thinks we're together.

"Chance, you'd be crazy to stop the momentum now."

"I'm not doing this, Derek. April's not one of your athletes. You can't mold her into a brand for profits."

"What if I mold her into your ticket out of the boonies?"

I freeze, my fingers tightening on the phone.

"Look, Chance, I don't really care who she is or why you were filmed. The point is you were. And it's good. You said she's a mechanic? Even better. You'll be the guy who supports women in male dominated industries. You'll have the internet eating out of your hands."

A big sigh erupts from my chest. I genuinely admire April and her career choice. I think she's amazing for opening her own shop. But every word out of Derek's mouth right now is making me feel smarmy.

"Remember what you said the day the suspension was announced?" Derek coaxes. "You said you'd do anything to get back to the league. You said you'd clean toilets with a toothbrush. Well, getting a pretty girl to date you is ten times better than that. *And* you get to save your toothbrush."

I start pacing, unable to keep still but also unable to deny anything he's pointing out. "There has to be another way."

"Right now, your reputation is in shambles. You're not The Clairvoyant. You're the guy who fights on and off the ice. You're a bad influence and a hockey pariah."

"I'm not—"

"If you weren't, why'd you sign with a no-name team?"

"I'm in the minor leagues to stay in shape," I argue.

"You're in the minor leagues because the Lucky Strikers are so insignificant, your bad press can't do them any damage. No one here is stupid."

I cough because that one hit me in the gut.

"Keep the girl by your side, Chance. Only good things will happen if you do."

"I can't. She hates me."

"Then make her un-hate you," he says, his voice going soft as it usually does when he already has the customer by the hook and he's starting to reel them in.

"*Derek, your meeting starts in five,*" a voice says in the background.

"Just a minute, Lotty. Chance, we good?"

"No."

He charges on as if he didn't hear me. "You want me in your corner again? That's the plan. Get yourself a steady girlfriend, show the world you've changed. Re-brand yourself as hockey's Prodigal Son. Once you get some brand deals going, get some sponsors back, once you show the league that the public's forgiven you, they just might forgive you too."

"I—"

"Good luck out there. I'll let you know once a big brand reaches out."

"Derek—"

There's a click followed by silence.

I fall despondently into the chair and run my hands over my face. Then I run my hands over my hair. Then I do both repeatedly until my hair's a mess and my face is red.

Charming women is easy... when they're interested. But how do I convince April to date me when I'm ninety percent sure she would save my Lamborgini over me if we both fell into the ocean?

CHAPTER EIGHT

APRIL

"I heard you're dating Chance McLanely."

I stop my inspection of the oxygen sensor and glare a hole at the rhinestone pink sneakers jutting beneath the car. "Don't start. I've had enough of that today."

"Do tell."

I push the creeper out into the open. Both me and the tool go skidding and the garage's bright white ceiling comes into view.

Lying flat, I stare up at my best friend. "For starters, I've been invited to group chats I didn't know existed."

Rebel drops to her haunches, a mischievous grin on her face. "Oh?"

"Did you know there's a Sexiest Men Alive society? Because I didn't. Not until I became the newest member of their group chat and they creepily asked if I could sell them shirtless pictures of Chance McLanely."

"Sexiest Men Alive society? Now that sounds like fun." Rebel grins.

I hand over my phone. "It's not fun to know a ton of strangers have your phone number."

"Whoa, that's a lot of messages." Her eyes widen. "They're all strangers?"

"Some of them. Some are people I haven't talked to since high school who suddenly want to grab a coffee."

"That's... surreal."

"Surreal's not the word I would choose. Sickening? Disappointing? Fake as a fern in the dentist's office?"

Rebel laughs in her restrained, lady-like way. "That last one would count as a sentence, not a word, no?"

"Don't lecture me. I'm not done venting."

Rebel makes a go-ahead gesture.

"Everyone has unanimously decided that I—an ordinary woman from an ordinary town—am extremely important. Not because of all my engine repair certifications, or because I have the monetary equivalent of a college degree in diagnostic tools. Nope, it's all because of a stupid article about a stupid hockey player that a stupid journalist didn't even bother to fact check!"

"Now, why would you lump me in with the stupid journalist and his stupid article?" A voice that does *not* belong to Rebel bounces around our empty garage.

I gasp and shoot to my feet. In my rush, I send the creeper skidding straight at the man in the doorway. He easily stops it with his foot and snaps it up with the toe of his sneakers.

"Cool." Chance inspects the creeper. "What's this? A skateboard?"

"What are you doing here?" I gape.

He sets the creeper down and walks deeper into the shop. Immediately, his large presence sucks the air out of the room and makes everything feel smaller.

My eyes slide down his frame like I'm following the lines of a wiring diagram for a 1996 Chevy. He's wearing a grey hoodie with his number and last name on the back. The fabric hugs his broad shoulders. Faded blue jeans go on and on until they reach his sneakers.

It is *very* unfair that the hoodie-jeans combo—which adds at least thirty pounds and an extra layer of 'frump' to my body—is dazzling on Chance.

"I came to see you," he says with a grin that shows nothing of our tense goodbye yesterday at the hotel parking lot.

"Now's not a good time," I say harshly, moving around to the other side of the car.

Rebel flashes me a 'what's up with you?' look and then approaches Chance with one of her killer smiles. "Hey, I'm Rebel, April's best friend and a mechanic here at The Pink Garage."

"Hey." Chance gives her hand a good shake, his eyes darting to me.

I'm tapping on my scanner, trying not to make it obvious that I'm watching him, but inside I'm holding my breath, waiting for him to take a *really* good look at Rebel and do what every guy who's come to our shop does—fall instantly for her.

I need to *see* the moment it happens. Because then, I can squash the tiny excitement that sprang to life at the sight of him.

"How did you hear about our shop?" Rebel asks, tucking her long, luscious hair behind her ear.

Any minute now.

"Oh, uh. I picked this up in April's car." He unfolds the pink flyer that sailed out of my car. Once again, his gaze darts to me.

Any minute, he's going to really pay attention to Rebel and bam!

"You were in April's car yesterday?" My best friend swerves to me, both eyebrows arched in a pointed question.

"She gave me a ride after my car broke down at the stadium."

"The stadium?" Rebel's steady tone reminds me of a parent who already knows her child is lying but wants to test how far they'll go with it. "And why were you at the stadium yesterday in *your* pick-up instead of the company car, April?"

I hurry over to Chance. "Let's talk outside."

"Sure." He seems confused but he lets me prod him out the door.

"Secrets among friends is bad manners!" Rebel yells after me.

"He's not my friend!" I yell back.

"Ouch," Chance says. "Did yesterday mean nothing to you?" He slams his fist against his chest in a melodramatic fashion. "Do you offer your passenger seat to every guy who can't find their engine?"

My lips twitch, but I force myself not to laugh. "Why are you here?"

"To check on you. But I think I can already piece together how well you're taking this."

"I know you're used to it, but for me, all this attention is…"

"Inconvenient?"

"Unwelcome."

"It's annoying for sure," he agrees. "But it sounded like you were angry."

"Because the rumors aren't true. Wouldn't you be angry if the whole world believed a lie?"

His eyes dart away for a second. "Actually, that's what I wanted to talk to you about."

I purse my lips. "You must be even more upset than I am. If you need my statement to clear things up, the answer is yes. I'll talk to whoever I need to and tell them I am absolutely, positively *not* dating Chance McLanely."

"Actually…"

"I'd tell them even if you were the last man on earth, it wouldn't happen."

He grimaces. "That won't be…"

"I'd tell them you and I have nothing in common and that we find it offensive to be associated together. I'm sure they'd back off."

"April!" He grabs my shoulders.

I startle, my heart clamoring to my throat as he stares desperately into my eyes with those ocean blue irises.

"I don't find it offensive to be associated with you."

Warning! Jello-knees en-route!

"And I don't want to clear things up," Chance says.

I stagger back. "W-what do you mean?"

"I mean." Chance licks his lips. "I want to fake it with you."

My brain misfires and cuts out everything between the 'I want' and the 'you'. So it takes me half a beat longer to get angry.

"I'm sorry. *What?*"

He opens his hands as if to explain and then wipes them against the side of his pants. "So… I can see you're not taking this well."

"How am I supposed to take this?" I screech.

"My agent called me last night. And he told me that the fastest way to get back where I belong is to fix my reputation."

"Your reputation has *nothing* to do with me."

"Us being together, you and me," he points between the two of us, "the internet loves it. Brands and sponsors love it. The fans love it."

"*I* don't love it."

He jogs in front of me when I start to stalk away. "Wait, I'm not expecting you to do this for free."

"I *cannot* be bought." I punch my finger into his chest. "Don't you dare fling money at me."

"I wasn't planning on it."

Moving around him, I stomp toward the shop again.

Again, he intercepts me. "If we work together—" He holds his hands up in surrender when I glare at him. "Big if, it wouldn't be on an employee-employer basis. We'd be partners. You know what a brand sponsorship is, right? I'd be the Pink Garage's ambassador."

"Why would we want you as our ambassador when no one else does?" I point out.

He flinches and I feel sorry for being so upfront. Then I push those feelings away and remind myself that he started this war by making such a ridiculous request in the first place.

"I may not have the same influence as I did before, but I can definitely point more attention your way," Chance explains. "You said you were competing with the Kinseys, right? I'd be your secret weapon."

He'd be a ticking time bomb.

"I'm not interested."

"*I am*," my sister's voice sounds behind me.

Not surprisingly, Rebel is blatantly eavesdropping on us but I'm surprised to see my sister there too.

"May, when did you get here?" I hiss.

"A few minutes ago. But you were too busy arguing to notice."

Rebel grins at me. "As an equal partner in this business, I vote yes to Chance being our ambassador too. A disgraced hockey player is better than no one."

"Thanks?" Chance scratches the back of his head.

"What'd you have to lose, big sis?" May coos. "Didn't you say you'd do *anything* to beat the Kinseys?"

Eyes narrowing, I glower at both May and Rebel.

Neither of them back down.

Chance starts looking hopeful.

With a giant sigh, I point to the bicycle that's propped against the side of the garage. "Time out, you two. Let's talk in private."

"What's there to talk about?" May tilts her head cheekily. "I say hand me a contract."

Rebel nods eagerly.

Steam coming out of my ears, I stalk toward my sister and best friend, wondering when the two closest people to me turned into traitors.

CHAPTER NINE

CHANCE

I KICK A ROCK DOWNHILL, STAYING CLOSE ENOUGH TO OVERHEAR THE ladies' conversation.

"Why were you spying on me?" April hisses.

"You guys were standing outside yelling for the world to hear. I thought you wanted me to listen!"

"April, you should consider the offer."

"No, I'll find another way to drum up business for our shop."

April plants both hands on her hips. Today, she's wearing a blue tank top and a jumpsuit that's peeled down to her waist. The outfit is fully utilitarian and yet seeing that contrast of her peaches and cream skin against the blue shirt and the way the tied sleeves emphasizes her tiny waist has me biting down on my bottom lip.

"How? We've been open for weeks and we can only fix the cars people sneak in at night. No one wants to go against the Kinseys."

"We'll prove ourselves eventually. We just need time."

"We don't have time. If we keep going like this, we'll forfeit on our loan and neither of us can afford that."

I wonder how much of a bad spot the shop is in. I could easily offer to pay the mortgage off but, I know, just as sure as the grass is green and the sky is blue, that April would beat me to a pulp with that wrench of hers if I tried.

"We don't even know that guy!" April hisses. "What if he's a psychopath? Would you sleep well at night knowing you sold me off to a psychopath?"

April calling me 'that guy' is only slightly less offensive than her thinking I could be a psychopath. She's right that we've only known each other for a day, but what about my behavior yesterday screamed I'd kidnap her and keep her in a basement?

Given how much you've been looking forward to fake-dating her, she may have a point.

Hm.

"He's a famous, well… infamous hockey player. The entire world has their eyes on him. What can he do right now?"

"It's the ones who've hit rock bottom that you have to watch out for." April fires back.

I snort out a laugh.

All the ladies stop and glare at me. I feel like a lone elephant in a pack of hunting lionesses. Shifting my expression into a respectful frown, I take a step back.

"Look at his face. I don't know a single psychopath that's as handsome as him."

"Oh? Do you regularly hang out with psychopaths?"

"Ladies, we can argue about this all day, but the fact is we have an opportunity here. Chance McLanely mentioning our shop just once would be explosive for business. April, you know it's true. However, you're the one who has to go through with it. You're the one who has to fake a relationship. May and I both have our opinions, but this is your decision."

"If it sweetens the deal any, imagine how crushed Evan would be to see you dating his favorite hockey player."

"Forget the shop. For that alone, I'd say yes to this."

"It would be nice to get revenge. But lying about dating someone just to get back at my ex feels so wrong and petty."

"Cheating is wrong and petty too. Seeing you upgrade to a hotter, richer, more famous hockey player boyfriend is what Evan deserves."

The women glance at me, see me watching and huddle closer, lowering their voices. After a few minutes, April and Rebel go inside while the newcomer approaches me.

I smile at her. "Hey, are you a mechanic too?"

"Uh no. I'm April's sister." She peers up at my face. "Your eyes are much bluer up close."

My smile widens. While April was chilly and guarded, her sister is the total opposite.

"I'm Chance and you are…"

"I'm May."

"May… as in April, May… June?"

"Yup." She bounces on the tips of her toes.

"Really?"

"June is our oldest sister, but she booked it out of here the moment she turned eighteen and rarely comes home." May shrugs. "What can I say? Our parents like the calendar."

"Wow." I'm still digesting April and her two sisters being named after months when May says, "You should come inside. It's hot out."

"Oh… yeah, sure."

I follow her into the shop and notice the lone car in the corner has been locked and the tools put away. Four chairs are stationed in the middle of the room.

May directs me to sit in the lone folding chair as the three women sit across from me in a line.

It feels like I'm about to be interrogated. My palms are insanely sweaty, and I want to pull out my fidget spinner, but I can't. Flicking an anxiety tool won't exactly help me bring the right image across.

"After a discussion with my team," April says crisply, "we've decided to give this a shot."

A grin unleashes on my face. It's too soon to be this happy, I know, but there's no controlling how pleased I am.

"In exchange, I'd like to service the exotic cars you supposedly own." She puts bunny ears around the 'supposedly'. "And I'd like it filmed for my social media accounts."

"Of course. Is that all?"

"For me? Yes. However, this agreement isn't just with me. It's with everyone here at Pink Garage."

The blonde woman in the pink jumpsuit straightens. "My expectation of this agreement is that you'll feature our shop on your social media profile for every date you and April have."

"And how many dates can we have?"

"Three," April says. "Pre-planned and pre-approved. Like I told you yesterday, I'm busy with the garage and you're busy with hockey. We don't need to be all over each other."

Three sounds like a pittance, but my role here is not as a negotiator.

"Speaking of being all over each other," April says, clearing her throat, "there will be no mouth-to-mouth kissing, touching above the bellybutton or touching below the waist. There will also be zero overnight stays at anyone's house."

I nod slowly. "Whatever makes you comfortable."

"I'm serious about that," April says, eyeing me like I'm a dog with no self-control. "We're going to write it down too, so you'll have to sign."

"Sure." I nod.

The women glance at each other. They seem surprised by my easy agreement, but that's fair. They don't understand my predicament or how relieved I am that this crazy plan is progressing forward.

"I don't want to disrupt your life any more than I have to. Whatever you want, whatever makes you comfortable, I'll respect it."

April's shoulders relax a tinge and I know it was the right thing to say.

"Finally…" May smiles the way my older sister's Labradoodle does when it's five a.m. and he's about to howl the entire neighborhood awake, "none of these no-touching rules apply around Evan."

April whips around. "May!"

"Listen, you can be as stiff as a board all you want otherwise, but with my sister's ex-boyfriend, I want you to *sell it*. Hard. I want him to think you guys are blissfully in love and you're about to get engaged tomorrow. I want him to really, *really* regret it, do you understand?"

April's mouth opens and slams shut in disbelief.

I chuckle.

"That'll be written in the contract too," May sings.

"No, it won't." April side-eyes her sister.

"Yes, it will." She turns in her chair and faces April. "Evan was cheating on you for a *year* and all you did was throw his promise ring in the lake and cry. It's bad enough that he had you fired from your old garage but what he did after—"

"May," Rebel warns.

April's sister glances at me and then pins her mouth shut.

This new information makes me stiffen. I already knew I despised Evan, but now I want to burn the ground he walks on and sprinkle disinfectant over the ashes.

April stares me down. "Do you agree to my terms?"

I walk over to her, noting how her chin has to tilt back several notches the closer I come.

"I do," I say quietly.

She blinks a couple times, swallows hard and then says, "Well, Mr. Chance McLanely, you've got yourself a girlfriend. For three dates anyway."

She stands, offers an oil-stained hand and then retracts it sheepishly. "Oh, I… let me wash my hands—"

I capture her fingers in my palm, swallowing them whole. Her callouses scrape against mine and something slips into place in my heart when I give her hand a squeeze.

In that moment, I make a silent promise to myself. I'm going to be the best fake boyfriend I can be.

Because this beautiful, precious woman deserves it.

CHAPTER TEN

APRIL

"When are you guys planning to have your first date?" May asks, taking out her phone and tapping down some notes.

Chance's deep blue eyes find mine. "I have a meeting with Max to prepare for the press conference on Friday but apart from that I'm free today…"

"How about you go out now?" Rebel suggests.

I panic. "Now?"

"Yeah." My sister checks her watch. "It's lunch time."

"I can't. I haven't finished inspecting the oxygen sensors." I hook a finger at the car behind me.

"I can do it." Rebel offers.

Before I can come up with an excuse, Chance shakes his head. "It's okay. We don't have to go on a date right this second."

My shoulders cave in from relief.

May finishes tapping on her phone and chirps, "I'll head home to type out the contract and forward it to you both to sign. Oh, I can't wait to get started." She rubs her hands together gleefully. "I say we aim for one hundred thousand new subscribers for the garage."

"One hundred thousand?" My eyebrows fly up.

"Go big or go home, baby."

I steer her toward the door. "How about you just go home?"

"You see how she treats me, Chance? I know my dear brother-in-law wouldn't be so rude."

"He's not your brother-in-law," I grumble.

But Chance disagrees because he stops May before she leaves and slips her a bill.

"Keep calling me brother-in-law and I'll keep these coming," he whispers loudly.

May kisses the ten-dollar bill and grins from ear to ear, "Chance, welcome to the family."

"You see that… utter bribery?" I stammer, pointing at where Chance and May are walking out together.

"He's funny."

"He's arrogant."

"He seems sweet."

"All men are sweet when they're trying to get what they want."

Rebel stares at me frankly. "He's not Evan."

"I know. I wasn't fake-dating Evan." Although, now that I look back at it, Evan was fake-dating me. Or fake-dating that hairdresser.

One of us was being fooled.

Rebel stares at me and a smirk tugs at her lips.

I hate when she does that. It makes me feel like she can see right through me.

"I know what you're thinking and you're wrong," I mumble.

"I haven't said anything."

"And please continue to do so."

She laughs in that boisterous, carefree way. "I think this will be good for you, April. Evan hurt you so badly, but he was awful to you before he cheated. I hate to think that he succeeded in turning you against dating for good."

"All Evan did was open my eyes to the truth."

"I'm afraid to ask what 'the truth' is." Rebel cringes.

"You know why I agreed to this so quickly? It's because love is a lie anyway. At least this time, I know that going in. Whatever happens between me and Chance won't be anything but a business arrangement. And that's fine with me."

I scoop up the creeper and lean it against the wall so no one accidentally slips on it. As I move, I feel Rebel's pitying gaze.

She wouldn't understand. Rebel's so beautiful that men fight each other to be with her. Her partners are so enamored with her, they do everything in their power to keep her happy.

While I, on the other hand, well… it's not like suitors were knocking my door down before Evan expressed interest.

Chance walks back into the shop.

"Did you forget something?" I ask.

"Yeah, your lunch order. I already got May's. She said it's Taco Tuesday. You ladies want the same?"

I blink slowly.

"I have a spa appointment," Rebel says, reaching for her hot pink purse. "But April will have five *carne asadas* and an *horchata*."

My eyes fling the word 'betrayal' at Rebel.

She smirks.

I glare back. "I think you over-rolled your 'r's, Bellie."

"That's the only thing I got out of fourrrrrr years of Spanish class."

I cringe.

Chance laughs.

Rebel blows me a kiss. "Remember not to close the hood of that truck, April. The latch mechanism broke and it won't be easy to open."

"Yeah, yeah."

"See you later." Rebel sashays out.

It's just me and Chance in the garage.

I find myself at a loss for words. After how unpleasant—okay, downright rude—I was to him at the hotel, it's a little embarrassing to find myself dating him less than eighteen hours later.

Fake-dating him, I mean.

Putting my jittery hands to work, I open the car hood, secure the jack so the vehicle is lifted off the ground and grab the creeper to return to my inspection.

I feel Chance's gaze hot on me and whirl around. He's leaning against the wall, surveying me with eyes half-hooded.

"You're still here? I thought you went to buy tacos?"

"May gave me the taco truck's phone number. I texted in my order and they said it'll be ready in thirty minutes."

"So you're just gonna stand there and... stare creepily for thirty minutes?"

"Define 'creepily'."

I press my lips together. "I'm sure you have better things to do than watch a woman in a jumpsuit fix an oxygen sensor."

"You underestimate how pretty you are in a jumpsuit."

I blink in shock, but Chance rolls right on.

"I find what you're doing very interesting, so don't mind me." He folds his arms over his chest, silently communicating that he's staying put.

All of a sudden, the air gets hot and sticky.

Flummoxed, I turn back to the car and reach for my jumper to unzip the top when I realize it's already unzipped.

Goodness, why is it so steamy in here?

Even when I wiggle under the car, it takes me a full five minutes to get back into work mode. Thankfully, the problem is a tough one to solve and as I go back and forth with my tools, Chance remains quiet and doesn't interrupt.

I get so engrossed in my research that when I hear his voice behind me, I startle.

"Our food should be ready. I'll pick up your orders and be

right back. Do you want anything else to drink? May texted that she wanted me to stop by The Tipsy Tuna for a smoothie—"

I launch forward and touch his arm. His bicep muscle is firm beneath my fingertips and I yank my hand back. "You don't have to go out of your way."

"It's just a smoothie." He smiles and my heart skips a beat. "I already gave my word to May. I can't take it back."

"Fine. Do what you want." Turning away, I mumble, "Why do you need all those giant muscles if you're going to let someone half your size push you around?"

"You think I have giant muscles?" Chance teases, edging around me to see my face which is probably a few shades brighter than the neon red, emergency triangle.

I turn in the other direction, avoiding his stare, but I can't avoid the creeper that's jutting from beneath the car. The wheels roll when I step on the lip of the tool and I lose my footing. On instinct, I reach for something to grab hold of. My fingers skim the car's hood and it goes slamming down.

"Watch out!" Chance yells, snatching my hand away from the truck's hungry mouth.

The good news is that I've spared my fingers from being chopped off.

The bad news is that my jumper sleeve wasn't so lucky.

"You okay?" Chance asks, looking down at me in concern.

I notice that one of my sleeves is being gobbled by the Chevy and I squeeze my eyes shut.

"What's wrong?" Chance's hands are all over me. "Are you injured?"

"I'm stuck," I moan.

"Huh?"

"Rebel warned me not to lock this hood. I should have been more careful."

"It really can't open?" Chance grunts as he shimmies the hood. It won't budge. "Isn't there usually a switch to open this from the inside?"

"It won't work," I warn him.

He climbs inside the car to pull the lever anyway. In the meantime, I tug at my jumper sleeve, hoping and praying that I can wiggle it out.

No dice.

"It didn't open?" Chance yells at me from the front seat.

I meet his eyes through the windshield and shake my head despondently.

He rejoins me and digs his teeth into his bottom lip, staring at my trapped sleeve like it's a car with a complex heating system and a busted radiator.

"Just go," I say with a slight tremble in my voice. "The tacos will get soggy and you said you have a meeting with Max."

"Both of those things can wait. I can't just leave you here." He scrubs his chin. "What if I get something flat to wedge the hood open?"

"It might damage the vehicle."

A crease appears between his eyebrows.

"I'll wait until Rebel gets back," I tell him. "We'll call the owner and get him to open the hood. I'd rather he do it himself than I do it and wreck his paint job."

Chance frowns. "You can't just stand here until the owner or Rebel comes."

"It's okay... I'll..."

The words get choked in my throat when the giant hockey player suddenly rips his hoodie off.

I shriek and turn away, but not before getting a peek at six glorious rows of abs that glisten and ripple down his torso.

"What are you doing?" I yell.

"Put this on," Chance says. With steady hands, he pulls the hoodie over my head.

His scent is just as sexy as his abs. It's a woodsy, clean cologne that I instinctively want to burrow into.

Feeling myself getting hypnotized, I sputter, "Chance, put your hoodie back on."

"I have a plan. Bear with me," he says.

I glare in his general direction, but since the hoodie is covering my eyes, I doubt it's effective.

"Put your hands through here." He guides me gently with his voice and his hands. "Yeah, like that. Good girl."

My glare turns laser-harsh.

Chance pulls the hoodie down fully and I'm finally free to glower in peace.

He chuckles when he sees my scowl and tugs the hoodie down so it's covering me to mid-thigh. "Huh. You're smaller than I thought."

"You're bigger than I thought. What size are you?" I wonder, lifting my hands and noticing how the sleeves swallow them completely.

Chance smiles secretly and says instead, "Take off your jumper."

My heart slams against my ribs and I whip my head up to look at him. "I beg your *pardon?*"

A wicked ghost of a grin on his lips, Chance looks down at me. "April, take your clothes off."

CHAPTER ELEVEN

CHANCE

I'M NOT SURPRISED WHEN AN OVERSIZED HOODIE SLEEVE IS AIMED AT my face. But since the woman attached to that hoodie is trapped against a car, all I have to do is step back to avoid the smack.

April hops like a little bunny, eager to land her palm on my cheek. Unfortunately, she's too small and too stuck.

Giving up on a physical slap, she hurls her words instead. "I don't care how much money you have or how famous you are, I am *not* that kind of girl. And you can forget about that contract, you creep!"

My laughter booms out of me before I can control myself.

Enraged green eyes blaze with fiery, hellish fumes.

"April, I'm not trying to make a move on you. Not that you'd be able to stop me right now."

She crosses her arms like an X over her chest. "Don't even *think* about it, bub."

I raise both hands in surrender. "That was a joke. Maybe not a good one but..." I shake my head. "Think about it. Once you take off your jumper, you won't be attached to the car anymore."

"Is that why you gave me your hoodie?" The suspicion slowly seeps out of her eyes.

"That and I really wanted to show off my muscles." I give her a crooked grin.

At the mention of my muscles, April sweeps her gaze down in an approving once-over. Her eyes stop at the band of my pants and she blushes from the tip of her head to all the way down her neck.

"They're not *that* big," she argues, her voice cracking underneath the weight of her lie.

"You're right. Big isn't what you said. I think the word you used earlier was 'giant'."

She clears her throat aggressively. "Turn around."

I raise an eyebrow.

"Are you going to watch me while I…?" She blushes. "Take my jumper off?"

Now it's my turn to stutter. "Oh, yeah. Right."

I face the door.

While the sound of her zipper rips through the quiet garage, I force myself to think about that play from the Lucky Striker's final game—the one that secured them eighth place—and not about the material sliding down her legs.

Defender 1 makes a pass on the strong side of the ice to the left winger.

April moans behind me.

The zipper makes another loud noise.

Sweat pops out on my forehead.

I take out my fidget spinner and give it a whack.

If the winger doesn't have an opening, the center has to be ready for the pass.

"Chance, um…" Her feeble voice rings out. "Chance, I… I think my zipper's stuck."

"What?" I croak.

"My zipper. It's stuck. I need your help."

Heart convulsing in my ribs and eyes on the ceiling, I turn around. "Stuck where?"

"Right where I bent it to tie the sleeves. I think it got caught in the fabric or... I don't know."

There's a thick cotton ball in my throat making it impossible to swallow. Heat fans up and down my skin and I know it is a *very* bad idea to touch April right now.

"Can't you try again?"

"I did try," she huffs.

"Let me call May," I say.

When it comes to undressing April, a sibling is a much better candidate than a 'disgraced hockey player' who's quickly discovering a roaring attraction for his new fake-girlfriend.

"Well?"

"She's not answering. Let me try again."

April's voice rings with impatience. "Chance, it is *sweltering* under this hoodie. I need to take it off."

Is this the same woman who was trying to slap me three seconds ago?

My heart is about to beat right out of my chest. "Let me call the blonde one."

"You mean, Rebel? If I could call her, I would, but she's at the spa so she won't have her phone on."

"Is there anyone else."

"No! What are you scared of?" she yells.

"I'm trying to be a gentleman!" I yell back.

"Chance, either take the hoodie or the jumper off, but you need to take something off. *Now!*"

"Oh, uh. Sorry. Bad time?"

Horror seeps into April's eyes.

I turn slowly around.

Max is wedged in the doorway. It's a thirty-two foot door built to let Mack trucks through and yet he makes it look like the door to a child's playhouse.

"I'll come back," he says, his ears the color of April's face.

"But uh, friendly advice? Ya'll should close the door when you two—"

"It's not like that!" April shrieks.

Calmly, I blink. "What are you doing here?"

"I was trying to call, but you weren't picking up. I figured you might be here with your girlfriend and I wanted to talk to April about fixing the Zamboni too so it…" His nose crinkles. "Why am I explaining? You're the one doing who knows what with the door wide open."

"We weren't doing anything!" April grunts.

I clear my throat. "Give us a minute, Max."

"Have all the time you need. I'll go wash my eyes out," he says, running away.

April groans loudly. "That… that didn't just happen, did it?"

"I'll explain everything to Max."

"The more you explain, the less he'll believe the truth."

I crouch down. "Let's just focus on getting you out of here."

Rolling up my hoodie so it's out of the way, I focus on the zipper. She's right. It is stuck and it takes brute strength to roll it free, but I finally get it done.

The moment the zipper moves, April shoves me. "I can take it from here."

She's got more arm strength than expected and I lose my balance, stumbling into some kind of machine with a hook at the end.

"Oh my gosh! Are you okay?" April reaches for me.

"Ooof. Yeah." I rub my back.

"I didn't mean to shove you that hard." She reaches out to help me up but, when her jumpsuit starts slipping beneath the hoodie, she grabs it to hold it up instead.

"It's alright." I wince. "I'll go talk to Max and make sure no one else sneaks into your shop while you're changing."

She juts her chin down in a sharp nod.

Massaging my back, I limp outside. Max is in his car with the engine running and the AC blowing a cool breeze.

"Turn this up." I yank the dial all the way to ten.

"Hey, hey! Gas prices aren't what they used to be, buddy." Max lowers the dial and stares at me. "Look, I don't have a problem with you dating, but this can't be a distraction from the game. You asked to be released if you got called back to the league. I asked you to give me everything you got until then."

"Nothing's changed."

His eyes dart to the garage. "Any girl who has you stuttering like that is going to mess with your head. When did you two meet? And if you say 'yesterday', I'm going to riot."

"I'll get the tear gas then."

His jaw drops. "You... you just met yesterday? As in... the mechanic I sent yesterday?"

I nod.

"You're already dating?"

I do a so-so gesture.

"What is that supposed to mean?"

"This isn't common knowledge but," I glance both ways and lower my voice, "my agent saw pictures of me and April circulating. The reaction from the public was good. Good enough that it might completely revamp my reputation and get me back into the league."

Max coughs. "How is that supposed to get you back into the league?"

"Right now, my image is wrecked. I'm in damage control mode and April is finally turning the tide of bad momentum."

"So what I just saw with you two—"

"I told you. It was a misunderstanding."

My phone buzzes.

It's May calling back.

"Who's that?"

"My sister-in-law. Gimme thirty minutes and I'll meet you at the stadium."

"Sister-in-law?"

"You know what I mean."

"What else can 'sister-in-law' mean?"

"I'm playing a part for the sake of my future." I hop out of the car. "It's not that serious."

Max yells at me through his open window. "I know what I saw between you two, McLanely. And if that was you fake dating, I don't want to see the real deal."

CHAPTER
TWELVE

APRIL

THE NEXT DAY, I WASH CHANCE'S HOODIE, FOLD IT UP AND PLACE IT in a bag. I need to return it to Chance but, every time I take out my phone to text him, I end up deleting the messages and putting it off.

Three days of indecision pass by.

Today's Friday and I'm *definitely* returning Chance's jacket. It's not that difficult. All I have to do is drive over to the stadium before the press conference, hand it over and it'll be fine.

Walking to the living room, I take out the hoodie and spread it out on the chair. "Come on, April. It's just returning a hoodie. You can do it."

"Yeah, you can do it," May says.

I yelp. "May! When did you get home?"

"Just now. Didn't you hear my keys jangling in the lock?" She kicks her shoes off and springs into the chair. "Ooh. This is nice." She grazes her hand over the hoodie. "And it feels so soft. Did Chance give you this?"

"No, he didn't." I snatch the hoodie from her, surprised by the level of possessiveness I feel.

May shrugs. "He hasn't stopped by the shop lately. Has he talked to you since you both signed the contract?"

I shake my head.

"Huh." May swings to her feet. "I'm making spaghetti. Want some?"

"No, thanks." I purse my lips and stare at the hoodie.

It has to be today.

Chance will get incredibly busy once the season starts, and I don't want him to think I stole his clothes.

Resolute, I return the sweatshirt to the bag and prepare to text Chance when my phone lights up.

It's Evan.

I sigh heavily and ignore the call like I've been doing all week.

Immediately, he sends a text.

Evan: I need to talk to you.

Evan: If you won't answer, I'll stand outside your house until you see me.

The thought of Evan showing up at my door gives me a headache, but I know he's good for the threat.

I text back.

Let's meet at the park across from the stadium.

After a moment's contemplation, I add:

You have five minutes. No more. No less.

* * *

EVAN IS ALREADY AT THE PARK WHEN I GET THERE. HE SHOOTS TO his feet and waves happily, as if we're meeting for a date and not because he's been harassing me.

Today, he's dressed in a T-shirt with the Kinseys' mechanic shop logo, jeans and a backwards baseball cap. I used to swoon when Evan wore his hair with that stupid baseball cap turned like that. But now, he just looks like a man who really wants the world to treat him like a child.

I start to open my door but my eyes catch on the bag in the passenger seat. At the last minute, I shrug into Chance's hoodie. Somehow, it makes me feel stronger.

That pinched look in Evan's eyes when he sees me wearing Chance's last name also brings a vast amount of satisfaction.

His hands tremble when he offers me a cup. "I bought your favorite. Strawberry lemonade."

"Your five minutes start now, Evan."

"April, sweetheart, I know you're mad at me, but I know we can start over."

I bark out a laugh.

"What happened with that girl was unfortunate, but I'm glad it happened because it made my feelings clear. It's *you*, April. It's always been you. And from now on, I choose *you*."

"You should have made that choice when we were, I don't know, actually together, Evan. Instead, you chose both me *and* someone else. That's called *cheating*. It's called lying and it's called backstabbing."

He rubs his unkept mustache and nods sadly. "I know. I was tempted away by someone who wanted to damage our relationship. But I see now that no other girl is as loving, as loyal or as sweet as you. *You* were the one who stayed with me when I had nothing and so you should be the woman by my side when I'm at the top."

I bark out a laugh.

Evan's eyebrows tighten.

"What do you mean at the top? You still have nothing, Evan. And what you do have is borrowed from your family."

Blotchy red spots form across his face and he narrows his eyes. "See that? If you were a little more encouraging April, maybe I wouldn't have—"

"Have what?" My heart feels like two giant clamps are squeezing it. Flashes of that awful conversation with him in the

Kinsey's mechanic shop sails through my mind. "Maybe if I were more encouraging? Maybe if I wore pink like Rebel? Maybe if I liked putting bows in my hair and putting on lip gloss? Maybe if my fingernails were clean? Maybe then you wouldn't have cheated on me?"

"T-that's not what I meant."

Folding my arms over my chest, I stare at him. "That girl dumped you, didn't she?"

His mouth opens and closes like a fish.

"She saw what a pathetic loser you are and she ditched you. And now you're running back to me, thinking I'm your fallback girl. Thinking I'll forget that you were cheating on me. Thinking I'll magically forgive those *awful* things you said to me after—"

"No, no, April, sweetheart, I'm so sorry. That's what I wanted to say. I'm sorry."

"Don't call me sweetheart!" I shriek, shaking my head so wildly that my ponytail slips out.

Evan blinks in surprise as my curls spring free and fall to my shoulders.

I raise my chin, my heart pounding. "You ignored me for weeks after we broke up. Let's keep doing that. I don't want to see you. I don't want to talk to you. Don't *ever* call my number again."

"April, you can't just throw what we had away." He grabs my arm.

"Hands off!" I growl.

Evan releases me, but he doesn't step back. "The end was awful, sure, but not every part of it was bad. We have three years of happy memories, don't we? Give me another chance. Let me show you why you were right to love me."

"I've moved on, Evan. I'm in a great relationship and I don't want to go back. Now get out of my way."

Evan snorts. "You expect me to believe you're actually dating Chance McLanely?"

The heat in his tone stops me in my tracks.

"Why haven't I seen you two in town together?" Evan challenges. "Every time I see him, he's alone or flocked by a bunch of female fans."

"We're busy. Not that I have to explain myself to you."

"You're lying," Evan says confidently.

He's right, but the fact that he's so sure about it is offensive and makes me want to punch him in the face.

"Do you know who Chance McLanely is? His family's loaded. With his background alone, he could have babes at the flick of a finger. Why would he want you?"

His words are like flying shrapnel from an exploding car and each one hits my chest with expert precision.

Evan tilts his chin up, talking down to me with his beady eyes narrowed. "You're the girl he's playing around with while he's in town. He'll never love you like I do."

I open my mouth to fire back at him when the sun suddenly disappears and a shadow falls over me.

"Since your definition of love involves cheating on your partner, then you're right. I don't love April the way you do."

I look up in surprise.

Chance winks. Backlit by sunshine, his thick black hair looks like velvet. Screaming blue eyes, piercing enough to rip through paper with a look, soften on me. "Hey, Tink."

"H-hi," I stammer.

My heart stalls in my chest when Chance slips a hand around my waist and pulls me against his chest. His strong, muscular arms lock at my hips as he secures me in a hug from behind. I'm being pulled into his universe of cool, earthy scents, the scratch of his jacket collar against the pulse at my neck, and his thick fingers that scrape the band of my jeans.

His warm skin sends electricity buzzing through my veins.

My heart *thu-dunks* in my ears.

He's way too big, way too strong, and way too *manly* to hug me from behind without a little warning.

I'm about ten seconds away from death by over-heating.

"What are you doing here?" I whisper, twisting my head to look up at him.

At first, all I see is the underside of a strong jaw before he looks down. "I was on my way to the stadium when I spotted you."

My lips inch up in a smile. "Great timing."

Chance returns my smile with a smirk that belongs on magazines.

"Ahem."

I glance over at Evan. His lips are trembling like a banjo string in the hands of a folk artist. Undoubtedly, the excitement from being this close to one of his favorite hockey players is warring with his jealousy over me.

I'm *feeding* on the chaos.

Yup, I'm a petty person.

"Evan," I speak with a hint of disdain, "I don't think you two have properly met. This is Chance, my *boyfriend*."

Evan sneers.

Chance totally ignores him. His eyes are gentle on my face.

"Tink."

"What?"

He sighs dramatically. "Why do you look prettier today than you did yesterday?"

I release a high-pitched giggle, playing it up in front of Evan. "Stop it."

Chance grins, his eyes twinkling. "I'm being honest."

There's a note of earnestness in his voice that takes me by surprise. Wow. He really *does* sound like he's being honest.

In the moment, it becomes abundantly clear that Chance is a much better actor than I am.

My competitive juices start pumping. I've never been one to lose.

At anything.

"Babe, you're embarrassing me." I laugh again and brush my

hand over his knuckles, sliding my index finger in and out of the hills and valleys.

Chance burrows his nose in my neck, making me giggle. "Ready to get out of here?"

"First, I have something to give you," I say, tapping his hand.

Chance's eyes make a quick beeline to Evan before he loosens his grip at my waist. Released from his back-hug, I turn fully to face him and rise on my tiptoes. My lips descend on his smooth-shaven cheek, pressing firmly.

A buzz starts in my chest as I feel his cheek beneath my mouth. Goodness, how can a man as masculine as Chance have such scrumptious skin?

I pull back quickly.

Chance's mouth falls open and he looks down at me in a daze.

"I thought you might need a good luck kiss before the conference," I explain, flashing a nervous smile.

A bird caws overhead, staring down at our frozen trio.

Chance has stopped breathing.

Evan is glaring.

I'm sweating because I have no idea what to do now.

The silence lengthens.

Pushing Chance forward, I grunt, "We should go or you'll be late for the conference."

Evan's scowl gets darker, but he doesn't stop us from leaving. Probably because it was easier to manhandle me than it would be to manhandle Chance.

As we move, Chance shakes his head and seems to come alive.

"Tink, let me drive you over."

"Wait," I tug on his hand when we pass my car, "I drove here."

He glances over his shoulder and notices Evan is still watching.

"Come with me," Chance says firmly.

He opens the car door for me and I slip inside, melting into the buttery, leather seats. The car still has that minty, fresh-off-the-lot smell mixed with the scent of Chance's cologne. I take a deep, intoxicating breath and then release all the painful memories Evan stirred up in me.

"Are you okay?" Chance asks, his blue eyes darkening with concern.

"Yeah."

"Do you want to talk about it?"

"No. But thank you for stepping in again."

"I hope there's not a next time, but if he ever calls like that, text me. Or better yet, the next time he calls, let me answer."

I laugh. "I don't think he'll call again."

"I'm serious, April," he says sternly. "I'm your fake-boyfriend. Protecting you is in the job description."

"I know how to handle a wrench, remember?"

"At least give me a heads-up. If I'd passed by too late, I wouldn't have seen you."

His stern look is equally hot and equally irritating.

I glance away.

An earnest Chance McLanely is far too appealing and I haven't built up enough of a resistance yet.

"The point is you *did* see me. And that was by design. I chose to meet Evan here knowing you were close by."

Chance's facial muscles relax. He starts driving. "Is that so?"

I squirm in my seat. "I'm sorry about your hoodie. I wanted to return it." I smooth my hands over the sweatshirt. "But it looks like I'll have to wash it again and return it another time."

"Keep it."

"I can't."

"Why not?"

"Because it's your hoodie. It literally has your name on it."

"Keep it." Slowing the car in front of the arena, Chance turns to me. He has an odd look on his face as he stares at the hoodie. "Yeah, keep it," he says again. "My name looks good on you."

CHAPTER
THIRTEEN

CHANCE

I think I might be losing my mind. Or maybe I'm more stressed about tomorrow's game than I thought.

Because I mean it when I tell April that I like seeing my name on her.

I like it a lot.

She laughs loudly, as if I told the funniest joke, and I let her laugh because it covers the fact that *I'm* not laughing.

I'm not even smiling.

I like seeing my name on her.

What does that mean?

That I want to own her?

No, not that.

It's just…

I have no idea. Nothing is making sense.

She kissed me on the cheek and my brain froze.

Every time I touch her, my heart palpitates.

I'm either in need of a cardiologist or something about this woman is messing with me.

I find a parking spot amongst all the news vans and April hops out of the car. "I'll check if the cost is clear and then hike back to my car. Thanks for the save."

"April!" I stride after her. "I have something to give you too."

She reels away like I'm a creep with a van offering candy to children. "That's not code for 'you're going to kiss me', is it? I just said that earlier because Evan was watching."

As usual, a grin tugs at my mouth. This woman is so charming that it's *painful.*

"Whoa." April's attention slips away from me and lands on a bright blue convertible sitting low on the concrete.

"I guess you found it first," I mutter.

"This is…"

"A '57 Bel Air. My dad handed me the keys the night I got drafted to the league." Dipping into my pocket, I let those very keys dangle in front of her nose.

April's green eyes widen until they take up half of her face. "No."

"It took a while to arrange someone to drive it out here."

"No."

"Dad gave the car to me in name, but it's still pretty much his baby and he didn't trust just anyone to drive it down."

"Noooo."

I chuckle. "Are you okay?"

"No. I mean yes. I mean… is this really a '57?" She walks around the vehicle in a slow circle.

The Bel Air sits proudly, blue paint shining and chrome sparkling. Dad kept it in pristine condition.

April's excited green eyes latch onto me and my chest puffs out like a peacock showing off all its feathers. Seeing her flip over the car makes me ten times happier than scoring a trick shot off the grid.

"Check out the engine." I point. "And it's in the *hood* this time. I double-checked."

"Don't tell me it's the original 283 engine. Just *don't.*"

"Okay." I shrug. "I won't... because I honestly have no idea what a 283 engine is."

April pops the hood, leans over and lets loose a high pitched squeal that has every dog in the nearby neighborhood barking.

"This is insane. I never... this is insane!"

"Is it?" I peer at the engine.

It's nice... I guess. But it's not 'lose my mind' nice.

"Look at that." She points to the hub of tubes, batteries and metal. "You can tell someone invested a ton here. They took care to restore the original with a custom rebuild. I mean, look at that. All the wiring is brand new. Do you know how long that must have taken?"

"I..." I run my fingers through my hair. "I mean, yeah. If you put it that way... probably a long time."

She scrunches her nose. "You have no idea why this is so cool, do you?"

"It costs a lot of money, so by that metric alone, it's really, *really* cool," I offer.

April laughs and it's the most musical, joy filled, addictive sound I've ever heard. I want to say something else that'll make her laugh but, I'm interrupted when a journalist walks into the parking lot and spots us.

Instantly, I'm on guard. "April, get in the car."

"What? Why?"

The journalist pulls out his phone and fast-walks in our direction. At the same time, two news vans barge into the parking lot.

There's no time to argue. I slip both hands around April's waist and hoist her up until her feet are off the ground.

She wiggles. "Chance, what are you doing? Put me down!"

"Unlock the car," I say urgently.

"What?"

"Now!"

The Bel Air beeps and I yank open the door with my free

hand, shoving April not-so-gently inside. She lands with a thump and an 'ow'!

"Are you okay?"

"Have you lost your mind?" April crawls into the driver's seat and threatens me with a fist. "I should—gah!"

The rest of her threat is drowned out by the stampede of journalists rushing around the car. Cameras flash. Questions fly at me from both ends. Reporters trap me against the Bel Air.

"Chance, does it feel like a step down to join the Lucky Strikers after playing in the majors?"

"Have you given up on getting back to the league?"

"Are you aware that Tom Sethberg is making a comeback?"

I try to shield April with my body, but it's hard to do since the Bel Air's driver side door is wide open. Once the reporters notice that April is nearby, their attention fastens on her. I've seen vultures pick at carcasses with more mercy.

"Is that your girlfriend?"

"How long have you been dating?"

"Is this really a publicity stunt?"

"April, close the door," I order.

"What about you?" She frowns.

I bend over. "I'll be fine."

"I'm not running away, Chance. Besides, isn't this a part of our agreement?"

She's right. Being my girlfriend does come with being in the spotlight, but I'm not shoving her at these vultures to sell the story. Not. Gonna. Happen.

More questions get hurled at us as the reporters press in closer.

Thankfully, I hear Max's voice. He's brought security guards and they're beating a path straight for me.

"Now's your chance." I jut my chin at the exits and shut April's door.

She starts the car. *Good girl.*

I step back and give her room. So do the journalists. At the end of the day, this is just a job for them and they don't want to get run over for a story.

Max pulls me behind him and two security guards flank me on either side.

"You good, Chance?" Max asks, eyes ablaze with the fierce protectiveness that made our college buddies call him the 'Good Samaritan'.

If anyone ever needed a sober driver, a wingman or a place to crash for the night, Max was the one to turn to.

I wait until April's driven off and then I nod. "Yeah, I'm good now."

With the help of the security guys, Max escorts me inside the arena. The whisk of blades against the ice and the *thuck* of hockey sticks fighting for the puck fills the air.

The team is on the ice, gearing up for our friendly scrimmage which will be filmed by the local news team after the press conference.

Gunner catches my eye and gives me a death glare before turning his attention back to the game and chasing down the puck.

"I already talked to Gunner and the rest of them," Max says, noticing my stare. "But I need to make this clear to you too. No matter what brought us here, we're here for a reason. We're a team. Once you hit that ice, you leave it all behind."

"If you truly believed we could leave it all behind, you wouldn't have told us to train separately," I grumble.

Max sighs heavily. "I didn't like it either, but the coach insisted it would cause less friction."

I frown at the man yelling plays at the wingers. "Coach Danvers, right? Where'd he come from?"

"Oh, you know." Max scratches the top of his head. "A city."

"What city?"

Max looks into the exposed beams in the ceiling.

"He's from Sethberg's city, isn't he?"

Max coughs. "I'm sure he'll be fair."

Neither of us actually believes that.

"I'm working on finding a new coach but, for right now, Danvers fits the budget and the timeline."

"He's spineless. And old school. I memorized his plays in three nights. The guy won't take risks on the ice, has poor substitutions and—"

Max tightens his lips. "We can't go into a season without a coach. Not if we want any chance of reaching the play-offs. More than just your future is on the line here, Chance."

I grit my teeth. In all honesty, Max didn't just scoop me out of the dung I dropped in because he wanted to be a good friend. He's hoping I can earn my keep.

"I get it, Max. I do. But for my reputation not to get any worse and for you to turn this team into a worthwhile investment, we need to actually win some games."

He shakes off the worried look and pastes on a giant smile. "It'll all work out. Besides," he hits my back. "I have The Clairvoyant on my side. He's worth ten Coach Danvers. Now, go change. You need to hurry if we're going to start that press conference on time."

I stalk away from Max, my head whirring.

He's a loyal guy. It's been that way since college, but if Max is letting his players and a biased coach call the plays for the Lucky Strikers…

We're going to need more than just my skills on the ice.

We're going to need a miracle.

CHAPTER
FOURTEEN

CHANCE

THE PRESS CONFERENCE STARTS ON TIME AND MOVES BRISKLY. WITH Max fielding questions, the vultures—ahem—journalists don't swarm or pick at me like I'm the deer carcass I passed driving to practice yesterday.

I discuss my expectations for the season and Max shares his grand plans for the Lucky Strikers. No one interrupts or butts in to take the conversation in another direction. Whether it's Max's intimidating size or the security team's shakedown, the reporters behave respectfully.

"How is it that you and April are trending more than the press conference?" Max complains after the reporters leave.

We're running down the hallway to the lockers since I'm ten minutes late for our in-house scrimmage.

I shrug. "Same thing happened when I was in the league. The media put my dating life under a giant microscope."

"Really? I didn't hear much about your dating life back then."

"Because you weren't paying attention. Sports fans stick to

the games and the stats. The general population wants details on our personal lives and they're the bigger audience, so *they* control what trends."

The invasion of privacy used to bother me. I *only* wanted people to care about how I did in the game, not what I was driving or who was in my passenger seat. But now, I can harness the power of the general audience to bring me back to where I belong.

Max sighs heavily. "I have to hand it to your fans. They're creative."

"Huh?"

"Look at this." He shows me a short video. Someone took the clips from me and April at the burger joint and compiled them with the footage taken of us today.

In the video, I'm smiling at April and tilting my head back in the middle of a laugh. She's staring up at me, eyes sparkling.

"Does she look at me like that?" I ask, pointing to the phone.

"Don't get excited, Chance. Everything looks more romantic when you slow down the speed."

I scowl and return the phone to Max.

He groans loudly.

"What did the internet do now?" I grumble.

"They gave you a couple name. It's '*chapril*'?"

"I think it's pronounced 'chay-pril'. And what's wrong with that?"

"They're using your couple hashtag along with the Lucky Strikers hashtag. Now my team will forever be linked to your relationship." He covers his face with his hands.

"They should have put her name first. ApeChance… oh. That sounded better in my head."

"Bro, do you hear me? You and April are now linked with the Lucky Strikers."

I slip out of my shirt and remove my jersey from the hanger. Seeing my last name and number on the back reminds me of April wearing my hoodie and I smile.

Then I frown.

Being in the spotlight comes with perks but it also comes with lots of bullying. I need to make preparations so I can protect April online.

"Since you're on there, make sure to report anyone you see talking trash about April."

His eyes bug. "You think I have nothing better to do than report trolls on your behalf?"

"Then send me a screenshot. I don't mind if they come for me, but I won't let them talk badly about her."

Max scrolls down and winces. "You plan to sue the entire world then?"

"If I have to. Our family lawyers are on retainer."

Max snorts but it slowly dies into a cough. "Oh you're serious?"

"Dead serious." I grab my gloves.

"I admire your 'go the extra mile' spirit, but they don't hand out trophies for fake boyfriend of the year."

I reach for my hockey stick and press the locker door until it clicks. "Shut up, man. What else are they saying online?"

Max follows me to the exits, reading out. "This article says you... whoa. Did you really give April that convertible?" He eyes me with a smirk. "If so, I hope my custom cruiser is coming in the mail."

I unclip the toy car linked to the side of my gym bag and toss it over to Max. "Here you go. No need to thank me."

Max huffs. "Forget it."

Chuckling at his disappointed expression, I head to the arena. Everyone is already warming up on the ice. A few of the players wave to me. I've met up with the rest of the team and gotten to know them over the past week.

Unfortunately, the friendliest faces on the ice belong to the weakest players. I accepted a pseudo-mentorship role, but it's been difficult training with skaters who still lose track of the puck.

Shaking out my limbs, I get on the ice and notice two cameras set up on either side of the bleachers. There's a camera lady standing at the entrance, speaking into a microphone.

Just then, Gunner skates past me and knocks into my shoulder, sending me sprawling forward. My hands windmill forward and it's only my instincts that keep me upright.

Without an apology, Gunner skates on and starts stretching.

The schmuck is my least favorite person and I especially despise him for being related to April's bum of an ex, but I can't lose my cool.

Not in front of a camera.

My agent told me to revamp my image and fighting a teammate on the nightly news won't win me brownie points.

Think about April and you'll be alright.

I grip my hockey stick, inhale a deep breath and think about April squealing over the Bel Air in the parking lot. A smile inches over my lips and, when I open my eyes, I don't have the crazy urge to shove Gunner into the boards.

"Hey, man." I skate up to Gunner who's using his hockey stick to stretch his arms behind his back.

He glares at me behind the visor of his helmet.

"Hate me or not, we're both here for the same reason." I nod. "Let's have a good game."

His stare turns ten times frostier than the ice. "Don't think we'll go easy on you because of the cameras, McLanely."

"Give it your best shot." I tap my shoulder where he'd knocked into me. "I'll repay you for that later."

He skates off.

Renthrow, Theilan and Watson follow him.

Looks like I won't be invited to the cool kids' table any time soon.

I glance out at the bleachers and notice Max, making a 'calm down' motion with his hands. Rolling my eyes, I skate to the opposite corner of the ice to get my stretches in.

The game starts and I know exactly what play Gunner,

Renthrow, and Theilan are going to make as if I was a fly on the wall during their strat meeting.

The defensemen are on my tail, forming a block whenever one of my teammates looks for an opening to pass me the puck. No matter where I go, there's always three guards, leaving my other teammates free.

Unfortunately, Gunner can skate circles around them and every time we make a move, Gunner takes back control of the puck.

Frankly, I'm impressed by the game plan. It speaks of preparation and effort.

Someone did his homework.

My team, who'd been banking on relying on me for the pass, lose momentum in the blink of an eye.

I'm not surprised when Gunner shoots and scores.

The horn blares.

The scoreboard blinks.

0, 1

"Keeping up, McLanely?" Gunner taunts, skating by.

I grit my teeth but make no comment. Instead, I gesture to my teammate.

Pointing to the blue semi-circle directly in front of the net, I instruct him, "Keep your eye on Kinsey. He'll try a backhand shot at the paint for an easy score."

The kid nods and skates off.

I yank another one by his jersey. "Renthrow and Theilan are going to attack like crazy. Don't pass to me until I ditch my tails."

He looks worried, but there's no time to baby him because the game's already getting hot.

Determination firing my blood, I speed into the attacking zone. Renthrow's flanking me but not for long because the minute our team takes control of the puck, I cut across the line.

Behind his visor, Renthrow puckers his lips in confusion, but it's too late. I've already outmaneuvered him.

Once I'm free, there's no stopping me.

The left winger passes for the assist and I line up the puck, sending it straight into the net with a beautiful *twuck!*

My teammates celebrate with pumping fists and wide grins.

Momentum is in our court now.

I pass Gunner and give him a little chin-up gesture, no words needed.

The scowl that mars his face is a perfect reward. After that, he skates like a fire is lighting under him, but my team settles into a groove. We beat the opposite team three to one, giving Gunner no time to get the last word in.

It's a sweet victory and I relish the sound of the whistle calling the game.

The coach looks about as happy as Gunner does to see me take the victory. That's a bad omen for the season but, I focus on the win and the interviewer that's waiting for me the moment I step off the ice.

It's not an annoying interview—I've had a few of those in my career—but after answering all those questions during the press conference, I'm camera-ed out.

Seeing my lack of interest, the journalist pries around for an 'exclusive' scoop on my past scandals, but I've done this interview song and dance enough to keep my answers short and diplomatic.

It helps that sweat is dripping down my face like someone turned on an invisible faucet above me.

After a while, she closes the interview with a sheepish, "Thanks for your time, Chance. Last question. What are you going to do to celebrate tonight's win?"

"Me?" I grin broadly at the camera, suddenly filled with a ton of energy. "I'll take my girlfriend on a date."

CHAPTER
FIFTEEN

CHANCE

Gunner and his crew are noticeably absent when I drag myself to the locker room. Despite their absence, or maybe because of it, the room is buzzing with excitement.

I step inside.

As one, the team turns their flush-faced, wild-haired, expectant eyes on me.

"There he is!" someone yells.

Whoops break out.

My teammates surround me.

"Nice job out there." I smile. "Palenski, I saw you with those assists."

He grins so broadly his chipmunk cheeks almost punch me in the face.

"Chance, you *have* to come with us. We're heading to the Tipsy Tuna for a round of beers."

"I got plans, but…" I open my locker and slip out my wallet, handing over a credit card, "you guys enjoy yourselves."

Their eyes widen.

Another roar of celebration erupts.

I notice that they're all clothed and changed out of their gear.

Shooing them out, I say, "See you on Monday."

The guys leave, talking excitedly. Some of the players on Gunner's team sheepishly wave at me. I wave back, showing I hold no malice.

Gunner, Renthrow, Watson, and Theilan are the ones who have it out for me. It's not fair to the others for them to tiptoe around us or feel like they have to choose sides.

Stowing away my hockey stick, I sit down to remove my gear. Once my hands are free, I grab my phone and check if April texted. I forgot to ask her to message me when she got to the garage safely.

Since there are no notifications from her, I reach out first.

ME: *Hey. Did you get back okay?*

ME: *I was thinking of you during the press conference.*

After a pause, I add a wink emoji.

APRIL: *I did. By the way, this is the garage's number.*

ME: *Okay…*

APRIL: *Rebel thought a customer was flirting with her.*

ME: *The flirting was intended for you.*

APRIL: *Then you swung and missed, hockey boy.*

I laugh and tap in her personal phone number to use instead.

ME: *How are things with the Bel Air?*

APRIL: *It's in pristine condition. All it needed was an oil change and it was good to go.*

ME: *Thanks for changing the oil. Was that canola or olive?*

APRIL: *Ouch. Was that supposed to be funny?*

ME: *Another swing and miss?*

APRIL: *:) Thank you for bringing it over. May says having it in the background of our videos will be great for 'engagement' online.*

ME: *I bet it will.*

APRIL: *It's ready for pick up. We're closing the shop in thirty minutes though, so if you don't get here in time, you'll need to pick it up tomorrow.*

I don't mind if April keeps the Bel Air overnight. It's safer with her than with me since I don't have a house to park it in front of.

Absently, I tap on her profile picture. The image is of her posing next to the Bel Air. She's wearing her mechanic jumpsuit with the oil stains and her leg is kicked up in celebration.

She looks so beautiful it literally chokes me up.

I massage my throat, unable to breathe.

Forget seeing her tomorrow, I need to see her.

In person.

Right now.

How much time do I have left?

I check the phone screen.

Twenty-nine minutes.

Tossing the phone, I strip out of my clothes and run into the shower like I'm being chased. The steam curls around me, floating through the air like grey ghosts. Steaming hot water spatters into the shower tiles at my feet.

I scrub my face and hair enthusiastically. Then I scrub down my stomach, grinning when I remember the appreciative gleam in April's green eyes when she saw me shirtless.

After the shower, I grab a clean towel, wrap it around my waist and return to my locker to grab a fresh change of clothes and some cologne.

Unfortunately, I can only locate the cologne. All my clothes have disappeared.

"What's going on?" I murmur. Tossing out all the things in my locker, I search every nook and cranny.

No clothes.

I check around the benches, behind the towel hamper and even in the garbage.

Not only *my* clothes, but all the worn jerseys from the hamper are missing too.

Aside from the towels, there is not a stitch of fabric in the locker room.

Gunner.

His name rings through my mind and brings with it a bitter taste in my mouth. What's with this middle-school prank?

I check the time.

Twenty minutes to go.

At this rate, I'll miss April.

Desperate and naked, I call Max.

There's no answer, which means he's still mid-interview with the local news.

"Bobby!" I hiss, through the door. My towel slips and I reach with one hand to snap it up before I expose myself. "Bobby!"

The friendly maintenance man doesn't show.

Wracking my brain, I search for another solution.

In the corner of the locker, an abandoned mascot head stares at me with unseeing eyes. I pick up the giant head and bring it to my waist, gauging its length and width.

Yup. Should be enough to cover the maker of my future children.

I secure the towel tightly, adjust the mascot head in front of me and tiptoe outside. I keep another gym bag in my car with an extra set of clothes, underwear and sneakers. If I can just get to the parking lot without being spotted…

"Chance?" Max's voice rings loudly in the microphone the reporter has stuck to his face.

The camera swings to me at the same time.

The reporter blushes.

The camera zooms in on the mascot head.

Since there's nothing to do but go with it, I straighten and wave a little for the camera. Unfortunately, removing my hand from the mascot head makes it unstable and the whole thing topples lower on my body.

Max springs forward and blocks me from the camera. "O-kay." He clasps his hands together. "I think our interview is over now. Can you turn that off?"

Bobby pops out of the hallway on the opposite end of the

stadium. His eyes widen and he scurries toward me. Max sees him coming too and sighs in relief.

"Is this your new mascot theme?" the journalist asks, eyeing me up and down like I'm a juicy steak on the grill and she hasn't eaten all day.

"Uh…" Max's eyes dart all around.

The side door screams open and a group of grey-haired older women march in, cackling loudly. They're all wearing thick leggings, neon-green headbands and knee pads.

"Who are they?" I squeak, petrified.

Max slaps his forehead with his palm. "I forgot. The rollerblading rink is closed for renovations so these ladies are learning to skate."

I grind my teeth in embarrassment.

Bobby arrives, his eyes still wide.

"Take Chance to my office. There are clean clothes in my locker. I'll see the reporters out; make sure they delete the footage." Max glides away, smiling broadly at the news team. "Where were we?"

The female reporter gives me one more interested look before allowing Max to tug her away.

"Where are your clothes?" Bobby hisses, tugging on my arm.

"That's my question too," I grumble.

From behind me, I hear snickering. Four familiar hockey players are in the bleachers, kicking their feet up and watching it all go down.

Gunner and his posse look smug.

My eyes narrow. *Real mature.*

"Let's try not to attract any more attention," Bobby says nervously. "Come this way."

"Ooh la la!" A raspy voice wheezes, stopping me and Bobby in our tracks.

"Well, hello, gorgeous! If this is your mascot, I'll come to the games!"

Grey heads bobbing, the roller derby ladies rush down to me, phones out and snapping a million pictures.

"Can I get a picture, hun? I'm a big fan."

Before I can give my approval, the woman pushes a paper-thin cheek to mine and takes a selfie.

"Me next!" Her friend squeals.

One by one, the ladies line up.

"Can you take it, honey?" A woman that smells like Vicks Vapor Rub hands her phone over. "I want to get that nice little V-line at your hips in the shot."

I almost choke.

So this is how it feels to be objectified.

"Whoa, whoa. Okay, let's break this party up." Max slides between me and someone's naughty grandma.

"But my picture!" Naughty Granny says.

"I'll take it," I say with a patient nod.

Max frowns.

The woman brightens.

I take the shot, making sure all of my abs are showing, and lead Bobby to the locker room. After handing him my keys, he retrieves my gym bag from the car and returns with it.

Max is waiting on the bench when I change into a T-shirt, shorts, and my gym shoes. His eyes are narrowed and he looks like he's been chewing a handful of thumb tacks.

Sighing heavily again, I check the time on my phone. April probably left the garage by now.

I missed my window.

"What happened?" Max demands.

I tell him about walking out of the shower and my clothes being missing.

"That's absolutely ridiculous!" he mutters.

While Max rants about sportsmanship, my phone buzzes.

DEREK: FreshButtFit, a luxury boxers brand, is interested in a meeting. Call me when you have a chance.

"I guess the picture's gotten out already," I mumble, stowing the phone away.

"The news team?" Max groans.

"It's probably the grannies."

"That stinks, Chance."

"Not really. I got an offer from a luxury boxers brand out of it so…" I shrug.

"I'll speak to Gunner tomorrow," Max says firmly.

"Don't bother." I take a sip from my giant water bottle.

"This was not only immature but totally uncalled for. What are we? In the fifth grade?"

"It's okay." I pat his shoulder. "There was no harm done."

"You were naked as the day you were born *and* it was all caught on camera, but you're not mad?"

"I didn't say that."

Max shakes his head. "I need to do something. As the manager of this team, I can't turn a blind eye."

I swing my gym bag over my shoulder and look back at him. "Turn a blind eye, Max."

"Why?"

My lips curl up cruelly. "So you can do the same when I get them back."

CHAPTER
SIXTEEN

APRIL

I park in front of the Happy Go Lucky nursing home. The acreage is bracketed by an apple orchard to the left and a stone pathway that leads to a sprawling garden, tended by the residents.

Despite the lush grounds, the buildings are straight-edged brick with glass doors, large windows, and golden door handles.

It's *the* most upscale nursing home in the county and, though I'm grateful I was able to get dad a suite here, I can admit that I was overly ambitious.

Dad was my rock growing up. I want him to have *the* best of the best.

However, 'the best' comes with a hefty price tag and right now, my purse is empty.

"I'm so sorry it's taken me this long. I'll have the money wired to you by the end of the month," I practice to myself in the car. "So sorry…"

Mid-speech, my phone rings.

Blushing despite being alone in the car and not *actually* talking to anyone about my money troubles yet, I pick up. "Hey, Rebel."

"Hey, I just wanted to let you know that Chance dropped by and picked up the Bel Air."

"Oh."

She sighs heavily. "I wanted one more day with her. Twenty-four hours wasn't enough."

The memory of Rebel squealing when I drove the Bel Air into the garage yesterday zips through my head. We both 'eeeeped' for three minutes straight, forcing May to get on her bike and pedal home to spare her eardrums.

"Chance said he has a fleet of luxury cars to drive down, so we just have to be patient," I remind her.

"That's the only reason I let him take her back," Rebel admits. "That and I felt sorry for him."

"Why?"

"He was physically standing still, but his eyes were looking all over the shop for you. When I finally told him that you weren't coming in today, he seemed devastated."

I roll my eyes. Rebel can be so dramatic.

"Poor thing. You should have given him a heads-up that you'd be gone. He was really looking forward to talking with you, April."

"About his car? I told him all it needed was an oil change."

"Not that, silly."

"Then what?"

"I think Chance missed you."

It's such a ridiculous statement that it makes me choke. "Me? Missed *me?*"

"That's what I said."

I wrap my fingers around the steering wheel and squeeze. "Might I remind you that he's *the* Chance McLanely. Hockey all-star, famous heir to a fortune, *Chance* McLanely?"

"And?"

"Aaaand," I stress, "if he'd be missing anyone it wouldn't be me. A supermodel? Yes. A social media influencer? Sure. A celebrity? Of course. But me?"

"What's wrong with *you*?" Rebel snaps, sounding ready to fight.

You're just too much like the guys, April. Sometimes, you feel like one of the bros to me.

Unwarranted, Evan's voice rings through my head from the day we broke up.

I scramble outside into the sunshine to escape the memories.

"Can we not talk about this?" I mumble.

"No, we're talking about this. I want to know. What do those women have that you don't?"

"Come on, Rebel. Let's be realistic. I spend more time in a jumpsuit than I do in a dress. I know more about cars than the average guy. And I come home with dirt under my nails that's impossible to clean off. It's embarrassing when I have to shake hands with people. Nothing about me is sexy or soft or ladylike. Does that sound remotely like someone a super famous athlete would want?"

"*Heck yeah!*" Rebel yells. I can picture her with her head tilted, blonde hair spilling down her shoulders and eyes ablaze. "Is having dirt under your nails a crime? Is it the same as going on a murdering spree? Or throwing old ladies off buildings? No! You're a mechanic. It comes with the job. And who decides what's feminine and sexy and soft and what's not? You look super cute in your jumpsuits. Supermodels and social media girls can't compete with your gorgeous natural curls and those adorable freckles! Absolutely not."

I bark out a laugh as I pass a row of shiny cars. "Aw, you're so sweet, Rebel. This is why I have a freakish amount of confidence. You know how to butter me up."

"I'm telling the truth."

"The point is," I wave my hand, "Chance is just a business partner."

"I know what I saw."

"Then maybe that's a sign to get your eyes checked," I tease.

Something glints in the corner of my eye. I notice a familiar convertible in the line of cars parked in front of the nursing home. Am *I* the one who needs to get her eyes checked? Why does that look like Chance's car?

"I'll call you later, Rebel." Hurrying up the stairs and through the revolving glass door, I slip my phone into my purse.

A receptionist greets me with a smile in the lobby.

"April, hi." She checks her watch. "You're a little late today."

My eyes dart around. "Oh… yeah. It was a busy day." I peer past the archway leading to a long, marble hallway. "Is my dad in his suite?"

"He's in the entertainment room with the other residents."

"Thanks." I push away from the counter and hurry to the entertainment room. It's the largest room in the building with wall-to-ceiling windows that let in lots of sunlight.

Usually, there are tables set up all over the room for residents to use their coloring books, knit or play bingo. Today, the tables are pushed against the wall and there are several rows of chairs facing a small, raised platform.

My gaze is immediately drawn to Chance and it's not only because he's dazzling in a button-down shirt that matches his screaming blue eyes.

Photographers surround the stage, snapping pictures of him as he hands out some kind of plastic-wrapped gift.

"Thank you so much," an unfamiliar man dressed in a flashy suit and a jewel-studded watch gestures for a grandmother to step off the stage. "Next!"

I ease into a chair at the back of the row, my eyes drifting from Chance to the banners on either side of the stage. They're images of a man with silver hair wearing nothing but Photoshopped abs and tidy-whities.

The label *FreshButtFitt* is plastered over the banner.

I gasp when my eyes return to center stage and I see Chance handing over a package of boxer briefs to my *father*.

"FrsehButtFitt is the brand for silver foxes like you." He winks. "Enjoy, my friend."

My father grins and hugs the boxers to his chest, skipping down the stairs like he won the last round of Bingo.

I gasp, covering my face with my hands. I'm not sure if Chance hears my gasp or if he just happens to look my way, but his eyes collide with mine. They widen in shock, allowing me to see the dazzling blue even from this distance.

"Chance? Chance?" The flashy suit guy gets Chance's attention. He does a distracted head shake, glancing at me once more before continuing to hand out the underwear.

My face is red. I can *feel* the heat cross my cheeks and down to my chest.

Fighting to act normal, I weave past the rows of chairs and stoop next to my father.

"Hey," I whisper.

His eyes dart to me and back to his gift.

"How are you?"

"Look what I got?" He shows me the boxers.

I laugh at his delighted expression. It's been a while since I've seen him smile like that. Usually, he's grumbling about the food they serve or the fact that someone took his keys and he can't find his car.

"That's great." I smile back at him.

"April?" A woman dressed in a teal blue nursing uniform touches my shoulder. "Miss Tina from admin is looking for you."

My smile shatters and I straighten immediately. Of course, the office is looking for me. I'm behind in my payments.

Unease swirling in my heart, I turn to dad. "I'll be right back, okay?"

Dad doesn't answer.

I follow the nurse, dipping and weaving through the residents who all smile and call me by name.

"April, you'll play a round of Bingo with us later, right?"

"Wouldn't miss it," I say.

"April, my dahlia's bloomed. I'll take you to see them."

"I'll go as soon as I'm finished," I promise.

As I move, I can feel Chance's eyes on me, but I refuse to acknowledge him. I'm afraid if he looks at me, he'll be able to read my mind and know my financial struggles.

When we get into the hallway and are free from prying eyes, I ask the nurse, "How has dad been? Is he eating better now?"

"No. He's still not touching his food. We had to IV him earlier this week."

I frown in concern. "Is his condition getting worse?"

"That's the strange thing. He's had several moments of clarity this week. He was even able to recognize one of his old friends from a photo."

My pulse quickens. "Do you think…" I lick my lips, "that maybe he'd be able to remember me?"

"He might, but we always caution family members to prepare themselves. There's no guarantee that he will."

I'd expected that answer but my heart sinks anyway.

"However, we're doing everything we can to improve his appetite. The chef makes him a special meal every day to entice him. We're taking the best care of your father."

Which is why you should pay what you owe.

But that last part echoes only in the silence of my guilty conscience.

Dad always taught us to pay our debts. Since opening the garage, things have been really difficult. It's the first time in my life I've ever been this behind on my responsibilities.

"This way, April." The nurse opens the door to the admin office and gestures for me to walk in.

Heart in my throat, I step past her. I need to assure the admin that I'm doing everything I can to get the money. *Everything.*

Pretending to date Chance and being thrust into the spotlight was for *this* reason.

So far, dating Chance has gotten my social media tons of likes, but it hasn't produced any new customers for the business. Even so, I'll work harder. I have to.

I'm staking my *life* on this fake relationship.

There's no other option than for it to work.

CHAPTER SEVENTEEN

CHANCE

THREE THINGS KEEP ME FROM RUNNING OFF THE STAGE TO TALK TO April.

Derek will kill me if I ruin this photo op.

The nursing home residents seem extremely excited about these free boxers.

And lastly, I got years of discipline and self-control as an athlete.

However, staying on the stage doesn't mean I'm focusing on taking pictures. I'm all-in, one hundred percent, *locked* on April.

When she excitedly greets an elderly man and smiles up at him like he means the world to her, I take notice.

Is that her dad?

He and April do kind of look alike.

"Alright, that's the last of them," Derek says, striding over to me and offering me coffee. "You can take a short break. We're going to shoot some b-roll for…"

I race off the stage so fast I smell the soles of my sneakers burning. My head whips back and forth. Earlier, April was called away by a nurse. She took this hallway, but I don't see her anywhere. Did she go into one of the rooms?

"Excuse me." I pull aside a nurse in the hallway.

She looks up with an astonished smile. "Me?"

I nod.

Her eyes soften and she bats her eyelashes. "How can I help you?"

"I'm looking for my girlfriend."

Her face instantly drops.

"She's about this high." I gesture to my chest. "With curly brown hair and green eyes like the ocean. What else?" I point a finger at the nurse's cheeks. "Freckles. She's got the cutest freckles—"

"No, I haven't seen her. And I'm really busy." She stomps away.

"Thanks for your time," I call to her back.

Lost and slightly disappointed, I return to the main hall and spot the elderly man April was speaking to. I brighten and head his way. I have a feeling she's still in the building and that she'll see this guy before she leaves.

"Hey." I slip into the chair beside the old man in the white T-shirt and over-alls. "I'm Chance."

"I know who you are," he says, excitedly pumping my hand up and down. "You just got drafted to the league."

My eyes widen and I flick a glance at the ground. Should I correct him?

"Let me tell you, buddy. The real work is just beginning. Here's my advice." He leans close as if dispelling a great secret.

I lean forward too.

"You've got potential. I can see you taking home the cup in a few years. Easy. But you can't get distracted by all the rigama-role. Keep your head down. Play a good game. That's all you gotta do and it's in the bag."

I cough softly. "Thank you, sir. I'll remember that."

"Mr. Brooks," a nurse arrives, "the chef has a surprise for you in the cafeteria. Why don't you follow me?"

"I'm not hungry." Mr. Brooks folds his arms over his chest.

The nurse's tone remains patient. "You promised you'd at least *see* what the food is before you reject it."

The old man looks away.

"Your daughter will be so disappointed if she hears you didn't eat."

"June?" His eyes brighten.

"No," the nurse blows out a breath, "April."

The old man frowns and flounces back into his seat. "I don't know who that is. I want June."

The lump in my throat turns into a boulder. I can just imagine April's heart shattering every time her dad doesn't recognize her.

I face the stubborn patient. "Mr. Brooks?"

"Yes?" He pins eager green eyes on me.

"I'd love it you could help me out with my game."

"Of course, son."

"How about we talk some more over…" I meet the nurse's eyes.

"Lasagna," she whispers.

"Over some tasty lasagna?" I finish.

He rubs his whiskers with thick, calloused fingers. Seeing his weathered hand moves me. I have a strong suspicion that *these* are the hands that taught April to fix cars.

I decide, right then and there, that if it's the last thing I do today, I'll make sure April's dad eats.

"If you're not interested…" I get up.

He grabs my hand. "I'm interested." Releasing his grip, Mr. Brooks gripes, "It's not often I get to talk about hockey. The company here is sub-par. No one watches the game with me." He rolls his eyes as if to say *what a disgrace*. "The cafeteria's this way."

The nurse shoots me a grateful look and I smile, following the old man as he and his cane patter into the cafeteria.

We take a seat and he immediately starts talking about hockey, but I stop him.

"Let's have a few bites first."

He watches me dig in and, when he doesn't follow suit, I gesture to him. "Do you mind joining me? I feel awkward eating alone."

His eyes narrow as if he can tell that I'm setting him up but, after a few beats, he picks up his fork.

April finds us when her dad's plate is clean and we're debating the top ten greatest goals of all time.

"It was Ovi!" I insist.

"Young man, I question your taste if you can't appreciate Orr's play in the nineties—"

"Dad?" she squeaks.

We both turn.

I greet her with a smile.

Mr. Brooks greets her with suspicion.

April clutches her bag. "What are you doing?"

"Eating," I say, showing her my empty plate.

"Yeah, I ate the food." Mr. Brooks brandishes his plate and grumpily scolds, "you nurses don't have to harass me."

April presses her lips together and I feel the overpowering urge to give her a hug.

After a deep breath, she nods. "Good job, Mr. Brooks. I'm so glad," her voice breaks, "so glad to see you eating."

He waves her away. "Can you excuse us? Chance and I were in the middle of a conversation."

As hurt spears through April's eyes, I clear my throat. "I should go. My team is probably looking for me."

"So soon?" Mr. Brooks frowns in disappointment.

"I'll be back," I promise him. "And hopefully, you'll be ready to admit that Ovi's one-handed no look was *the* most spectacular goal of this century."

"Orr is the most iconic goal and I will take that to my grave," he fires back.

I wave goodbye and gesture for April to follow me into the hallway. She walks with her hands slipping into the front pockets of her over-alls and her eyes on the ground.

"Are you okay?" I ask when we're alone. "You seem tired."

"I'm fine," she says. And it's the most unconvincing 'I'm fine' I've ever heard. "Thanks for…" She gestures to the cafeteria with her eyes downcast. "His lack of appetite has been a concern."

I want to ask her when her dad got sick. How she's been handling seeing the man she admired slowly turn into someone who doesn't recognize her. I want to ask what happened with June and if it hurts to know that his eldest daughter is the only one he remembers and calls for, despite it being April who's here visiting him.

But I don't say any of that because I doubt she'd answer.

"It was fun. He's a hockey fan, so we had that in common."

She nods distractedly.

"Which makes me wonder why *you* didn't recognize me." I tilt my head. Outside, I'm smirking but inside I'm filing through my list of jokes. How do I get her to smile again?

"Dad didn't force me to watch the games so I never did." She shrugs. "I would rather watch a ScannerDanner video or read up on a new diagnosis tool."

"That… sounds like fun."

She lets out a breathy little laugh.

It's not a full-on belly laugh but at least her shoulders aren't as tense.

I take a step closer to her, my sneakers a breath away from her steel-toed boots. Her mouth falls open slightly and she sucks in a sharp breath. I look down at her, forcing her to tilt her head back to meet my eyes.

She doesn't flinch or move away despite how near I am to her.

"April," I say softly.

"Mm?"

"I'm not supposed to do this…" I watch as her eyebrow quirks, already anticipating the worst. "But because it's you, I'll sneak your dad a few more boxers. Let me know if you ever need more."

Her dewy eyes collapse into slits as she lets loose a real, sincere laugh that comes all the way from her stomach. Embarrassed, she covers her mouth to hold it back but it spills from the sides of her palm.

"Yeah, what's up with that?" April chuckles. "The very *last* thing I expected was to walk in here and see you as the ambassador for underwear."

"I guess you haven't heard what happened yesterday," I reply with a dry grin.

"What happened yesterday?"

"Forget it."

"Now I'm curious."

"Let's just say, I've been getting lots of compliments on my… glutes."

She giggles.

I straighten and meet her eyes with a satisfied smile.

"What?"

"I really like that."

"What?" She arches an eyebrow.

Your smile, the way you blush, the way car oil stains your fingertips, the way you breathe.

"Your freckles," I say instead. There. That's a non-creepy response.

A blush steals across her face. Like clockwork.

She brushes her cheeks as if trying to sweep them off. "They're ugly."

I am personally offended. "No, they're not. They're magnificent. Why would you say your freckles are ugly?"

A nurse passes by and gives us a curious look.

The tension returns to April's body and her smile disappears again. "Stop joking around. I shouldn't be laughing right now."

"Why not?"

"Because..." Whatever she was about to say, she decides not to share and instead gives me a polite nod. "Because I'm letting out my 'only in front of family and friends' laugh."

"Oh? And which one am I?" I step forward and she shuffles back. "Family?" Another step. Her back hits the wall and I brace a hand next to her head. Leaning down, I add, "A friend?"

Her eyelashes bounce like a chihuahua on a trampoline. She bites down on her lush bottom lip. "I... you're not either."

"What if I want to be?"

"I'm confused. Which one do you want to be?"

"I don't want to choose."

"But—"

"A 'boyfriend' counts as both, right?"

Her eyes widen slightly. Her nose flares. "That position's filled."

"Lucky guy."

"Stop joking around."

I sweep my thumb over one of her freckles. "What if I'm serious? What if... I've been thinking about you all day and I really want to take you out on a date. Soon."

"How soon?" she answers sassily despite her very obvious blush. "I'm kind of busy."

My lips curl up in amusement. "We're heading out of town for a week—Max has us training with another team, and then I have a photoshoot so I'll fly out and be back by Saturday night."

"Isn't that Saturday your first game?" she asks.

I flash her a disarming smile. "You've been keeping up with my schedule."

"I'm just worried you'll be too tired to parade around town with me. Wouldn't the Sunday be better?"

"I won't be able to wait until Sunday." I stare into her eyes that are the color of expensive, turquoise gemstones. "Let's have dinner after the game. That way, whether we win or lose, I'll end the night happy."

If she blinks any faster, she's going to create hurricane-force winds with her eyelashes and then she'll start levitating off the ground.

"There you are, Chance! I was looking everywhere for you." Derek's voice attacks me like a swarm of bees.

I groan and hang my head, slowly removing my hand from the wall and freeing April. The moment my agent sees her, he brightens like she's his next big paycheck and hurries over to her.

"Nice to finally meet you, er, what was your name again?"

"I'm April," she says. The red stain still hasn't left her cheeks.

"Ah yes." Derek winks. "The pretend girlfriend."

Instantly, the air between me and April gets tense.

Not that Derek notices.

He keeps yammering. "You're doing a fantastic job by the way. Really killing it. I knew *this guy* could sell it." Derek clamps a hand over my shoulder. "He's so charismatic, every girl he dated thought she was 'the one'."

I wince.

Derek laughs. "But you? You were a wild card. So I'm relieved you guys have enough natural chemistry to pull this off." He wiggles a finger. "But don't get too carried away. The moment I get this man back to the leagues, it's over."

April's open, trusting eyes instantly shifts with suspicion and I pin my agent with a dark, flaming look. With one word from Derek, what little trust I was starting to build between me and April just crumbled.

And now I'm back to square one.

CHAPTER
EIGHTEEN

APRIL

My pride stings like I stepped in a beehive and attacked the queen.

Smarting and feeling a little exposed, I answer the guy in the flashy suit harshly. "Thank you for the reminder, but I've never forgotten what this is."

Lies. Lies. All lies!

If I were Pinocchio, I'd be balancing a limbo stick on my nose right now.

The truth is that I *did* forget.

Not just that.

While Chance had me backpedalling to the wall like a cement truck on a construction site, my brain slipped out of my head and splattered to the ground. I'm surprised I didn't slip on brain fluid.

Thankfully, I'm not alone in catching the Chance-flu. His agent made it clear that there have been a long line of women before me.

So honestly, this isn't my fault.

It's Chance's fault for being so freakishly charming.

Chance spares the flashy suit guy a dark look and says, "April, this is my agent Derek. Derek, this is April."

"April. *Aw.* What a nice, wholesome name for a small-town girl."

His words are polite enough but the tone behind them feels extremely condescending.

I'm not the only one who picks up on it because Chance's thick eyebrows form an immediate and strict V over his eyes.

"*April* is the name of a talented mechanic running her own shop and building a successful business." In a blink, the intense expression is gone and he smiles at his agent. "That's, I think, what you meant to say."

"Uh, right. Yes… right. Well, it's a pleasure to meet you, April the talented and successful mechanic." Derek side-eyes Chance as if to say *happy?*

Chance responds with a proud smile.

I walk backward. "I need to go check on my dad, but Chance about that date…"

He looks at me expectantly.

"Text me the details." I raise both fists in a tiny cheer. "As per our agreement, I'll have my game face on."

"Wait. April…"

I do a quick wave and rush back to the cafeteria. Peeking through the swinging doors, I see Derek and Chance talking and then both men head to the exits.

Relief drags a sigh out of my chest and I lean over to catch my breath.

The look in Chance's eyes when he told me he wanted to be my boyfriend *felt* real. Stirrings of something I thought had died with my last relationship whooshed to life. While his bicep bulged to my left, his cologne swirled around me and his fathomless blue eyes carried me away like a tide, I wanted so badly to feel all the gooey feelings.

But feelings aren't an excuse to make bad decisions.

And Chance McLanely?

He's a bad decision in the making.

I take a few more deep breaths until I'm back in reality where I belong. Fixing the straps of my jumper, I look around the cafeteria for dad.

He's nowhere to be found.

Heading through the balcony doors that lead to the backyard, I look past beautiful rose bushes and hydrangeas until I see him at a wooden bench reading a book.

"*Auto Fundamentals* is a great one." I sit beside him and the bench creaks.

He adjusts his glasses. It's so strange to see him wear them. Dad hated working with his bi-focals in the garage. '*The darn glasses slip down my nose all the time. It's impossible!*'

I'll never forget the day I bought him his first, prescription goggles for Christmas. He hugged me like he'd gotten a brand-new car.

Dad turns a page. "It's always good to brush up on the basics. Cars might change in the future but…"

"Principles never change," I finish.

He lets out a disbelieving laugh. "How'd you know that?"

Because you've told me that a million times, dad. "I had a great teacher."

"You're an auto mechanic?" He looks astonished.

"I am. I have my own shop and everything."

"There's another shop in town other than Kinsey's?" He arches an eyebrow.

"Yes, there is."

"Impressive. I always thought he needed some stiff competition, but I wasn't brave enough to start anything on my own." He closes the book, leaving his thumb inside to mark the page. "Where'd you learn the trade?"

"I went to a technical college, but I was working on cars before then. I used to follow my dad around when he did jobs. Eventually, dad handed me a wrench and told me to join him."

He nods wisely. "Cars don't care what gender you are. When they're on the last leg, when they're in pain, they just need a solution."

"Yes, they do."

"Your dad sounds like a good man."

"He is," I croak, my voice tight. "You remind me of him."

My father shifts in discomfort. Lips pursed, he points down to his book. "I should get back to it."

"Sure. I'll visit next week." I take a step away before turning back.

He looks up.

"Can I give you a hug?" I blurt.

His bushy eyebrows cave in and he studies me curiously.

"Would that be okay?" I clasp my hands in front of me, trying not to fidget.

Dad lifts a shoulder in a half-hearted allowance. I surge forward, wrapping my arms around him and hugging him tight.

'Your account balance is too high. The higher-ups are beginning to discuss discharging your father'.

'I want to start over with you, April'.

'Don't get carried away. Chance is like this with all the girls.'

"There's so much I wish I could talk to you about. I miss coming to you for advice. You always had all the answers."

Dad's strong fingers curl around me and he pats my back. Gently, he pushes me away so he can look down at my face.

I look at him too, noting the wrinkles that have seeped around his eyes and mouth. The liver spots that plague the back of his paper-thin skin. The green eyes that used to shine strong and vigorously, but now swim with confusion.

"I have a daughter too. Her name's June and you know what I'd say to her if she were here?"

I sniff. "What?"

"Life can throw all the curveballs it wants. Sometimes, you'll dodge 'em and sometimes you'll get knocked down. But eventually you're going to pick yourself up and what you do when you're on your feet again, well, that's the most important."

"What do I do?" I whisper.

"Simple. Return to the principles, to the foundations that never change. And you build from there."

My lips tremble as I smile. "That's good advice."

He nods.

Picking myself up from the bench, I wave goodbye to my dad and wipe the tears away.

"Leaving already, April?" A nurse asks as I walk through the cafeteria to get back to the main hallway.

"Oh, yeah, I need to stop by Mrs. Armstrong to watch her dahlia's and then I'm gone."

"Did you square everything away with the admin?" She gives me a knowing look.

Embarrassment tries to claw its hands into me, but I always feel ten times taller after a pep talk from my dad. So this time, I just smile and nod breezily. "Yeah, I did. I'm on it."

"Great." She waves.

I leave the cafeteria, find Mrs. Armstrong, coo over her dahlias and then I'm ready to head back to the garage to strategize a solution with Rebel. My dad's nursing home fees need to be paid and I'm going to pay it if I have to drive two counties down to find customers.

"I know! She's so short and stumpy. And her hair! It's so wild? Does she not own a flat iron?"

"I have no idea what Chance sees in her. She wears those dirty jumpers everywhere. It's like she wants *to be mistaken for a hobo."*

"Famous athletes date anyone that breathes. Maybe he wants something different."

"By different you mean a hobbit?"

Bursts of laughter follow the statement.

I slow my steps as I walk past the nurse's lounge where three women are standing around a coffee bar, mixing cream into their coffees.

"Like I said, athletes date anyone with a skirt but they don't ever marry girls like her. He's going to dump her for someone more on his level."

"No one even talks about them online anymore. She's so boring looking that sports guys don't care and the female fans don't admire her either."

"They don't even look good together, so why bother?"

Another round of laughter rings out.

The nurses glance at the door and I hurry past, my heart hammering against my ribs and angry tears forming in my eyes.

For a moment, I'm back in that garage with Evan as he listed all the reasons a man would cheat on me. *'You don't even TRY to look nice, April. It's like you want everyone to forget you're a woman. How could any man be attracted to that?'*

I run to my car, crawl inside and slam the door. Wrapping my fingers on the steering wheel, I lean my head against it and squeeze for all I'm worth.

In the chaos, the shame and the embarrassment, I hear my dad's voice.

Return to the principles and build from there.

I straighten and stare unseeingly through the windshield. Dad's advice will take too long, and there's no guarantee it'll work. Right now, with so much at stake, I don't have time to build on foundations. I need results fast. And that means playing the game by the world's rules. Not mine.

Pulling out my cell phone in a flash of angry determination, I text May to come to the garage.

Next, I call Rebel.

"Hey," she says chirpily, "how's your dad?"

I talk right over her. "Rebel, remember you said I could always raid your closet. No questions asked?"

"Uh... yeah?"

I start my car and reverse out of the parking lot so hard that I spit stones and gravel. "I need to borrow a dress."

CHAPTER NINETEEN

CHANCE

I sulk in the backseat of Derek's rented BMW, giving my fidget spinner a moody flick. My agent glances at me in the rearview mirror before darting his gaze back to the road.

He taps his finger on the steering wheel three times and sighs out loud. "What's going on with you and that mechanic?"

I say nothing.

The spinner makes a soft, whirring sound as the fans blur in front of me.

"Are you seriously into her?"

Another flick.

"Come on, Chance. I haven't seen you in ages. What's with all the angry glares?"

"You haven't seen me because you tossed me like garbage after the suspension."

"What's the point in bringing up the past? I came back, didn't I?"

I scowl.

"Look, I know what you're really mad about. It's because I

said the wrong thing in front of that girl—" At my dark look, he rectifies, "that strong, independent female mechanic." He waves a hand dismissively. "I apologized for my comment about her being a small town girl but the thing is… she *is* a small town girl. I wasn't wrong about that."

"Aren't you tired of running your mouth, Derek?" I growl.

"How am I the bad guy for reminding the both of you not to get attached? You think this is a romance movie, bro? There is *no* way you can have her *and* the league."

I hunker lower in my seat.

"Do you plan on giving up and staying here in the middle of nowhere?"

"Of course not," I say firmly.

"And you think April will leave her town, abandon her family and close down the shop she worked hard for so she can follow you to the city?"

I open my mouth and then slam it shut.

Derek straightens his shoulders and gives me a *'that's what I thought'* look.

I give the fidget spinner another flick.

"You have enough on your plate without throwing women into the mix. Your team can't even make the playoffs in the *minors*. I've seen the tapes."

"This time is different. They have me."

"Hockey's not an individual sport." He drills a finger into his temple. "Your teammates stripped you naked and hung you out to dry. Does that sound like a team that'll be in sync on the ice?"

I lean back and stare out the window. "I have a plan to fix that."

"What are you going to do?"

I let the expectant silence ring.

"At least give me a hint."

"'An eye for an eye'." I watch him. "Isn't that what you taught me?"

A slow, proud grin twists his lips. "That's right. You're

Chance McLanely and *no one* messes with you. If these chumps won't like you, at least make them fear you."

Tired of the conversation, I put away my spinner, slip my earbuds in and lean my head back.

But all I can see when I close my eyes is April's hurt expression when she ran away from me in the hallway.

* * *

BY NOW, EVERYONE ON THE TEAM KNOWS MY WARDROBE malfunction was the work of The Wicked Wizards of the West—that's my new name for Gunner, Renthrow, Watson, and Theilan.

It doesn't escape my notice that the WWW become extra vigilant when I'm around. They startle when I pass by, are extra quiet when I enter a room, and they keep their gym bags nearby when they change in the showers.

They're not the only ones holding their breaths.

Everyone on the team is tense.

They know payback is coming.

Watching the WWW squirm is its own delight. Power struggles were a regular part of life in the league and, as the New Guy, I constantly had to prove myself to establish my place on the hierarchy.

This time is different.

None of these guys intimidate me.

But they *do* annoy me.

"Come on, come on, Renthrow!" I throw my arms up as the winger skates past me on the ice, acting like he doesn't see me.

Unfortunately, while the WWW are keeping things low key off the ice, *on* the ice, it's a total mess. It's the last day of our scrimmage and we still haven't found our mojo.

I rush into position, my fingers clenched around my stick. Gunner looks over at me like he wants me to trip over my own skates, and I return the glare. Our rivalry, while obvious when we were doing in-house scrimmages, is like a giant, throbbing *toe* sticking out in the away games.

The team we're practicing with is way less experienced than us and yet we win over them by too close of a margin. If this week's been any indication of how we'll function during official games, we don't have a fart's chance in a gas chamber of making it to the playoffs.

More winded from irritation than actual exhaustion, I puff out a smoky, white breath and return my attention to the puck. It skids into the pocket and I head there. A blur to my left catches me off-guard and I swivel just as Gunner cuts me off to attack the defense.

I grit my teeth, fighting to hold my temper. Gunner may have given up the center position to appease Max, but he still plays like he's waiting for a breakout pass. This is the second clash this week.

My head whips around to the coach who starts whistling and, suddenly, finds something on his shoes way more interesting than our game.

I bite back a groan. Playing on this team is like paddling upstream with nothing but a palm leaf while surrounded by man-eating sharks.

The opposing team steals the puck and shoot past me, heading for our goalie. I skate close to Gunner and make a back and forth caper. He narrows his eyes, sweat dripping from beneath his helmet.

I make the gesture again.

He shakes his head and shrugs.

Argh!

Up ahead, Watson is on his knees at the goal, preparing for a scramble. He narrowly deflects the shot. The flash of sheepish realization on his face tells me he knows, if they'd been a little more aggressive, the net would have eaten the puck.

Exhaling again, I assess my teammates. There's no way we should be battling this hard for the puck. Both I and the WWW are extremely competitive. In the game, at least, we should be able to set aside our differences.

"They're attacking our zone in the middle," I yell at Renthrow as we skate to the boards.

He gives me a quick nod and I take off toward the puck, but it's not easy to break the pass. After having their butts handed to them all week, our opponents are giving it their all.

The coach starts noticing the other team's determination and he makes constant substitutions. I hate every second I'm on the bench and I catapult out of the box when I'm put back in the action.

We play down to the wire. Even I'm winded by the time the last buzzer sounds.

The scoreboard declares that it's our win, but neither I nor the WWW are smiling.

After high-fiving our opponents, my teammates shrug out of their gear and head to the showers. That's when Bobby appears, wearing his usual flannel over a white undershirt, khakis and heavy work boots.

"Bobby?" Gunner checks his phone. "What are you doing here so early?"

His eyes nervously meet mine before darting away. "We, uh, the bus needs to leave now."

I mentally face-palm.

Note to self, *never ask Bobby to lie again.*

Gunner narrows his eyes in suspicion, but Bobby grins nervously and keeps talking in that cajoling tone of his. "I thought you guys would be eager to get back? If not, I can leave and come back in an hour or two… or three…"

Roars of disapproval break out from the other players.

I can't blame them. While the hospitality of the team here has been impeccable, it hasn't been fun sharing three run-down bathrooms with twenty men or sleeping in a bunk bed that was built for someone under six feet.

"I wouldn't mind showering at home and crashing on my own bed," Gunner admits with a shrug.

The other WWW members nod along.

Bobby and I both breathe out in relief.

"Gunner, Renthrow, Watson, and Theilan," he calls. I try not to make it obvious that I'm lingering while he takes the WWW aside. "Before you get on the bus, I'd just like to confirm the schedule. I was told to take you four to the arena. Did you get the email from Max?"

The email he's referring to is a dud account that I created on my phone while the other guys were asleep two nights ago.

"Yeah, I got it," Theilan says.

The rest of the WWW grunt in acknowledgement.

Bobby's smile gets a little less nervous. "I'll drop you off at the arena first."

When the conversation breaks up, I drop to one knee, pretending to tie my shoe.

"Whoa!" Bobby says loudly. "Chance, I did not see you there." His stilted, acting voice makes me inwardly cringe.

"Hey, Bobby. Drive safely, man." I bump his fist.

"You're not coming?" Gunner asks, giving me the stink eye.

"Nah." I shake my head. "My agent is picking me up for a photoshoot. I'll come in a little later." Smiling a little wider, I tell Gunner, "I didn't know you cared so much about my schedule?"

He rolls his eyes and stalks outside.

The rest of the WWW pass me without comment.

When Bobby turns to follow them, he gives me a little nod.

I nod back.

The WWW are about to be served a little taste of revenge.

CHAPTER TWENTY

APRIL

"You know those makeover scenes in the movies where the main character walks into a store and two minutes later she walks out with all her shopping bags?"

"Yeah?" Rebel calls.

I shove the dressing room curtain aside. The hooks make a *tsk* sound as it travels the length of the metal rails. "Why is *my* makeover scene taking seven days?"

"Because this is real life, not a montage, silly. Now spin." Rebel sticks up two fingers and makes a 'twirl' gesture.

I do a three-sixty. "Have I mentioned how much I hate shopping?"

"That you have." Rebel shakes her head at my outfit and her glossy blonde hair ripples with the movement. She shoos me away.

"I asked you for a dress. A single dress. I feel like I've tried hundreds of dresses since then. One of them *must* be acceptable enough." I stomp back into the dressing room.

"Stop whining!" May yells at me, capping her bottle of water.

She turns sideways in the couch and lets her legs dangle over the edge. "How does Rebel put up with you?"

I push my head out of the dressing room curtains to give my sister the stinkiest of stink eyes.

She sticks her tongue out at me.

Rebel waves me back into the dressing room. "Try on the red one!"

"The sparkly red one with the low cut? No thanks!"

"It's not a low cut. It has a perfectly respectable V-neck and yes, you *will* wear it because your date is tomorrow and we have literally run out of time."

"None of this would be necessary if you'd just lent me a dress," I grumble, slithering out of the short white dress with the poofy skirt and capped shoulders.

"April, I'm several inches taller than you and we have two different body types. You wouldn't fit in my clothes."

"Are you calling me fat?"

"No, I said we have two different body types." Rebel's voice rings with exasperation. Even though I can't see her, I can imagine her pouting her lips and rolling her eyes. "You need to find a silhouette that's flattering for *you*."

"At the very least we should have gone to a thrift store. I don't have money for this," I grumble.

May pipes up. "Ah-ah, as the head of marketing, we're using everything in our budget on this dress. I just *know* we're going to make it all back within a week."

I purse my lips because none of us *know* that. I had one crazy idea in the heat of the moment and now, instead of snuggling in bed watching car repair videos and reading car manuals, I'm stuck visiting every dress shop in the county.

I'm starting to regret letting May and Rebel in on my plan to get more customers. If I'd just kept my thoughts to myself then, when I inevitably stopped being angry about the comments I overheard, this particular idea would have died a quiet and natural death.

Unfortunately, my sister and best friend are here to keep the vision alive.

I frown as I shimmy the red dress up my hips. It's a little snug, so I grip both ends and give it a tug like I'm wrenching off a stubborn bolt on the engine.

"Why are you grunting?" Rebel asks. "Is it too tight?"

"Yeah!"

"Stop tugging!" she yells.

I stop immediately.

"Why did you yell?" May complains.

"Your sister can twist the lug nut off a tire with her bare hands. Imagine what she'll do to fabric if she gives it her full strength." Rebel's heels *click-clack* outside and then I see an arm stick over the top of the stall. Her bracelets dangle to her wrist as she wiggles her fingers. "Give me the dress. I'll ask if they have a size up."

I shove the shimmery fabric into her hands. "Maybe look for some other alternatives while you're out there. That red is too much."

"I know it's a lot for you since you prefer dark colors…"

"Dark colors don't get dirty," I remind her.

"… but there's something about this dress, your skin tone and your new highlights that I think will really work together."

As her heels click away, I swivel and face the mirror in all my half-clad glory. I'm wearing a bra, like an actual one and not the sporty variety that I prefer and my hair is now a gorgeous chocolate brown with highlights.

One of the first places Rebel dragged me to was the hair salon —thankfully, not the one in town where Evan did most of his cheating. The hairdresser originally only wanted highlights done to my curls, but I was so emotional that I proudly told him to do whatever he thought would be the most dramatic change.

I sat in the chair as the flat iron sizzled like bacon and my curls disappeared before my eyes. Now, I have straight, silky hair that's so slinky, it slips out of every ponytail clip I own.

Twisting back and forth, I marvel as the bronzy highlights play peek-a-boo with the light. The new color weaves in and out of my dark hair like the sun kissed the top of my head and promised I'd live in an everlasting summer.

It's nice.

I do miss my curls but… I don't hate it.

"Here you go!" Rebel shoves the replaced dress over the top of the booth. "You got it?"

"Yeah!"

I shimmy into the red dress and breathe out in relief when it eases over my hips with no resistance. The zipper moves smoothly and I fly out of the dressing room without even looking at myself.

Rebel rises slowly.

May dribbles water down the corner of her lips.

"Are you okay?" I ask my drooling sister.

Eyes locked on me, Rebel trots closer.

"What?" I run a hand down the dress. "Is it that bad?"

"Shut up and turn around." Rebel grips me by the shoulders and forcibly turns me to the mirror.

I stare at the woman in red and my jaw nearly disconnects from my body.

Whoa.

* * *

Rebel holds the front door of the store open for me as I walk out with two shopping bags—one holding the dress and the other bearing the shoes, earrings, and bracelets that May insisted was 'in the marketing budget'.

I have a feeling my sister is putting her own personal funds into this. Since I'm the one who *gave* her the marketing budget, I know exactly what we have available.

And this is way over that price.

"I can't wait until Chance sees you," Rebel says, strutting down the sidewalk like it's her own personal runway.

May laughs gleefully. "He's going to die, come back to life and then die again."

"I'm not doing this for Chance," I point out.

"I know. He's just collateral damage." May winks.

They burst out laughing uproariously. I chuckle on a less shoulder-shaking and knee-slapping scale.

Despite being one hundred percent invested in this makeover for the sake of my business, I feel a tinge of excitement at the thought of Chance seeing me all dolled up. I may not be a socialite, an heiress or a supermodel, but I do clean up nicely.

I'm smiling to myself, when a shadow falls on my path. I look up to witness the automotive kingpin of our small town glowering down at me.

Stewart Kinsey is a bear of a man in his early fifties. But don't be fooled by his thick limbs and giant hands. He's limber enough to squeeze his beer belly underneath a car and change the oxygen sensor in a jiffy.

Stewart's cold eyes trail the shopping bags and then move to my straight hair and the cherry gloss Rebel foisted on me because 'cracked lips aren't cute'.

"Brooks! Fancy seeing you here."

"Mr. Kinsey." I nod stiffly.

His eyes jump to Rebel who scowls in response. "How've *you* been, pretty lady?"

Rebel's stare is so frosty it feels like a sudden winter blizzard has descended. "Mr. Kinsey."

"Call me 'uncle', darling." He sidles toward her. "Why, I remember when you were knee high." Kinsey grins like a shark. "And your mama brought you with her while she was cleaning the garage. Every year, you look more and more like her."

Rebel jerks forward.

I step in front of her before she can lunge "It looks like you were on your way to something, Mr. Kinsey. We won't keep you."

May and I grip one of Rebel's arms and steer her away from Kinsey.

"Oh, Brooks!" Kinsey calls.

I stop, but I don't turn around.

"I think you're doing a good thing, changing your hair and dressing up for that hockey player. Doing your best to be a rich man's wife is a much easier job than being a mechanic. That's for sure." He chuckles like he's dispensing the wisest advice. "Well, it's not like your garage was doing that well anyway. Let me know when you start selling your machinery. No need to make a big fuss. I'll take all those diagnostic tools off your hands."

Rebel whips around, her eyes ablaze.

"Come on." I tug on her hand.

"Are you just gonna let him talk to you like that?" Rebel hisses as we drag her around the bend.

"Arguing won't change a Kinsey's mind," I remind her, my gut churning. "Only beating them fair and square."

"We *have* to make the garage a success," Rebel says, her eyes brimming with angry tears.

"We will," I promise her, my hands shaking slightly. "We will."

CHAPTER
TWENTY-ONE

CHANCE

A STACK OF COMPUTER MONITORS BLINK TO LIFE IN FRONT OF ME. I fall into the office chair and it makes a loud creak. Leaning forward, I scrape my thumb over the monitor showing the arena's front entrance.

"Hm." I rub my thumb and index finger together, noting the dust coating both. "Does Max not have security at the arena?"

My phone buzzes with a text.

Derek: I sent the girls over like you wanted. They should be arriving by now.

Right on time, a van drives into the parking lot. Tall, beautiful girls dressed in tights and crop tops pile out of a van.

Checking my phone for the time, I balk.

Where's Bobby?

I send a frantic text to the Zamboni driver, but there's no response.

Plucking out my fidget spinner, I give it a whirl. If Bobby's late and we miss this window, the crux of my plan falls apart.

"Come on, come on," I whisper, as if I can wirelessly communicate my wishes.

I open my eyes and see movement on the monitor. Scrambling forward, I tap into the video feed of the street. A giant bus rolls into the camera's line of sight.

My shoulders sag in relief.

Bobby's arrived.

The cheer team is still moving up and down from their truck to the arena, carrying their pompoms and camera equipment. My gaze naturally flicks over the girls, but it's with nothing more than respectful appreciation. Ever since I met April, my interest in other women saw a significant dip.

Thankfully, the WWW have not yet been bewitched by a curly-haired female mechanic like I have.

My teammates dismount the bus and notice the girls. Gunner and Renthrow don't slow their stride as they head inside the arena, but Theilan and Watson do a double take. The girls smile at them. They smile back and wander over to make small talk.

My phone rings.

I answer, eyes on the feed.

"Chance," Bobby talks in a nervous rush, "phase one is complete. I got the four of them here. What do I do now?"

"I already put the sign on the locker door. Gunner and Renthrow should notice it right away." As I speak, the guys are turning the bend and approaching the locker room.

I tap the speaker icon, set my phone on the dusty surface of the desk and click to the security feed with a full view of the hallway.

Gunner is stalking ahead with a scowl. Rain or shine, he always looks like someone cut him off in traffic. For someone whose family owns the whole town, you'd think the guy would be a lot less grumpy.

Renthrow stomps beside him and throws a Hello Kitty gym bag over his shoulder. His muscles bulge like he's training for a bodybuilding competition, so the cartoon-themed bag looks extremely out of place as it flaps against his back.

"Call Theilan and Watson inside." I tell Bobby. "Then stay out of sight for a bit."

"Aye-aye, captain."

The phone clicks off.

On screen, Gunner and Renthrow stop in front of the door to the locker room. Gunner is the first to notice my *'Changing Room for the Jumping Diamonds'* sign. He points to the paper and says something to Renthrow.

"Isn't there a way to get audio?" I click around the security feed program, but none of the icons make sense. I went to school for hockey, not cyber security.

To be fair, I don't know how to do the thing I *did* technically get a degree for. Studying business administration was a way to keep mom off my back while I partied for four years.

How I scraped by in those classes that I never showed up for is a mystery that I *could* solve... if I checked dad's bank transactions. But some secrets are better left buried.

I'm determined to at least get a decibel of audio going but my phone rings, distracting me.

Thinking it's Bobby, I answer without looking.

"Not yet, Bobby. I'll call you when we get to phase three."

"What's 'phase three' and who's Bobby?" Mom demands.

I startle and nearly drop the phone on the desk.

"Hello?" Mom squawks. "Chance?"

Gingerly, I hold the phone properly to my ear. "Mom?"

"What mischief are you getting into over there?"

"Me? I... I was... ah," I cough loudly, "mom, I'm in the middle of something. Why'd you call?"

"Can't a mother check on her son, the underwear model?"

I groan loudly. I've been so focused on April, the team, and doing everything I can to get back to the league, that I didn't think of what would happen if those pictures reached my parents.

"You saw?" I cringe.

"I waited and waited, thinking *surely* Chance will call with an explanation on why he's parading around with his buttocks ablaze, but *nooo*," she stresses, "I'd no choice but to pick up the phone and call you myself."

"There was a bit of an accident…" Something on the screen distracts me. Theilan and Watson have joined Gunner and Renthrow in the hallway. They're all heading to the second locker room.

"Accident? What accident?"

"Nothing too serious. But unfortunately, it happened in front of a news team."

I set a six minute timer. I've been observing the WWW all week. On average, they only take about six minutes to shower.

Putting mom on speaker, I navigate to my messenger app and type out new instructions for Bobby. After I press 'send', the monitor picks up Bobby's location. He's on the ice, taking pictures of the dancers. The girls crowd him, pushing their cell phones at him and flashing practiced smiles.

"A news team? We should sue them! There's such a thing as citizen's privacy, you know."

Bobby, answer your phone.

"Put your lawyers away, mom," I mumble, checking the monitor. "We don't need to sue anyone."

"As a mother, it is my job to protect my son's buttocks—"

"Mom, can you *stop* saying 'buttocks'? *Please?*" I swipe my phone from the desk, sneak out of the security room and look both ways.

"Would you prefer the term 'no-no zone'? Bodunk-a-donk? Rumparoony—as the kids say?"

"Which kids? I would pay to know which kids are saying that." I tiptoe down the hallway.

"If you can't even say the word, Chance, why on *earth* would you galivant around in such a manner, embarrassing yourself and your family for the whole world to see?"

I'm getting close to the second locker room.

Lowering my voice, I whisper, "I'm sorry, mom. It's my fault. It'll never happen again. Now, I really need to go."

"Wait, I have one more thing to discuss. Who's that girl you keep getting photographed with?"

I tense. "You're asking like you haven't already run a background check."

"That's not very nice, Chance," she says dryly. "And of course I've run a background check. I know more about that woman than you do."

"Mom…"

"Her name is April Brooks. She went to a *trade school*," mom sounds mildly disgusted. "Her dad is in a nursing home and she's struggling to pay both his bills and her garage's mortgage."

That stops me short. "April's struggling to pay her dad's bills?"

"She looks very different than the women you usually go for, Chance. And don't get me wrong. That's not a bad thing. I'm just a little concerned that such a woman would be with you for your money."

I check my watch. Three minutes.

I'm running out of time.

"April's not like that. She's amazing."

"But—"

"Things are different with her," I tell mom firmly.

"So you're bringing her to the gala?"

I crane my neck to see into the locker room. "Yes, yes. You'll see her then."

"Chance, darling, if you're ready for 'different', I can introduce you to so many women—"

"I'll call you later, mom. Love you."

Tapping the 'end call' button abruptly, I slip my phone into my pocket and sneak into the locker room.

Two minutes.

I run like a track and field athlete at the Olympics. My fingers dig into fabric. Shoes. Gym bags. I even snatch the team's flag from the wall. Rolling them into a giant ball, I scurry out of the locker room just as one of the faucets in the shower squeaks off.

"No way you got so many numbers," Theilan is saying to someone.

Watson's voice rings with pride. "I got ten, bro."

"Call them. I bet half those girls gave you dupes." That voice belongs to the Hello Kitty man himself, Renthrow.

"Wait right here. I'll get my cell phone and prove it." Footsteps slap the ground and a moment later, I hear, "Did anyone move my cell phone?"

Holding back laughter, I dash to the security room. By the time I drop comfortably into the chair behind the monitors, the action is already taking place.

Renthrow's head is wedged into the hallway while his body is hunkering behind the door. His eyes are wide and he's craning his neck as far as it can go. Mouth wide, he appears to be yelling for someone.

Poor guy is yelling at empty air.

Gunner's head pops out under Renthrow.

Theilan and Watson follow.

They look like four peas in a naked little pod.

Gunner is the first to realize he's being watched. His chilly stare angles upward at the security camera. I do a chin-up gesture, returning his glare with a greeting.

The four heads disappear.

A moment later, Gunner steps into the hallway. I burst out laughing when I see the tiny speedo he's wearing. I left the speedos in the locker room long before they arrived at the arena. They're sparkly, pink, and several sizes too small.

Eyes narrowed, Gunner turns and gestures to the others. Slowly, the rest of the WWW file out. Theilan is covering his speedo with both hands as he inches along in embarrassment. Watson keeps picking at the material, walking crookedly.

Renthrow is at the front of the pack, but today, he's not

walking like he's leading an army. Instead, he's crouched over, making small, shuffling movements, and jumping at every sound.

From the camera, I see a trio of dancers moving in their direction. Gunner glances back and forth nervously.

The rest of WWW freeze.

As if an alarm went off, the men make a sharp turn and scramble back to the locker room. Theilan goes sprawling. None of the others go back for him. He looks over his shoulder with wild eyes, crawls desperately on all fours and pushes himself to two feet again.

My stomach is about to split apart.

Tears leak from my eyes.

No wonder they were laughing so hard when they pranked me. I'm enjoying the show and I don't even have audio.

Vindicated, I head back down to meet them.

As I get closer to the locker room, I hear Gunner saying, "Renthrow, you take a hit for the team. Go find some clothes and I'll get your daughter those tickets to *Star Princess Girl* that you've been asking about."

I freeze in my tracks.

Renthrow has a daughter? Since when?

So then... is the Hello Kitty themed gym bag and slippers not his aesthetic? Does it have something to do with his kid?

"Theilan should go. He's the one who isn't afraid of showing off his body online."

"Making exercise videos on the beach is *not* the same thing," Theilan objects. "Watson should go!"

With a grin, I step into the room. "That won't be necessary."

"You!"

"Where the heck are my clothes!"

A pack of glittery-speedo-wearing athletes charge at me, all yelling at the same time.

Renthrow moves to grab me by the collar, but I stop him by lifting my phone.

"Smile for the camera, boys."

Immediately, they halt in their tracks, cover their faces and yell for me to put the phone down.

Gunner glares at me, but even he backs off.

"You think this is funny, McLanely?" Watson clips through gritted teeth.

"*You* thought it was funny. When you did it to me."

A harsh, self-reflective silence falls on the room.

There's a reason 'do unto others as you want done unto you' is a golden rule. It's because it's true.

I lift my phone higher.

"Ah!"

"Don't!"

But instead of taking a picture, I call Bobby.

Thankfully, he answers.

"Can you bring the clothes I left in the security room?" I say into the phone.

"I'll be right there," Bobby answers.

Gunner straightens his shoulders, his glare thick enough to melt paint. "Was this all a set up? Even those girls?"

"The girls were part of the ruse, yes," I say calmly.

Renthrow's bushy eyebrows tighten over his eyes. "We were never supposed to retake photos for the website, were we?"

"Nope. That was sent from a fake email account."

Watson scoffs. "This is where your prank ends? Nice try, McLanely, but you didn't go as far as we did."

I say nothing.

Gunner inhales sharply. With a dark frown, he looks at Watson. "He could have if he wanted to."

Awareness rolls over Watson's face.

Renthrow narrows his eyes.

"I don't want a war." I step forward with my eyes on the lockers behind them. It's difficult to have a serious conversation when my opponents are wearing ridiculous, bedazzled pieces of fabric.

"You asked for one the moment you took over the team without earning it," Theilan says.

"Maybe. Maybe not. But fighting each other won't get any of us what we want."

Someone snorts. Could be Renthrow. It came from his direction.

"You think hating my guts will win you any games? It won't. Our real enemies are the players who come on that ice thinking they can keep us from the trophy."

Bobby hustles into the room then. I nod to the players and he instantly gets the message.

"Get dressed." I tell them as Bobby dishes out their clothes. "You look silly in those speedos."

That comment earns me dark looks across the board.

Gunner shrugs the shirt over his head and flings a heated stare at Bobby.

"Bobby, how could you betray us like this?" Theilan says.

Bobby shrugs. "You each got one chance to torture each other. Now, you're even and we can finally focus on the season."

Gunner sits on a bench to tie his shoes, his glare a little less severe. "We knew you were going to get us back someday. We were waiting all week. As far as revenge goes, this isn't bad."

"Thank you."

"But it could have been worse," he allows. "So why didn't you make it worse?"

"Because as much as I believe in giving as good as I get, there's something more important than that."

"Which is?" Renthrow grunts.

"Protecting my team at all costs."

Watson gasps.

Theilan glances away.

Renthrow studies me as if he doesn't know what to do with me.

Gunner shakes his head disbelievingly. "We know why

you're here. We know you're not sticking around. Don't bother acting like we're a team."

"That's exactly why I don't want to waste time fighting with you. You don't have to like me. We don't have to be friends, but what we are—whether we like it or not—is teammates."

I stride right up to Gunner.

He leans back, eyeing me warily.

"Honest truth? Off the ice, you suck."

He bares his lips in a snarl.

"But," I offer my hand, "on the ice, you're my family."

Gunner smacks my hand away.

I offer my hand again, determined.

Gunner studies the hand, rises to his feet and stares me right in the eyes. "Dream on, McLanely. You suck on *and* off the ice."

I laugh, seeing the olive branch for what it is.

Renthrow slaps me on the back. "Where'd you find these speedos, man? They're awful."

"I ordered them online. They were pretty customizable. I almost got one with each of your names on 'em."

"You couldn't get them a size bigger?" Theilan squirms, his mouth twisted in discomfort.

"Yeah, sorry about that."

Watson points at Theilan and guffaws. "You really do look awful. I wonder how many of those girls would have texted back if they saw you like this?"

"Are you kidding? I could bag twice as many girls in this speedo."

Renthrow waves a hand at the door. "You've still got a chance."

"I said I *could*. I didn't say I *wanted to*." Theilan grins and runs into the shower with his bundle of clothes.

Watson, Renthrow and Gunner follow him.

At the last second, Gunner turns back and looks at me with his cold stare.

I tilt my chin up, waiting.

"I'm dumping your gift in the trash," he says. "Unless you want it back."

I make a disgusted face. "You can keep it as a souvenir."

He narrows his eyes and moves toward the shower. Then he stops and looks at me again. "We usually head over to The Tipsy Tuna on the weekends. Just to let off some steam."

My eyes widen in shock. That was definitely an invitation to join them, but do I have to? I wanted to go see April after this.

As the silence lengthens, Gunner's face hardens. "If you have something better to do…"

Gunner strikes me as the petty type. He will never make another offer if I reject this one. "I could use a drink. Who's buying?"

"If you want us to pretend tonight never happened…"

I chuckle. "I guess I am."

CHAPTER
TWENTY-TWO

APRIL

Rebel stretches her arms over her head and then rotates her neck to the left and right. She mindlessly reaches for her granola bowl and somehow picks out only the m&ms to toss into her mouth.

"This is *exhausting*," she says.

I resurface from the engine I'd been half-buried in and glare over my shoulder. "Quilting is tiring you out?" I point between me and the stubborn engine. "Really?"

"First of all, this isn't quilting. It's embroidery. Second of all, don't start huffing at me. You're the one who wants to work until eight p.m. on a Friday night. I'm only here for best friend moral support."

"You're here because you don't want to go grocery shopping." I wiggle my wrench at her.

She throws her hands up as if to say 'guilty'. "Being an adult is over-rated. Why do I have to buy my own groceries? Why aren't my cupboards magically re-stocked without me doing anything?"

"You know there's an app that hires someone to grocery shop for you?"

"It's cheaper if I just get in the car and do it myself."

"So do it yourself."

She sinks lower into the chair, groaning, "Noooo."

I smirk at her dramatics and remove my gloves.

"What are you sewing anyway?" I wonder.

"Can't you tell?" She holds the stitching up.

I scrunch my nose. "Is it… a dog?"

"No, it's a polar bear. Where do you see a dog in this?" She shakes the embroidery close to my face.

"I guess… if I twist my head to the side and close one eye, it does kind of look like a dog."

Rebel tucks the bowl to her stomach. "That's it. No granola for you."

I let loose a loud, unladylike guffaw. The sound echoes around the garage. When I realize my voice is echoing because we have no cars in the bay and no potential customers in sight, my laughter dies and my smile freezes.

Rebel sees my panicked expression. "Hey, what's wrong?"

"Nothing." I shake my head. "I'm just frustrated with my progress on the car."

"Don't let it get to you. I even splurged to update our auto software and couldn't figure it out. From the diagrams, we'll probably need to take the car apart."

"Before we take anything down, I need to locate the problem first. The car hasn't been showing any of the symptoms the customer described." I pull my ponytail out, scoop up all my hair again and fix it into a bun. In direct defiance, the bun slips right out of the clip and caramel-streaked strands fall around my shoulders.

My hair has a mind of its own whether it's straight or curly.

"I'm going to take the car for a test drive. The symptoms might show up if I move around town."

"Or you could, you know, *not*."

"Are you coming or are you going grocery shopping?"

Rebel skates across the garage and jumps into the passenger seat.

I climb in and start the car.

"My back is killing me." My best friend makes a fist and punches her lower back. "How those ladies in the embroidering club walk around without hunching over is mind-boggling."

"Why are you even *in* the lady's embroidering club?" I flick the indicator and turn onto Main Street.

Her shoulders tighten. "Is there a reason someone like me can't be in a club like that?"

"If you enjoy it, I guess… I just know those ladies tend to be the prissy, uptight types."

"It's a club for people who enjoy sewing. And I happen to be one of those people."

I slant her a suspicious look.

Rebel pretends not to notice. Tapping a manicured finger on her necklace, she muses, "Where should we go? The park? The lake?"

"It doesn't matter where we go. Can you record the screen please? I want to study the engine levels later."

Rebel accepts the computer from me with a disapproving sound. "Seriously, April? Do you not have an off button?"

"The *only* reason this client came to us is because no one else could fix his problem. So even if it means I stay up all night with the help of energy drinks, I'm repairing this car."

She sighs heavily. "I'm not saying we don't fix the car, but the thing is… you need balance. Even May is hanging out with her friends tonight."

"And I'm hanging out with you."

"Exactly. Which is why," she thrusts a finger forward, "forget the lake or the hills. We're going to The Tipsy Tuna."

* * *

The Tipsy Tuna is a wooden bar and restaurant next to the lake. It's got a long pier where the wealthier townsfolk who own boats can jet over, dock and enjoy a perfectly fried snapper.

The rest of us regular folks park in the parking lot.

It seems like everyone has the idea to eat at The Tipsy Tuna tonight because it takes me forever to find a parking spot. I finally locate an open space, but instead of getting out, I keep studying the engine levels.

"Come on," Rebel whines, tugging on my arm.

"Just a second." My eyes are glued to the screen. I press the brakes, listen to the engine roar and watch the lines on the diagnostic program jump. Concerned, I turn to Rebel, "This shouldn't be happening. See? This is the fuel injector line and this is—"

"April put that laptop away before I turn *you* into a tipsy tuna."

With a sigh, I slap the laptop closed and follow her outside. "I didn't plan on going inside tonight. I didn't even wash my hands before coming here."

"They have a bathroom." She drags me up the stairs, her blonde hair trailing in the wind. "Besides, the only way we're not walking in there is if you want to go home, shower and change into one of your new outfits."

"Nope. I'm good in my jumper."

"Then let's go."

I trail her, keeping a frown on my face as protest. But internally, I'm grateful for the break.

Regardless of what Rebel thinks about my work-life balance, I do enjoy going out every once in a while. The Tipsy Tuna has a great, friendly atmosphere and I love all the sea food platters. Except their tuna dishes. Which is ironic.

Golden lights beam from the windows. I can hear the laughter and trendy pop music blasting.

Just before we reach the entrance, the door bursts open and two extremely beautiful, tall women strut out. They're wearing crop tops with some kind of bedazzled star and leather shorts with stockings and cowboy boots.

"Excuse us," they say, giggling.

Rebel and I step aside so they can pass.

As we enter the bar, we exchange quiet looks with eyebrows raised.

'Is there a festival going on?' I silently communicate.

Rebel pushes out her lips and shrugs. *'Don't think so.'*

Inside The Tipsy Tuna is *crawling* with gorgeous women dressed in the same star logo crop-tops, shorts and stockings.

"Let's order," Rebel says, pointing to the counter.

We wade through the mass of human bodies and are greeted by Mauve, Bobby's wife.

"Hey, Mauve."

"Hey, sweetie." Mauve lifts a dark hand and uses the back of it to wipe the sweat on her face. "Haven't seen you in a while."

"That's because she lives inside the garage," Rebel teases.

"Ah, yes. Bobby told me all about how you swooped in to save the day with the Zamboni."

"It was nothing." I wave.

"You two are very talented ladies." She winks. "Now, what can I getchya?"

We give our orders and Mauve slips into the back.

Bopping my head to the beat, I glance around. I'm glad Rebel convinced me to do this. I'm already feeling a lot calmer.

In the corner of my eye, I notice a guy pat his friend and point in our direction. He's not the only one. Many of the male patrons have taken notice and are staring at us.

Well, not *us*.

They're staring at Rebel, who looks like a model as she casually sits, one leg folded over the other and neat pink nails drumming the shiny bar. If my profile looked that stunning, I'd walk around sideways for the rest of my life.

"Doesn't it get exhausting having this much attention?" I

squirm. I'm not even the one they're looking at, but it still makes me self-conscious.

"What?" Rebel leans toward me.

I start to repeat myself, but my words are swallowed up by a loud and sudden roar. It's coming from the game section at the rear of the bar.

We both crane our necks to get a better look.

I immediately notice the Lucky Strikers jerseys. With their cool confidence, fancy jackets, and towering height, the hockey players are hard to miss.

"Gunner's here," I point him out to Rebel.

As expected, her eyes go dark and she scowls. Suddenly, her expression clears and she points, "I think that's Chance."

"Chance isn't here."

"Are you sure?"

"He would have texted me if he was back," I say confidently.

I felt awkward around Chance after Derek's comments in the nursing home. It was my intention to avoid him until absolutely necessary. However, Chance texted me while he was away, and it felt rude not to answer. Then eventually, I started looking forward to answering.

We've texted every day since. We don't talk for long, since we're both pretty busy, but I *know* he would have let me know if he was here.

"No, April." Rebel's somber gaze makes me uneasy. "It really is him."

I look over just as Chance tosses a dart and hits the bulls eye. A cheer erupts from the crowd and, suddenly, a tall, gorgeous woman with the most magazine-worthy curves and shampoo-commercial hair throws her arms around him, hugging him tightly.

My heart wrenches in my chest and I spin back around as if I caught my mom and dad kissing.

Rebel looks furious. "Why didn't he tell you he was back?

And who's that girl?" She smacks her hand on the bar and scrambles to her feet. "I'm going over there."

"No." I pull her down.

"But, Chance, he—"

"He what?" I meet her gaze desperately, ignoring the pain gushing through my heart. "Needs to report his every move to me? Can't hang out with other women? He's not my real boyfriend, remember?"

"Then why do you look so upset?" Rebel asks.

"I'm not." I slither off the bar stool. "It's too loud in here and I need to get back to work."

"April…"

"I'll wait for you in the car."

Hurrying out of The Tipsy Tuna, I tell myself I'm being foolish. Why am I in pain when I meant every word I said to Rebel?

Chance owes me nothing.

He and I are barely friends.

At best, we're co-workers.

It doesn't matter to me if he didn't tell me he was in town. It doesn't matter if he finds that girl more attractive than me. It doesn't even matter if he goes home with her tonight.

It means nothing at all.

CHAPTER
TWENTY-THREE

CHANCE

The scent of sweat, iron and wet mats fill my nostrils. I push the weights higher, holding the bar up until my face turns red. With an exhale, I bring it down to my chest and push up again.

My body's burning.

Sweat leaks from my crown to my chin.

I flare my nostrils, breathing through the exercise.

"Chill out, man." Max looks down at me with concern. "If you keep this up, your arms will be noodles. Forget getting on the ice, you won't be able to hold your hockey stick."

I grunt and push the iron bar up, ignoring him.

"Chance. *Stop.*" Max's firm command is followed by him grabbing the weights and forcing them into the cradle while I'm still holding on.

The urge to grab the weights back and push myself to the limit fills me. Working out is my go-to when I'm *really* stressed. Right now, I'm filled with the kind of anxiety my fidget spinner can't handle.

"What's going on?" Max demands, tossing me a clean towel.

I dab at the sweat on my face and arms. In the gym's mirror, I see a man with dark, wet hair sticking to his forehead, cheeks a ruddy red and eyes a little wild and lost.

I look insane.

Pulling at my grey tank, I control my breathing so my chest stops pumping like it's filling up a tire. Then I shake my hair so I look a little less like a wet dog.

Averting my eyes to my cell phone, I open the screen.

No new notifications.

Navigating to the message icon, I open to April's number.

The messages I sent since last night blare up at me.

Me: Hey, April. I forgot to mention I'm back in town.

Me: Hey.

Me: Are you asleep?

Me: Morning, April.

Me: I stopped by the shop in case you were there and wanted tacos.

Me: Are you at your dad's?

Me: Don't forget our date tonight after the game. I'm really looking forward to it.

"Ugh," Max's voice sounds close to my ear.

I look over and find him cringing at my texts.

"Hey!" I pull the phone to my chest.

"Why are you blowing up April's phone?"

I glare at him, my mouth wired shut.

Max clips his nose. "Do you smell that? Smells like desperation in here."

"You must be smelling your BO."

He laughs loudly. "I never thought I'd see *the* Chance McLanely get ghosted. Is this karma for all the hearts you broke in college?"

"Ghosted means you won't see them again. April's right here in town. We have a date tonight."

He smirks. "You don't sound so sure."

I open my mouth to disagree and then realize I don't have a

leg to stand on. April's been ignoring my texts since I came back and that's not a good sign.

Reaching for my water bottle, I chug all the contents and wipe my mouth with the back of my hand.

"I wouldn't be desperate if she was answering her phone," I grumble.

Max makes the disgusted sound again.

I shove him.

"You *do* remember that *you two aren't real?*" Max hisses the last part of the sentence. "Why are you bothering the poor girl?"

"I'm not bothering her."

"What do you call sending eighteen messages?"

"It was eight."

"You should have stopped after she didn't answer the first one. Instead, you stalked her shop—"

"I brought her food."

"That's what all the stalkers say."

I resist the urge to punch him.

Squeezing the towel until it screams for mercy, I ask, "You really think April's ignoring me on purpose?"

"Everyone is glued to their phones these days." Max points out. "In this era of technology, not texting back is a choice."

I worry my bottom lip.

"Did you do something to offend her?"

"No, nothing." I scratch my head. "I mean…"

Max leans in. "What?"

I think of that day at the nursing home. Trapping April against the wall. Testing the waters by admitting I like her freckles and her smile.

"Maybe…"

"Maybe?" Max urges.

Did I push too hard?

I close my eyes and think of that pretty flush spreading across her cheeks. Her calloused fingers digging into the wall behind her. Her pretty green eyes sparkling at me.

No, it wasn't that.

Was it Derek's stupid comments?

The first thing I did after that day was send April a text apologizing for my agent. But that was a week ago and April assured me that it didn't bother her. Had she been lying? Was she just bottling up her true irritation all this time?

"What?" Max yells, startling me from my thoughts. "What did you do?"

"I don't know for sure, but whatever it is… I'll beg her to forgive me."

Max snorts. "Then prepare to have your butt handed to you. Without the mascot head to hide behind this time."

"I can't fix it unless she tells me what I did wrong!"

"When in the history of womanhood has a lady ever come out and communicated what she's feeling?"

"The least I can do is let her know I *want* to fix it. We should work out our issues like a real…I mean, a healthy, fake couple." Eyebrows tightening, I growl, "I'm gonna call her."

Max yanks my phone away.

I lunge for it.

He fakes a toss. "You want me to throw it out the window?"

Slowly, I lower my arm.

"Think clearly, Chance. When a woman is mad, the *last* thing you need to do is keep calling her."

"I'll show up at her place then."

Max plants a hand on my shoulder and forcibly pushes me back into the bench. "Have you never been in the doghouse before?"

"No."

"Really?"

"Women tend to just," I flash my warmest smile, "love me."

"Okay, Romeo. Out here in the real world, you don't harass your girlfriend into talking to you. Give her some space."

"And if that doesn't work?"

Max rubs his chin in thought. "Show up with roses, not tacos. Or at least do a taco bouquet. Show some effort."

I sigh, accepting defeat.

He slides the phone over to me. From the shift in his demeanor, I can tell he's about to broach a serious topic.

"You think the team's ready for tonight?"

"As ready as we'll ever be." I'm still thinking about April, so I don't sugar coat the truth. "I made some progress with Gunner, but we still haven't found a rhythm on the ice. It's inevitable that we'll get in each other's way. Plus, the team is still divided between the two of us. We don't have one, clear leader, and it's confusing for everyone."

Max flinches. "I was hoping you two would have worked things out at the bar yesterday."

"How do you know we were at the bar yesterday?"

"This is a small town. Everyone saw you, but even if they didn't, you think I wouldn't know you invited a dance team to tour our stadium? Seriously?"

He has a point.

"I allowed it because I wanted you to get revenge out of your system."

"Bobby said the same thing." My eyes widen. "Did you tell him to cooperate with me?"

"Like I said, it's *my* team, Chance."

Huh.

Max checks his watch and then slaps me on the back. "Come on. I'll get you a heat pack. After all those reps, your arms are going to kill you tonight."

Max is half-right.

But it's not my tired arms that try to murder me before the game.

I'm exercising on the ice, earbuds in my ears so I can tune out the noise from the crowd when someone nearly bulldozes me down.

"Sorry, sorry." The opposing goalie says, eyes locked on something in the stands.

"Watch where you're going." I glare at the distracted, young player before continuing my reps.

It's difficult enough to get in the zone with all the noise. It feels like the entire town is here tonight. If Max isn't coded for a safety violation tomorrow, I'll be surprised.

Someone skates up to me and a firm, insistent tap hits my shoulder. I whirl around, eyebrows tightening.

Theilan is behind me, wearing the blue and black hockey gear and a wry grin. Pointing up at the stands, he speaks with words that are muffled through his mouth guard, "McLanely, I think that's your girlfriend."

My first instinct is to dismiss him, but something prompts me to swing around.

That's when my heart stops beating.

A woman in a bold red dress is floating down the stairs. Reporters are stampeding around her, trying to film her angelic descent. An awed silence falls on every row she passes by, a quiet wave rippling through the entire arena.

Even from this distance I can see the delicate jewelry sparkling on her wrist. When she reaches up to tuck a lock of her straight brown hair behind her ear, I get a glimpse of dazzling silver earrings.

There's no way that's April, is it?

I've always known April to wear baggy shirts and shorts or T-shirts under oil-stained jumpers. She would never wear a dress that showed so much of her beautiful, creamy skin.

Not only that, but April's hair is full of gorgeous untamable curls.

This woman is…

Not my fake girlfriend.

I'm about to turn away when a pair of unmistakable, gemstone-green eyes collide into me.

I skate back like someone pushed me into the boards.
My heart stops again.
Forget seeing a cardiologist, there's no escaping the truth.
April Brooks is here… to kill me.

CHAPTER
TWENTY-FOUR

APRIL

THIS IS *THE* MOST MORTIFYING MOMENT OF MY LIFE.

Everyone is watching, filming, pointing *at me*.

Why, oh why did I think this was a good idea?

"April, over here! Over here! One more picture!"

I smile and wave, so, *so* grateful that Rebel forced me to practice my picture-taking skills.

Inhale.

Exhale.

Play the game, April. Play the game.

Camera lights flash in my face.

Questions yell from all around.

Overwhelmed, I look for somewhere to point my attention and unwittingly catch sight of Chance on the ice. He looks like an intimidating mass of gear and muscle. How tall is he again? He seems bigger than usual. Is it because of the skates?

My fingers curl into fists and I force myself not to notice how his dark, Prince Eric hair is mostly hidden under a helmet with pieces sweeping just over his vivid blue eyes.

"Excuse me." Rebel waves her hands wildly in front of the flashing cameras. "The game's about to start. April will answer all your questions later."

I rub my shoulders, shivering. The air conditioner is *blasting* in the arena. I knew it would be cold, but I didn't anticipate it'd be Arctic-tundra cold.

Yeah, yeah. I'm aware it's my fault. It was a risk not to wear a jacket, but I had to make sacrifices for my grand entrance.

"*Excuse* me!" Rebel sounds like she's reaching the last of her patience. "You can't do this here!"

The reporters ignore her, continuing to swarm me.

Footsteps thump on the bleachers above and I glance up, noticing a bunch of security guards pouring into our section. A bear of a man charges ahead of them. He looks like he could pick all the journalists up and kick them out himself.

"Hey, April. I'm Max, Chance's friend."

"I remember you," I mutter.

"Chance sent me to escort you down to better seats." Gesturing with an arm the size of a cannon, the bear-man says, "Follow me please."

I grab Rebel's hand, dragging her with me. I'm not sure if Max's invitation included my best friend or not, but it does now.

The security guards hold the reporters off while Max weaves through a series of brightly lit hallways. We make it to the lower ring of the stands, closer to the ice.

"I still have some things to take care of." Max checks his watch and a slight, disgruntled look crosses his face. "So Bobby will escort you to your seats."

"Thank you," I say, sensing his barely-restrained impatience.

He smiles tightly and dashes off.

I remember Chance mentioning that his best friend is the owner of the team, and it strikes me then that Max probably had better things to do than rescue a teammate's girlfriend from reporters.

"April!" Bobby appears before us, smiling brightly. He's

dressed in the team colors, blue and black. "And Rebel. Don't you ladies look lovely?"

"Thanks, Bobby." Rebel tosses her hair.

"This way." Bobby takes the lead. "Watch your step, April. Don't trip in that pretty dress."

I smile, happy to be in the company of someone who *isn't* sticking a camera in my face.

"Is this the VIP section?" Rebel teases, following Bobby down the stairs.

"Unfortunately, we don't have one of those. Chance requested that you sit on the glass, but not too close since it can be overwhelming for your first game. This *is* your first game, right?" He peers at me.

"Uh, my first game in person? Yeah."

Bobby nods as if he needed the confirmation. "I think right around here is good. Not too close, not too far."

He gestures to seats that I know for a fact were *not* empty because when I tried to purchase tickets two days ago, only three spots were left in the entire stadium.

Rebel and I plop in.

The differences between our former seats and these upgraded seats remind me of the time I bought a super expensive, high-resolution scanner. It's a mix of wide-eyed awe and a dash of *'I can't believe I lived my entire life without seeing these details? Is THIS how the graph of the TPS waveform is supposed to look?'*

There's a flurry of movement on the ice. Tall players skate past wearing fancy hockey uniforms. Excitement is a thick cloud in the air and it's extra intense this close to the action. I can totally understand why these seats are considered the best. Right now, it's as if I'm *on* the ice with the players.

"Do you ladies need anything to eat or drink?" Bobby asks.

I shake my head, feeling self-conscious. "I'm sure you have better things to do than get food and drinks for us, Bobby."

"That might be true, April but," Bobby leans in to speak conspiratorially, "Chance lost his mind when he saw you tonight. If Max and I didn't scramble to your aid, he would have jumped over the boards and run to you himself."

I glance at Rebel. "The boards?"

"You see those?" She points at the tall, transparent panes separating us from the ice.

Whoa. There's no way Chance could have scaled something that tall... right?

"Unfortunately, Chance can't run into the stands when the game's about to start. You understand, right?" Bobby scans my face as if one hint of dissatisfaction from me will result in Chance beating him up.

My heart coughs like an engine with faulty wires. "Y-yes."

"Great. So drinks?"

"No, we're good." I swallow hard.

Bobby flashes one more, friendly smile and runs off.

"Chance is really playing up his 'role' tonight," Rebel says, her lips pursed.

"Isn't it clear from last night that we're *both* acting?" I rub my hands over my shoulders, kick my feet and blow on my palms to give them warmth.

"It's just so hypocritical."

"I'm doing the same thing. So technically, if he's a hypocrite, so am I."

With a shrug, she admits, "You're right, but I just want to hate him in peace. This has nothing to do with being rational."

That makes me smile.

Just then, I catch Chance looking at me.

Immediately, my grin falls flat and I dart my gaze away.

"Uh, I'm freezing," I mumble. My teeth are chattering so loudly it sounds like a badger whittling a stick.

Rebel smacks her forehead. "I forgot your jacket in the car. Hold on a sec, I'll be right back."

"Do you want to share my blanket?" a girlish voice asks before my best friend can dart away.

I look to my right and notice a little girl, no older than six or seven, sitting two seats down. She has dark hair, twin dimples and chipmunk cheeks. The little darling is wearing leggings under a tutu along with a varsity jacket. Her funky outfit instantly gains my approval.

She pokes her head forward, entrancing me with warm brown eyes. "You can borrow it if you want."

"Oh, sweetie. It's okay. My friend will get my jacket for me."

She unrolls her blanket and stretches across the two people sitting between us. "My daddy says it's nice to share."

My heart melts into a little puddle.

I accept the hot-pink offering. When I unroll it, I see a bunch of Hello-Kitty cartoons over the fabric. It might not exactly be my taste, but it *is* warm.

"Thank you," I say. "What's your name?"

The two people between me and the little girl scoot back to facilitate our conversation.

"Gordie."

"Gordie? Is that short for something?" I ask.

Everyone in our vicinity gasps.

The woman in the row behind us shoots me the stink eye.

Rebel smacks my arm. "It's for Gordie Howe. As in 'Mr. Hockey'?"

I stare blankly at her.

"He pretty much invented the Gordie Howe hat trick?"

I got nothing is what my stilted expression says.

Rebel throws her hands up with a disappointed sigh.

"Well, thanks anyway, Gordie." I tell her, settling the blanket on my lap.

"Oh, you had a blanket?" A haggard voice sounds above me.

I look up.

Bobby is bent over our row, panting with enough force to crack a rib bone. He grips the back of a chair.

"Chance..." he gasps, "wanted me..." he sucks in a breath, "to bring you his jacket."

I blink pensively. "Are you okay, Bobby?"

"Yeah. Just…" He straightens and stretches his back. "Not as sprightly as I used to be. Anyway, can you take this? I need to go help Max."

"Sure. And I'm sorry about all this, Bobby."

He waves away my words and stumbles up the stairs like a drunken deer at midnight.

The stares, this time, are ten times more judgmental than when I walked in wearing a bright red dress.

I sink lower in my seat.

The spectators at the beginning of the row pass Chance's jacket down to me.

I hear someone mumbling, *"Who is she? A princess?"*

"This is why I'm never getting a girlfriend. You just turn into their slave."

"Like you could ever GET a girlfriend."

The comments get fainter and fainter until the jacket finally lands in my lap.

I stare at the fabric.

McLanely is printed largely and in all caps across the back.

Rebel leans over, sees the jacket and snorts. "It might as well read 'property of Chance McLanely. If lost please return to owner'."

I silently agree.

"Are you going to wear it?" Rebel asks.

I say nothing.

"Do you *want* to wear it?"

Want isn't a part of the equation.

Rebel frowns. "You don't have to. You have an alternative." She picks up the Hello Kitty blanket.

Shaking my head, I shrug into the jacket and almost moan in relief when I feel the warmth. The blanket was nice, but it only covered my legs so my arms were still freezing. Not only is Chance's jacket warm, but it still smells like him too.

Not that that's a bonus.

I'm just saying…

I hand the blanket back to Gordie who stands in her chair to smile at me. "You don't need it anymore?"

"Uh, no. My… my friend gave me his."

"Cool." She turns and shows off proudly. "Look, I'm wearing my daddy's jacket too."

On the back of the blue and black gear is the name 'RENTHROW'.

I smile politely at her as the lights go dim.

The game's about to begin.

Chance and his team are going to skate around on the ice for about two hours and then…

And then whether his team wins or not… we have a date.

CHAPTER
TWENTY-FIVE

CHANCE

"You with us?" Gunner grunts, skating to center ice for the face off.

I glance at April, taking her in for the last time. Once the game starts, the world around me will become a blur except for my teammates and the puck.

"Yeah." I nod. Seeing April in my jacket makes it easier to concentrate.

I close my eyes, visualizing the rink the way I always do. A sense of calm, of familiarity, of *home* falls over me.

This is where I belong.

I open my eyes.

The opposing team faces us down for the puck drop.

Gunner points two fingers at the board and nods at me. It's a signal letting me know that they'll keep me away from the offside—which is my biggest trigger. I hate being smashed into the boards, especially by the opposing team. Fifty percent of my fights in the league started that way. It's like dynamite on a gasoline keg.

Just focus on keeping it together tonight.

My limbs are loose. My stick, secure in my hands.

The referee drops the puck.

I'm off like a gunshot.

A thrill runs through my veins as I skate past my opponents, but it's not long until I'm picking up the other team's defensemen. They swarm me like fleas on a dog.

No surprise there. Clearing me from the ice and pushing me into the penalty box was a common strategy for my past opponents.

The team we're up against isn't known for a great defense, but they're wicked aggressive on the attack. Our main plan tonight is keeping control of the puck.

And me?

Well, I need to keep control of my temper.

The cold prickles in my throat, turning the air around me heavy. The lights in the arena are bright enough that I can see the sweat percolating on the defenseman's chin as he blazes a line straight for me.

Ice sprays beneath my skates when I stop abruptly. He tries to sweep the puck from under me, but I'm ten moves ahead of him. It's already on its way, headed to Renthrow who takes control like he was built for the ice.

I'm on the move, ready to skate over the line the moment Renthrow crosses with the puck.

The opposing team claims it back and we're on the defense.

I'm heading into the scrimmage when someone blows into my shoulder. I'm hit from behind with enough force to jerk me forward. My head whips up and I glare at number thirteen, a bulky guy with dull brown eyes. He sneers at me from behind his mouth guard.

The ref doesn't call it and that, plus the obvious targeting, sets my blood boiling.

Deep breath, Chance.

Getting myself together, I skate ahead just as Theilan clears the puck. We're back in control of the play and I do an about face, skating into the fray.

The moment Theilan passes and I have control of the puck, the opposing team flies at me. Hockey sticks dart around my legs, fighting to take the puck. In the chaos, I feel a hand shove into my back.

The ref calls the infraction.

But the spark's been lit.

My nostrils flare when I notice number thirteen smirking at me. He skates close by and, if his words weren't lost to the wind, I'm one hundred percent sure he'd be heckling me.

Skating ahead of him, I follow the play until we get to our defense zone. There, thirteen skates off with the puck.

Red clouds my vision.

I meet Watson's eyes. The goalie is dressed in thick knee pads and a strong helmet. But even with all the gear, his concern shines through. He does a slow downward gesture with his hands. *Calm down.*

I heave a breath, shaking my head.

The coach calls me in during the time out, probably seeing what Watson is seeing.

"Cool off, McLanely," he says, patting my back when I climb over the boards. "They're coming for our throats tonight. You won't do us any good in the sin bin."

I'm replaced by another forward, who's ten times slower than I am. On pins and needles, I watch the game proceed without me.

Gunner makes the first score, and the crowd goes ballistic.

I resist the urge to look up at April. I wanted to earn the first point of tonight's game, but the opposing team made it impossible by closing me off every time.

If Gunner had been as targeted as I was, he wouldn't have made the first goal.

It's a selfish thought and I brush it away. Ego has no place in the game. What matters is we're in the lead.

But it's not for long.

The other team scores too.

We're head to head.

As the momentum falters, the coach makes a flurry of substitutions.

I'm back in the game.

A fire lights under me and I cut down the ice, skating with my eyes on the goal. Renthrow and Gunner flank me on either side, waiting for a prime opportunity to score.

Renthrow gets control of the puck first and he passes to Gunner who gets stuck at the point, an area just outside the opposing team's blue line. Gunner should *not* be so close to the boards, but our defensemen are on the other side of the rink.

Gunner passes and I take possession of the puck. An opposing defenseman skates toward me and I instinctively flick my stick. I don't even realize it's a flip pass until I hear the faint roar of the crowd and the announcers screaming about the play.

"Did you see that? McLanely did not come here to waste time!"

Head whipping back and forth, I calculate the best opportunity to shoot straight past the goalie. A shadow breaks my concentration. It's number thirteen flying at me.

I shift my weight from my left leg to my right. Instinctively, I send the puck hurtling toward the goal just as thirteen slams me into the boards.

My helmet ricochets off the clear surface. Beyond me, the crowd grimaces and I hear a collective 'ooh'.

The puck skids against the goalie's stick and deflects.

I missed.

Faintly, I hear the announcers goading me.

"Oh, that was a nasty slam."

"Are we about to see a classic McLanely meltdown?"

"They better get that penalty box ready, Stu."

I lunge forward, not thinking about anything but teaching that smuck a lesson. Penalty box or no, who does he think he is?

My hands are outstretched and ready to grab number thirteen by the back of his gear. On the way, I catch a glimpse of a bright, sparkling red dress.

April.

"I don't like violence in the middle of the game."

It's what she said to me the first day we met.

My body slows and my hands lower before I realize I've made the decision to stand down. My eyes skim past number thirteen who's on his way to the penalty box.

I look through the crowd.

And then I see her.

April.

She's on her feet, eyes glued to me. Her mouth is open, her brows knitted, her hands clasped in front of her. My jacket is slipping down her shoulders, revealing more of her beautiful red gown, but she seems oblivious to the cold.

Suddenly, the rest of the world rushes in.

I hear the screams of the crowd. Feel the biting cold of the rink. Taste the sweat above my upper lip.

"You okay?" Gunner yells as he skates past me.

I rejoin the game, my heart pumping and my hands shaking.

"Can you believe that? Chance McLanely walked away from a fight."

"Someone learned his lesson after leaving the league."

"I never thought I'd see the day McLanely avoided the sin bin!"

Pushing the noises out of my head, I take advantage of the opposing team's crippled state. They're down a man and I'm going to make it hurt.

My first score is a punishment for scheming to lock me in the sin bin.

The second score is specifically to number thirteen who slammed me into the boards and robbed me of my chance to score a goal and impress April.

My third score is just because I'm in a good mood, the game's about to be over and that means, my date with April will begin soon.

Five… four… three… two…

The buzzer goes off and I raise my arms, grinning at the scoreboard.

Gunner, Renthrow, Theilan and Watson converge on me, followed by the rest of my teammates who scramble over the boards to make a dog pile.

"*McLanely has done it again! He's on fire!*" the announcers boom.

The celebration continues with lots of roaring from my teammates.

After three minutes of being suffocated by hockey sticks, hockey gear, and men that weigh more than motorcycles, I'm allowed to surface.

The first pair of eyes I look for are April's. She's smiling in the stands, her cheeks flushed pink from the cold and her straight hair flowing down her shoulders.

Tearing off my helmet so there's nothing obstructing my view of her, I blow her a kiss.

A bunch of 'awws' break out from the crowd.

Cameras flash all around.

We've got the attention of the entire stadium.

I smirk at her, an eyebrow arched. She sees me staring and her brows lift in response.

Telepathically, I invite her to join me.

Do you dare?

A bright, adventurous smile skirts over her face and she scoots out of her row. For a second, April disappears from sight and then she pops up in the entrance to the ice.

I skate toward her. My cheeks hurt and I realize it's because I'm smiling too broadly.

Seeing this woman running toward me… my heart is about to burst.

Is this what heaven feels like?

With the crowd chanting my name and confetti spraying

down, April springs into the rink and I catch her, skating back slightly before regaining my balance.

"Congratulations," she says.

"Than—"

My 'thank you' is cut off when she cradles my face and kisses me.

CHAPTER
TWENTY-SIX

APRIL

I kissed Chance for publicity.

That's what I keep telling myself as my hands tighten around his neck.

After the kiss, he lowers me to my feet, allowing my body to slide down his hard, muscular chest and sweaty hockey gear. His cheeks are red from the game. His hair is damp and clumped together in a way that makes me want to run my fingers through it.

Resisting the urge to do so, I press my hands into his shoulder gear as the world swirls with brighter colors.

How tall *is* this man? It feels like I've been sliding down his torso for *hours*.

Every torturous inch lights me up inside. I know it's still sub-zero degrees in the stadium, but it feels like I'm stuck in a barbecue grill being slow roasted.

I'm on my feet now and my neck is already aching from looking up at him. Chance's eyes are half-hooded, allowing me to admire just how abnormally long and *pretty* his black eyelashes are.

He tilts my chin up with his coarse hockey glove. The scratchy material on the underside of my jaw is strangely alluring and a lump gets caught in my throat.

"Thank you for coming," Chance says, as if it really means everything to him.

"No problem," I say hoarsely.

When he bends down as if he'll kiss me again, my eyes widen.

"Chance, how does it feel to be back on the ice?"

"Chance, where are you going after the game!"

We both freeze as reporters yell at the star player, eager to get the first post-game interview.

Out of sorts, I push away from Chance. It's too strong of a shove, however, and my heels end up skittering on the ice. Arms windmilling, I struggle to catch my balance just as Chance grabs my elbow.

He waits until I'm settled before ripping his glove off and sliding his hand down the length of my hand.

His grip on the hockey stick during the game had been strong and sure, even in the midst of all those other players attacking him. But now, his fingers are as gentle as silk.

His touch eases down my elbow, streaking a path of mini-lightning bolts.

By the time he finally captures my palm I'm about to hyperventilate.

Ducking my head, I shuffle back to the entrance.

Chance doesn't let go of my hand and maintains my pace. He'd been moving like a Bugatti at full throttle on his skates, so I'm surprised he's able to go so slowly.

I grip him tightly, walking on stilts.

Okay, two-inch heels aren't exactly classified as 'stilts', but since I *never* wear heels, they might as well be.

"You want some skates?" Chance teases when he sees me wobbling.

"Absolutely not. I'm deathly allergic to falling on ice and balancing on razor-thin blades," I mutter back.

Chance chuckles and keeps a steady grip on me until we get to non-slippery ground. The moment Chance steps onto the platform, he's surrounded by his teammates, the coach, and reporters. It's his moment to shine, so I slip away to find Rebel.

Thankfully, she sent a text letting me know she's in the parking lot.

As I hurry past the chairs where we were sitting, I look for Gordie, but I don't see her anywhere.

Outside, everyone stops and stares at me, but I don't slow down. Hoofing it to the parking lot, I locate my best friend's car and dive in.

"Well, hello, hello," Rebel says darkly. I'm hit with a pair of judgmental blue eyes.

I raise my hands in surrender. "It's not what you think."

Rebel humphs.

"Everyone was watching. It was the perfect time to make a big splash. Really end the night with a bang."

"It ended with a bang, alright."

My heart thuds because she has no idea. Kissing Chance McLanely felt like I strapped my heart to two boxes of fire crackers, set a match and then forgot to run away.

Words escape my mouth, faster and faster. "I *know* there's going to be a buzz online about this. There were so many out-of-towners here too. You'll see. We're going to be booked tomorrow."

Rebel purses her lips.

"I have everything under control," I shriek in a voice that sounds like someone slowly losing her mind.

"I didn't say anything."

"You're literally looking at me like I left your car doors open in a thunderstorm."

"Am I?"

"I didn't kiss him because I wanted to," I insist. "It was a business decision."

"April, I want to believe you."

"But?" I sigh.

"I totally believe in your plan and I love that you're finally pampering yourself. You one hundred percent deserve to spend money on you and feel desirable and beautiful, but it's just… Chance is… well, he's like a really bad cold and you don't have immunity."

"I took my flu shot," I argue.

"I don't want you to get hurt," Rebel says, giving my hand a squeeze.

Uncertainty steals the strength from my words, but I force my chin up. "He's a good actor, but so am I. I can handle this, so stop looking at me like I'm a car wreck on the freeway."

My phone buzzes.

I glance down and see a text from Chance.

The reporters won't let me out of here, his text says. *Can I pick you up from home?*

Rebel blows out a breath. "Was that him?"

"Yeah." My smile trembles a little.

"April…"

"Can we just go? Please?"

Looking unsure and very concerned, Rebel starts the car and drives in silence.

* * *

I WANT TO CHANGE OUT OF THIS DRESS AND INTO SOMETHING MORE comfortable. Unfortunately, May refuses to let me change.

"Are you crazy? You look like a million bucks right now. Why would you go celebrate with Chance in your over-alls? That makes no sense!" My sister shakes her head as if I'm a lost cause.

"I don't know where he'll take me tonight. It might be something casual."

"With you, in *that* dress, he better drive out of town to one of those fancy restaurants everyone posts about."

I'll admit that the dress looks great and, maybe if it was the start of the night, I'd agree with May. However, the thought of being 'on' for another fake relationship performance exhausts me. As exciting as the hockey game was—despite having no idea what was happening on the ice at all—it took a lot out of my social batteries.

"Don't look so upset," May coos. "Come take a look at this."

"At what?"

May turns her cell phone toward me and scrolls through a page full of article headings.

"It's not only the sports magazines. Celebrity gossip mags are talking about you too. Plus your hashtag has almost a million hits."

My heart jumps to my throat. "Did you say… a million?"

"People love a heart-warming romance and you gave them a show." She navigates to another page full of pictures.

It seems like everyone is talking about our kiss. There are images of us from different angles too—up high, to the left, and to the right. In every image shot, Chance's hands are low on my waist and my hands are tight around his neck.

Covering my eyes, I turn away. "Can you not?"

"What? You two look great! And that kiss? It was hot."

"May…" I groan.

"But next time, don't mush your lips against his like that," May coaches. "It's not as aesthetically pleasing as him cupping your mouth with his bottom lip—"

"Argh!" I grab the nearest weapon, which so happens to be a pillow, and throw it at her. "Stop."

She easily dodges my fluffy blue missile. "Why are you acting shy? You weren't a scaredy cat when you ran out on the stadium to make out with Chance McLanely."

"It was a *kiss*, not making out. And he *called* me on the ice," I defend.

"Sure, he did." May smirks.

I reach for another pillow to throw at her, but she hands me her laptop instead.

"Check it out. The garage's website is getting a ton of new inquiries."

"Wow, that's a lot," I mumble. Tapping the laptop keys, I skim the emails.

May nods proudly. "Tomorrow morning, I'll send an online form for people to fill out. Then I'm going to post a message announcing you have a tight schedule, so if they want a consult with you, they need to pre-pay. That will drive up the demand for the garage *and* get you money immediately so we can pay off some bills."

I look up at May's earnest grin. "Squirt, I think you might be a genius."

May rolls her eyes at the nickname. "Even if only a conservative percentage of these inquiries pan out, you'll be extremely busy tomorrow and next week. And then, when you fix all those cars, showing what an amazing mechanic you are, the word will spread even faster."

"It really worked…" I breathe in awe.

"Seriously?" May arches an incredulous brow. "It was *your* plan."

Yeah, but thinking up a plan and actually seeing it become a success are two different things.

In a daze, I fall into the sofa.

May scoots close to me. "Unlock your phone. If the garage is getting this much buzz, I can't imagine how your personal accounts are doing."

I check my social media and notice my follower count has blown up even more.

The top comment catches my eye.

'*How many are here from tonight's kiss video?*'.

The comment has thousands of likes, proving that many of my new followers came from tonight's game.

I keep reading.

My smile slowly disintegrates.

She looks so much better now than she did in those old over-alls.

Who did her makeup? Or is it plastic surgery?

She looked like a total bumpkin before. But now I can see what Chance likes about her.

They look good together.

May reads over my shoulder and, when she sees the comments, she yanks the phone from me. "Why are people so mean? You looked good before too."

A knot forms in my throat, but I force the unease away.

My plan worked.

Getting all dolled up, attending Chance's game, even kissing him, it was all to save my business and, ultimately, keep my dad safe.

I did the right thing.

And once business picks up, this weird feeling in my stomach will go away.

CHAPTER
TWENTY-SEVEN

CHANCE

AFTER THE GAME, I SHOWER, CHANGE INTO A FRESH SHIRT AND I'M on my way to April's. Enroute, Derek calls and I can *hear* the smile on his face.

"Chance, you were on *fire* tonight."

"I know."

"That flip trick was insane!"

"*That's* what impressed you?"

"Of course, of course." His tone changes into one of a proud parent. "You avoided the penalty box. How'd you manage that?"

It was because of April, but I'm not telling my agent because it feels like something I should tell April first.

Derek doesn't seem to mind my silence. "Holding back was the right move. Everyone's saying you've been rehabilitated by love. Cheesy, right? But hey, cheesy sells. And that's not all, Chance. Some big players are taking notice of you. Did you see Spellman tweeting about the game tonight? He's got lots of clout with the league."

"Yeah?" I click the indicator, driving down an uneven, gravel path.

"Mark my words. You'll kick that team of nobodies to the curb and fly back to the top in no time. I'm telling you. I can smell the blood in the water already."

I cringe at the term 'nobodies'. Theilan, Renthrow and Gunner played far too skillfully tonight for that.

My tires spit gravel as I park the Lambo in front of a modest bungalow. Warm yellow lights glow from the porch and an old, sturdy tree stands guard. Leaves dance gently in the breeze. May's bike leans against the front porch that wraps around the side.

"Derek, I'm at April's. I gotta go."

"Tell her I said hi," Derek croons.

Yeah, I don't think April would receive Derek's greetings kindly.

"And buy that girl something nice, Chance. She's playing her part to a T." He snickers. "Who knew there was such a stunner under all those baggy clothes?"

I bristle.

Derek says goodbye and hangs up before I can call him out.

He's not the only one making comments about April's appearance. The woman sent a ripple through the entire stadium, which was probably the point. That red dress was designed to be noticed.

But I don't particularly like the way she's popping up on so many radars.

Especially when those radars belong to eligible bachelors.

The whole town is mesmerized, as if they've never seen her before. But the thing is, *I* saw her before. And I thought she was jaw-droppingly gorgeous with curly hair and over-alls too.

The front door opens.

April stalks down the stairs and I scramble out of the car, hurrying to open the passenger door for her. She hasn't changed out of the dress and I'm surprised by that. I thought she'd switch into something more comfortable as soon as she went home.

Not that I'm complaining.

My eyes slide over that mouth-watering outfit. The fabric is shiny and soft and it hugs her in all the right ways. The dress, paired with her fancy straight hair, makes me feel like I'm with someone totally different.

April stares at the ground and I know I should say something, but my eyes catch on her mouth and my steps falter.

Soft. Subtle. Pink in the moonlight.

I think I'm obsessed…

When we kissed earlier, her lips were a bright burning red that singed right past my skin to my heart. She left her mark. Literally. I had to wipe her lipstick off my mouth during the post-game conference.

"Hey." April pauses. Her eyes shift to my T-shirt and jeans. Back-pedalling, she gives my outfit a long scan. "You're casual."

"And you're…" *Hot enough to burn a cat's paws on the sidewalk.* "Not," I finish lamely. Realizing how unimpressed I sound, I clear my throat. "I mean, you look amazing."

Her eyebrows knit.

I cringe. *Real smooth, Chance.*

"I mean it. You look beautiful."

"It's the makeup." She waves a hand in front of her face. "Take me swimming and I turn back into a pumpkin."

A frown crosses my mouth. Why does April seem on edge tonight?

"You were never a pumpkin, April," I assure her.

She gnaws on her bottom lip, and I realize we have yet to make eye contact. Tilting my head and stepping closer, I test whether she's really avoiding me.

April drops back a step, her eyes on the ground.

Why won't she look at me?

"It's getting late. We should go." She dives into the car like she's being chased. I try to close her door for her, but it's yanked out of my grip as April slams it shut herself.

Inside, the air is icy. April stares straight through the windshield, her fingers pulled into fists on her lap and her mouth pressed into a thin line.

"Are you feeling okay?" I ask.

"Yeah." She tosses the word at me.

"You can rest tonight if you're not up to going out."

"No, I'd rather get it over with."

Ouch.

April can be… prickly, but she's never been like this.

I pin my mouth shut and turn down Main Street. It's surprisingly heavy with traffic. Must be from all the spectators going out for drinks and revelry after the game.

The sound of fabric rustling brings my attention back to April. Streaks of silver light falls on her as we pass under a streetlight. I stare at an exquisitely made up face, mesmerized. Big green eyes. Button nose. Not a hint of freckles.

Why did she cover up her freckles?

I wrack my brain for a way to break the ice. Nothing comes to mind so I turn on the radio. Twelve inches to my right, a red-painted fingernail taps out a rhythm on her skirt.

Focus on the road, Chance.

What perfume is April wearing? It's a light, flowery scent that fills the car and makes my head spin.

Eyes ahead.

April swings one leg over the other. Red fabric parts and reveals a tantalizing slit. Have mercy. Since when did this dress have a slit? Is she trying to murder me?

"Chance, what are you doing! It's a red light!" April screams.

I wrench my gaze back to the road just in time to slam on the brakes. A drunk crossing the street yells expletives and shakes a beer-clad fist at me. Lifting a hand in apology, I studiously ignore April's mad-dog stare drilling into the side of my face.

The Lambo purrs as I switch lanes.

My heart is banging on my ribs like a drummer at a rock concert.

Squeezing the steering wheel even tighter, I force my attention on the new sign in the town square. They're advertising a food drive. That's good. Very humanitarian. I should probably donate some cans. I'll first need to buy some cans since I'm still living in a hotel and don't currently have groceries... that perfume—what on earth is it? It smells so good.

I press the tab on my door and my window rolls down. Air. I need some air.

"Can you roll that up? My hair is..." April tries to corral the strands. "It can't take that much wind."

I close the window. Cans. Food cans. Can drive. Charity. What cans should I donate?

In the corner of my eye, April is raking her fingers through her mane. Her hair, it's a different color, isn't it? I can't exactly tell. It's still brown, but not the same brown as before. Her hair smells good too. Every time she flicks it, I get a whiff of fruity shampoo. Does every part of her body smell insanely good?

I can't think about her body parts.

Leaning forward, I turn up the music.

April turns it down. "Chance, you're being weird. Do you not want to do this?"

"I do."

"Then do you want to tell me where we're going? Because unless there's a new secret restaurant on this road, it seems like we're going to the library."

She's so pretty even when she's asking questions like she wants to start a fight.

"Just wait. You'll have your answers soon." I accelerate down the road.

Her silence turns even icier.

I wish she hadn't flicked off the radio.

April swings her right leg over her left this time. The split inches up even further. Her perfume drowns my senses in a fruity-floral bliss.

I'm glad when the library rises in view or I would have had to stop the car, throw myself outside and take a walk.

Her eyes meet mine for a split second before darting away. "We *are* at the library."

"Come on."

I lead her inside using the keys that I got from Ms. Glennice, the sweet, older librarian. The light flickers on and illuminates rows and rows of books shelved neatly in wooden bookcases.

The smell of air freshener and worn pages fills the air. For a small town, the library is surprisingly sizable and well-maintained.

"This way," I say, gesturing for April to follow me.

She remains in place, her arms folded over her chest.

"Why are we here?" she demands. "Aren't we going to show off our relationship in front of the town tonight?"

"Is that what you want to do?"

"Isn't that what *you* want?" she fires back.

"I want you to have a good time," I admit. "I want to talk with you, eat with you and get to know you."

She bristles. "Like a *date*-date?"

I don't understand why she's so mad. I thought that was obvious.

Patiently, I tell her, "Isn't that what this is?"

She turns her face away and takes three deep breaths. When she faces me again, she looks guarded, even a little angry. "Chance, I'd appreciate if you didn't blur the lines here."

My eyebrows shoot up. "Blur the lines?"

"Yes, you and I… we can't 'hang out' just because." She gestures between us. "We're business partners. That's it."

"Business partners?"

Her chin snaps down in a sharp, decisive nod.

"Business partners can still enjoy each other's company, April."

"That's not what I meant." She frowns.

I study her intently. "I'm not going to apologize for wanting to spend time with you if that's what you're waiting for."

Fire crackles through her usually sweet eyes. "Of course not. Why would I expect the great Chance McLanely to apologize?"

Her tone makes me tense. "I'll apologize if I did something wrong, but I didn't."

"You're going against our contract!"

"You broke the contract first."

She blinks at me in surprise. "*Excuse* me?"

"Was that kiss a part of our 'terms'?" I lean against the bookcase in the reference section and watch as the wheels behind April's eyes turn at a fast clip.

Her neck becomes splotchy and the red is quickly mirrored in her cheeks. It could be a trick of the light, but I think I see a hint of my beloved freckles too.

"That…" April tosses her long hair off her shoulders. "That was nothing."

"Nothing?"

Her chin inches higher. "Yes. Nothing."

My heart pounds as I study her face.

"People kiss all the time for absolutely no reason at all." Her eyes lift to the ceiling and I can tell she's just spouting whatever's popping into her mind. "We're both adults and there's no need to make a big deal out of something meaningless."

"Oh, really?" I step toward her.

She steps back. "Although, I will admit that I could have gotten your consent beforehand. Men have rights too."

Her eyelashes flutter. Her cheeks brighten even more.

I suddenly have the urge to kiss this woman and never, ever stop.

But April looks too horrified by my approach.

Her back hits the bookshelf. Her head twists around as if she needs visual confirmation that she's trapped.

I press my hand on the shelf just above her head and lean

down until our faces are separated by mere inches. Her breath catches as I sweep my eyes over her, from head to toe and back.

"W-what are you doing?" April stammers. She presses up on the tips of her toes as if she wants to climb the bookcase backwards.

"That kiss really meant nothing?"

Her eyes dart away. "That's what I said."

"You can kiss anyone without feeling anything for them?"

"Y-yes."

"Prove it." My eyes lock on her lips.

Her breath escapes in panicked spurts, but I show no mercy when I add…

"Kiss me."

CHAPTER
TWENTY-EIGHT

APRIL

The lip of a bookshelf digs into my back. It's a dull pain and I focus on that sensation to keep from getting lost in Chance's dark ocean eyes.

Breathe, April.

I shoot a look at the exits. Chance sees where my eyes have gone and his expression loosens in amusement. It's a subtle change, a simple twitch of his lips.

But I can tell he's laughing at me.

Come on, April. Dig yourself out of this hole.

I try to speak in a normal voice, but it fails spectacularly. "We're not in high school, Chance. This isn't truth or dare. I don't have to prove anything."

"So it *did* mean something."

"No, it didn't."

"Then why are you blushing?"

"Because I'm angry."

"You really are a terrible liar, Tink."

I'm not a fairy, but there *are* a couple of winged creatures flapping around in my stomach, all of them enamored with the man whose face is way too beautiful and way too close to mine.

My head has gone completely blank and I have no idea what to do next. The hesitation makes me feel even more vulnerable.

When it comes to fight or flight instincts, I'm a fighter.

Usually.

Except when I'm backed up against bookshelves by pro-hockey athletes.

Throwing all my weight forward, I shove at Chance's chest. He steps back easily, allowing me to flee a couple paces away.

"That isn't funny," I scold him.

"That wasn't a joke," he answers, his voice low and silky.

I attempt to swallow but my throat is dry and I just end up coughing. "I already apologized for kissing you."

"I *don't* accept your apology."

My eyes narrow on instinct. "Don't be petty."

"It's up to the victim whether he forgives or not."

I bark out a dry laugh. "Victim?"

"Unlike you," he traces his lips with a finger, "I don't share these lips with just anyone. I'm a very modest man."

I roll my eyes.

"I'm hurt that you don't believe me." Chance shakes his head.

My mind conjures the memory of him and the girl he was hugging at The Tipsy Tuna. "We both know you don't have a problem getting close to women," I snap.

Chance frowns. "What is *that* supposed to mean?"

"Nothing."

A muscle in his jaw jumps. His smile disappears and is replaced with an intensity that sends my head reeling. "Is that why you stopped answering my messages? Do you think I've been talking to other women?"

"Just drop it, Chance."

"It's only been you," he says firmly. "There's been no one else, April."

Liar!

My heart beats faster and faster. If he keeps talking, if he keeps explaining himself, I'm going to believe him. I'll pretend that I didn't see what I saw with my own eyes that night. Like a total idiot, I'll succumb to the Chance effect.

And after Evan, I'm not signing up for another 'bad boy who can't keep his pants zipped' package.

"You don't have to explain anything," I say firmly. "I don't have any expectations of someone like you."

His eyes flash. "Someone like me?"

"Yeah, someone like you."

"And who exactly am I in your eyes, April?"

Chance's voice has a dangerous edge, but I don't back down.

"You, Chance McLanely, are a man who always gets what he wants, especially with girls, and for the first time ever, you met someone who isn't swooning every time you flash those pretty blue eyes or whip out your charming smile."

"You think my smile is charming?"

I glare at him. "Is that all you heard?"

"That's all that matters."

I throw my hands high. "You're full of it, Chance McLanely."

My wrath is building to a boil. I'm angry with Chance for making me feel this way. Angry with myself for being unable to control these feelings despite my best efforts.

And through it all, he keeps looking at me with this penetrating gaze, like he's so close to breaking down my walls and seeing right through me.

"Just so you know, the attraction isn't one sided," Chance says with a smile.

My jaw clenches and my blood simmers. He really thinks this is all a joke.

"There is no attraction. There has *never* been an attraction." I point an accusing finger, stalking in front of him. "This is me drawing the line with you. Sorry to disappoint, but I haven't fallen for any of your tricks."

He massages his forehead like I'm a wayward student who refuses to get the lesson. "You think… all this time, I've been playing tricks?"

"I think none of this matters and this conversation is pointless. After the way you played tonight, you're definitely going back to the league and you and I will never see each other again."

His voice is a thin, restrained sound, like I'm stretching out his last nerve. "So in your mind, you'd never date me if it wasn't for the contract."

"Exactly!"

"You think the absolute worst of me."

"I do!" I agree vehemently.

"And yet…"

"And yet?"

His eyes narrow slightly and he leans down, dropping his voice to a taunting husk. "I don't believe you."

My mind churns with chaos, grasping at straws for a way to prove my point. And finally, it settles on a desperate, impulsive, half-baked way to end the argument once and for all.

"Fine," I spit. "I'll prove it."

Digging my fingers into his collar, I wrench him down until his face is a breath away from mine. His wide-eyed stare is all I see before I close my eyes and surge in for a punishing, battle-cry of a kiss.

Our lips smash together for a brief, angry dance. The urge to deepen the kiss overwhelms me, but I shove him away instead.

He stumbles back, his chest heaving and his eyes ablaze.

My chest is pumping up and down and I stammer, "S-see?"

Chance stands frozen, staring at me beneath his fringe of dark hair. I notice his hands curling into fists and then releasing, working in time with the muscles flexing in his jaw.

I blink rapidly, willing my feet to run. To take me out of there. To free me from his addictive stare.

It was so ridiculously stupid to kiss him. What exactly did that prove? Why did I let my temper get the best of me?

I press a hand to my wildly beating heart and lie straight to his face. "I feel nothing. It means nothing."

Slowly, torturously, Chance's gaze slides up my body and pierces me.

"You shouldn't have done that," he whispers darkly.

My heart tumbles over itself because *I know*.

There's no use running now.

His biceps contract beneath his T-shirt and, seconds later, I'm getting swept into his arms. I gasp when our bodies collide, lining up flush against each other.

My head tilts back and I anticipate Chance grabbing my face and kissing me hard enough to bruise, punishing me in the same way I did to him.

Instead, he brushes his thumb against my cheek and grinds out, "Where are they?"

"W-what?"

"Your freckles?"

The breath knocks out of my lungs. Something bright and dangerous flares to life behind the ice wall I'd built around my heart.

"And your curls?" Chance touches a lock of my hair. "Why did you change what was already perfect?"

My fight or flight alarm bells are blinking a persistent red.

Mayday, mayday! Get out of there.

But I can't move.

Not only because Chance's fingers are digging into my hips but because my knee-caps have suddenly decided they're full of Jello.

"So beautiful." He breathes the words in my ear and now I not only have Jello knee-caps but also Jello shins and Jello ankles.

His eyes darken. "I've wanted to tell you that since the first time I saw you in those over-alls, carrying that toolbox."

His touch lingers on my cheek and then slides behind my ear. The exploration is so excruciatingly light that my heart *pains* me. For some reason, the way he's watching me, like I'm something too exquisite, too precious to hold, makes me emotional.

His face muddles out of focus as tears crop in my eyes.

I don't want to hurt again, and Chance McLanely… oh he could make me *hurt*. Not only that, he could *destroy* me.

"Are you crying?" Chance's voice rings with worry.

"I'm not," I sniffle.

"You are," he says, gently scrubbing his thumb under my eyes.

What on earth is happening to me? I've lost full control of my body and mind.

Chance McLanely is a wizard and he's casting a spell on me. A spell that reaches completion when he leans in and presses a kiss to my eyelid.

His smell of peppermint and cologne fills my nostrils.

Leaning in, he kisses the other eyelid with lips so whisper-soft that a pin drop would be louder.

"Don't cry, Tinkerbell," he soothes me.

My head swims from the heat of his body, the heaviness of his hands, and the thick *something* that lingers in the air. It's the hint of promise, the weight of a moment that could change the course of my life forever. As if Fate itself is sitting in front of us with popcorn, eyes glued to the TV screen.

I can't do this.

I *can't*.

After everything with Evan…

I'll never forget the bitterness of rejection. The way my heart shattered when I saw the truth in all its glory—I am not good enough as a girlfriend. I am not good enough as a woman. I am *not* the kind of girl men find it easy to be faithful to, especially ones like Chance who'll constantly be surrounded by more dazzling, more sensual and more feminine options.

Breaking away with all my strength, I shake my head.

"No. I… I'm not going to do this with you. I want to break the contract. I can't do this. I won't."

"Good. I was thinking the same thing," he says.

I nod stiffly. "I'm glad we're in agreement."

As I turn away, Chance pulls me closer. His lips chase mine down like a predator to a prey.

I don't have time to blink, don't have time to figure out what to do with my hands—whether to push him away or drive him closer.

His kiss deepens, and I respond in kind. Tasting him, matching the rhythm of his mouth's brutal strokes. My thoughts are drowned out by the harshness of my breath, by the storm of emotions that swell like a raging tide.

It's so, so wrong…

But it feels so right.

With our lips still connected, Chance walks me backwards. His hands twist my hips, spinning me away from the bookshelf. It's his back that collides with the column of books.

His mouth disconnects from mine as the entire bookshelf rocks, but my arms and my mouth follow him like magnets, obliterating the distance he created as if I have a personal vendetta with it.

Chance grins against my greedy mouth, slowing down the kiss so he can speak right to my lips. "Still think this is 'nothing', Tink?"

"Don't misunderstand. I'm hating every second of this," I grind out.

He not too gently twists me around again so it's *my* back against the bookshelf. I'm spine to spine with an Ancient Gaelic Language dictionary. And, when Chance holds me tightly and nips on my bottom lip in displeasure, sending a spurt of pain and heat straight to my stomach, I start speaking a Gaelic tongue of my own.

The room is spinning around me.

Chance McLanely's kiss is literally *rocking* my world.

Apparently, the bookshelf feels the same way because a sharp slice of pain splits apart all the hot sensations flooding from his mouth to mine.

"Ow!" I scream.

My hands fly to the top of my head and my gaze sails to the ground, taking in the giant book titled *Special Species: World Research Edition*.

It really did feel like the entire world took a sledgehammer to my head.

"Are you okay?" Chance's eyes bulge.

I whimper in pain, holding my hand to the center of my scalp. I think the edge of the book nicked a brain vessel. It hurts so much.

"Come over here." Chance leads me to the center of the library where the light is much brighter. He whisks his fingers into my scalp, gently probing. "I'm sorry, Tink. No matter how good the kissing was, I shouldn't have pushed you against the bookshelf."

I can feel my face turning into a full-on tomato. "Seriously? *That's* what you're apologizing for?"

Chance's lips twitch before he curbs the smile and says solemnly, "I don't see any blood. Let me get you some ice."

I scowl at him. "They don't keep ice in the library."

There used to be an ice machine left over from the water factory but it broke last summer, flooding the room and ruining hundreds of books.

Unfortunately, Chance doesn't listen. He insists on leading me through the library and out into the open air.

Then he leads me to the reading gazebo a few paces from the library's back door.

And what I see there makes me gasp out loud.

CHAPTER
TWENTY-NINE

CHANCE

APRIL'S REACTION TO MY SURPRISE DOES NOT DISAPPOINT. HER EYES sparkle and her mouth parts on a stunned gasp.

The moment would be perfect... if there wasn't a bump on her head the size of a hockey puck.

"This way. Watch your step." I guide her up the gazebo stairs. The structure's been outfitted with beautiful string lights, fresh flowers, and a thick rug that was flown in from an exotic country that I've forgotten the name of.

I have to hand it to the event planner, the fluffy decoration was the right call. It feels like we're sitting on a cloud.

April sinks into the soft fibers and leans against the sturdy picnic baskets containing our dinner of fancy sandwiches topped with *imported* olives (or so was listed on the bill), baked chicken, and cheese platters.

I dive into the ice box, bypass the wine chilling on top, push past the lemonade and beer coolers, and scoop out a few cubes. Looking around for a cloth to wrap the ice in, I disentangle the fancy tablecloth wrapped around the cutlery, drop the ice inside and tie it up.

"Here." I press the makeshift ice pack against April's head.

She barely registers the movement.

"April, honey, you need to hold this where it hurts."

She absently presses the ice pack to her crown, too busy tracking every inch of the gazebo to scold me about calling her 'honey'. Although now that I have, I'm definitely calling her that again.

"Is that… a candy stand?" April points to the M&Ms, Oreos, and mini chocolate bars arranged in rustic, wicker baskets. Each basket carries a silver scoop and a tiny, handwritten cardboard sign bearing the treat's name.

"And gummy bears!" April dumps the ice pack and crawls toward the treat.

I hiss in disapproval. "We'll tend to your wound first, then we can eat."

Despite my firm tone, happiness glows in my chest as I watch her excitement.

April obediently settles back in the rug. "Chance, did *you* do all this?"

"Yes," I answer.

Her eyebrows crash down in disbelief. "Really?"

"I paid someone, so technically—"

Her mouth puckers. "That doesn't count."

"It does count."

"No, it doesn't."

"Whoever pays a sniper to assassinate someone is ultimately responsible for the crime."

"They're technically both responsible for the crime, and this is not nearly the same as hiring a hit on someone."

"I think the law would disagree with you," I answer.

"And I think you're the one who should have gotten smacked by a good book."

"The Good Book?" I peer up at the starry skies, not surprised at all that the Lord Himself had to step in earlier. There was probably no other way to get my hands off April.

"No, I said *a* good book. You're impossible." April rolls her eyes.

"And you're cute and injured. Ice pack."

April huffs but she does as she's told.

While she moves the ice pack around her head, I take a small, transparent bag and scoot over to the candy bar.

"Which one?" I ask.

"Oreos. No, the M&Ms. No…" April peers at the selection with eyes narrowed. "They're all my favorites."

"I know." I scoop out the M&Ms first then grab three more bags and fill those with the Oreos, gummy bears, and chocolate bars.

"How did you know?" April moves her narrowed gaze from the candy to me.

"Because I've made it my mission to know everything about you."

"It was May, wasn't it?"

I laugh at the way she's totally unfazed by my flirting. "Hold the candy. I'll take over with the ice pack."

April willingly trades the ice pack for the treats.

"You won't be able to eat dinner later if you eat this first," I warn.

"Who said I was staying for dinner? I plan on storming off as soon as I'm finished." She pops the candies into her mouth.

I chuckle. "If you leave early, you'll miss the best part."

"What's the best part?" Her eyes glow with interest.

My gaze drops to her mouth.

A dazed look enters her eyes and her chewing slows. With a start, April glances away and keeps munching.

"When did you plan this?"

"Since the moment you agreed to the date," I admit.

I did hours of agonizing research, chatted with May about

April's preferences and scoured internet dating forums, before I settled on what I wanted to do tonight.

"What made you think I'd be into something like this?" April gestures to the string lights.

"It's more like I thought of what you *wouldn't* want. You didn't strike me as someone who'd like to spend her evening at a stuffy restaurant, or at a movie, or looking across a table at someone for two hours. You like your space. You like the outdoors, and most importantly…"

"I like books?" She fills in.

"Mechanic books, yeah. I spent hours scrolling your social media." I shake my head slowly. "You strange, strange woman."

She laughs and then catches herself. "Is that the surprise? Did you want us to read car manuals at the library?"

Since it seems like the perfect moment, I reach into a nearby basket and pull out a long, heavy box.

"What is it?" April asks when I deposit it into her lap.

"Something I got through the library. Open it." I gesture.

She undoes the bow, pulls off the top and her eyes glaze over in surprise. "Chance, this is…"

"The original edition of *The Ultimate Bugatti E-Type*. Five years ago, you posted that you wanted to read it. Last year, you reposted the memory saying you still hadn't gotten a chance."

"This book is super rare and out of print. There are only a handful of copies in the world and they only lend it to select libraries."

"I knew someone who knew someone." I shrug. A perk of dad being such a car head is he has a deep network of connections in the automotive space. "Ms. Glennice was also a big help."

She's still blinking up a storm. "Chance, I can't believe this. It's too much." Despite her words, her fingers close tightly around the tome, as if her body can't bear to part with the book.

"Like I said, it belongs to the library." I shake my head. "As much as I wanted to keep it so every time you wanted to read, you'd have to see me, that didn't work out."

Her lips quirk. "That sounded like the plan of a supervillain."

"The best villains have a good reason for being bad."

She tilts her head. "Am I your villain origin story?"

"That depends."

"On what?"

"Whether you have permanent damage from that book falling on your head."

She chuckles and looks down at the rare book again.

Her ice pack has melted by now, so I shake out the non-liquid pieces in the grass and scoop out some more from the ice box.

"I'm okay," April says, touching my wrist when I try to put the ice pack back on her head.

"Are you sure?"

She nods.

I retreat and shake out my hand to get some warmth back. Holding the ice for so long started to burn my palms.

"An outdoor picnic is a budget-friendly idea." She glances around. "But I'm almost afraid to ask what you spent on all this."

"It doesn't matter."

"It does matter." She frowns. "You even hired someone to decorate."

"That's a given. I don't waste time doing things I'm not good at. And decorating… is not a skill of mine."

"Chance…"

"April, the last thing you and I need to talk about right now is money." I give her a knowing look. "Not when there are more pressing topics."

"Like what?" She licks one side of the Oreo biscuit.

I track the motion. Reaching over to steal an Oreo from the package, I say, "That kiss, for instance."

I'm smug about it, expecting April to choke on her Oreo in response.

But instead, she turns to me, blinks frankly, and says, "Which one?"

And suddenly, I've got an Oreo stuck in *my* throat and it's April who has to find me a bottle of water. I accept it and chug thirstily.

She hovers over me. "Are you okay? I don't know CPR, so if you're not, I'll have to call an ambulance."

I massage my throat. After croaking out a weak 'I'm okay', I crawl over to where she'd been sitting and lean against the baskets. April gauges my position and sits on the opposite end of the gazebo.

To be fair, it could be because she wants to be closer to the Oreos.

But I think she's just avoiding me.

"This entire idea was beautiful, Chance. And this book is…" She blows out a breath. "I really appreciate everything you've done for me."

Instantly, I brace myself for words I won't like to hear. April's somber tone is the exact one my general manager used when he let me go from the team.

"But," April's fingers tug at the bristles of the rug, "but I—"

"You don't trust me."

She swallows and ducks her head. "That's not it."

I set down my bottle of water and close the distance between us. Gently, I take her hand and say, "I respect that you don't feel the same way and I won't force you to change your mind."

Her eyes flit to me, full of relief.

"But," I add and now I see *her* bracing herself, "I'm an athlete and there's not much anyone can do to stop me when I put my mind to something."

"And what exactly have you set your mind to do?" She scrunches her nose, probably imagining the worst.

I rub my thumb over her knuckles. "You'll see."

"Chance…" She groans.

I release her hand and climb to my feet. From this vantage,

she looks so small and fragile that I want to scoop her into my pocket and protect her with my life.

"I'll take you home so you can read that in peace." I point to the book.

She chews on her bottom lip.

"Or we can stay here and follow my original plan—me feeding you strawberries while you sit on my lap and read."

"I'll read at home!" April blurts.

I laugh at her startled expression.

April stands too fast and nearly trips on her dress. I steady her with a hand to her elbow and release her just as quickly. When her back is turned, I scoop out a few more sweets for her and follow her to the parking lot.

I say nothing as I take her home and she seems uncomfortable with the silence, sending me constant looks as if she's trying to figure me out. More than once, I notice her open her mouth and then slam it shut.

When I finally get her home, I offer her the sweets and send her off with a wave. "Tell May I said goodnight."

A furrow between her brow, she opens the door. "Uh, yeah. Goodnight."

I watch her scramble to her front door and, in the quiet of my car, I whisper, "See you tomorrow."

CHAPTER
THIRTY

APRIL

May grills me about the date with Chance as soon as I get home, but I'm too exhausted to do a blow-by-blow of the night's events. Honestly, I'm not sure *what* happened in that library.

At first, Chance and I were arguing…

And then we were kissing…

And then he was whisking me into a transformed gazebo ripped straight out of some magical wonderland…

And then… he… threatened me?

What exactly have you set your mind to do?

You'll see.

Those cryptic words haunted me even in my dreams.

Now I'm awake, the sun is pouring through my window and I'm lying in bed, staring at the ceiling, totally puzzled.

Chance McLanely is a determined man. No one gets *that* good at a sport—at anything really—without a single-minded dedication, bordering on obsession.

As someone equally obsessed with her career, I'm well aware of the downfalls of that kind of mindset. When I encounter a problem with a car, I don't sleep or eat until it's solved.

I can't imagine what Chance has up his sleeve, but I know it will be just as intense as his playing on the ice. It was hard enough resisting him *before* he made liking me his primary objective. I don't know how I'll survive this.

Suddenly, my bedroom door bursts open and May barges in. Her ponytail swishes behind her as she marches around my bed.

"April, you need to get up *now*!" My sister bounces to the windows and throws the curtains back.

I wince at the dangerously bright sunshine. Groggily, I demand, "Unless someone's dead or something's on fire, close that window and let me go back to sleep."

"Get. Up."

"What time is it?"'

"It's seven thirty."

"What? It's so early!"

"You need to get dressed and go to the garage. Rebel's already down there doing the intake process, but she'll need help."

"Why is Rebel at the garage? We don't open until nine."

A sheepish look crosses her face. "The thing is, I made a mistake with the schedule. Customers brought their cars at five thirty this morning—"

Sitting straight up, I stare at May. "Did you say… customers *actually* brought their cars in?"

"Yes!"

"This early?"

"Mmhm!"

"This isn't like all the other times when we got tons of new followers but no actual clients?" My fingers scrunch in my dark blue comforters. "People actually showed up?"

"Yes! Now get up! I'm serious. Rebel called me in a panic when she wasn't getting through to you. It sounds like it's chaos out there."

I launch out of bed, take a quick shower and see May following me through the door.

"I can't give you a ride to the bus stop, May. I need to go straight to the garage."

"I know. I'm coming with you."

I check my watch. "Don't you have a class in twenty minutes?"

"I'll skip it."

"Absolutely not." I shake my head.

"But this is partly my fault. I should at least go help." My sister's mournful eyes hit me right between my chest.

"You know what dad would have said. Education comes first."

"But—"

"You're going to be late as it is. Here." I reach into my pocket and drop some bills into her palm. "Take a taxi. It'll be faster than your bike."

"At least eat something before you go."

I gratefully accept the banana May flings at me on my way out the door.

"Have a good day!" she yells, waving at my back. "I'll come help after my morning class."

"Thanks!" I yell back.

On the way to the garage, I call Rebel.

She answers with a harried, "Finally! I thought my brain was going to explode."

"Why didn't you call May sooner?"

"I thought I could handle it. Plus, I figured you'd be tired from your date with Chance, which I'm totally getting all the details for later. If I survive till later, I mean."

"I promise. I'll leave nothing out." I eye the road carefully as I remove one of my hands from the steering wheel to peel the banana.

Main Street is stirring to life. The florist's shop, manned by Ms. Shirley and her wheel-chair bound son, Sterling, is already open. So is the bakery run by three generations of Canoughays. And as I pass by, the smell of fresh sourdough bread fills my nostrils.

"How many cars are in the shop right now?" I ask, taking a bite of the banana.

"Twelve."

"*Twelve?*" I squawk and the banana rolls right out of my mouth and plops into my lap. I fish around my overalls for it. "You're joking. Our garage only has the capacity for six cars, and that's if we park three on the street."

"I know! I managed to get three in the bay but the rest of the vehicles are still waiting outside. It's like a parade in the road. I've been praying for tons of customers since the day we opened, but not *all at the same time.*"

"Is this really all because I wore a stupid dress last night?" I grumble.

"That *and* I think May forgot that we don't actually have twenty-four hours in a day. On the form, our business hours started from twelve am to twelve pm rather than from eight o'clock to five. People started showing up at five this morning."

"They've been waiting since five a.m?" I parrot.

"That's what the one-star review on our business page says. And another customer who decided to wait until I came to open the shop said the same."

"*Excuse me, when is it my turn?*" a voice booms in the background.

Rebel answers distractedly. "Just a minute, sir!" Then with a more frantic tone, she whispers, "April, are you on your way over here?"

The truck roars as I push it even harder. "I'll be there in ten."

"Oh goodness. Ten minutes to forever."

I hang up with Rebel and tear it down Main Street, glad that it's too early for the sheriff to be about or I'd surely get a ticket.

When I arrive at the garage, I notice several cars already parked on the grass and a few out on the street. There's also a short line of vehicles idling on the road. I count five of them before squeezing into a parking spot between two trucks.

Rebel runs out with a clipboard. She's still wearing pink shorts and a white tank top. She must have been too busy to even change into her jumpsuit.

"What should we do?" Rebel grabs my shoulder. "We're at capacity here. We simply *can't* accept any more jobs right now." She checks her pink-gemstone wrist watch. "It'll be time for another few customers in the next hour. I'm drowning, April."

"First, take a deep breath." I inhale and exhale.

Rebel follows me. "Now what?"

"Let's shut it down." I twirl my hand in a circle. "We can only do what we can do."

Her eyes double in size. "We can't send them away!"

"Why not?"

"We're already getting bad press because we weren't here at five." Rebel fumbles with her phone as if she wants to show me and then gives up halfway. "April, we don't have a choice but to make this work. If we accepted people's money and didn't deliver, this will turn into a nightmare. All the effort you put in to get clients—"

"It's fine. We can recover."

"Reputations don't 'recover'. The bad reviews will ruin us."

I scrub my forehead and turn in a slow circle. *So many cars.*

Rebel studies me with her bottom lip tucked between her teeth.

I push out a breath. "Okay, let's..." I massage the bridge of my nose and then an idea hits. "The lifts! Let's put a car on the two lifts and then raise them high enough that two more cars can fit underneath."

"That means we can fit four cars in the bays." Rebel's eyes brighten. "April, you *genius!*" Her smile dims. "But that leaves seven more."

"I'll drive another three cars around back." The backyard is where we usually park cars that won't move for a while because the parts they need are being shipped in from a warehouse. "It'll be tight, but I think I can make it work."

Rebel bobs her head, the color returning to her pale cheeks. "Three can stay outside, so that leaves…"

"One." I smile. "And if you can point out which car has the easiest problem to fix, I can get it out of the shop in about thirty minutes."

"That sounds—" Rebel's words are cut off by the sound of a car honking. Two more cars have joined the lineup of waiting vehicles in front of our garage.

I cringe and check my smartwatch. "It's time already?"

"They're early." She groans.

"How many more is that?" I count silently in my head. *Three more cars.*

We do *not* have the space to accommodate three more vehicles either in front of, behind or beside the garage.

Rebel swallows loudly. "Uh… let's get someone to park the cars at the mart. We can explain it to Maddy. He's sweet on my mom and I think he'd turn a blind eye. We could even ask one of the bag boys to drive for a few extra bucks."

"I'm not asking a bag boy to drive someone's car from our garage to the mart. If they crash it, that won't be good for business either. We need someone we can trust."

"I'll see if any one of my cousins are free," Rebel says.

"I'll call Bobby."

I hurry to phone Bobby, but he doesn't answer.

Rebel returns to me, her mouth twisted in a frown.

"No luck?" I ask.

"The bag boys are looking like a great option."

"We can't, Rebel."

"Then who do we call? We don't have a lot of options."

I let out a deep sigh. "I'll handle that part. You can get started on the forklift."

She runs to park the cars.

My heart starts pounding as I lift my phone. Despite being

under immense pressure, I take two seconds before I dial his number.

Chance answers as if he'd been waiting for my call. "Hello?"

I say nothing.

"Tink?" Chance's voice is full of amusement, but it quickly spirals into panic the longer I stay silent. "April?"

"I… need your help."

Without a beat of hesitation, without a single question, Chance answers, "I'll be right there."

CHAPTER
THIRTY-ONE

CHANCE

April may need to rent a bigger garage. Especially if business keeps booming like this.

I return after dropping off my fourth car and it seems like there are still new cars showing up at the garage.

"Whoa! It's Chance McLanely!"

Shouts erupt as fans spot me heading in April's direction.

I'd intentionally remained out of sight earlier. April needed me to be a driver, not a pro athlete and if I'd stopped to take pictures before getting the task done, she would have been in big trouble.

"Hey." I flash my practiced smile.

"Can I have a picture?" A skinny guy with a long beard and a beanie rushes over to me.

I peer over his head to look inside the garage. The women seem busy. Rebel is running around frantically, coordinating all the vehicles and April is working on a car. Right now, she's perched over an open engine, her eyebrows furrowed in concentration.

"Can you give me a minute, bro?" I ask. "I need to check if April needs me for anything else."

"Of course. Of course. #ApeChance for life." He flashes two fists.

That 'ship name' sounds even sillier coming from his lips.

Inside, the garage is *packed* with vehicles. I turn sideways to squeeze past cars that are parked nose to nose. Unfortunately, there's no path that leads straight to April, so I have to catapult myself over a pickup.

It's too bad April's so concentrated on her work that she missed an action-movie moment.

I stop in front of her, admiring the way the baggy work overalls try—and fail—to hide her figure.

"Tink."

"Mm?" She bends further into the engine. Her shiny brown hair slithers across her face and she shakes it back.

"Any more cars I need to move right now?"

"Uh..."

Her noncommittal response tells me her mind is one hundred miles away.

"I'm almost finished working on this one," April mutters, tossing her hair back. "Give me ten more minutes."

If I were a mad scientist, I'd build a time machine and give her all the time in the world. Since I'm just a regular Joe, all I can offer is a massage, coffee, and possibly a hug.

"Dangit." April scowls at a car plug and violently wrenches her head to keep her hair away from her face. In direct defiance, her silky-smooth mane falls right back into place.

She gets enough of it and angrily yanks out her hair clip. A swath of chocolate-brown strands get yanked out too.

"Hold on, Tink. Let me," I say, stepping right up against her and reaching for the clip.

She pulls away. "I can do it myself."

"Relax, I know my way around a hair tie."

Her eyes narrow. "Lots of practice?"

"Not the way you're thinking," I tell her. "I had shoulder-length, Fabio hair in my high school 'searching for identity' phase."

Her eyes widen and, for the first time since the chaos at the garage began, she smiles. "I can't imagine that."

"Don't try. It's as hideous as you'd imagine. I'm no Fabio."

The smile grows.

Her eyes sparkle harder.

Everything around me blinks out of focus as I stare at her.

April's unique smell of flowers mixed with engine oil fills my nostrils and I take a deep breath. *Dangerous territory.* I could get drunk on this fragrance alone.

"Let's see what you've got," April whispers, offering the clip to me.

"Hold still." I gently but firmly guide her head straight and gather all her hair into my grip. Tongue sticking out in concentration, I make one loop with the clip and then another. After that, I half it and secure the base so there's a bun at the end and a plume of hair sticking up like a feather.

"There." I turn her around and inspect my work with pride. "You won't have hair in your face anymore. This held up under three hours of drill training."

"Thanks," she says, inspecting the bun with amusement.

Her eyes slowly track past me to the crowd that's waiting outside. More fans seem to have gathered and they're staring into the garage. Some even have their phones out.

She gnaws on her bottom lip. "Do they want to complain about the wait too?"

"Uh, no. They want pictures with me."

Her entire body sags with relief and the desire to hug her wells so strong that my arms ache.

"Pictures are a good idea." Her voice has a thoughtful note. "Maybe fan service will improve their mood and make them forget the long wait."

"It probably would."

"Do you mind?" She gives me a sheepish look.

Doesn't she know that I'd give her the world if she asked? This is nothing.

"No, I don't mind. I can even play field hockey with them if you think that'll help."

She laughs softly. "There are so many cars out there, we won't have space for you to play field hockey."

Oof. If I wasn't sure before—which I totally was—seeing April smile cements how much I like her.

Rebel's voice cuts in. "Hey, Mr. Hockey Player! Get away from our star mechanic! She has no time for the likes of you!"

Guilt streaks across April's face and she hurries back to work.

Outside, the crowd welcomes my return with applause and overlapping compliments. I give each individual my undivided attention.

It's a strategy that works. Despite the long wait, everyone is all smiles by the time they leave.

I head back into the garage to cool off. After taking what feels like a million photos, my cheeks are aching and I'm pretty sure my bottom lip has a bit of a spasm.

April looks up and back down again quickly. "Was it *that* exhausting?"

I shake my head. I can't compare my state to hers. She's been powering through this crisis like a champ.

A bike bell rings in the distance. A second later, May's footsteps rush through the building.

"I'm here!" May coos, bringing a bright smile and fresh energy to the frantic garage. "Oh, hey, brother-in-law."

"Sister-in-law." I grin. I've always liked how clearly May can read a room.

"Don't start with that," April warns.

Rebel strides close to us, dabbing at the sweat on her face with a pink handkerchief. "Great, May, you're here. I need you to type out these order forms and organize these part requests." She drops a stack of documents into May's arms.

"I've been tied up with office work all morning and I'm itching to get my hands dirty." Rebel pauses. "Metaphorically of course."

"Ay-ay, captain." May carries her workload to a desk.

Rebel takes command of a car on the opposite end of the garage, so I sidle close to April.

"Need some help?"

She glances up, eyebrows tightening into a V. She looks so disoriented that, for a second, it seems she doesn't recognize me. Finally, her eyes clear and she shakes her head. "No, you've done enough. Thanks, Chance."

I've been dismissed, but I pretend to miss the social cue.

"I can stick around in case you need more of my transportation services," I say. "Weren't you booked for the entire day?"

"Rebel contacted the clients scheduled for this afternoon and rescheduled them for tomorrow, so we're not expecting any more arrivals. Besides, don't you want to rest today? You had a big game last night."

"Max graciously allowed us a morning off. Training isn't until three."

Her eyes widen. "You're still training today?"

"It's hockey season. There's no day off."

She makes another sound from her throat and concentrates on her work. I peer over her shoulder, watching as she fiddles with wires—taping some together, pulling on others, and testing a few with a meter.

April's eyes pass over me and back to her toolbox. "You're still here."

"Do you need something from in there?" I point to the open lid.

She sidesteps me, but it's a small space and her shoulder ends up brushing my chest. "I got it."

I watch, fascinated, as she returns with the tool and gets to work on the engine.

"How did you clear the garage out so fast this morning?" I

ask. Every time I returned from driving to the mart, she had sent someone on their way.

"We catalogued the vehicles based on the reported issues. That way, we could work on the ones that were a quicker repair." She brushes a thumb over her nose and leaves a grease streak.

I take a nearby towel. "Really? What's considered 'quicker to repair'?"

"Some vehicles only need an oil change. That takes 'bout twenty to twenty-five minutes… what are you doing?"

"You've got something on your face." I grip her chin and swipe the towel over her nose.

"Aww, so cute!" May yells from across the garage.

"Chance, if you distract April one more time!" Rebel threatens.

I throw both hands up in surrender.

April blushes slightly and almost stumbles as she returns to the car.

I follow her. "If what the vehicle needs is a simple oil change, why did people bring it to you? Was it just to meet you?"

"No. To them, it *was* an issue that couldn't be fixed."

"Huh?"

"Not knowing the answer doesn't mean the answer isn't simple." She wiggles a plug in the engine. "Their mechanic probably changed the fuel regulator but didn't change the oil. So the vehicle would still have the 'check engine light' on, despite having a new fuel reg."

"Fascinating. A new part wasn't enough to fix the problem."

"Right. So, the fuel gets into the oil because of a bad fuel regulator. So then that bad fuel gets into the base of the engine and when the engine is running, it sucks in oil through the PCV valve, which sucks it back into the engine."

I bob my head like I understand a word she's saying.

"The PCV circulates unburned fuel mixture back into the engine to protect the atmosphere. If the oil mixes with the fuel because of a bad regulator, then it'll pass more than the vehicle is designed to handle."

"And that's bad, right? That sounds bad."

She chuckles. "Yes, that's bad, Chance. Now can you step aside so I can work?"

This time, I can't pretend to not understand when I've been dismissed.

Rounding the garage until I get to May's workstation, I observe her filing away invoices and logging client names into a database.

She glances up with mischievous eyes. "April chased you away?"

I shrug because admitting defeat isn't my style.

May stops working for a moment and looks across the bay at her sister. "She wasn't always like that, you know."

"Prickly?" I clarify.

"Skittish," May says.

I look across the garage to April, wishing I could be the calm to her storm.

"You know why I'm so angry with Evan?" May balances her chin on the palm of her hand. "It's not just because he was a douche canoe who cheated. It's because him cheating destroyed my sister. April was so confident and sure of herself before that relationship. After…" May blows out a sad breath. "It's like she's a different person."

"Was she friendlier?" I ask, trying to picture a smiley April and failing.

"Not exactly. She was always sarcastic and careful around people, but now it's really difficult for her to trust anyone. She has this giant wall around herself, but it's not just to keep people out. It's, like… like she wants to keep her pain and self-doubts *in*."

"What are you two whispering about over here?" Rebel butts in, peering at May and I with suspicious eyes.

"Nothing!" May chirps and gives me a secret look.

I take out my keys and walk to the door. "How about I work on some lunch for you ladies?"

"I'll have a triple cheeseburger from Phil's!" May yells immediately.

"A salad for me. Hold the olives," Rebel recites before settling on one of the rolling cots and sliding underneath a car.

"And for you?" I ask April.

She doesn't seem to hear me.

I walk closer and touch her shoulder. "April, I'm getting lunch."

"Not hungry."

"You need to eat," I argue.

"No time," she grunts.

I narrow my eyes.

She does a quick glance up, sees me glaring, and sighs. "You're not going to let this go, are you?"

"If begging won't work, I'll resort to threats."

Her lips twitch. "What kind of threats?"

"Either you eat willingly, or I sit you in my lap and feed you myself."

The blush appears like a dear and expected friend. "I'll have a burger."

"Good girl."

I stroll out of the garage, glad that understanding auto-repair is not a pre-requisite to being April Brooks' boyfriend.

CHAPTER
THIRTY-TWO

APRIL

AFTER THE KISSING, THE LOVE CONFESSION, AND THE SHOWING UP like a knight-in-shining armor *right* when me and my garage needed him the most, I thought I'd be seeing Chance every day.

But Chance and the Lucky Strikers leave town again for a series of away games and, just like that, he's MIA for weeks.

I'm surprised by how much I miss his playful smiles and flirty banter.

And I *really* wish I asked him how he managed to tie my hair without it getting loose.

"Nurse," dad's croaking voice lifts me from my thoughts, "he called B-24."

I place the sticker in a hurry and dad lifts his hand. "Bingo!"

Groans of disappointment sweep through the room, growing in direct response to dad's excitement. Dad eagerly points to the front of the room where the bingo prizes are stacked, a silent command to wheel him there.

I wrap my fingers around the handles of his wheelchair and push him forward.

"This one." Dad collects the package of *FreshButtFit* boxer briefs. "Chance McLanely wears these."

I wouldn't presume to know what underwear Chance prefers. I haven't allowed myself to even imagine him in anything close to boxer briefs. But I'm pretty sure his tighty-whities wouldn't have an 'accident guarantee' padding.

Dad smirks proudly. "I spoke to him, you know."

I don't correct my father. He's been really excited since Chance's visit. Which means his non-stop chatting about June reduced significantly.

"McLanely is playing the Southern Foxes this weekend." Dad informs me.

"You've mentioned it," I answer dryly.

Somehow, dad knows every detail of Chance's itinerary. In his mind, he even knows what Chance eats for breakfast.

"Why are you suddenly so interested in Chance McLanely?" I ask, genuinely curious.

"The better question is why aren't *you* interested in Chance McLanely?"

I humph. Dad sounds exactly like May.

A nurse smiles politely at us. "Mr. Brooks, it's time for your checkup with Doctor Reese."

Dad holds his bingo card to his chest. "I can't go yet. This is another winning hand. I'm sure of it."

"Dad, I mean, Mr. Brooks," I clear my throat, "I'll play this hand for you. You can take over when you get back."

Dad surveys me with narrowed eyes. "Alright." He gives in. "But don't get up. Not even to use the bathroom. That's how they get'cha."

I offer him a wobbly smile and promise that I won't get up even if my bladder's about to explode.

Dad is wheeled away and I play the rest of the round.

After the game ends, dad still isn't back yet, so I go in search of him.

I find his nurse tending to another patient and wait until she has a moment before asking, "Is my father still with the doctor?"

"Oh, he was tired after the check up so he retired to his room. I'm sorry. I should have informed you but I got caught up."

"No worries." I smile. "Everything's okay with him?"

"The doctor's very happy that his appetite improved."

"That's a relief. I was concerned that he would never get his appetite back."

"He's been eating every bite, three meals a day." She leans in with a warm smile and says, "Your father claims if he doesn't eat, Chance McLanely will nag him."

How far has dad's sickness progressed that he thinks Chance sincerely cares about what he eats? I want to ask her, but I'm afraid to.

"Thank you for taking such good care of him," I say politely.

As I head to the lobby, the receptionist catches sight of me.

"Goodbye, April!" she waves. "See you next time!"

"See you too!" I wave back enthusiastically.

The receptionist freezes and keeps her stare on me all the way through the exits.

I bet she thinks I'm acting strangely, but in all truth, this is who I've always wanted to be. Someone who smiles at the receptionist. Someone who walks into the nursing home with her head held high, knowing her bills are paid.

Whoever said 'money doesn't buy happiness' has never been in debt from staggering medical bills.

Humming under my breath, I saunter to my truck and climb in.

Just then, my phone lights up.

"Chance, hi." I let the engine run so the air conditioner can cool me down.

He sounds tired. "Did I catch you at a good time?"

"Yeah, I was just leaving my dad."

"Did you tell him hi for me?"

"I'm not sure if I should."

"What do you mean?"

"You're dad's new obsession. He mentions you all the time." I check my watch. Chance is on the other side of the country so he's several hours ahead of me. "Is the game over?"

"It is." He answers in a strained voice.

"Oh no, did you lose?"

"We won… *but* I spent most of my time in the sin bin."

"Really?"

His tone hardens. "It was my first time all season that I got two penalties in a row."

I sink deeper into my seat. Although I don't know much about hockey, I've heard the sports re-caps praising Chance for avoiding penalty calls. "What happened?"

"Their defender said something about you."

"What did he say?"

"I'm not repeating it."

"If you do, I'll probably laugh."

"It wasn't something to laugh about." Chance sounds about ready to throw a few more blows.

"Relax, Chance. I've been in garages my entire life. I know how guys talk."

"*Boys* talk like that. Men should mind their words. Especially when the woman they're talking about is mine."

"That sounds very possessive."

"I said what I said."

My lips twitch. "My point is, there is *nothing* those players can say about me that I haven't heard before. I'm not a sensitive flower you have to protect. At least, not on the ice where it's obvious they're just mocking me to push your buttons."

He says nothing, but I can imagine him glaring into the silence.

"It bothers me more that you let them use *me* to get to you. I want to be your strength, not your weakness."

The pause, this time, is even longer.

"Chance, you still there?"

"April, you keep talking like that and I'm flying back tonight. Forget tomorrow's game."

I snort. "Max will drag you back by the collar before you get to the airport."

"How do you know him so well?"

"Just focus on tomorrow's game, Big Shot."

"Big Shot?" His voice rumbles with satisfaction. "I like it."

"I was being sarcastic."

"You gave me a pet name."

"It was an insult."

"I think you're getting soft on me."

"I am *not*." I squirm when I catch my eyes in the rearview mirror and see a weird glint of interest. Prattling on, I say, "I mean it, Chance. Whether we like it or not, we're publicly linked. As you can tell by all the testimonials people are leaving for the garage, I'm a *very* talented mechanic with a thriving shop. So at the very least, you shouldn't embarrass me on the ice."

Chance laughs loudly. "Oh, April. I miss you so much."

My mouth clamps shut before I tell him the same thing.

"I'll text you after the post-game celebrations," Chance promises. "Call me before you go to sleep."

"It'll be like three am for you."

"Call me," he says firmly.

My heart tumbles like a turbine shaft in a storm. "Okay."

We hang up and I press a hand to my chest. Why do I feel so warm inside? Is it because of that quick conversation with Chance or am I still giddy after paying off dad's nursing home bill?

Hoping for a distraction, I search Chance's name online and look for his latest game. I want to read more about the fight he mentioned.

Immediately, millions of hits pop up under his name. But instead of finding articles about the Lucky Striker's latest win, I find a more appalling headline.

FINA SPOTTED AT STRIKERS VS FOXES GAME

McLANELY'S GLAMAROUS EX… BACK FOR A SECOND CHANCE!

Right beneath the articles are images of a leggy blonde with the *most* stunning cheekbones I've ever seen on a human being. Paparazzi pictures show her cheering at all of Chance's games.

Instantly, my mood sours.

Dragging the stick shift into position, I drive to the garage in a hurry. There's a fire burning in my chest and, though I tell myself it means nothing, it's hard to convince myself that's true.

CHAPTER
THIRTY-THREE

CHANCE

THE NEXT DAY, WE PLAY THE KONGE CRUSADERS AND WIPE THE floor with them. Theilan immediately sends out a group text inviting everyone to a local bar to celebrate.

"I'm gonna bow out," I inform him, stripping off my jersey.

Theilan slams his locker shut and wiggles his eyebrows. "Got other plans?"

"Yeah."

He narrows his eyes. "What you doing?"

"Calling April."

Theilan boos. "I thought you were about to say something else."

"What else would he say?" Gunner grumbles, walking past us in a towel.

A big, mischievous grin cracks Theilan's face. "Nothing. It's just... April's allllllll the way back in town."

I reach for my gym bag. If I wasn't surrounded by my teammates, I'd call April immediately. She might be sleeping by the time I get back to the hotel, and the thought of not hearing her voice for a full day sends me into a tiny panic.

Theilan stops me as I turn to the showers. "Are you really staying in and calling your girlfriend tonight?"

I squint at him. "You'd rather I write a letter and send it by carrier pigeon?"

Chuckles break out.

Theilan's eyes dart around.

We're on better terms now, but there's no hiding his desire to compete with me. Being extremely competitive is a hazard of the trade. As athletes, something in our biological code urges us to be the best in the room.

It doesn't bother me anymore. Theilan and I have found our own rhythm on the ice—which is what matters.

"All you've done on this trip is play hockey and chase after April. Were you this lame in the league?"

Watson saunters into the room, scrubbing his damp hair with a towel. "All Renthrow does is play hockey and video chat with his daughter. I don't see you ragging him about it."

"Yeah, but that's his kid. April's just a girlfriend."

I slam my locker shut and spin around.

Gunner immediately shoves a sock in Theilan's mouth. "Shut it if you want to live."

Theilan spits out the sock. "Did you just—"

"It's better than McLanely's fist." Watson points out.

I smirk at Watson and Gunner's protectiveness. Theilan is young, impulsive and looks up to Gunner like the guy's the town hero. In a sense, I guess he is.

Every time I forget that Gunner's family is a big deal around Lucky Falls, I see the way everyone defers to him and remember that he's the small-town version of Prince Harry.

Theilan falls back, but he's still grumbling. "At least help a brother out and send me her number."

"Whose number?" I grunt. He better not be talking about April.

"That smoking hot babe who's been following you around."

"Did you get a puck to the head?" I scoff. "What are you talking about?"

"I'm talking about the blonde who's been at every game, staring at you the entire time."

I squint at the bright, fluorescent lights, trying to come up with a visual.

None come to mind.

Gunner gives me a disbelieving look. "Even *I* noticed her."

"Does she stand out that much?" I don't usually look in the crowd during or before games. Unless you count that time I couldn't stop staring at April.

Gunner nods. "She came up to me at the bar last night and asked why you weren't at any of the afterparties."

I frown. "Sounds like a stalker."

"I'd let her stalk me any day," Watson coos, reaching over to fist bump Goode, another defender. "The girl's got some bazookas on her, if you get what I'm saying."

Deep-throated and appreciative laughter breaks out in the locker room.

I take another step toward the showers. "Even if I did know her, I wouldn't set any of my female friends up with the likes of you, Theilan."

Theilan grins. "I don't need your help."

"Why's that?" Watson teases.

"She's probably heartbroken that McLanely's not interested. And as a young, single, caring man, I'm going to teach her the best way to get over someone." Theilan wiggles his eyebrows suggestively.

"My man!" Watson slaps Theilan's open palm.

Theilan throws one leg over the bench and starts yapping to Watson. "I looked her up, man. Her entire page is just her wearing these tiny little outfits. She's just my type, super blonde, legs for days, this mmm…" his eyes roll back, "this Russian accent. Can you imagine that accent whispering in your ear?"

I crash to a stop. "Did you say she has a Russian accent?"

"Ring a bell?"

I immediately change directions, heading to my locker instead of the showers.

"What's up?" Gunner asks, his eyes following me.

The entire locker room goes silent, watching as I yank out my gym bag from the locker and rifle through it.

I feel a calm presence behind me and notice that Renthrow is standing close by, on guard. His hair is damp on his forehead as if he didn't get a chance to dry it yet. His eyes mirror the same concern in Gunner's.

Ignoring all of them, I grab my cell phone, open a search engine and tap in the name of an old acquaintance.

There. It *is* Fina. Her latest posts are selfies taken at my games. She even has a few smeary photos of me on the ice with heart-eyed emojis around my head.

I cringe at the flashy headlines and ugly comments underneath the posts.

Chance looks better with Fina.

Fina, go get him! I'm rooting for you!

Fina and Chance McLanely would be such a power couple.

Renthrow reads over my shoulder. In a low voice, he assures me, "It's just gossip. It's not that serious, McLanely."

I answer him with a grunt.

Gunner mouths to Renthrow, "What's going on?"

I leave Renthrow to explain, put the phone to my ear and stalk out of the locker room.

"Come on, April, pick up," I murmur as the phone rings.

The tunnels are packed with crew members.

"Hey, Chance!"

"Chance, great game!"

I rummage up a smile for the staff and duck into an empty room just as April picks up.

"Hey, Chance," she says.

I sigh in relief. She's not ignoring my calls. That's a good sign.

"Did I wake you?"

"No, I'm at the garage."

I check the time on my phone. "You're working this late?"

"I couldn't sleep." A banging sound punctuates the words. She must have me on speaker.

"Why couldn't you sleep? Did something happen?"

"No," she says tightly.

I release a breath.

"How was your game today?" April asks.

"Great. We won."

"I know. I saw the news."

"Did you, uh," I pull my collar away from my neck, "did you read anything else online?"

"Like what?"

"Irrelevant news."

"Why would I read it if it's irrelevant?"

Silence rings between us broken only by a loud *bang!* And the sound of metal dragging on the floor.

"I just… wanted to remind you that you shouldn't believe everything you see online."

Bang! Bang! Bang! "I'm not an idiot, Chance. I'm well aware of that."

I'm not one to hold my tongue. However, I *need* to be cautious. If April hasn't seen the articles about Fina, I don't want to alert her. And if she has, I want to assure her that the pictures are nothing but an empty publicity grab.

The banging stops and April's voice sounds closer to the phone. "Did you get to celebrate with the team tonight?"

"Absolutely not. I called you right after the game. I didn't even shower," I answer firmly.

"You don't have to do that."

"Shower?" I force a chuckle. "Are you saying I have permission to stink—"

"You don't have to report to me after every game."

I'm so stunned, it takes me a minute to answer.

"I'm not 'reporting' to you, April. I enjoy talking to you. There's no one else I'd rather be speaking with right now."

"Really? *No one* else?"

There's an undercurrent of accusation here.

I'm swimming in dangerous waters.

I lean against the wall and rub my eyes. "You saw the articles about Fina."

"That Russian social media model who wears bikinis in the winter? Never heard of her."

"Then how do you know she's Russian and an underwear model?"

"Maybe I'm a fan."

"*Are* you?"

There's a long silence.

I break it first. "There's nothing going on between me and Fina. We hung out once or twice a few years ago, but we were never that serious. I haven't seen or spoken to her since—"

"Like I said, you don't have to explain anything to me."

"I know it bothers you."

"It doesn't bother me."

"Then why are you in the garage beating the living daylights out of an engine? April, there's no need to be jealous—"

"I am *not* jealous?"

"But you *are* angry."

"I'm numb, Chance. Totally and completely numb. I know how men are. I grew up around mechanics and if you think locker room talk is indecent, you haven't heard a garage full of sweaty, oil-stained men. I told you before that I'm not a dainty little flower. I'm well-aware of the reality of the world. So you don't have to console me. Whatever you're doing on the road, it's none of my business."

"I haven't done anything—"

"Don't bother. It's not like I'm there with you to verify anything, so I'd rather we don't waste each other's time."

I really, *really* don't like the sound of that.

"I should go. I was just finishing up here," she grumbles.

"April, wait…"

The phone clicks.

She's gone.

I drill my thumb into my forehead hard enough to bore a hole in my skull.

The internet is an evil, swirling vortex of gossip, sensationalism and fake news, and none of it ever mattered to *me*.

Until now.

Because that evil, swirling vortex of gossip matters… to April.

CHAPTER
THIRTY-FOUR

APRIL

Sweat drips down my nose and plops against the open collar of my jumper. I mindlessly brush my knuckles against my forehead and keep inspecting the spark plug for a solution.

I could coat the tips with engine oil or…

Hey, Tink. You really shouldn't be working so hard.

I push Chance's imaginary voice out of my head.

I could replace one of the tips with a new plug that I *know* is working…

Have you taken a break yet, Tink?

Ergh! I toss the wrench back in the toolbox and it lands against my treasured scanner with a *clang!* Grabbing a dirty rag, I wipe off each of my fingers, scrubbing them as if I'm scrubbing Chance out of my brain.

Sadly, I'm unsuccessful at both forgetting Chance and getting the stains off my nails.

Ever since I read about him and Fina, I can't stop thinking about him. It's like my brain is stuck on a bad song. Like I'm running as fast as I can, but I've landed in quicksand.

I don't know why I'm like this. Chance's latest scandal is proof that holding him at arm's length is the right decision. Women will always flock to him. He's *the* Chance McLanely—a Beast and a Beauty on the ice. With his Prince Eric hair, his eyes the color of a midnight ocean, his warm, inviting personality...

Gosh! Why is it so hot?

I undo the top of my mechanic jumper and shimmy out of the sleeves. As the jumper peels away, the sleeves land against the bumper of the car. I stare at the sleeves, recalling the last time my jumper was trapped in the hood.

Take it off. Chance had said, his eyes a deep, dark blue.

Prickles run up my skin.

My heart pounds.

I slam my fist against my chest. "Behave."

Chance-related adrenaline spikes are not allowed.

Thinking of him is not allowed either.

I keep working until the engine in front of me starts to blur. Setting aside the wrench, I straighten, plant my hands on my hips and stretch my back. Spine-cracking sounds fill the garage.

"You should take one of those ancestry tests," Rebel says, walking up to me with a popsicle extended.

I spin to face my best friend. "Huh?"

"Check your DNA. You might be part bubble wrap."

I muster up a smile for her as I accept the popsicle.

Rebel jerks her chin at the door of the garage and walks steadfastly toward the coffee station there. I follow her and plop into the chair around a pretty metal table. Rebel's latest needlework—two wonky rose-shaped coasters—decorate the metal top.

"Why is it so hot lately?" I whine, pulling at my white tank top. "You'd think we were welders instead of mechanics."

Rebel eyes me, saying nothing.

I squirm under her steady gaze. "Why are you staring?"

"What's your deal, Brooks?"

"I don't understand the question?" The popsicle wrapping rips away easily and I go to town on the cold delight.

"Chance called me. He wanted to know if you were okay."

"Really?" I say as casually as I can.

"Are you ignoring his calls?"

"Did he say that?"

"He didn't have to." Rebel tosses her hair over her shoulder. "Why would he be calling me if he could reach you?"

"I'm not ignoring him. I just… told him I'm busy and I'd rather we keep in touch through text."

"Are you responding to his texts then?" Rebel grills me.

I clear my throat. "When I have the time."

She makes a frustrated sound in the back of her throat. "April, I love you, but sometimes, I could just…" She makes a squeezing motion towards my neck.

I press a hand there, turning slightly away.

"Do you really believe Chance is seeing Fina behind your back?" Rebel demands.

I choke on a chunk of tangerine-flavored ice.

Not even a flicker of mercy crosses Rebel's face as she watches me fight for my life. It's like she *wants* me to die a violent death for ignoring Chance.

"I showed you what happened on the cameras." She arches a perfectly trimmed brow. "Do you need me to re-send the video from that night?"

"No," I mumble, wiping the corner of my lips.

A few days ago, when the gossip sites started whispering about Chance and Fina, Rebel flew into a righteous rage.

"I'm going to expose that cheating, lying, backside of a camel for who he really is!" she ranted.

Rebel stormed off on her valiant quest for the truth, only to return with a sheepish frown and footage from The Tipsy Tuna exposing that:

(a) Chance barely talked to any of the cheerleaders we saw that night;

(b) the cheerleader who'd pounced on him for a hug had done so without invitation and was quickly brushed off by Chance.

"He was innocent," Rebel says, as if I need the reminder. "I can't vouch for him on any other night, but *that* time, he did what a guy who respects and cares for his girlfriend is supposed to do."

"I know," I say quietly, setting the popsicle down on the open wrapper.

"Then why are you being like this?" Rebel wrinkles her nose. "From that short phone call, I could tell that Chance is losing his mind not talking to you. And you don't look that great not talking to him either. It's obvious you both like each other and so far, he hasn't shown himself to be a cheating scumbag like Evan. So what gives?"

"I... I don't know how to explain it."

She crosses her arms over her chest and sasses, "*Try* me."

The words in my head rush too fast and I'm not sure how to present them in a way that she'll understand. Rebel has *always* been beautiful and confident around men. On their part, men have always been attracted to her.

Every time I mention my insecurities around her, she scolds me or tells me to have more confidence. As if I can just shimmy on down to the confidence store and buy another bottle of good ole' self-esteem.

"Is there some other piece of information that I'm not aware of?" Rebel insists. "Did you catch Chance flirting with girls while he was with you? Did he make eyes at a waitress in front of you? Did he hide his phone when you walked in the room? Has he shown you any red flags?"

I dig my dirty nail into the loose thread of the coaster. "No."

Rebel's eyes narrow to slits. She leans forward, waiting for more.

"I *do* believe Chance is a good guy. I believe he was telling the truth when he said he hasn't spoken to Fina. And the fact that I trust him *that* much after Evan is already such a giant surprise."

"Then what's the problem?" Rebel throws her hands high, an empty popsicle stick in hand.

"Right now, we're just pretend. But the closer we become…" I trail off. "Dating Chance McLanely comes with the price of sharing him with the world," I admit quietly. "I can't do that again. Unknowingly sharing my ex-boyfriend with my hairdresser was hard enough. I don't want to share Chance with all the crazy, possessive fans chasing him around at every game. I don't want to date someone who'll constantly get nasty messages and late-night invitations from models and socialites. I know who I am and I know that it would drive me insane no matter how much I like him."

Rebel sighs. "I guess I can see that."

"Chance is a great guy. And maybe… if things were different…"

Her eyes fill with compassion. "Different how?"

"If he were a normal guy who moved to town, just another farmer or coal miner or cowboy…" I shrug because it's a foolish exercise. Chance is the *farthest* thing from a normal Joe. "The problem isn't him, Rebel. It's me. I'm too broken to handle everything that comes with his fame and hockey career."

A cool hand covers mine and Rebel says, "That's what you decided?"

I hesitate to nod. "It's a choice I wish I could make."

"What does that mean?" she asks softly.

"I thought all the feelings would go away." My heart thumps harder in my chest. "It didn't. Despite telling myself it won't work and that I'm only setting myself up for pain, something's changed. The more I tell myself all the reasons I can't have him…" Tears shimmer in my eyes as I admit, "the more I want him anyway."

Rebel chuckles through her own tears. "Is this why women

date bad boys we *know* aren't good for us? Do we all suffer from the same temporary insanity?"

I smile despite all the rolling emotions in my gut.

Just then, I hear May's voice and the cheerful *bbbbrrriing!* of her bike bell. Stones and sand scatter as my little sister skates her bike to a stop in front of the open garage door. She hops off and runs to me, her chest heaving.

"May?" I jump to my feet. "What's wrong?"

"Chance," she heaves for breath, "viral video…" Another gasp. "Online."

"What?" Rebel bends her head to hear May better.

I leap forward, already imagining the worst. "What happened to Chance?"

"Just. Watch!" May shoves her phone at me and then collapses into an exhausted heap on the floor.

CHAPTER
THIRTY-FIVE

CHANCE

Cameras flash directly on the podium. From this high up, it's like looking into a sea of exploding stars. After so many years of this circus, I'm still not used to the way cameras actively try to blind us.

Questions erupt from all corners of the conference room.

I only respond to one.

"Chance, why have you been refusing to do after-game interviews? Are you trying to build suspense?"

"You caught me, Harry. That's exactly what I'm trying to do."

Harry Winsbury pauses. He's a sports journalist with The Millenial Times. Nice guy. A bit overzealous but only because he loves hockey as much as the players he writes about.

I feel a hand land heavy on my shoulder. To my left, Max is grinning painfully. His eyes beam a frantic 'what are you doing?'

I shrug his hand off and look at the cameras.

"There's something I need to address, but I wanted to wait until you were all here before I spoke up." I nod to the line of cameras filling the room. Every major broadcasting network is present and waiting.

"And what exactly is this news you want to share?" Harry prods.

"Don't tell me you're trying to retire?" another reporter barks out.

Harry throws them the stink eye.

A low roll of disgruntled murmurs erupt from the journalists. It's a bit surprising that the media is so sympathetic to me. It wasn't too long ago that I was being burned at the stake.

"Never gonna happen," I reply. "You'd have to drag me, kicking and screaming, off the ice. I'm never giving up on hockey."

Loose, uncomfortable chuckles tell me I may have been a little too intense saying that. Too bad. I mean every word.

"This isn't about hockey, but it is about something equally important to me." I clasp my hands and set them on the table. "As you all know, I'm in a relationship."

"Don't remind the ladies, Chance. We didn't bring enough Kleenex," Harry yells.

The room fills with laughter.

I do not join in. "That's the thing, Harry. I do want to remind the ladies. And the men. I want the entire world to know this. I am a taken man and I have zero interest in anyone but the woman I fell in love with."

Max's eyes are drilling holes into the back of my head.

Harry's jaw is on the floor.

"The first time I met her, my car had broken down. Like a total idiot, I rejected her when she offered to take a look at it. Despite that, she offered again. That's who she is. A woman who'll help a stranger on the road. Who'll take thirty minutes to fix a car when I can't even name the parts of an engine. Who'll give her life to take care of her family. Someone honest to a fault, whip-smart and so beautiful that sometimes all I can do when I'm in front of her is stare."

I adjust the mike and lean closer so the words reverberate through the speakers.

"Her name is April Elizabeth Brooks. It's her and no one else."

"Tell 'em your truth, McLanely," Harry encourages.

I shake my head. "This isn't my truth, Harry. This is THE truth. Immutable. Unobjectionable. And Unchangeable." I pause for dramatic effect. "Now... any questions?"

A giant bear paw of a hand covers my phone screen and lowers it to the backseat. "Put that down," Max says, dramatically covering his eyes. "Oh, I have a headache."

"There are worse things to say at a press conference," I remind him, pausing the video and putting the phone away.

Max just groans.

I check my watch and cringe. With the way traffic is crawling, I could miss my flight.

Scooting forward, I tell the chauffeur, "I'll pay triple your fare if you get me to the airport on time."

"Yes, sir." He salutes and shifts gears.

Max's eyes take up half of his face. "What do you mean you're going to the airport? You're not heading back to the hotel?"

"No." My phone buzzes and I take it out, distractedly explaining, "I'm heading back to town now."

"What about your luggage?"

"Oh, right." I look up and give him a pleading stare. "Could you handle that for me?"

Max grumbles, "Why would I, the owner of the team, take care of your luggage?"

"I'm not asking the owner of the team," I reply, noticing that Derek is calling. "I'm asking my best friend from college."

Max sulks in his seat, but he's such a giant guy that he can't even slouch properly. "I'm charging a transportation fee."

"Send me an invoice." Sliding the phone to my ear, I smile. "Derek, that was fast. I *just* left the press conference."

"You think you can say anything in front of the media and I wouldn't know about it? I make half my entire salary from that pretty mug of yours."

I laugh at my agent's excited tone. "I know what you're going to say and I'm going to correct you ahead of time. What I did today was not brilliant marketing. I meant every word."

"Doesn't make a difference to me. The only thing that needs to be real in my life is money. Speaking of, *FreshButtFitt* has been hounding me day and night. They want to lock you down for another five years."

"That's a gamble. What if I'm no longer relevant in five years?"

"McLanely, everyone with eyes can see that your trajectory is heading in one place and one place only—up. Besides, the currency those companies are looking for is influence, and you have more now than before your suspension."

"Because of me and April?"

"The family man image doesn't hurt, but it's your incredible ice time too. People are watching what you're doing with that team from Podunk Town and they want more."

"Lucky Falls."

"I wouldn't say it's luck, Chance. We made an intentional, targeted effort to clean up your act by involving that female mechanic—"

"The *town*, Derek. The name is Lucky Falls."

"Right, right," he admits, his tone indicating that he's already forgotten. "I've been invited into some rooms, Chance. I can't give you any more information now, but I've got a great feeling about this."

"What's with the mystery, Derek?"

He laughs. "I'll let you know when I have more. Just keep on doing what you're doing."

"'What I'm doing' is playing the game I love and heading back to town to see my girlfriend."

"Exactly."

I sigh in satisfaction. "I'm really living the dream."

"Because of who?" Derek coos.

"My hard work and my incredible agent?"

Derek laughs. "This is a ruthless world and you made the right combination of choices to survive in it." A chair creaks in the background and I can picture Derek leaning back as he often does when he's trying to lecture someone. "Some people have influence with no skill. Some have skill with no influence. You've got both, McLanely. That's a magical combination."

"Thanks… I guess."

"*FreshButtFitt* isn't the only company that's itching to work with you. I'll send over some contracts. Take your time deciding your next move."

"Whatever it is, it won't be with underwear," I warn him.

He laughs.

I end the call after promising to get back to him on the contracts.

Max glances at me and then at the window, squinting into the sun filing past the windshield. "That your agent?"

"Yeah, Derek."

"Mm." A thoughtful, worried look crosses Max's face. "What'd he say about the press conference?"

"It was good for my image. I'm getting more brand deals. The usual."

"Mm."

"Yeah."

Max starts cracking his knuckles. It's so loud that the driver jerks the car in shock.

"Sorry, sorry."

"Sorry. That was me," Max admits sheepishly.

"I thought something had fallen off the car. Everyone okay back there?" He peers at us through the rearview mirror.

I flash a thumbs-up. Through the window, I notice we're almost there at the airport. Right on time too.

"Did Derek have any updates from the league?" Max asks casually.

"No, why?"

He shrugs. "If you hadn't taken control of the narrative at the conference today, that question would have come up."

He's not wrong. I feel like that's the number one question on everyone's mind since the season started.

"Your fans are even starting to petition for your reinstatement," Max adds.

"The league won't be bullied by anyone, not even my fans. Nothing's certain yet."

Max nods. "Either way, a deal's a deal. If you do get called back…"

"I'll let you know." The taxi rolls to a stop and I pull out a few hundred-dollar bills. "Don't ship me off just yet, Max. We still have the play offs." I climb out of the car and swing my backpack over my shoulder.

"You might not make it to the playoffs with us," Max mumbles.

I freeze at the resigned tone of his voice.

He sees me watching and smiles. Waving a hand, he motions, "Go give April a hug. We'll talk more when I get back with the team."

I hurry inside of the airport, an unsettled feeling in my stomach. It's not until I'm already boarding the airplane that I realize what it is—unease.

For the first time since I was suspended from the league and drafted to the Lucky Strikers, I'm not excited about returning to where I belong.

CHAPTER
THIRTY-SIX

APRIL

WATCHING THAT VIDEO OF CHANCE PROUDLY DECLARING HIS feelings for me to the entire world cracked my heart in half.

No, it's more accurate to say that it cracked the protective chasm around my heart.

And now my heart is beating, open and vulnerable to the elements.

Beautiful. He called me beautiful in front of the entire world.

"April, are you wheezing?" May squeezes my shoulder. "Do you need to sit?"

"I'm fine," I breathe.

Rebel peers at me with eyes that can see right through me. "Did it change something? His speech, I mean?"

Admitting that it did would make me a hypocrite. I'm well aware. A few seconds ago, I'd been very firm about how broken, insecure, and unsure I was about a relationship with him.

One love confession from Chance later and I'm still all those things but, somehow, they don't seem to matter.

"Can you handle the afternoon clients for me?" I ask Rebel in a daze.

"Of course."

Without another word, I grab my phone and purse and take off running.

"Is she doing it? Is she finally getting out of her own way?" May asks Rebel in excitement.

I don't hear my best friend's response, but I'm pretty sure she's smiling.

Sunshine bounces against my straight hair, leaving its heated fingers on my shoulders and cheeks. The grass is withering from the humidity, and yet the heat of the day is *nothing* compared to the burning meteor that tore a hole through my chest.

It's her and no one else, he'd said with a sure look in his eyes. *So* sure. How can Chance be so certain when life is so unpredictable?

It's total and utter *foolishness* to believe that two people can be faithful to, serve, honor, and protect each other for the long term. It's even more insane to believe that two people can actually like *and* enjoy each other's company for decades.

And yet, I think... with Chance...

Every cell, every fiber, every bone in my body longs to believe that it's possible if it's with him.

The drive to the airport feels like it takes hours. Chance isn't picking up the phone and I'm slightly panicking as I rush to a customer service desk.

"How can I help you?" the perfectly dressed woman in the tailored suit asks.

I lick my lips. "Can I... I'd like to buy a ticket? Can I do that here? Or..." I fumble with my phone and it almost crashes to the ground. "Do I need to buy a ticket online?"

She looks me up and down. "Yes, you can purchase a ticket here."

"Great." I sigh in relief.

"By the way, you look familiar." She taps a manicured nail on her chin. Her eyes rove my dirty mechanic jumper, my wind-torn hair and makeup less face. "Are you that mechanic? The one who's dating Chance McLanely, the hockey player?"

I smile in discomfort.

"Oh my goodness." Her eyes do another slow rove. Her nose turns up in distaste. "Wow… you really *are* a mechanic, aren't you?"

I wipe my hands over my hair, hoping to clean up a bit. The move only brings her attention to the dirt under my nails and something inside me splits.

You're just too much like the guys, April. Sometimes, you feel like one of the bros to me. That dark voice in my head amplifies my own desire to hide.

I tuck my hands behind my back. I should have gone home and changed before rushing to the airport. I smell and I'm too dirty…

She's so beautiful that sometimes all I can do is stare. Chance's words from the press conference wash over me.

I inhale deeply and remember why I'm here.

Chance believes in me. He believes in us.

I've never done something as impulsive as buying a plane ticket to visit a man, but I've also never met anyone I wanted to trust more.

Being with Chance for real will bring me face to face with my insecurities. I'll be constantly placed under a microscope. Constantly having to defend why I'm 'good enough' to be with him. If he was brave enough to take that leap in front of the entire world, why can't I make a decision within my own heart?

Lifting my chin, I stare the rude woman right in the eyes. "I was gapping spark plugs on a six-liter engine—that's a big engine by the way—when I suddenly missed my boyfriend and wanted to see him. Hence why I'm here." I set my elbow on the desk and she leans back. "So can you please help me with that? You *are* a customer service rep, *aren't you?*"

I make sure to deliver the question in the same, condescending tone in which she'd given to me.

The woman nods tightly. "Of course. Can I have your ID?"

My heart thumps in a wild craze and my palms leak enough sweat to flood the desk. Yet, I feel looser than I have since the breakup with Evan.

I never used to care what people thought of me. But after Evan demolished my self-confidence—no, after I *allowed* Evan to demolish my self-confidence, things changed.

I miss the old April. I miss the *real* April.

I want her back.

As I'm rummaging in my purse for my ID, my phone rings.

It's Bobby.

"Hey, Miss April," Bobby says in that good-natured drawl, "I really, *really* need your help. The Zamboni's gone in again and the children's figure skating competition is coming up this weekend. I need that truck back on track. I can't have the little ones getting hurt on uneven ice."

"I'm a little tied up at the moment. Could you call Stewart Kinsey?"

"Kinsey's not picking up the phone. I think he found out you fixed the Zamboni last time and now I'm on his 'blocked' list."

I remain quiet.

Bobby presses, "If you can't help me, I don't know what I'll do."

I chew on my bottom lip. Although I want to see Chance *now*, I can't bear the thought of anyone's precious son or daughter getting hurt when I could do something to prevent it.

"Alright." I sigh. "I'll be right there."

"You won't be flying with us today?" The clerk arches a brow smugly.

I debate buying a ticket for later today, but I don't know when I'll be done with the Zamboni. I thought I'd fixed it properly last time. If it's broken down again, there might be a deeper, more complex issue that I can't solve before the flight.

"No thank you."

Turning away, I return to my car and drive to the stadium. On the way, I call Chance again but it goes straight to voicemail.

I back into the stadium's parking lot. There's a giant banner of the team hanging on the front of the stadium. Chance is slightly ahead and in the center of the group.

"Why aren't you answering?" I grumble to the humongous image.

With a slight shake of my head, I grab my tool box from the truck bed and enter the stadium. The lights are off, which is strange. Did Bobby forget that he called me down here? And where's the Zamboni?

"Bobby!" I call, moving carefully down the stairs in the dark. "Bobby, where are—"

My words are cut off when the spotlights over the stadium burst to life. They illuminate the Zamboni that's working very well as it vrooms over the ice in a peculiar pattern.

I slow down, inhaling sharply. From this vantage, looking down at the ice, the Zamboni is leaving a mark behind.

What is that?

I back up the stairs to get a higher view and the pattern becomes clear.

It's the shape of a heart.

I cover my mouth with a hand. Why is Bobby doing this? I know he's head-over-heels for his wife, so that must mean…

"Tink," Chance's deep voice rumbles behind me.

I spin around, jumping so far in the air that it really seems like I can fly. "Chance, what are you doing here? I thought the team wouldn't be back in town until tomorrow."

"I left early." He takes a step forward. The rest of the stadium is still dark, but the light bouncing from the ice illuminates his handsome face. "I missed you."

My throat pulls tight. All the things I wanted to say to him get lost between my head and my lips. Breathlessly, I gesture to the ice. "Is that for me?"

"Yeah." He tilts his head. "I wanted to do something special for you. Next time, I'll set up candles and rose petals everywhere."

I squint in thought. "Is it legal to light candles in an ice rink?"

He pauses and thinks about it. "You know… I'm not sure."

I laugh, my shoulders, neck and back loosening. My heart is finally at ease seeing him and I… I'm just so happy.

His eyes soften on me. "Whoa."

My lips freeze. "What?"

"Your smile just made my heart flutter."

I laugh and shake my head.

"I'm being serious," Chance insists.

I chuckle again, unable to stop smiling at him. Now that I think about it, I started smiling and laughing a lot more after meeting Chance.

Chance remains a few feet away, but his gaze is so tenderly caressing that it feels like he's touching me when he says, "I really missed you."

I take a step forward. "Me too."

"Yeah?" He seems surprised.

"I saw the press conference."

"I meant every word."

My fingers fall to the pockets of my jumper. Pressure builds in my head and I take another step forward. "Chance?"

"Yes, Tink?"

"There's… something I need to tell you."

CHAPTER
THIRTY-SEVEN

CHANCE

ALL I WANT TO DO IS GRAB APRIL AND GIVE HER A BIG HUG.

Every day that I was apart from her was torture. Standing this close to her after so long away feels like diving into cool, turquoise waters after wandering around in the desert.

It takes every ounce of self control I have to follow her to a seat and sit beside her without holding her hand.

However, I know it's the right move when she looks up and gives me a brave smile. Whatever she has to say is difficult enough for her and I don't want to crowd her space.

"Um…" Her voice trembles slightly and she rubs her hands on the oil-splotched legs of her jumper. "So, as you know, I was dating someone… before you."

I work to keep the jealousy from my face. Now that I've admitted my feelings for April, the thought of any other man having her—in the past or in the future—makes me want to put a ring on her finger immediately.

She swallows, clears her throat and says, "That person cheated on me, as you already know."

I do know.

And Evan is very lucky there are laws against tying someone to a lamppost and shooting them with a hundred hockey pucks.

"Evan and I met in high school, but we didn't seriously date until I graduated vocational college. I started working with him at the garage and he'd stay back late at the shop just to eat and work on cars with me."

I nod, listening intently even though I wish I could erase all visuals of Evan flirting with April over the open hood of a car.

"I thought we were happy." April wrings her hands together and I debate offering my fidget spinner. "We both loved cars. We could talk about turbo engines and compressors and faulty brake pads all day long. I thought I'd found the one."

She starts pulling on her fingers and, this time, I do offer her the fidget spinner.

Her lips inch up as she accepts the device from me and she gives it a flick. "Thanks."

"You're welcome."

As the plastic toy whirs, I survey April closely. "How long had you been dating before you found out about the other woman?"

"Three years. They'd been together for a year by then."

I curl my fingers into fists. "The next time I see Evan, he's getting a long overdue punch to the face."

"It's old news," April says, shaking her head.

I don't believe that. After what May told me about how April's self-confidence was crushed, it feels like that betrayal is still fresh.

"The other woman was," April sighs heavily, "the complete opposite of me. She always had long, painted nails. Her hair was always in a new style—probably because she's the town's hairdresser."

I make a mental note to boycott Lucky Fall's hairdressing salons. All of them.

"And she dresses really well."

"That's not a valid reason to step out on your partner," I grouch.

"I'm not saying that to excuse Evan. But it did show a glaring fault in our relationship. One I should have been aware of from the start. It took me ending things with Evan for him to truly be honest with me."

"What did he tell you?"

"He said I'm too much like the guys. That… sometimes, I feel like one of the bros instead of his girlfriend."

"Idiot," I mumble. One look at April's delicate cheekbones, full lips, and sweet smile and it's clear as day she's a woman. No amount of T-shirts, jumpers, or steel-toed work boots can disguise that fact.

April ducks her head. Watching her, I realize that she truly believes she's somehow inferior because of her career and style. And it makes me angry to think those words have been inscribed in her heart and a weight around her neck for such a long time.

I blow out a breath and say as gently as I can, "You know that's not true, don't you? You are incredibly beautiful, April."

"Thank you." The fidget spinner whirs as she gives it another push. "I think I would have been able to get back on my feet again. But right after blowing up at Evan, I was called into my boss's office."

She pauses.

"Stewart Kinsey. Mr. Kinsey owned the only garage in town at the time. My dad had worked there before he got sick and I'd been hanging around the garage since I was knee-high."

Another pause.

"I really looked up to Mr. Kinsey, not just as a good mechanic but as a family friend. I enjoyed working at his shop too because it felt like," a slow flick of the spinner, "I don't know, like my dad was still there with me."

I nod in understanding.

"But after I freaked out at Evan, Mr. Kinsey fired me."

"He fired *you?*"

She nods. "He said I was too emotional, that I couldn't do the grunt work the other guys could and that everyone felt like they had to watch their mouths around me because I was 'too sensitive'. Mind you, I usually let all their crass jokes slide unless it was *really* demeaning to women." She stops the fidget spinner suddenly. "Evan had complained that working with his ex would be too awkward. It was just an excuse for Mr. Kinsey to side with his family and get rid of me."

I shake my head in disgust.

"After that," April adds, "Mr. Kinsey offered me some… personal advice." She takes a giant breath and seems to prepare herself to speak again. "He said that I shouldn't be surprised that Evan went looking elsewhere. He said that men are visual creatures and seeing a woman all covered up like me wasn't what men wanted."

Inside, my blood starts boiling.

"He said if I wanted to be happy, I had to lower my expectations. After a long day's work, a guy doesn't want to come home to someone like me." She extends her arms to show the stains on her hands and nails. "I should just accept that if a guy had to choose between a feminine lady and a dirty mechanic covered in oil and sweat…" April nibbles on her bottom lip, "he wouldn't choose the mechanic."

I explode to my feet. "Where is he? Where's this Kinsey guy?"

April grabs my bicep. "What are you going to do?"

"I don't know? Drive my car through his shop window?"

She laughs.

I sit back down, my eyebrows taut. "I'm open to suggestions."

"Chance," she says with a smile.

I can't even look at her pretty face. I'm filled with so much righteous anger, I might start a political rally and change a few state laws.

"Chance, I'm not finished."

I look over at April. She's sitting on the bench, her face upturned and a small, hopeful smile on her face.

"Evan's actions and Mr. Kinsey's words really hurt me. I believed that maybe I *wasn't* enough. Pretty enough. Feminine enough. Sweet enough to be in a relationship. Maybe I wasn't the type of woman that a guy would be interested in. Even if he *was* interested, I wasn't the type of woman a guy could be faithful to."

"That unworthy feeling got worse when you and I," she points between my chest and hers, "started faking our relationship. Everyone on the internet criticized my looks, so I changed it. But when I started dressing more like the woman Mr. Kinsey had described, I felt even worse about myself." She gestures to her jumper. "*This* is the real me, but people only started paying attention and believing we were really together when I hid it."

"I'm sorry, April. I should have known. I should have protected you better."

I don't realize my fingers are tightening into fists until April starts prying at each digit. When my fist is unclenched, she smoothes her hand down my palm and links her fingers with mine.

Stunned, I look from our joined hands to her beautiful face.

"You once told me you don't hand out apologies unless you mean them. I know you're being sincere, but I won't accept your apology this time, Chance. This is not your fault. You've done nothing but make me feel valued and protected."

My lips curl up. Those words mean the world to me.

April chuckles. "If it were anyone else, I wouldn't have gotten to this point. Believe me, I was looking for any reason to mistrust you, but you haven't given me a single opportunity to doubt your character."

I squeeze her fingers and then bring them up to my lips to kiss the back of her hand. The harsh scent of engine fluid and whatever oils and grease she was working with fills my nostrils. But it doesn't bother me at all.

"I really, *really* like you, April." It's more than that, but she only opened the door to her heart a crack. I don't want to barge in with another love confession and overwhelm her too soon.

"I like you too." She leans forward. "For real."

Joy explodes in my chest and I whoop like a maniac.

April teeters back with laughter and watches me with a big grin. "Are you that happy?"

"I worked so hard to hear that… Of course, I'm ecstatic."

April scoots forward and wraps her arms around my neck. Instantly, my grin tempers into a quietly pleased smirk. Having her close is almost better than ice time.

Nope, it's *way* better than ice time.

I rest my hand on her waist and pull her a little closer. "What's the first thing you want to do as my real, official girlfriend?"

"Mm." She tosses her head back, exposing her beautiful neck to me. "Now that we're official, how about we seal the deal?"

CHAPTER
THIRTY-EIGHT

APRIL

"When you said 'seal the deal', this is not what I had in mind," Chance mutters, staring at me as I wobble forward on the skates Bobby lent me.

Behind him, the ice glints white and frosty. It's a regular ice rink, but it might as well be the Siberian tundra in my eyes.

My safety-pad-covered knees quake at the thought of stepping onto the ice.

A chill inches up my spine despite the two layers of Chance's sweater and numbered jacket shrouding me from the cold.

I try to take a step forward, but my brain communicates 'time to panic' and my limbs revolt.

Both legs start wobbling.

Arms, windmilling.

Balance and gravity are in a heated battle and the former is losing.

I bend my knees and wiggle my arms, knocking the scarf around my neck askew. "Chance!"

Warm, calloused fingers close around my elbow. I manage to remain upright with Chance's grip firm around me.

"You good?" Chance asks. I have no idea how he got to me so fast, but he's not even winded.

"Yeah." I blow out a breath. With his help, I take a shaky step forward.

"Didn't you tell me you were never going to skate?"

"I said I was allergic to falling on ice. But things change. I can't be your girlfriend and not even know how to handle myself in an ice rink."

"I'm your boyfriend and I don't know how to fix cars," Chance points out.

"Don't worry. I have a bunch of beginner friendly engine repair tutorials all picked out."

Chance groans while I laugh maniacally. However, that laughter turns to whimpers of fear when I take another step toward the ice.

"I got you," Chance says, holding my elbow for balance.

I windmill my arms, moving jerkily. "You said this wasn't what you were expecting? What did you think I meant?"

Chance tilts his head, eyes rolling to the ceiling as if contemplating whether he should share. Finally, he returns his dark blue eyes to me and says, "Kissing."

Heat rams straight through my cheeks. I wrench my elbow away from his hold and immediately regret it. The slices of iron death attached to the bottom of my shoes slip out from under me and gravity tries to body-slam me into the ground like a WWE wrestler on a Tuesday night match.

Chance quickly wraps his arms around me. I end up flopping into his chest, which is really just a mass of bricks underneath a soft white T-shirt. It hurts almost as much as getting bonked in the head with thick library books.

I ease back a little.

Chance leans forward, bringing his face even closer to mine. A cheeky smirk tugs on his lips. "Ah, this is good too."

I can literally feel my scalp blushing.

I clear my throat and push him away, not too far though because letting him go would mean face-planting in a violent display of flailing arms and legs. "If it's this hard to walk already, I'm not sure it's a good idea to get on the ice."

Chance accepts the subject change and the slight distance between us with grace. He slides one giant hand through his hair and the soft black strands shift messily in all directions revealing, yet again, that there is not a single hairstyle he can't pull off.

Except maybe the Fabio one he had in high school.

"I've got you," he says confidently.

Chance leads me to a bench just behind the boards. He sits beside me and laces up his skates like a fireman shrugs into gear at the sound of alarms. In what feels like a second, he's on his feet again—having gained an unnecessary set of extra inches—and offers his hand to me.

I hesitate. "It's okay. I can do it."

"Don't trust me?" He arches a brow, his lips quirked upward.

"No, it's not that. But… can you help me *and* stay upright yourself?"

"I skate better than I walk," he returns cheekily. "You'll be fine."

With a cloud of doubt swirling around me, I set my hand in his and totter behind him. The moment I set one leg on the slippery ground of hardened water (or whatever ice rink floors are made of), I immediately regret it.

"No, no, no. I need to go back," I whine.

Chance turns to face me so gracefully, I'd believe it if he said he was a figure skater before he signed up for hockey. "April, just breathe and put both feet on the ice."

"I can't. I can't." My brain is sending up red flag after red flag. Ice was *not* meant to be walked on. If humans were designed to go gallivanting on slippery slopes, we would have been born with metal plates jutting out of our toes so we could glide.

"April…" Chance tries to pull me forward.

I resist.

The tug of war costs me dearly. While I have one foot anchored on the solid part of the ground, my other foot is on the ice and surging ahead like the *Titanic* at that iceberg.

"Chance!" I squeeze his hands for dear life as I drop into a mid-split. "Chance!" Frantically, I climb my way up his arms to stop my slow descent.

He tugs me back to my feet with the strength of his bulging biceps alone and then returns my hands on his.

"Tink, sweetheart, I got you. Just follow me."

I slowly allow my other foot to join the first on the ice. Chance holds my hand and skates backward at a glacial pace. I follow him like a newborn deer testing out his legs. Each of my skates seem to have their own engines because one foot keeps veering right while the other keeps sliding left.

Chance snorts.

I shoot him a glare that's sharp enough to cut. "Are you laughing at me?"

"No, ma'am," he says, pulling in his lips.

I murmur grumpily, "I haven't done the splits since my middle school cheerleading tryouts and here I am about to do two of them in a day."

Chance's eyebrows shoot up. "You tried out for cheerleading?"

"You try being an awkward eleven-year-old who loves fixing engines with her dad *and* the younger sibling of the most popular girl in school. It was a very confusing time."

"Did you make the team?" he asks.

"I got laughed out of the gym."

"I'm sorry."

"It's fine. Dad let me drive on the backroads after try-outs, so it turned into a happy memory. Besides, I would have hated every second of being a dancer. I was happy leaving that to June."

"This is your first time talking about her."

"About who? June?"

"May mentioned that you three are a quarter of the calendar."

I laugh.

"But," he adds, "that's kind of all I've gathered." He smiles and shakes his head. "So *June* was the most popular girl in school?"

"Don't sound so excited." I give him the stink eye.

"I'm just intrigued. You're so…"

I scrunch my nose. "So what?"

"Feisty."

"Is that a compliment?"

"Of course, Tink." He laughs. "And May is chirpy and optimistic. So I kind of pictured June as a combination of the both of you."

"Well, she wasn't. June was—is—extremely beautiful, but she's kind of cold too. Didn't like having her sisters hanging around all the time. Was super independent. She and dad argued a lot growing up. Even so, I don't understand how it was so easy for her to leave town and never look back."

My heart burns the way it always does when I talk about my older sister. Our family shattered the day she left and we've carried on, but it's never been quite the same.

"Sounds like you miss her a lot," Chance says carefully.

"Miss her?" I scoff loudly to ignore the pang in my chest. "I cut her off when she stopped answering my calls. Dad and May are the sappy ones. Dad can't remember us, but he mentions June all the time and May…" My throat wells with emotion. "Anyway, that's enough of my family drama. What about your family?"

"What about them?" Chance asks, skating a little faster.

I side-eye him because I notice he's increasing the pace, but I don't stop him. As long as he doesn't let me go, we'll be good.

"What's your family like?" I add.

Chance narrows his eyes in thought as we take a curve. Does he have eyes in the back of his head? How has he not turned around to check that he isn't crashing into the goalie net?

"We're pretty normal. My mom and dad are both business owners. My sister is married and lives out of state. We don't get together often enough to have drama."

Thanks to my internet search I'm aware that Chance's parents are more than simple 'business owners', but I don't think correcting him about how he views his family's wealth is the right thing to do.

"Hm." I move my attention from him to the crisp feel of the wind on my face as we skate. Being on the ice no longer feels as awkward since I'm not in fear of landing hard and cracking my knee.

This isn't half bad.

"I think I can try on my own," I tell him.

"You sure?" Chance asks, watching me closely.

I nod.

"Okay. Move your feet out like this." He shows me. "And if you feel like you're about to fall, don't make your movements big and wild or you might land backwards. Instead, fall forward, okay?"

"Okay."

He releases my hands and I wobble a fair bit but manage to keep going on pure momentum. Chance finally stops skating backwards and moves beside me.

"Speaking of my family," Chance says casually, "my mom supports a non-profit children's organization."

"How nice," I mumble.

"They have a ball every year to raise donations."

"Oh." A 'ball' sounds like a 'rich people' word. Why not just call it what it is—a party? "That's nice." I keep my concentration focused on gliding my feet the way Chance taught me.

"I was wondering if you'd come with me," he says.

My eyes whip up to his. "As in meet your parents?"

"Well… yeah."

At that moment, I lose all my balance and catapult to the ice.

CHAPTER
THIRTY-NINE

CHANCE

AFTER THE FALL, APRIL LOSES INTEREST IN SKATING, SO I TAKE HER to the local bookstore for some hot chocolate.

She's already blasted through the book I gave her on our date, so I offer to buy a book for her. At the promise of more mechanic books, a smile finally returns to her face.

One hour and a surge of selfies with unexpected fans later, we walk out of the bookstore carrying an untouched cup of not-so-hot chocolate for me and a history book on the development of the car manufacturing press for April.

"Are you sure you're okay?" I ask, glancing over. I'm driving April's truck. I wasn't letting her drive after watching her hit the ice earlier.

"Mmhm. While you were taking pictures with everyone, I read a couple pages. Did you know that the first car manufacturing company started in France in the 1900s?" Her eyes dance with delight.

April's eyes should be studied. They're a shade of green so deep that a man could drown in them.

"Wow," I say with as much exuberance as I can. "The 1900's? That's… that's really interesting."

April bursts out laughing.

I rub the back of my neck sheepishly.

"Please continue to be a terrible liar, Chance. It's a very trustworthy trait."

My lips tug up in response. I love when April laughs. It's the equivalent of a hundred tiny, fairy wings beating all at once. Or maybe that sound is just the beating of my grateful heart.

Reaching over, I take her hand. "I should have been holding on to you when I invited you to the ball."

Her smile dims. "Yeah, meeting the parents is a big deal."

"I already met your dad," I point out.

"That's different. Dad is a hockey fan, so you had an unfair advantage."

"You have an advantage too." I rub my thumb over the back of her knuckles. "Me. I'm crazy about you."

She groans. "That's not enough to convince your parents."

"My dad loves cars, so you two will hit it off right away. And mom… uh… will respect my choice someday."

April narrows her eyes. "Is your mom that scary?"

"She's," I search for the right term, "opinionated, but you have nothing to worry about."

April flops against the headrest. "What do I even wear to a ball? I'm not Cinderella. I don't have a fairy godmother crouching in the bushes, waiting to transform my jumper into a dress."

"Just wear your overalls if that's what you're comfortable in." I shrug.

"I am *not* wearing overalls to a gala. I'm a female mechanic; I'm not socially unaware."

I chuckle. "I don't care what you wear, as long as I get to pay for it."

"Absolutely not."

"I insist."

"Me too." She tilts her chin up. Today, she's not wearing any makeup and her generous freckles spread out across her fair skin like her face was brushed by the stars.

I want to grab her cheeks and kiss the daylight, moonlight—heck, all the lights—out of her.

Instead, I grip the steering wheel and drive up the gravel path that leads to her home.

"We'll continue this conversation later," I promise.

She shakes her head in exasperation.

I stop her as she leaves the car. "Oh, before I forget, the gala is this Saturday."

"*This* Saturday? And you're just telling me?" Wedging the book beneath her elbow and waist, April hops out of the truck and taps on her cell phone. "I need to call Rebel. I have no idea how we'll fit dress shopping in between all the repair work at the garage, but if anyone can make it work, she can."

"Here." I pull the keys out of the ignition and jog to her. "Take these inside with you."

"It's okay. Drive it back to your hotel. I'll ask Rebel to pick me up tomorrow."

"That's too inconvenient. I already planned to call a cab."

She wraps her hands around mine and pushes the keys toward me. "Chance, you played the Mutteneers last night, hosted a press conference early this morning, and flew straight back to town which means you got little sleep. I don't want you standing on the side of the road waiting for a taxi, which you won't get because none work all the way out here."

I move closer to her. "If you're so worried about me, you can invite me inside and watch me sleep."

Her face flushes in embarrassment. Despite that, she raises her fist valiantly. "Have I told you how good I am with a wrench?"

I laugh and step back a safe distance away. "Thanks for letting me drive the truck. I have training early tomorrow morning—Max's way of punishing me for taking off early—but

I'll leave the keys at the front desk. They shouldn't give you any problems."

"Got it." She waves sweetly. "Bye."

I wave back, wishing I could ask her to stay with me a few seconds longer.

April doesn't feel the same yearning because she skips up the stairs, opens her front door and disappears inside without looking back.

If that's any barometer of her feelings, I am far more into her than she is into me. Surprisingly, that doesn't bother me at all.

I trudge back to the truck, and a heavy sigh floats past my lips.

What is this strange feeling? I put a hand to my chest and my heart pangs with sadness.

I just saw April, but… I miss her already.

Whoa, I'm in deep.

I slam the door shut and turn the ignition when April's front door bursts open and she blazes down the path in quick-booted strides. Urgently, she yanks the passenger side door open and swings into the passenger seat.

"Did you forget something?" I peer at the floor mat, ready to use my phone's flashlight app and help her look around.

To my surprise, two soft hands land on either side of my face. My eyebrows shoot straight to the roof of the car as April leans in and plants her soft, pink lips on my cheek. The kiss is gentle enough to rival a butterfly's wings.

Before I can react, she straightens, looks at me in harried silence, and then backpedals fast. I watch her scurry back to her house and slam the door shut like someone's chasing her with a saw.

Slowly, I lift a hand to the cheek that she'd kissed.

I'm over six feet and almost two hundred pounds, but I feel light enough to float straight to space.

After a few minutes, I start the car and avoid looking at

myself in the rearview mirror. I already know what I'll find in my reflection—the sappiest smile known to man.
Oh-ho. You're a goner, McLanely.
There's no point arguing with the truth.
In the stillness, my phone rings and I check to find my mother's name blazing across the screen.
The smile drifts off my face and I inhale a deep breath before answering. "Hey, mom."
"I am really *very* tired of calling you first, dear."
"I meant to call, mom. We've been traveling to games almost every day. I didn't realize the minors were this busy."
"Is that all you have to say to me?"
I pinch the bridge of my nose. "You saw the conference?"
"I own a TV, cell phone and have working internet. I believe anyone within those categories in the United States of America and some parts of Canada saw your interview. It was everywhere."
"Are you calling to congratulate me then?"
"I wouldn't say that," she responds tartly.
A sigh erupts from my chest. Driving around with April, I hadn't been tired in the least. In fact, I could have played a full game *and* gone to the gym for cardio training. But three seconds on the phone with my mother, and my entire body feels drained.
"Calling someone 'family' before the world is a serious claim, Chance. You practically swore you'd make that woman a McLanely one day."
"I know what I said."
"Marriage is no spectacle, son. You know how seriously we take our commitments in this family."
"'Until death do us part'. I'm aware of the terms."
"A union such as marriage is not just about commitment. Of course, that's a *part* of it, but there are more responsibilities. What of your trust fund? The company that you and your sister will inherit that feeds thousands of employees? The holdings? The land titles? It's acceptable to ignore such things when

dating, but these are all considerations you should have when moving to the next level."

"Mom, I have never cared about inheriting the business, the holdings, the land titles, none of it. All I want is April and the health and strength to play hockey until I retire. That's it."

Her tone is even, but a scolding lingers just beneath the words. "If you're grown enough to speak of marriage, then you should be grown enough to understand that would-be-husbands can't always do as they want."

I keep my tone as respectful as I can. "I know that I can't always do what I want, mom. But big decisions like my career and my future wife are *mine* to make."

"Fine." She huffs. "I didn't call to argue. I wanted to confirm that you are, indeed, bringing that woman to the ball."

"Her name is April and yes I am."

"I'll let the planners know," she says stiffly.

"April is a sweet girl, mom. I'm confident you'll fall as hard for her as I did."

"Perhaps," she says dryly. "But remember, darling, marriages can fail and wives can return to their maiden names, but you will *never* stop being a McLanely. At the end of the day, that is what *I* am confident about."

I hang up with my mother, feeling unsettled and wondering if I should bring April to the ball or keep her a safe, far distance from my mother.

CHAPTER
FORTY

APRIL

"Eep! A shopping day! I'm so excited!" May screeches, strutting into the giant mall that we drove two hours to visit.

"I've shopped more times this month, than I have for my entire life," I grumble.

"You're welcome," Rebel says cheekily, gliding across the floor. As she walks, at least three men—two of whom are with their wives or girlfriends—turn to watch her.

"Let's go in here!" May grabs my elbow and steers me toward a fancy outlet.

My eyes double in size. "No way. We do not need an overpriced dress from an overpriced brand like that." I drag both of them to the side so we're not stopping traffic. "Before we continue, I need to tell you guys my budget and style. Something simple and right for the occasion is all I need."

"Re-*lax*, April. We can buy whatever we want because I have *this*." May fans out a credit card.

I hiss, "May, no! Another credit card? You *do* realize that just because the garage is doing better now, that doesn't mean we can spend unwisely. Between the garage's mortgage, our house bills, dad's nursing home fees, and your student loans, we don't have that much left over."

My sister flashes a smug grin. "This isn't mine. It's Chance's."

Instantly, my stomach wrenches. "We are *not* using Chance's money."

"Chance left very clear instructions. We're going to buy you whatever you want—that includes shoes, accessories, purses, *underwear*." She giggles.

I scowl at her, blushing fiercely.

"And," May continues, "Rebel and I are to treat ourselves to the fanciest lunch as a reward for our assistance. Chance's exact words."

"You can't spend someone else's money."

"Why not?" My sister counts off on her fingers. "He's my brother-in-law, he told me I could, and he has lots of it."

A weight presses deeper into my chest. It's been there ever since Chance invited me to the party a few nights ago. He definitely downplayed his family's resources by saying his parents simply 'run businesses'.

Even my little sister is aware of his family's reputation.

How can I stand before them knowing I'm just a mechanic from a small town no one's ever heard of?

"Chance's stuff is his stuff. Mine is mine." I lift a thin envelope from my purse. I visited the bank early this morning and drew out some cash for this shopping day.

It's a hack I learned from my dad. "*Plastic is too fake,*" he used to say. "*These cards don't really tell you what you have and don't have in your account, so it's too tempting to swipe. With cash, when you're out, you're out. That's the way to do it.*"

"How much did you bring?" Rebel asks, leaning over May's shoulder.

"Enough," I say mysteriously.

May thumbs through the money in the envelope. "What is this supposed to buy? Socks?"

"I'm sure we can find something nice with that," I argue. "It might take a lot of work, but if we go through the clearance racks…"

May meets Rebel's eyes.

The two nod decisively.

I shriek when they pounce on me. Rebel grabs my left arm, May grabs my right and they both drag me into the fancy store.

"Can I help you ladies?" A sophisticated clerk with slicked-back hair and white gloves approaches us.

"Yes." May gestures widely to me. "This is Chance McLanely's girlfriend and she's attending a fancy dinner with him. We need to make her *fabulous*."

The man's eyes glitter. "I know you. Your pictures with Chance are all over my feed. Someone even made a song for you two."

"Oh… uh, thank you?" I shuffle awkwardly.

"Come. We just got in a new stock from our hottest designer. These dresses only come in threes. That means, it's very unlikely that you'll see anyone else wearing what you do."

I look to Rebel for backup, but my best friend is grinning from ear to ear and skipping behind the clerk like she's Dorothy on her way to the Wizard of Oz. May is keeping up with her, hanging on the man's every word.

I force myself to tag along with them and try on every dress they thrust on me. Unfortunately, we end up leaving that store empty-handed because I don't really love any of the outfits there.

As punishment, Rebel and May spend hours dragging me from one store to the next.

My feet are about to fall off by the time we enter the last boutique hidden all the way at the back of the mall. A tall, pretty woman with flaming red hair greets us.

"Oh my word!" she says in the sweetest accent. "You're April Brooks!"

I give a stiff wave in response. I'm still not used to people recognizing me.

"Can I take a look over here?" Rebel asks.

"Of course."

Rebel breaks away and flutters her fingers through the dresses on the rack.

"Are you a Chance McLanely fan?" May smiles proudly, as if she and Chance really are family members.

"Well, the truth is…" The clerk leans closer and points to me. "I'm more a fan of your friend."

My jaw drops at her response. Usually, people recognize me from my pictures with Chance and ask me a million questions about what it's like to be a famous hockey player's girlfriend. I always feel like I have to perform for them so I don't disappoint whatever expectations they have of me.

This woman doesn't give me the same awe-filled look as the others. Instead, her smile is friendly and sincere.

"Why are you April's fan?" May asks incredulously.

"Because, from what I hear," the woman meets my eyes, "you're a real good mechanic."

Rebel cranes her neck to look over at us.

May's smile tweaks to a hundred-megawatt grin. "That she is," my sister says, tilting her chin up. "By chance, have you brought your car to their garage?"

"Not me. My sister-in-law. I don't know if you remember her," the woman says.

I glance over at Rebel.

My best friend hikes her shoulders and does a little shake of her head.

"Well, anyway, she was having lots of trouble with her car and every mechanic she went to couldn't fix the issue. Even worse, some of them straight up scammed her." The woman gets teary-eyed, "My brother, uh, my brother died a few years back so it's just been his wife and their kids. I'm the only one of my family who lives close to her."

I nod in understanding.

Rebel abandons the clothing rack and moves closer to hear the woman's story.

"She's had a lot on her plate and the car breaking down was just the last straw. Unfortunately, we couldn't find any mechanic who would take us seriously. The moment we walked into a garage, all the mechanic saw was two clueless women and... well, you know how the story goes."

I purse my lips, wishing it were different. It's no secret that some unsavory mechanics take advantage of women who come to the shop alone. It's why I always advise my female friends to bring a man with them when they visit a mechanic, even if that man knows nothing about auto repair.

"Anyway," she waves a hand, "long story short, my sister-in-law felt safe dealing with your garage. She said you were patient while explaining what her car needed and that, when you pointed out everything that was wrong, she didn't feel like you were trying to overcharge or scam her."

"I'm really happy to hear that," I say, smiling wide for the first time since Rebel and May trapped me in this shopping mall.

The woman clears her throat and says sheepishly, "Oh, look at me yapping. I do have a habit of oversharing, but what a miracle that you just happened to walk into my shop after doing that for us. I'm so grateful that I can't keep it in." She rubs her hands together. "Now, tell me what you're looking for."

"The thing is... I'm going to a party," I explain.

"A really fancy party with lots of fancy folks," May adds.

The woman sizes me up. "Are you a dress gal or a pantsuit gal?"

"I feel like dresses aren't as comfortable, but I'm a little too shy to wear a pantsuit for an occasion like that."

"You're not the bold type?" She teases.

I shake my head 'no'.

"I got just the thing."

The woman disappears into the back and returns with a beautiful navy outfit. The filmy material is loose with an incandescent shine that feels almost fairylike and I immediately think of Chance teasing me about truly being a fairy when he sees me in it.

"At first glance, it looks like a dress with a soft silhouette, but check this out." She separates the material at the bottom and I gasp. The woman laughs at my reaction. "It's just fancy pants, ain't it?"

"That's super cute!" Rebel chirps.

"Try it on!" May pushes me toward the dressing room.

I shimmy into the jumpsuit and immediately feel comfortable. While the red dress from my first Lucky Striker's game had been flashier and more attention-grabbing, it hadn't felt like *me*.

"I like it," I say the minute I step out of the dressing room.

"Whoa." Rebel nods in appreciation. "It fits you so well."

"That color looks amazing on you!" the woman tells me.

May takes a picture and the 'click' is loud in the silence.

I frown at her. "Why'd you do that?"

"Chance wants to know what color your dress is so he can match his tux to it."

"Chance? As in *the* Chance McLanely?" the woman giggles. "He's going to wear a tux that matches a dress from *my* store?"

"Your store?" I ask, eyebrows climbing. "Are you the owner?"

"That I am." She walks around the counter, bundles the jumpsuit and sets it in a branded bag. "We just opened a few weeks ago."

"Congratulations," I tell her.

May hands over Chance's credit card.

The owner pushes it back. "It's alright."

Taking the card from May, I set it in her hand. "I know how it is when you're just starting a business and things haven't picked up as yet. Please take it."

"Well… alright," she mumbles reluctantly. "But at least take this necklace. It'll go super well with the dress."

Rebel inspects the necklace and nods her approval. "I like it. It'll elevate the look."

I accept the bags, the card and my receipt from her. "Thank you."

"No, thank *you*. You fixed my sister-in-law's car when no other mechanic could. Now, she doesn't have to worry about getting herself and the babies safely to and from home. That means the world to me." She wraps her hand around mine. "Everyone might say you're lucky to be with Chance McLanely. But my sister and I believe that Chance McLanely is lucky to have you."

Something hot presses the back of my eyes, and I duck to hide the emotion.

Chance McLanely is lucky to have you.

I tuck her words deep in the pocket of my heart, somewhere I can easily reach it. Tomorrow, I'm putting on this jumpsuit and entering Chance's world. To survive there, I'm going to need all the encouragement I can get.

CHAPTER
FORTY-ONE

CHANCE

I book first class tickets for me and April and it feels amazing to treat her to this luxury. Plus, it's cute the way she fumbles around with the hot towel the airline attendant delivers to us.

"What am I supposed to do with it?" she whispers to me.

"Put it on your face like this." I demonstrate.

April places the towel on her face and yanks it off immediately. "It burns."

I stifle my laughter.

Streaks of red course over April's cheeks and she swats at me. "Don't laugh. I told you it would have been better if I drove."

"You'd be exhausted driving all the way. And I know you didn't want to close your shop early or leave Rebel to do all the repair work alone."

Her mouth opens and then slams shut. She can't argue with the truth.

Throughout the flight, April continues grumbling about the

plane's amenities. I grin hard each time she discovers something new—like the fact that the wine is complimentary or that the seats can recline.

"I don't think you should have shown me first class," April says later, as we breeze past the crowds waiting in the general line. "Way to set the bar too high, McLanely."

I chuckle at her scrunched nose and angry expression. My ultimate goal in life is to spoil April Brooks, and I'm just getting started.

April stuffs the complimentary blanket, slippers, and water into her backpack as she says, "The next time I fly, I'll be in economy and it'll be even worse because now I'll *know* how first class flying feels."

I maneuver the suitcases with one hand and capture hers with the other. "Stick with me, and you'll always fly in comfort, Brooks."

"Sounds like you're bribing me to date you," she says.

"Hey, whatever works."

"I'm not with you for your money, Chance."

Her tone is so fierce that I squeeze her hand. As I'm about to assure her that I was just joking, a teenager dressed in a loose shirt and khakis rushes up to me.

"Hey, Chance. I'm a big fan. Do you mind if I take a picture?"

I shoot April a worried look. She'd been concerned about being photographed and I'd assured her that I was rarely approached in the airport. In such a crowded space with people constantly on the move, everyone tends to mind their own business.

I take a step back. "I'd love to, but my girlfriend and I just got off a flight…"

A soft touch on my hand stops me. April juts her chin subtly forward, giving her consent.

We take the picture and I reach for April's hand again when another group comes up to me. What was a two-minute request from one fan, turns into a two-hour stream of photo-taking for me.

By the time the crowd dissipates and I come up for air, I've lost track of April.

I swivel around frantically until I locate her a few feet away.

She's sitting in one of the waiting chairs. The giant, floor-to-ceiling windows pour buckets of sunshine over her, giving her hair a golden halo. She purses her lips in concentration while reading. Slender fingers slide between the pages of the book I'd purchased for her at the bookstore.

I lift my phone and snap a picture. As if she heard the silent click, April's head whips up and she takes me in. Her green eyes soften.

"You coming or going?" I ask.

"Huh?"

I take the seat beside her, wedging my large arms against hers. "If we're heading in the same direction, I'd love to take you to dinner."

Clarity flashes through her emerald-green gaze and she prissily turns her nose up. "I have a boyfriend."

"Man." I sigh in defeat. "Lucky guy."

April laughs and it's so pretty that I snap another photo.

She tugs the sleeve of my T-shirt in an effort to claim my phone. "Delete that. I look awful."

"You look like sunshine." I turn and show her the photo of her laughing face. "No matter how harsh winter gets, I can look at this picture and it'll take me to a warm summer day."

She ducks her head into my shirt and groans. "Don't tell me you write poetry too."

"I don't, but I might start now." I rub a hand down her hair. "I've found my muse."

April looks up, but her pale fingers are still entwined in the collar of my outer shirt. "You're such a flirt."

"Only with you, Tink."

Her eyes scan beyond me. "Is anyone looking at us like they want to secretly come over and ask for a picture?"

"No." I check the airport waiting area. "I don't know what happened today. People usually don't recognize me at—"

April leans into me, covers my mouth with hers and gives me the longest, sweetest kiss she can manage. It comes to an end only when she runs out of breath and I'm seeing black spots in front of my eyes.

"Sorry." Her face a fire-red, April hides against my chest again.

I sigh happily and nuzzle my cheek against her hair. "Don't apologize. I'd be happy to pass out like this any day."

"Pass out?" April groans. "It was pretty long, wasn't it?"

"You can kiss me as long as you like, Tink. I'll go around with smelling salts in my pocket the way my old aunt Edna used to."

She bursts out laughing and shakes her head, raining cute punches at my chest. "I just can't with you, Chance McLanely."

I capture her hand and kiss the back of it.

Just then, my phone rings.

"It's my dad," I announce.

Immediately, April turns as white as a sheet and leans away from me.

I allow her to have her space and answer, "Hey, dad."

"Traffic was absolutely brutal, but we've arrived." Dad's cultured voice rings with anticipation. "Which gate was it again, son?"

"He's here," I whisper to April.

She stands and shuts her book, worrying her bottom lip.

I stand too. "Dad, I told you that you didn't have to drive. You could have sent the chauffeur."

Beside me, I sense April stiffen.

"Your mother had need of the driver today," dad explains. "And I wanted to be there." The sound of a horn honking rings behind him. "You still haven't told me a gate number."

I look for signs, trying not to run anyone over with my suitcase while moving forward. After giving dad the information, I escort April through the exits just as a shiny car glides to a stop in front of us.

April gasps loudly. "Is that a vintage Impala with a 283 Tri-Power V8 engine?"

"A 230… what?" I mutter, stumbling behind her.

"A lady who knows her stuff." Dad smiles. "You must be April. Nice to meet you. I'm Randal."

"Hi." April shakes his hand, eyes glued to the car.

"Have you worked on a tri-power engine?"

"Worked on? Yeah, but not in a beauty like this. I've only seen vintage Impalas in public auction videos. I never thought I'd be able to ride one in real life."

Dad preens so hard, if he were a peacock, all his feathers would be ruffling.

April walks around the car, her hand hovering over the paint but not actually touching it. "What a dream. Look at the grill and the tail fins are more subtle than the later 80's models. It's got to be a what? '60?"

"It's a '65. Most people don't recognize it right away because the design is so understated, but that's exactly why I like it. Now, if you pop the hood, you'll see the original husk, painstakingly remodeled by the best customization garage in the US. And if you walk this way…"

I clear my throat. "Hello? Dad? It's me. Your *son*."

Dad whirls around in shock. "Oh yes. Chance, welcome back!" He hurries back to the sidewalk and gives me a hug.

I peer down at dad's salt-and-pepper hair, smelling a rat. "You offered to pick me up so you could show up in the Impala, didn't you?"

"It's rare to meet a like-minded individual with good taste in automobiles. Leave me alone," he whispers.

I shake my head and lug the suitcases into the trunk myself.

Dad and April spend so long admiring and discussing the car

that an airport traffic officer threatens dad with a ticket if he doesn't get moving.

On the freeway, the two continue chatting excitedly. I can't even get a word in. It continues all the way through lunch on the rooftop of a five-star hotel *and* when dad invites April over to view the rest of his fleet.

My sister is at the house when we arrive, and I'm relieved to see her—if only to remind myself that not everyone in the world speaks in horsepower and car lingo.

Dad quickly makes the introductions but leaves no time for my sister to edge in and take April from him.

"This way, April," dad urges, leading her down to our third garage where we keep the 'just for Sunday drives' vehicles. The two soon disappear, their conversation overlapping in a noisy clamor.

I patter to the kitchen, smiling.

My sister is there, wearing a fancy red dress.

"Your girlfriend's been kidnaped," she says dryly, pouring herself a glass of wine.

I shake my head when she offers to pour one for me. "Did you see how April skipped behind him? She's a willing participant."

My sister sips and then looks at me thoughtfully. "She's cute. A little rough around the edges but more sincere than any girl you've been photographed with."

"What do you mean by rough around the edges?"

"You know…" she lifts her fingers.

"I really don't."

"It doesn't matter what I think about her. What do *you* think about her?"

I don't hesitate to share because talking about April is my second favorite thing. Talking to and holding April is my number one—of course. "She's amazing. She's everything I've ever wanted. Sometimes, I look at her and she's looking back at me with those eyes, and I have to pinch myself to make sure I'm not dreaming."

"Ew. Gross. I've never seen you so in love."

"Get used to it, sissy. April's not going anywhere."

She peers at me over the rim of her glass. "Did you really mean all those things you said in the press conference?"

"I did."

"Does she feel the same?"

I pause. "April's not someone who makes hasty decisions. We're both taking this seriously."

My sister snorts. "So she's not as crazy about you as you are about her."

"I'm working on getting her there."

"Mom won't help your cause. She doesn't like any of this."

"I know."

"She's decided to pretend that you didn't say what you said. That's why she's not here right now."

"I know that too."

My sister stares at me. "What else do you know?"

"I know she'll have her claws out at the gala tonight."

"And did you prepare April for that?"

I wish I could, but I have no clue how. "You know… I think I *will* have a glass," I say instead.

My sister pours one out for me and lifts her cup. "I wish you luck, brother."

I clink our glasses together, knowing I'll need much more than luck when facing my mother tonight.

CHAPTER
FORTY-TWO

APRIL

CHANCE'S HAND ON MY BACK IS A STEADY, COMFORTING PRESENCE as we step into the gala.

My eyes bounce back and forth, dancing from the well-dressed guests to the lavish decor. Every fresh sweep brings something new and breathtaking to my attention.

As a mechanic, I've grown used to the strong smell of engine fluid, the inevitable dirt that stains every outfit, and the aversion to light colors like peach, cream and white.

But tonight, my humble existence has been blown open. I enter a lavish universe I've never known.

Soft lights expand from low-hanging chandeliers suspended by delicate beaded chains. Tall, white-dressed tables are laden with skinny champagne flutes and expensive branded gift bags. To the right, a fully functioning buffet with heated pans and a feast of desserts tempts my eyes.

Chance presses a kiss to my temple. His swirling cologne is as intoxicating as his voice when he asks, "You okay, Tink?"

"Yup, I'm fine," I say as calmly as I can.

"You look amazing tonight. Have I told you that?"

"About five hundred times," I say, relaxing a bit. Chance is trying to make up for every bad word that's been said about me on the internet. Not even my dad was this adamant about complimenting me growing up.

"You look like a dream," Chance whispers in my ear. "There. Now it's five hundred and one."

I laugh.

That dazed look enters Chance's eyes again and he sighs happily. "There's the smile I've been waiting for."

I push at him, trying to hide my blush. "You're hovering."

"You're glowing," he counters.

"I don't need to be rescued or overseen tonight. I'm an adult. I know how to conduct myself in public."

"At least one of us does. I find these things awfully boring," he admits. Stopping, Chance looks down at me, his blue eyes alight with mischief. "Should we just skip out now?"

"Do you really want to leave? Didn't you give your mother your word that you'd attend?"

He glances to the side, guilty.

"You don't have to be so worried about me," I add.

"I'm not worried about you. I'm worried about *them*." Chance flashes the room of wealthy donors, celebrities, and powerful influencers a suspicious look.

"Chance!" A group of aged businessmen gesture for him.

"And so it begins," Chance mumbles. "Last chance to run now."

I smile and nudge him forward. "Go."

To my surprise, Chance slides his hand down my arm and links our fingers together instead. He pulls me to the group.

"Gentlemen." He nods.

"So the prodigal son returns!" A man with thinning hair and a beer belly grins. "Are you finally ready to put that business degree to good use and join your father?"

"Dad is far from ready to retire and I'm all-in on hockey at the moment, but we'll see what the future holds," Chance says tactfully. "Have I introduced you to my girlfriend April? She's a brilliant mechanic and entrepreneur. Her garage in Lucky Falls is flourishing."

"How nice," the men say, sipping their champagne and looking away.

"Lucky Falls? Where is that?" another asks with mocking laughter in his tone.

"It's a beautiful place full of small-town charm. When you're ready for a change of pace, I invite you to visit," I say sweetly.

Chance looks down with a surprised look.

I blink up at him, proud as a peach.

"Excuse us. We have a few more guests to greet," Chance says. He sweeps me away from the group of country club curmudgeons, his hand dangerously low on my back and his grip tight on my hip.

Heat slides through my stomach when he growls in my ear, "Who was *that* April?"

"*That* was the April who spent most of her life being the only female in the room." I tilt my chin up boldly.

Just because I'm not used to being fancy doesn't mean I can't hold my own in a strange environment. I'll admit, Chance met me at a time when I'd forgotten who I was. After Evan, I was floundering to find my way again. But I have *always* been brave. If I was the type of woman who backed away from spaces she didn't 'fit in', I never would have become a mechanic.

"*That* April is sexy and I *really* want to kiss her." Chance pulls me closer to his side, looking greedily at my lips.

My breath catches in my throat. The tension between us is taut enough to drop a V12 engine from a suspended truck.

"April!" A familiar, joyful voice interrupts us.

Chance and I ease apart. At first, I'm annoyed that my kiss was postponed, but the moment I see Randal, my face lights up like a Christmas tree.

Mr. McLanely and I spent hours discussing vintage vehicles,

automobile history, and debating the latest innovations in the auto space. Though he's much older and richer than me, it feels like I've known him for years.

Chance definitely gets his charm and friendliness from his dad.

I start to greet Randal when a slender hand carrying a rock the size of a small planet suddenly appears around his elbow.

"Randal, there you are. And Chance, wonderful, you made it." The newcomer gives Chance vapid air kisses. To her husband, she says, "You disappeared in the middle of Croxby's egregious investment pitch. How could you leave me with that infuriating man alone?"

"Sorry, dear."

"Come. The president of Continuum is looking for you."

"Wait, Corinth," Randal remains in place, "you haven't met Chance's girlfriend yet, have you? This is April."

"Hi," I say, staring at Chance's mom.

I'd imagined a woman with angry eyes, deeply red lips, and deep wrinkles hewn from years of scowling at children. But the regal silver foxette in front of me is… not that.

Corinth's face is smooth as a baby's bottom. Except for the faint lines around her pretty blue eyes, her peaches-and-cream complexion would make it nearly impossible to tell her true age. While her long, black dress is quiet and simple, the thick material paired with a tweed jacket and white pearls screams 'expensive'.

This woman does *not* have to open her mouth or wave around gold bars to prove she's wealthy.

"Hello, please do enjoy yourself," she says with a smile faker than the five dollar 'pure silver' earrings dangling from my ears. Turning abruptly, she motions to her husband. "Dear, this way."

Chance steps forward. "Mom, I know you're busy tonight, so I'd like to take you, dad and April out to lunch tomorrow before we fly back."

"I'll have to check my schedule, Chance. You know this is an awfully busy season for me. You understand, don't you?" Her cooing tone has a steel band beneath the surface.

"Your mother can't sit still for a minute." Randal pats her hand affectionately. "April, Chance, why don't you stay with us tonight?"

My jaw drops.

Chance lifts both eyebrows.

"In separate rooms, of course." Randal grins. "If you're at home, we'll be sure to spend some quality time together in between your mother's appointments."

"Er, I don't know about that," Corinth hedges.

"I don't mind." Chance looks down at me. "Tink?"

The thought of sleeping under the same roof as Chance makes me nervous, but I figure it's not so different from sleeping under the same roof in a hotel. Plus, a hotel doesn't have Randal's fleet of impressive vintage cars.

"Okay." I agree.

Annoyance flashes over Corinth's face before she tucks it away like a seasoned pro and nods along. "Lovely. I'll see you at home then, son. April. Randal, this way."

"That's my cue." Randal laughs good-naturedly and follows his wife.

Chance blows out a breath.

"Were you that nervous?" I tease, although to be fair, I'd been on pins and needles the entire time too.

"That went better than I expected."

"What did you expect? A mud fight?"

A faint, half-grin tugs at his lips. He runs a thumb down my cheek. "You're staying over tonight, huh?"

"I am taking the guestroom at your *parents'* house," I correct him as my insides quake at his touch.

"It's also *my* house. Since I grew up there. And my bedroom is…" he presses his cheek to mine, "right upstairs."

My heart thuds so loudly, I'm sure it can be heard above the live jazz music. The word 'bed' and 'room' should never leave Chance's mouth while he's looking at me like that.

"Why is it so hot in here?" I fan my face, stepping away.

Chance laughs, eyes sparkling harder than the chandeliers. "I'll get you something to drink. I'm guessing you're okay with sparkling cider?"

I nod.

He struts away and I can't help watching him.

Half the room can't help watching him.

He's a magnificent human being, inside and out.

But especially out.

Rather than brush his hair back like many of the guys did tonight, Chance's hair is effortlessly wind-swept with just a few pieces hanging strategically over his strong forehead to hint at an intentional style.

The haircut highlights his square jaw and side profile that has been the inspiration of many an online fangirl.

Not to mention, Chance McLanely's broad shoulders were made for hockey uniforms and tuxes.

As I'm drooling over him, Chance turns back to look at me. It's too late to pretend I wasn't staring and I note the quick concern that flickers over his face before he realizes that I'm just ogling him because he's unfairly beautiful.

Internally, I groan. He's going to tease me about being unable to keep my eyes off him when he returns with the drinks. I just know it.

Chance finally breaks eye contact but, just as he takes a step, he collides into someone holding a champagne flute. Instinctually, his hand reaches out to grip the woman's arm and steady her.

"I'm so sorry," the woman says, brushing him down. Wine is seeping into the white fabric and exposing his chiseled abs.

"It's okay," Chance says, gripping her hands to stop her. "It's my fault. I was… distracted."

The woman looks up.

Chance freezes.

My shoulders go tense at his reaction and I tilt my head to get a good look at the woman. The moment I see her, my heart drops straight to my toes.

Those impossibly high cheekbones, puffy lips, and Victoria Secret body are unmistakable.

It's Fina, Chance's ex-girlfriend.

CHAPTER
FORTY-THREE

CHANCE

I'M QUICK ON MY FEET, SO WHEN I SPIN AROUND AND SEE SOMEONE barreling toward me, I try to dodge them. Strangely, sidestepping doesn't help and we still ended up colliding.

"I'm so sorry," a feminine voice says.

I remove my hand from the elbow where I'd been offering support.

The stranger looks up at me and I reel back. "Fina?"

"Hi, Chance." Red lips stretch wide in a sultry smile.

Looking down, I realize she's still rubbing my chest. I remove her hands immediately. "What are you doing here?"

"What do you mean?" She raises thin eyebrows and speaks in a thick accent. "I receive invitation. Same as you."

I jerk my head around to April. She's staring at me in concern, but that look turns to horrified shock when Fina glances over my shoulder to see where my gaze has gone.

"Your girlfriend?" Fina says, a question in her tone.

Without a word, I offer her my pocket square to clean up and promptly move past her.

A trio of waiters descend on the mess of broken shards and spilled champagne. One holds a mop and the other steps in my path to offer me a dry towel. Stalking ahead, I let the towel hang limp from my hands.

People move out of my way.

The jazz band stops playing.

The entire room watches my every move, but I barely register any of them. My attention is on one person and one person only.

"Chance." April gapes at me, tilting her head back. Her hands flutter to her throat. "What...?"

Gruffly, I grab her hand and lead her out of the ballroom. She stumbles behind me, hurrying to keep up in her heels.

When I realize she's struggling, I slow my pace but only by a bit.

"Chance, are you okay?" My mother blocks my path, her eyes wide. "I have a set of extra clothes in our room upstairs. Your father couldn't decide between his two tuxes until the last minute. Take this and dry off before you catch a cold." Mom offers me a room card.

Angry words froth at the tip of my tongue, but I don't release them. I wasn't raised to disrespect my mother, and I refuse to lift my voice at a woman no matter the reason. Also, the conversation we need to have about her inviting Fina can wait. This is neither the time nor place for it.

"I'm okay," I tell her flatly.

Her eyebrows hike and she looks dumbfounded.

I pull April along, throwing the doors of the ballroom open and heading down the hallway. Soon, I feel a little tug. April is trying to free herself from my grip.

"Chance, slow down. Where are you going?"

Forcing myself to ease the pace, I tell her, "I didn't know Fina was going to be here."

April's thick eyelashes bounce up and down. She shakes her head as if I'm not making sense. "Chance, your shirt is soaking wet. At least take your mom's advice and change into something dry."

"It's fine." I've endured worse than this. Sweating profusely on an ice-cold rink is a hazard of the trade. I can survive a little champagne on my shirt.

"You're so stubborn," April mumbles. Her energy shifts from befuddled to emboldened. She quickens her pace and leads me to the elevators. When the doors open, she taps the button for the upper floor.

The doors remain open.

April taps again. "Why isn't it closing?"

"You can't go to the hotel suites without a room card." And since I didn't take the card from mom, the only place we can go is down to the basement parking lot or lobby.

"Oh." April makes an embarrassed little sound and flicks mom's keycard against the slot.

Immediately, the doors beep and slide closed.

I frown at her. "When did you get that?"

"While you were dragging me away like a caveman. I accepted it on your behalf."

I sigh heavily. "April—"

"Chance, I'm not going to repeat myself. You're changing into dry clothes. Whether or not we return to the party is up to you, but that part is non-negotiable."

I study her as the numbers on the elevator panel get higher and higher.

"What?" April asks, brushing her hair back.

"Aren't you angry?"

Her eyes flick to me. "Angry?"

"Yeah. About Fina."

She scrunches her nose as if the thought had never occurred to her and my heart releases a breath so heavy it rattles my ribs and lungs.

"Why would I be angry about Fina?" Understanding dawns and she pokes her finger in my chest. "Is that why you were so weird with your mom? You think I'm upset that Fina is here?"

I wrap my hand around the finger poking my tux. "Trust is hard to earn but easy to lose. My dad taught me that." I shrug. "Well, it was his advice for networking in business, but it applies to relationships too." Dropping my tone to an earnest husk, I explain, "Earning your trust was so difficult, April. I won't do anything to make you doubt me. And I won't tolerate anyone who tries to attack the trust I earned."

April tosses my hand off and folds her arms over her chest, but her stern frown thaws a little.

The doors open and she stalks out first.

I follow her, trying to figure out how to get out of the doghouse. On the one hand, I'm thrilled that April seems unaffected by Fina's appearance tonight. On the other hand, it seems like I might have overreacted, thereby extinguishing the very flame I was trying to protect.

April presses the room key to the door and it opens with a beep. Once inside, she slides the plastic in the cradle behind the door and the lights click on, brightening the dark room.

Her eyes sweep over the suite, eyebrows climbing. I've been in a million suites like this while traveling, not only for hockey but also with my parents growing up.

However, I try to see the suite from her eyes.

The penthouse overlooks the frantic city center. Many stories below, cars wind through the streets and pedestrians rush out to meet friends or go on dates after work. From this height, the activity below is hard to pinpoint. Everyone outside of this room looks like a tiny, moving dot.

Skyscrapers beam hues of red and yellow, creating a canvas of manmade stars that stretch as far as the eyes can see.

The room itself is huge with a salon boasting overstuffed leather chairs, a thick rug, and a mini-bar for entertaining guests.

"Go find your dad's shirt. When you take off this one, give it to me. I'll wash it."

"You don't have to do that," I tell her.

April narrows her eyes in warning.

I obediently step into the next room and locate dad's shirt. It looks a lot smaller than my current one. Setting it on the bed, I unbutton and shrug off my clothes. Checking the tag on dad's shirt proves my hunch correct.

"Hey, April," I step out with both dad's shirt and my ruined one in each fist, "I don't think this will fit."

Utter silence is all that greets me.

I glance up. April is sitting on the edge of the couch, her eyes glued to my chest. I warm beneath her innocent and unrestrained observation.

I've done a few shirtless photoshoots for magazines—and there was also the recent debacle that landed me my *FreshButtFit* deal—so I'm used to being stared at while half dressed. But I've never been this happy showing off my physique.

"I think I'll have to dry this one." I dangle my ruined shirt from the edge of my fingers, intentionally flexing my bicep in the process.

April shoots her gaze to the ceiling, her cheeks flushed. "Hand it over. I'll wash it in the bathroom sink."

"Do you want me to check the mini-fridge for a water bottle?" I ask.

"What?"

"To put on your cheeks?" I tease. "Blushing that hard seems like it hurts."

"I'm not blushing." April shoots to her feet and snatches the shirt from me, running off.

I chuckle and follow at a safe distance.

April steps into the bathroom and I'm thankful that the toilet and sink are separate. There's no door for her to lock me out or I'm sure she would have.

"It's not even your first time seeing me shirtless," I point out.

April ducks her head toward the sink and studiously ignores me as she places the shirt under running water.

I smile and lean against the wall, just watching her. She curled the ends of her hair and the thick, brown locks dance against her back with every scrubbing motion. The navy dress fits her like a glove, hinting tastefully at the curves hidden beneath the fabric.

She's exquisite and so beautiful that I wish I could keep her to myself and not share her with the party downstairs.

"April."

"What?" she sputters, refusing to look at me.

"April."

This time, she spins around. "*What?*"

"Nothing." I fold my arms over my chest and don't miss the way her eyes dip down before they sail back to my face. "I just like saying your name."

She quickly turns away, but I can see her blushing prettily in the mirror. Her hands work, scrubbing my shirt together. "It's not that fancy of a name. In fact, it's barely a name. It's literally the fourth month of the year."

I purse my lips. "It's a beautiful name because it's *your* name. There doesn't need to be another reason for it to be special."

April stops scrubbing. My shirt floats in the sink, surrounded by suds before it drifts down to the bottom of the water.

I shuffle closer to her. "April?"

Her fingers dig into the sink and her head hangs low.

Panicked, I grip her shoulders and turn her around.

There are tears in her eyes.

April… is crying.

CHAPTER
FORTY-FOUR

APRIL

THIS IS BEYOND EMBARRASSING. LIGHTYEARS, EONS BEYOND horrifying.

I do not cry.

I didn't when June took off.

Didn't when dad was diagnosed.

And I didn't when I found out Evan was cheating—though, technically, I did cry in the days following that.

But at least then, my heart was broken, I was unemployed, and a good cry session was long over-due.

Tonight, none of those circumstances apply, so I have no idea why I'm leaking tears now.

"Oh, sweetheart." Chance pulls me into his chest and gives me a hug.

I inhale his intoxicating, spicy cologne and the tears, despite my best attempts, fall faster.

Get yourself together, April!

Not only am I having the most horrifying cry fest of my life, but I'm doing it against a 6'4" hockey player's six pack abs.

What even is this madness?

I sniffle and pull a little away from Chance. He refuses to let me go so, while still in the circle of his embrace, I tilt my head up and use the power of gravity to keep the tears in.

"Let me get you a tissue," Chance says. Rather than release me, he walks me backward toward the sink, plucks a tissue while keeping one hand secure around my hip, and dabs under my eyes.

Next, he grabs another tissue and moves to press it around my nose so I can blow. Embarrassed, I take the tissue from him, turn my face to the side and make an elephant-like noise that threatens to blow the roof off the suite.

When I'm done, Chance holds his hand out, palm up.

"Er, I'll throw it away," I mumble.

He allows me to step across the bathroom to the trash and doesn't touch me again when I return. I'm grateful for his thoughtfulness. Right now, I can use the space. My head is spinning and I kind of wish I could hide under the bed until the horror fades.

"You want some time alone? I can go downstairs," he offers.

"Dressed like that?" I sniff.

Chance spreads his bare arms wide, looking down at his body. "It would spice things up, don't you think?"

I laugh through the tears.

He smiles and studies me with a soft, warm look. "I don't ever think I've made a girl cry by calling her special before."

"Yeah, well, there's a first time for everything." I reach for another tissue. "I don't know what came over me, I just…" My words falter and, sensing I need encouragement, Chance comes over and squeezes my hand.

"I think… for a long time, I haven't felt very special at all." Emotions well in my chest again. "I was the invisible presence in people's lives. No one really saw me."

Chance remains silent, taking in everything I say.

"Like June… she just up and left without even telling me.

And then dad got sick and he couldn't even remember my name…" I sob and the hand squeeze turns into a back rub of encouragement. "Wow, this is a trauma dump. I'm sorry."

"No, I want to hear it. I want to know what hurts so I can make it better. And if I can't, I want to make it feel lighter." Chance swipes his thumb over my cheek, chasing away a tear. "Don't cry, baby. It breaks my heart."

My lashes quake, burdened by the tears. The tip of my nose burns.

I can't describe what I'm feeling, but there's a tide in my chest. A wave crashing into me. It feels… monumental.

"Are you real?" I look up at Chance in hushed wonder. "Are you really real?"

"If I'm a figment of your imagination, then you need a psychiatrist. And an exorcist."

I chuckle, glad that he's joking around. I'm so off-kilter that nervous laughter is the best I can do right now.

Chance presses a kiss to my forehead and then cages me against the bathroom sink, setting both hands on either side of me. "I'm not perfect, if that's what you're asking, but I also," he brushes a lock of my hair aside, "have never been more ready to choose a woman the way I want to choose you."

His sweet words are a balm and the tears stop flowing at last.

"You're mine, April Brooks. I'm not saying that to be possessive. You're my responsibility, you're my partner. You're my 'I'll get up in the middle of the night and come right over if you call'. You're my 'I'll hand over wrenches and spanners and whatever tool you ask for even though I don't know anything about cars'. You're it for me."

I wrap my arms around his neck. "You know… a spanner is just another name for a wrench."

"Really? Wow."

I laugh again, louder than I have all night. "I can't believe you didn't know that."

"That's why *you're* the mechanic, and I'll just hand you the tools," he responds. "Once I figure out what the tools actually are, of course."

My laughter fades as I stare into Chance's eyes. The heat of his bare arms on either side of me chases away the cold. His face is so close that I can see the outline of each of his impossibly thick eyelashes.

Heart laid bare and my emotions at an all-time high, I step into him. Chance McLanely might not be a figment of my imagination, but his chiseled features are a work of art so captivating, it's almost fantasy.

Fingers trembling, I trail a line over his forehead.

Chance sucks in a sharp breath.

I move down the slope of his nose.

His eyes flutter closed and he sighs happily.

I brush across one cheek and then the other.

Trace the angles of his sharp, defined jaw.

Finally, my exploration arrives at his mouth. Soft. Firm.

My own mouth parts on a sigh as I let my touch linger there.

Chance's eyes flash open. They're stormy, pupils dilated until the blue bleeds into black. He stares me down ferociously with equal parts craving and hunger.

My heart thumps in my chest.

Heat zings down my spine.

That heat roars to inferno levels when he lifts a hand and grips my chin between his calloused thumb and forefinger. I expect him to drag me closer and ground his lips against mine, but instead, Chance turns my face away with a deep, reluctant groan.

"I'm not going to kiss you, April. Not like this."

"Why not?" I ask, surprised by the disappointment spinning through me.

His voice escapes on a tortured moan. "Because… I don't think I can stop at a kiss right now."

I can't breathe.

I also can't see him because he's turned my face aside. My

only view is of the lamp sconce on the bathroom wall. Fighting to turn my head back toward him results in Chance stepping fully away.

"Chance…"

"You keep giving me those eyes and I won't be able to control myself." He shakes his head and takes another giant step back. "I'll call the concierge desk and ask someone to send up a T-shirt."

Just then, there's a knock at the door.

"I'll get it," Chance says, hurrying into the other room.

I follow, unwilling to let him out of my sight. The view of Chance from behind is just as appealing as the view of him from the front. Ropes of muscle and sinew contract and release as he reaches to open the door.

"Mom?" His voice rings in surprise.

Corinth steps into the room, immediately shifting the energy with her poised stature and sharp eyes. She stares pointedly at Chance's undressed state before her gaze swings to me in clear accusation.

I blush, despite the fact that Chance didn't even kiss me. We were both thinking about it though and it seems that Corinth can sense that.

"While you two were *entertaining* yourselves, several people have been asking about you downstairs." The word drips with torrid meaning.

Chance doesn't correct her and I'm not sure she'd listen even if I defended myself.

She hands over a pressed white shirt on a hanger. "I asked my assistant to bring you a shirt. It occurred to me that your father's may not fit."

"Thanks." Chance accepts the shirt and looks back at me. "I'll change into this quickly. It won't take me long."

I nod at him.

"I'll head back down," Corinth announces, turning away as if she can't stand the sight of me.

"Wait." I stop her when she steps through the door.

Corinth swings her head around, her shrewd gaze making me want to put myself in time-out. I square my shoulders instead and dig deep for courage.

I may not have her money, power, and connections, but I am not inferior to her… even if it feels like it.

"Corinth, I'm not sure what I did to offend you, but I'd like to clear something up. I lo—" My eyelashes flutter as I realize what I was about to say. I amend, "I care deeply about your son. If I didn't, I wouldn't be with him. After everything we've been through, Chance has proven himself to be trustworthy, dependable, and disciplined. I don't know what your intention was inviting Fina but—"

"Darling, do you think I have so much time to waste as to sabotage my son's relationship with you?"

She cackles and I start to feel very, very foolish for thinking I could confront her and win.

"I am not interested in getting to know you, not because of your occupation or your lackluster background. It's because you won't be around next year." She wags a manicured finger. "See, I know how this will end. Your relationship will implode on its own, without any effort from me."

Her words are sharp enough to cut. Outside, I keep my expression steady but, on the inside, my confidence shakes.

"You see, Miss Brooks," Corinth's heels click on the floor as she looms over me, "the mistress you should fear is not another woman." Her eyes flash knowingly and she offers a prim smile. "It's hockey."

CHAPTER
FORTY-FIVE

CHANCE

AFTER THE GALA, I TAKE APRIL HOME. SHE CLAIMS TO BE TIRED SO I drop her off at the guest room, press a kiss to her forehead and force myself to walk away.

Mom barely shows her face the next morning and skips out on lunch due to a mysterious 'prior arrangement', but at least dad and my sister make up for mom's coldness. They're both warm and accommodating to April.

Dad drives us back to the airport and hugs April so fiercely, it's like he's sending his daughter off to war.

On the flight, April is quiet and contemplative. While I want to press, I leave her to her thoughts and sort through my emails.

Derek sent a barrage of potential brand deals. How does he expect me to play hockey and keep such a full schedule? I won't have any time to train, to date April or even to sleep if I do them all.

On the bright side, the cloud of bad press from my suspension is fading away like sunshine after a heavy rain. If these deals are any indication of public sentiment, I may be getting good news soon.

After dropping April off at home, I head back to the hotel. It feels ridiculous to still be paying for a room here and I make a mental note to look for houses ASAP. The closer to April's, the better.

I crash into bed and I don't rise until the next morning for early practice.

"Good to have you back, Chance," Max says, his bear-like hand swinging into my back in a friendly pat.

"Saw your pictures online, McLanely. You look good in a monkey suit!" Theilan calls in-between drills on the ice.

I laugh and shake my head.

When I sit down to put my skates on, Max is beside me. "How did your mom react to April?" He asks in a low voice.

Max is well aware of my mother's... temperament. His family situation is similarly complicated, except it's his dad that has the high expectations, while his mom is always smoothing things over between them.

"As well as can be expected," I admit, tying up my laces.

"That bad, huh?"

"Mom just needs time. In a couple years when April and I are married with kids—"

"Kids? Who *are* you, McLanely?"

A silly grin crosses my face. "You'll get it when you fall in love too."

"Love? No thank you." Max shudders. "I have my hands full." He gestures to the hockey team on the ice. "I can't afford to be distracted with all this chaos."

I push to my feet, balancing expertly on my skates. "I wasn't looking for April either, but once I found her, there was no going back. It might be like that for you too."

"Maybe, maybe not. Either way, I'm happy for you, Chance. If anyone can make the long distance thing work, it's you and April."

"Long distance?" I arch a brow.

Max freezes and I watch as his soul flees his body for a second. "Uh, I mean… the long away games."

"No, that's not what you meant." I narrow my eyes. "You know something."

"I need to make a call." He fumbles for his cell phone.

I block Max's way. After a few seconds of my intense staring and Max's squirming, he finally breaks.

"Your agent called. He wanted me to send over the contract you'd signed with the Lucky Strikers."

Shock rushes through my system. "What?"

"He told me not to tell you. Said nothing's set in stone yet but…"

I break into a wide grin. "Are you serious?"

"Yeah, man." Max leaks a smile.

My mind runs at a million miles a minute. Derek isn't the type who'll miss an opportunity to make money. And he definitely isn't the type to make a move that will *lose* money.

If he's already reaching out to Max for negotiations about my contract, he's got something solid in the works.

I'm still thinking about Max's words when I get on the ice.

"Heads-up, MC." Renthrow shoots a puck, his skates making a *skkkt* sound as he stops abruptly.

Instinct kicks in. I instantly get in position for a wrist shot, sending the disc straight into the net.

"Hey-yo!" Theilan lifts his hockey stick, skating past in celebration.

Gunner smirks. "Show off."

I laugh and shake my head.

Renthrow partners up with me for the next set of drills.

"Did you miss me, Renthrow?" I tease.

"Not as much as the others. They were grumbling about not being invited to your party."

"Wasn't *my* party," I answer, already starting to breathe hard from the drills, "but yeah. I'll invite everyone next time."

"Heard that!" Theilan says, skating past.

"You better not play with me, McLanely. I'll be waiting for that invitation," Watson adds, following right behind Theilan.

I grin wide as Renthrow and I complete another set. Strangely, I wouldn't mind having the guys at one of mom's boring parties, especially if April chose not to go and I was attending solo. It would liven up the night and I might actually enjoy myself.

The coach—who still seems to dislike me but has learned to tolerate me because of my skills on the ice—blows his whistle.

Renthrow and I change directions and join the others to practice cycling the puck.

As we get into formation, I seamlessly rotate with Gunner over to the vacated defensive position. He catches my eyes and I understand him perfectly, moving ahead. Despite our rocky start, Gunner and I have developed the best rapport on the ice.

I have a fairly good relationship with all the skaters. The pressure to one-up one another isn't as harsh here as it is in the majors. Whether that's by design or a by-product of most of these guys growing up in Lucky Falls together, there's a layer of care beneath the competition.

Gunner rotates positions again and I know he's about to cycle the puck in the zone. In two moves, I skate ahead of him, accept the breakout pass and send it back. Gunner goes to the net and the satisfying *whiff* of the puck hitting the rope fills my ears.

"Nice!" Renthrow compliments us, moving back to the line.

I grin. Power plays like this one are strategic, but I've never remembered enjoying a free-form play with any other team.

After practice and a shower, I send April a text asking if she wants to meet up for a late lunch.

APRIL: I ate already. Maybe dinner instead?

I glance up.

Gunner catches my eye first and he jerks his chin at the door.

I text April back to tell her I'll have lunch with the team and that I'll swing by the garage at closing. After pressing 'send', I jog to catch up with the guys.

We take over the Tipsy Tuna the moment we arrive. Theilan, Watson and the rest are boisterous and cheerful. Renthrow drags two tables together without even asking. The rest of the team swagger into the restaurant and find their seats.

"Aren't you a sight for sore eyes," Bobby's wife says, smiling down at me as she takes our orders. "Welcome home, Chance."

Something rearranges in my chest. Warmth shines through her honest smile. I see a few grey and white heads bobbing around the other tables. All the old regulars seem to agree.

I'm used to getting recognition and special treatment when I go to shops and restaurants. But here in Lucky Falls, I feel my presence is more appreciated than my hockey stats.

"We missed him too. He's been too busy dating to hang with the likes of us," Theilan announces, grabbing both my shoulders and shaking.

I laughingly brush him off and give my order.

"So the usual?" She responds, scribbling furiously. "I'll be right back with those." She winks and darts off.

I gaze at her back in a daze.

Gunner, who's seated to my left, passes me a napkin. "What are you staring at?"

"I… have a 'usual'," I say. "I've never had a 'usual' before."

Gunner shakes his head as if he doesn't understand and doesn't want to either.

"By the way." I turn to him when our drinks are served. "There's something I wanted to ask you."

He gestures for me to go ahead.

"It's about your uncle," I say, watching him closely.

Gunner's bored expression shifts at the mention of his uncle.

His thick eyebrows hunker low.

"What about him?" he asks in a strained voice.

I pause and choose my words carefully. Although I haven't

mentioned it to April, everything she told me about her ex boss's sleazy 'advice' as well as the unfair firing lingered in my head.

I've been meaning to bring it up with Gunner. Pursuing a legal fight against his family is something that would divide the team and ruin our hard-earned truce, so I've been hesitant about making a decision.

"Some information came to light about him and his behavior with April when she worked there," I say vaguely.

Gunner's lips tighten until they almost disappear from his face. "What kind of information?"

"The kind that I could give to a legal team."

His jaw clenches. I can't tell if he's angry with me or with his uncle.

I wait for a response.

Gunner offers none.

I'm searching for another way to ask my question when the door opens. The bell above jangles and a blonde woman wearing pink mechanic over-alls saunters in. I recognize Rebel instantly and glance over her shoulder to see if April is with her too.

Unfortunately, she isn't.

When I turn my attention back to Gunner, I'm stunned to find him looking at Rebel, a rare ghost of a smile tugging at his lips. A moment later, his hand pulls into a fist and he forces his gaze away. Something dark seems to overshadow him and his smile putters into a taut frown.

"What were you saying about my uncle?" Gunner asks tightly.

"It's fine. We can discuss it another time." Curiosity tugs at me. "Do you know Rebel?"

"It's a small town. Everybody knows everybody."

Rebel laughs with Bobby's wife at the bar and reaches for a package of something. Probably drinks for her and April.

I raise my hand, intending to get Rebel's attention so I can pay for those drinks. If April is enjoying a refreshing lime soda in between fixing cars, I want her thinking of me.

As my hand starts to climb, Gunner clamps his fingers around my wrist and stops me. Rebel sails out the door, undisturbed.

I frown. "What's wrong? I thought you knew her."

"We're acquainted, but we're not… friendly."

"Why not?"

"Even in a small town," his eyes flash to mine, darkening by the second, "people have their secrets."

Before I can ask more, Gunner stands abruptly.

The others turn to look at him too.

"Where you going?" Theilan grins.

Renthrow points at the waitress approaching us with heaping platters of burgers and fries. "The food is here."

"I'll catch you later," Gunner grumbles, his eyes on the ground.

Shocked, I scoot my chair in so he can make his exit.

Gunner passes by but suddenly stops and lifts his gaze to mine. I stiffen. The guy's always been a closed book, but now I get the feeling something bad will happen if that book is ever opened.

"About my uncle," Gunner says in a low determined voice. "Do what you must."

With that, he stalks out of The Tipsy Tuna and lets the door bang shut behind him.

CHAPTER
FORTY-SIX

APRIL

'THE MISTRESS YOU MUST FEAR IS NOT A WOMAN, IT'S HOCKEY.'

Corinth's warning follows me like a dark cloud and puts me in a strange mood for a few days. However, on the third day, I find my equilibrium again.

After being cheated on by my ex—who was with an actual woman behind my back—I decide that hockey isn't that horrific of a mistress.

Sure, Chance will be away from me for weeks at a time during hockey season.

Sure, there will be plenty of women like Fina who want his attention when he's on the road.

Sure, lots of those women will be gorgeous and tempting.

But…

I trust him.

The gala last week proved that he can control himself and not jump on every woman he's attracted to, even if that woman is me.

Of course, I'm not delusional. I'm aware there will be *some* drawbacks to competing with hockey for Chance's attention, but I decide not to let Corinth's harsh prediction get in my head. I'll simply enjoy being with someone who cares about me and who I care equally for.

The weekend rolls around again and Chance asks if I can clear my schedule to help him look at properties.

May knocks on my room door while I'm getting ready. She pouts, "Are you sure you don't want me to film you today? This will make *such* great content for your channel."

"Chance and I are *really* together now," I say, tying the lacings on my fresh white sneakers. They're the only white items I own and are exclusively for special occasions, like on dates with Chance. "We don't need to film everything about us anymore. I don't like sharing too much either."

The town provides enough candid pictures of me going grocery shopping or working in the garage to satisfy the fans.

At first, the secret picture taking was mildly annoying, but now it's just plain scary the way our privacy is infringed upon.

Two days ago, someone took a picture of Chance, dad and I at the nursing home. They uploaded it and the picture immediately started trending.

Chance got the picture taken down quickly but, on the internet, nothing ever disappears.

"The poor ChApril fans are *starved*, April." My sister drapes across my bed in a dramatic fashion. Her long hair brushes the ground. "*Starved*."

"I'm a mechanic, not a social media influencer. I don't live my life for the ChApril fans." I walk over to the writing desk where I keep my beginner friendly makeup items. Since I don't have anywhere to store the makeup and brushes, I keep them in a little mug on my desk.

"The garage is doing better now, so we don't need everyone's attention. We just need the attention of those who want their cars fixed."

"You're no fun," May whines.

There's a knock on the front door.

"I'm not ready yet!" I panic, whirling back to the mirror with my eyeliner pencil in hand.

Despite my precision when working on cars, it freaks me out to have a pencil that close to my eye and I keep having to wipe away the scraggly lines and re-do them.

"I'll get it." May pulls herself up and sends me a cheeky grin. "The great thing about you dating Chance is that whenever he brings something for you, he always brings something for me too."

"That's because you harass him," I scold, giving up on the eyeliner. It's not like Chance likes me for my makeup skills anyway.

"It's not harassment. It's a mutual exchange. Chance understands the brother-in-law assignment."

I reach for something to throw at my sister, but she's already laughing and dancing out of the room.

Hurrying through the rest of my routine, I head to the living room.

Chance is sitting in our sofa, which is average-sized, but he's so big that he makes the couch look like a child's. I do a quick once-over. He looks scrumptious in a white button down and loose cream-colored trousers. I have a hate-hate relationship with colors that are easily soiled, but Chance seems to love them.

"Hey," he says, lighting up at the sight of me.

"Hey."

"I have something for you."

I squeal when Chance presents a book on the history of driver-less cars. "I love it! Thank you!"

"You should have brought her flowers too," May says, lifting a small bouquet of wildflowers. "If you keep bringing her books instead, you're going to run out of books eventually."

"I'll get creative when that time comes," Chance says, his eyes never leaving mine. "You look amazing, April."

"Thank you." I do a little spin. Today, I felt like wearing a dress. It was long, blue, pretty and it called to me from the back of my closet.

I've never been the type to wear dresses but, since dating Chance, I've found myself gravitating to this style more. I feel a lot more girly and soft when I'm with him and my clothes are a reflection of that.

Chance waves goodbye to May and sets his hand on the small of my back. I love the warmth of his touch and I can't help snuggling into his side as he walks me to his car.

"Are we meeting the realtor at the first house or at their office?" I ask.

"Ah-ah." Chance corrects me when I naturally open the door for myself.

I chuckle as he pops the door with a flourish and gestures for me to slide in. I sit first and, to my surprise, Chance scoops in and gives me a quick peck on the lips.

"I couldn't resist," he breathes, touching my nose.

I laugh and watch him jog around to the other side of the car. It takes me a moment to realize that I haven't wiped the smile off my face yet.

What has gotten into me?

I've only ever dated Evan, but if dating is like this, I can see why everyone is so obsessed with being in a relationship. I truly enjoy spending time with Chance. We text throughout the day. We date every night—either going out to eat or hanging out at the garage.

So far, I haven't tired of his company. In fact, I crave it.

Chance clicks his seatbelt into place and starts the car. "The realtor is meeting us at his office. It shouldn't take long to get there."

"What exactly are you looking for?" I ask him, observing the trees that thicken along the side of the road.

He reaches for my hand. "I originally wanted a property close to you."

I snort. "That was your main objective?"

"Yeah." His eyes crinkle from the force of his smile. "But then I started thinking that… this could potentially be *our* house. And I thought of what you needed."

My heart picks up speed like an over-spinning engine.

"You'd want to be closer to your dad. That's a priority. It couldn't be too far from the garage. May would need a room too, since she'll want to come over all the time and it'll be convenient if she can just sleep in her own room there. An attached garage is a must, of course. Somewhere we can store all the vintage cars I'll buy for you and another garage where you can work on cars just for fun on the weekend."

Shocked, I sputter, "I don't think that house has been built yet. At least not in this town."

"We'll see." He winks.

I reach for one of the fidget spinners he keeps in the center console. "Maybe… you should think about what *you* want in the house first. Before you think about what I need."

"What do you mean?"

"I mean… we just started dating. We shouldn't rush anything."

Immediately, the energy in the car shifts from playful to serious.

"I'm not asking you to move in tomorrow, April," he says in a cautious way, as if any sudden movements and I'll jump out of the car.

"I know. I wouldn't move in tomorrow if you asked either."

He winces and I wonder if that sounded meaner than it had in my head. Chance continues steadily, "I just want you to know that you're in my future."

"And I appreciate the thought. I really do, but—"

"But you still don't trust me," he says flatly.

"It's not that…"

"It's okay." He drums up a sad smile before focusing on the road. "I got ahead of myself. I'm sorry if you feel I pressured you."

"You didn't, Chance."

He doesn't look at me and the sad smile is starting to deepen into a sad expression.

I touch his shoulder. "Chance."

"Yeah?"

"Look at me."

"I'm driving."

I balance my elbows on the center console and rest my chin in my palm. "Just for a second."

He reluctantly allows his gaze to rest on me. It's only for a moment, but it's enough that a smile tugs on his lips.

"Don't be angry," I coax him.

"I'm not angry."

"You look angry."

"I'm not. I care about you so much, April. I can't imagine life without you." He taps a finger on the wheel. "I'm an athlete. I tend to see a goal and go after it, ignoring everything around me. But just because a life with you is my goal doesn't give me permission to ignore you and what you want too."

I smile.

Chance brings my hand to his lips and kisses it. "You're not angry with *me*, are you?"

"No. I feel… very safe."

He arches a brow.

"My trust was at a deficit after my previous relationship. But every time you do something for me or you restrain yourself for me or you show me who you are, trust coins fall into my trust piggy bank."

"Your trust piggy bank, huh?" Chance grins.

I rest my head back and admit, "If you keep going like this, soon that bank will overflow."

"And what happens when it does?"

I shrug. "Guess you'll just have to keep putting in the coins to find out."

He laughs. "I like that."

I nod, proud of myself for what feels like an awesome description of how I feel.

Chance flicks the indicator. "You'll need a bigger pig by the time I'm done."

I chuckle and keep holding his hand until we get to the realtor's office.

The moment we arrive, Chance opens my door for me and I start to climb out when my phone rings. It's an unknown number.

"It might be a client," I tell Chance.

"Go ahead and take it. I'll head in first."

I settle back in my seat. "This is April Brooks."

"April, this is Derek."

"Derek?" I swivel around as if the obnoxious agent is hiding in the backseat.

"Is Chance around?" Derek asks excitedly.

"He just left but I can call him back."

"No, no. I'm glad I got you alone."

"Why?" I ask, bracing myself.

"I've got great news."

"What is it?" I ask.

Derek pauses for dramatic effect. "Chance's suspension has been lifted! Even better, his team wants him back ASAP before the upcoming season."

"What? That's fantastic!" I squeal.

"Yes! And you know what's even better?"

"What?" I gasp.

"They want him *now*."

"Now?" I squeak, my celebration dying and my hand sinking to my lap.

"This is your win too, April. Thanks to you, Chance can finally leave Lucky Falls for good."

CHAPTER
FORTY-SEVEN

CHANCE

THE REALTOR LEADS THE WAY TO THE LISTINGS HE'D INITIALLY FOUND for me and promises to take me in a different direction if I don't fall in love with any of them.

By the third listing, I understand where his confidence comes from.

Every house offers a unique charm—whether it's the lakeside property with the priceless view or the sprawling acreage where I can, in the far off future, build April her own garage.

My eyes light up every time I step inside a foyer with an open floor concept, or picture making breakfast for April in the state-of-the-art kitchen or think of cuddling April in front of the fireplace.

But I'm alone in my exuberance. April is quiet and unengaged the entire way through.

'Not this one' is what her trembling lips seem to convey.

Not this one.

Not this one.

With a head shake of disinterest, we're off to the next until we're out of options.

The realtor promises to get back to me with new listings by the middle of the week and he drives off in a cloud of disappointment.

I take April to lunch where she seems to bounce back to her normal self and nothing appears out of the ordinary until our appointment with the realtor the next Wednesday.

"I'm not feeling well," April says groggily into the phone.

At those four words, my boyfriend powers activate. "What is it? Flu pain? Stomach pain? Headaches? Hold on, I'll clear out a pharmacy." I prepare to throw my hockey stick down in the middle of the hallway and run to her. "I'll be there in fifteen minutes."

"Chance, n-no. I'm just tired. I'll be fine."

"That's okay. I think the realtor's flexible. I can call him and reschedule for tomorrow."

"No, tomorrow isn't good for me."

"How about Friday?"

"That won't work either."

"Saturday?"

"Can't."

"Sunday?"

"I have a... thing."

I frown. "Is everything okay?"

"Of course."

"Did something happen with the garage that you didn't tell me?"

As far as I know, April's had to turn down jobs. As her stellar reputation spreads, more and more people want to work with her. At this point, she's booked until next year.

"No, it's not the garage."

"Your dad then?" I press.

Mr. Brooks looked fine when April and I visited last week.

His nurse assured us that his appetite's improved and he spent the entire visit talking to me heartily.

"Chance, I told you nothing is wrong."

April sounds… angry with me. But I can't remember doing anything wrong.

"April," I drop my voice so my teammates can't hear me, "ever since we saw those properties, something's been off with you."

"Off how?"

"I don't know. It just feels like there's something you're not telling me."

She remains silent.

"If you have concerns, let's discuss it. I'm on your team, Tink. No matter what. Nothing between us will change."

A little sigh flutters through the phone. "I'm busy, Chance. I'll talk to you later."

Then the dial tone rings coldly in my ears.

* * *

The metal weights clank loudly matching the sound of my loud grunts. Sweat stings my eyes, but my hands are wrapped around a steel rod, so I just let it sting.

"Whoa, whoa, whoa."

The weights suddenly lift from above me and Max deposits them back in the cradle.

"What are you doing here?" He checks his watch. "Practice was over hours ago. Shouldn't you be on a hot date with April?"

"She's busy." I sit up and roughly wipe my face with a towel.

"Oh. Well, then… that means you have time to join us at—"

"She's been busy a lot lately," I tack on.

"It's understandable. She's making a name for herself as one of the best mechanics in town. Now, about tonight, if you're not doing anything—"

"I think I messed up."

Max releases a long-suffering sigh. "What did you do?"

I swing my legs over the bench. "I think she knows I'm keeping something from her."

Max looks interested now. "Something like what?"

"I'm leaving soon." It's supposed to be an exciting admission, but my heart drags to the ground.

Max's eyes dart all over. "I didn't tell you anything."

"No, it wasn't you." I think back to the call I had with my agent three days ago. "Derek let it slip that I'm doing a commercial for the EB Sports channel."

"But don't they only hire athletes from the league... oh?" Understanding dawns in Max's eyes.

"I don't know how to break it to April. Especially now that things between us feel strained. How am I supposed to tell my girlfriend I'm moving across the country and I'll probably only see her once or twice a month?"

"No idea. But the longer you drag it out, the worse it might be." He shrugs.

I groan and run a hand down my face.

Max encourages, "If your relationship is strong and you really believe that she's the one for you, then you'll work it out. Somehow."

"Yeah, I guess so." I stare at the sweat-droplets on the ground, deep in thought.

Max slaps me on the back and then grimaces. Wiping his hand on his shirt, he offers, "Hey, how about you think of a way to tell April at The Tipsy Tuna?"

"Great idea. I'll buy a couple burgers and drinks for April and swing by the garage to check on her. She said she was tired this week. Maybe she hasn't eaten yet."

"Er, yeah. Great idea. Let's go." Max juts a thumb at the door.

After shifting out of my sweat-soaked shirt and loose basketball shorts into a fresh T-shirt and sweatpants, I follow Max's car to The Tipsy Tuna.

I'm not surprised at all when I see the crowded parking lot.

It's the weekend and there's not that many places people can go after work.

Max waits for me at the top step.

I frown at the dark windows. "Something's weird."

"What is?" Max asks, shuffling from one foot to the next.

"I don't know. I can't put my finger on it."

"Yeah, yeah. Let's go inside." Max tries to nudge me forward.

I look up. The sky is a dark, swirling black with rain clouds looming like a volcano about to erupt. Bringing my attention back to The Tipsy Tuna, a thought strikes.

"There are so many cars here, but I don't hear any music or see any lights inside." I frown at the dark window panes. "Maybe something's going on in there." I shake my head and point back to my car. "I don't think we should go in."

"For crying out loud, let's go, McLanely." Max grabs my arm and drags me into The Tipsy Tuna.

At first, the room is entirely dark.

A second later, the lights blare on, confetti explodes around me and a host of happy faces yell, 'surprise!'

I look over at Max in shock and there's a silly grin on his face as he points to the sign above the bar.

It says 'Congratulations Chance'.

"Congratulations for what?" I ask Max.

"For getting your suspension lifted," Derek says, stepping out of the crowd with a document in hand. "You did it, Chance. You made it back where you belong."

"Whoop, whoop!"

A ruckus goes up from my teammates who are around a table, nursing beers and wide smiles. Even Gunner is there, and he lifts his beer high in salute.

"When did you do all this?" I turn in a slow circle.

"Oh, it wasn't me." Derek grins, pointing a finger. "It was her."

At that moment, April steps forward with a cake. There's a

firework candle popping cheerfully from the middle. The words 'McLanely 33' is written in blue icing.

The candle sends soft orange light all over April's face. She beams with a smile and my world is alright again.

"Is this why you were so busy lately?" I ask her incredulously.

She nods and then moves the cake closer. "Blow out the candles."

I blow and take her hand, mouthing, 'thank you'.

She scrunches her nose cutely.

Derek drags me away to snap a few photos and I make sure to call April a few snapshots later so we can take a few together.

Later that night, May finds me with a disgruntled look on her face. "Hey, Chance, why don't I see any of the pictures you and April took tonight on your social media page?"

"I don't know. My team will probably upload them later," I assure her. "If not, I'll tell my agent to fire my publicist and hire you instead."

"Really? Yes!" She pumps a fist.

I start to walk back to the bar where the rest of my teammates have taken up residence when I catch April's eye. She has her purse strung over her shoulder and she gives me a little wave.

I immediately barge over to her. "Are you leaving already?"

"Yeah." She smiles softly. "I have to open the garage early tomorrow."

I swing a look back at the guys before making my decision. "I'll drive you."

"Absolutely not. You were drinking," she reminds me.

I frown because she has a point. Normally, I'm much more conscious about that, but all I could think about was being with April.

"I'll ask around to find a driver—"

"It's alright." She steps back. "Tonight is about you and hockey and those guys understand that world way better than I do."

"I don't care." I wrap my arms around her to keep her close. "I'd rather be with you."

She inhales and leans her head against me. "Me too. But think about the Lucky Strikers. I'm not losing a boyfriend, but they're losing a teammate." She arches an eyebrow. "I'm not losing a boyfriend, am I?"

"Absolutely not. Never."

"Then it's decided. I won't stop you from enjoying your night."

"Let me at least walk you to your car," I offer.

Taking her hand, we step out of The Tipsy Tuna. It's windy and I notice April hugging herself for warmth. Shrugging out of my jacket, I swing it around her shoulders.

April protests. "You keep giving me your hoodies. Do you have any left?" She laughs softly. "May's warming up the car. I don't need this for such a short walk."

I wrap my fingers around hers. "Keep it until you get to the car."

"Okay." Despite not wanting my jacket, she burrows into it like a turtle hiding in its shell.

"Thank you. For the party."

"It was Derek's idea. I think he just wanted the pictures of you being chummy with your teammates to prove you're leaving the Lucky Strikers on good terms." She shakes her head with a wry grin. "But I was happy for the privilege. You deserve this, Chance."

I stop in the middle of the parking lot and look down at her. "I, uh," rubbing the back of my neck, I admit, "I thought you were angry with me."

"Why would I be angry?"

"To be honest, I knew this was coming a while ago. It wasn't official, but… there are some things we need to discuss. About us. About how we're going to do this. I know long distance is difficult but I'm going to do everything—"

April places both hands against my cheeks and stares at me with her sparkling green eyes. "We're going to be fine. Do you hear me, Chance? You and I? We're going to be okay."

CHAPTER
FORTY-EIGHT

APRIL

It's been two weeks, three days, and sixteen hours since Chance left.

I'm okay.

This is totally okay.

I lived my entire adult life without him. A few months ago, I barely even knew he existed. And he definitely had no clue I existed.

I can survive a long distance relationship.

Sure, I brighten every time I see someone wearing the Lucky Strikers hockey jersey, thinking Chance is back.

And maybe I do drive by the houses we saw together, imagining a life where Chance actually bought a property in Lucky Falls and stuck around.

But I'm fine with the way things are right now. We call and text as much as our schedules allow which is...

Well, it's *not* that often anymore.

But he *did* fly out to see me a few days ago. It wasn't a long visit since he was actually on a layover and had to leave a few hours later, but it was something.

I'm perfectly fine…

This is…

The wrench in my hand clanks to the ground and the noise rings louder than a gong. *What on earth?* I stare at the tool near my foot. I want to pick it up, but I can't. The more I command my hand to move, the more my body rejects the assignment.

I lift my hands slowly and look at them. My fingers are wonky, like someone stretching a picture until it becomes pixelated.

My head constricts.

This is not okay.

Not at all.

Rebel's returning a car to a client. There's no one else in the garage to call out to.

I stumble backward, my knees growing weak. And not in the 'I'm watching Chance in a tuxedo' kind of weak-at-the-knees.

The room spins like a top on a merry-go-round. I hunker over the trunk of the Corolla I was working on. The weight of my body doubles and I slouch, losing all my ability to balance.

Black spots dance before my eyes.

Out. I need to get out.

Instead of moving forward, I drop to my knees instead. Panicked and desperate, I fight to keep my eyes open despite the pull to close them. Using the car's bumper as my crutch, I lift myself up.

If I can get to my feet and get to the door, maybe I can call for help.

I push with all my might, but my head is stuffed with cotton and my limbs are over-cooked noodles. Hands slipping off the car, I feel myself dropping backwards with no cushion to dampen my fall.

Just before I hit the ground, the back of my neck snaps against something cold and sharp. My tool box. I hear the faint sound of my name over the explosion of pain in my skull. But by then, it's too late. Everything goes black.

When my eyes peel apart again, it's because the ground under me is shaking. Is it an earthquake? It's too noisy to be heaven. Though, technically, it would make sense that heaven is noisy given the multitudes of people up there.

"You'll be okay, April. You'll be okay!" The frantic voice sounds like Rebel.

I agree. I *will* be okay. I promised Chance that I would. Me not being okay would mean I'd be going against that promise.

Bright lights blur on the ceiling.

Wait, now that I think of it, why is Rebel in heaven with me?

"Carbon monoxide poisoning."

Those words sound awful and they're coming from an unknown male voice. I doubt angels would be discussing carbon monoxide poisoning.

Besides, heaven smells distinctly like antiseptic and vanilla air freshener.

"Paramedics… oxygen… procedure…"

Something is tight around my face. An oxygen mask?

They definitely don't give those out in heaven.

I want to tell everyone I'm okay, but my mouth won't open. I'm way too tired to do anything but fall back into unconsciousness.

* * *

My eyes open with a start. Where am I?

"Sh, it's okay," Chance's hushed voice reaches my ears.

He's leaning over me with a damp rag and pressing it gently against my forehead. So gently, it's like he's afraid I'll shatter to pieces if he adds any more pressure.

"Chance," I whisper with relief, reaching for his hand.

He takes my fingers in his. The warmth of his touch brings

tears to my eyes. It's been so long since we held hands. I forgot how tenderly Chance holds me.

My entire life, I've fought to be taken seriously and present myself as a tough, knowledgeable mechanic. But with Chance, I've never felt like I had to fight or force myself to be tough. I could just... be.

"Where am I?" I ask out loud. "What happened?"

"You're in bed at home. You're sick with the flu," Chance says.

I glance at the discarded tissue paper and the empty flu medicine packets on the ground. "Really?"

He nods and his dark, Prince Eric hair flops forward. "May said you don't get sick often, but when you do it's *bad*. You've been struggling to breathe for two days now."

I blink once. Then twice. The dream where I fell in the mechanic bay felt *so* real. I can't believe it was just a figment of my own, sick mind.

"Did you have a bad dream?" Chance asks as he wrings the excess water from the rag and sets it neatly against the edge of a bowl.

"You can say that."

"Was the nightmare that I wasn't there when you needed me?" he teases.

I crack a small smile. "What *are* you doing here? Don't you have that commercial this week?"

"It's later today," Chance says.

I try to shoo him away. "What are you doing here? You need to get to the airport."

Chance doesn't look flustered at all. He instead takes a cup of orange juice from the desk and offers it to me.

I push his hand away.

He insists.

I finally accept the drink. "How long until you have to leave?"

"Not sure."

His answer makes my insides twist and wrench. "Let me drive you back to the airport."

"You're not strong enough to drive. Even if you were, I'm not flying out today."

"Chance, you can't ditch your commercial. Derek was very clear. You're on probation with the team. You have to fulfill all your obligations before they announce that you're back officially."

"Skipping one commercial won't hurt me."

"Really? Because I read the contract and you'll be next to bankrupt if you don't. They were very clear about the penalization fees."

He clears his throat and mumbles, "I knew I shouldn't have shown you the contract."

"You have to go."

"Then... I should probably head out now. I'm already late as is."

Immediately, a lump forms in my throat. Despite telling him to leave, despite knowing he *has* to and it's what we agreed on, my heart screams with pain and I feel a distinct sense of loss.

Chance braces one hand on my headboard, leans over and plants a gentle kiss on my forehead.

"Feel better soon. And call me."

I nod, watching him turn.

The moment he starts to leave, my hand takes on a mind of its own and I'm suddenly shooting out my arm to grab the hem of his shirt.

Chance turns around with a startled expression.

"Don't leave," I whisper brokenly. "Please don't leave."

"I'm not going far, April. I'm just letting the doctor know you woke up."

Who said that?

That voice doesn't belong to Chance.

The fog clears from my mind and I look up in shock. Instead

of falling into heart-stopping blue eyes and a mischievous, white-toothed smile, I see Evan's weasel-like face.

"Evan?" I croak.

"I'm here, April."

I realize I'm still clutching the hem of his shirt and I throw it away like I'm touching something radioactive.

Where am I? The ceiling bears a harsh, fluorescent light. Gone are my bedroom curtains and the tissue papers on the floor. My dark comforters disappeared too. Instead, I'm in a hospital cot and wearing a loose hospital gown.

"I'll be right back." Evan nods at me and then disappears.

I lie in the silence, stewing in thought. Was what happened in the garage reality? Did I faint for no reason? And what about Chance? Did I even *have* the flu?

Harried footsteps explode in the hallway.

The door whirrs back.

Rebel shrieks. "April!"

May sighs. "Oh, thank God!"

I brace myself as Rebel and May descend on me. My best friend checks me over while my sister grabs my hand with tears in her eyes.

"I'm so glad you're up," May wails. "I was so scared."

"Ladies, please give the patient some space." A spritely, older man with wispy white hair and glasses enters the room.

Rebel and May both obey and take a tiny step back.

"W-what happened?" I ask, struggling to sit up.

To my surprise, Evan bounces over and fluffs my pillows. "You were rushed to the hospital after getting carbon monoxide poisoning. You've been unconscious for three days."

"*Three days!*" I blanch.

Evan's bottom lip trembles and then he bursts out laughing. "No, it hasn't been long, but I've always wanted to be the boyfriend of a coma patient."

I wish I had a wrench so I could smack him.

"Why is Evan here?" May says harshly.

Rebel folds her arms over her chest. "I literally left for one second. Who let you in?"

"I heard April was rushed to the hospital, so I ran over."

My brain is so confused.

I ignore everyone and focus on the doctor. "You're saying I got carbon monoxide poisoning and I've just been here. In the hospital. Unconscious?"

"That's right." The doctor nods. "Your friend called an ambulance. You were unconscious for about an hour."

"But that doesn't make any sense. We have an exhaust fan at the shop for this very reason."

He nods to Rebel. "Your friend confirmed that a bird had gotten caught in the pipe and blocked the fan. Carbon monoxide doesn't have a smell or taste or anything to warn that dangerous gas is leaking. You'd been exposed to a dangerous amount before your friend arrived. On top of that, you had a small gash from where you'd fallen against the edge of your tool box."

I reach under my head. Indeed, there's a big gauze there.

"I can't believe I was out for an hour. That's…" I blow out a breath and shake my head. "What happens now?"

"The poison is no longer in your system and your wound—thankfully—is not so severe. Everything in your scans came back alright. Even so, we'd like to keep you for observation, just in case."

"Keep her two days if you have to," May says earnestly. "I want to be *sure* she's alright."

"The nurse will be in to check your vitals, but the fact that you're up and talking is a really good sign." The doctor nods.

"When can I leave?" I ask, lifting the hand with the IV drip.

"If you rest tonight and there aren't any anomalies in the scans you take tomorrow, I foresee you being able to recover quickly."

"Thank you, Doctor," Evan says as if he's my doting boyfriend and we never broke up.

Rebel follows the doctor out. "I have a few questions about any symptoms we should look out for…"

May walks closer and offers me my phone. "I called Chance, but he wasn't picking up, so I left him a message."

"He's probably busy."

Evan pats his chest. "If you were my girl, I'd fly right over if I heard you were in the hospital. What good is a man who isn't there when you need him?"

He has a point.

I ignore that thought because the *last* person I want to take relationship advice from is my cheating ex.

"You heard the doctor, Evan. I need to rest."

"Sure, sure. I'll be here tomorrow to check on you."

"Don't bother," May tells him tautly.

After Evan leaves, May fluffs my pillows again and cranes her neck to look at my phone. "Has Chance answered yet?"

"No."

"That's so weird." A wrinkle appears between her brow. "I sent a text from my phone and yours. It said he read it. You don't think Evan's right and he's ignoring you, do you?"

"No, Chance and I are fine."

"Yeah, but why isn't he answering you back? I'm not asking for him to fly over because of this, but not even a text back when his girlfriend is in the hospital?" She firms her lips. "I'll send him another text."

"Don't bother. He'll call tomorrow. Bright and early. I'm sure of it."

But when tomorrow comes, the person who hurries to my bed side is Evan.

And I don't even get a text back from Chance.

CHAPTER
FORTY-NINE

CHANCE

It's been two weeks, four days, and two hours since I left Lucky Falls.

Returning to my old team isn't easy.

To be fair, it never was.

Competing at the highest level always comes with a cost. My teammates and I weren't close before, but they're *definitely* not pleased that I caused them to play with one less member right before the biggest game of the season.

Can't exactly blame them.

Suffice it to say, the cold welcome Gunner, Theilan, Watson and Renthrow gave when I first joined the Lucky Strikers is as warm as a Caribbean cruise in comparison.

At least Derek is keeping me busy with brand deals so I don't have to think about how much I miss my previous teammates.

That night, I finish up with a photoshoot for a famous men's haircare line and head straight off the set to get my cell phone.

"What time is it?" I ask Derek.

He checks his watch. "It's eleven pm."

I do a quick mental calculation. It's too late to call April. As much as I want to hear her voice, I hate disturbing her when she's already asleep.

"Phone?" I hold out a hand.

Derek hesitates a second before handing it over to me.

I give it a quick glance, see that there are no new messages and slip it into my pocket. "How did the pictures turn out?"

"Great." Derek slaps me on the back. "You're doing great, Chance." He reads me a list of the weekend's schedule while I wipe all the makeup off my face. "I've been testing the waters to see if the fans would object to your suspension being lifted. So far, there's been a great reception. Once you officially announce it at this weekend's press conference, you'll have a world of support. It's only up from here."

I nod distractedly.

"You need me to drop you off?" Derek offers.

I nod. "I'm going to the arena."

"You're training this late?" Derek raises an eyebrow.

"I have five AM training, so I'll be able to get a bit more sleep if I'm already there."

Derek drops me off, and I sleep until I hear my teammates filtering in for the morning.

After a laborious five AM training, I shower and catch a cab to my hotel room. Since I've been so busy with hockey and my brand deals, I haven't had time to find an apartment.

April joked that I moved from one hotel to another. And she'd be right. Despite being back in the city where I spent most of my life, I haven't felt *settled* once. It's like I'm suffering from a jet lag that won't go away.

The sunshine is bright in an uncharacteristically cloudless blue sky.

I snap a pic of the horizon and the skyscrapers standing proudly in the distance and send it to April with a text.

Morning, beautiful.

I roll the windows down and allow the wind to blow through the car. The sunshine is warm on my face.

My phone buzzes.

APRIL: *It's afternoon here.*

I stare at the text from April and something odd tugs at my gut, but I can't put my finger on it. Wishing her 'good morning' despite the time difference is a running joke between us. She usually acts amused. This time, her response feels cold and angry.

Am I overthinking it?

It's difficult to pick up someone's tone over text. Maybe April's response was meant to be taken playfully.

But why didn't she use an emoji?

The cab stops in front of the hotel and I hop out. Taking the elevator, I send her another text.

Have you eaten yet?

Hours go by and April doesn't respond. I head to my meeting with the team's nutritionist and physical therapist, swing by a taco joint for some grub and come back to the hotel later that night.

April *still* hasn't responded.

I don't know what that means. Is she busy? Did she not see the message?

Reaching for a fidget spinner to focus my thoughts, I call her. The phone rings and doesn't connect the first time. After it goes to voicemail, I debate how much of my dignity and pride I'm willing to give up for a woman.

I decide that I'd rather have April than either pride or dignity and call her phone one more time.

She answers.

I nearly collapse against the kitchen wall in relief. "April, hey. I've been trying to reach you."

"Have you?"

I frown at the note of tension in her voice. "Yeah, was it a busy day today?"

"No. I stayed home today."

"That must have driven you crazy, you work-a-holic." I shake my head. "You must not have felt well."

"Yeah... I guess."

"You need to take better care of yourself when I'm not there, Tink. I can't do everything for you," I joke.

"I know how to take care of myself, Chance. I'm not a child. You don't need to scold me."

Shocked, I pull the phone away from my ear and then set it back again. "That's not what I meant, April. Not at all."

"What did you mean then?"

"I just..." I stammer over my words because I have no idea why we're fighting right now. "Babe, let's video-chat. I don't think you're in a good mood and anything I say will be used against me."

"I don't want to video chat with you right now."

I wince. "You *are* angry."

"I'm just surprised you have so much to say given how long it took you to get in touch with me."

I try to diffuse the tension with a joke, "Aw. Are you upset because you miss me?"

There's a long pause. It's so long, that I start to feel extremely uncomfortable.

"Is this how you usually are?" April asks, her voice bare of all emotions. "Or is it just with me?"

"I don't understand the question."

April doesn't clarify. She doesn't say anything at all.

Something cold slips down the back of my neck and I go into full emergency mode. "April, if this is about me taking so long to respond to you, I was busy. It's not like it was intentional."

"I know, Chance." She sounds resigned. Exhausted.

And it scares me.

I start pacing around the granite island countertop that I never use. "There is *nothing* that I would like more than to pack up and run to you every time you call. My entire heart, my entire being is with you in Lucky Falls. I would give anything to hold you right now."

"Anything?"

"Yeah, anything."

"Anything but hockey," she says.

My entire body freezes. I grip the phone tighter. "What does that mean, April?"

"Nothing. I'm just clarifying your statement."

"That's not fair. I'm not asking you to leave your friends, your family, and your garage behind to be with me. I know how much they mean to you and you know how much hockey means to me. This is our reality."

"I can tell what reality is. And I didn't ask you to give up hockey either."

"Then what was—" I bite my tongue because my voice is rising.

The urge to get defensive and fight builds in my chest, but I tamp it down. We're both, obviously, tired and one of us has to be level-headed.

"I know this is difficult, April, but we agreed that, for the time being, we'll have to make some sacrifices. There isn't a better alternative right now."

There's silence again.

My heart climbs like a monkey to my throat. "Let me see you. Let's video chat."

I half expect her to disagree but she turns her camera on and I hold up the phone so I can see her properly.

April's sitting in her couch. The lighting isn't the greatest, but she seems extra-tired. Her hair is pulled back into a messy bun and there are dark circles under her eyes. I wasn't lying when I said I wish I could hold her. Right now, the urge is multiplying in strength.

"Are you okay?" I ask. "Did something happen?"

She looks down. "No, I've been resting since I came back from the hospital."

"Did you just say the hospital? Why were you at the hospital?"

"May sent you a bunch of texts. And I tried calling too."

"Did you? I didn't see any texts on my phone." My heart is like a puck throwing itself against my ribs repeatedly. I rush through my text messages and call logs to confirm. "I swear to you, April. I had no idea. I can show you my screen right now. I didn't get any of your messages. Were you sick? What happened?"

"It's nothing. I'm fine now."

"Then why were you in the hospital?" I yell.

She sighs heavily. "Chance, whether you knew or not, I don't think anything would have changed."

"I would have flown back to Lucky Falls. I would have made sure you were okay. There's no way I would have filmed that commercial yesterday or gone to training this morning if I'd known."

"Then that's even worse. You can't come running over every time something happens to me."

"I don't think that's the full truth, April. Isn't that why you're angry?" I point out. "Because I didn't run over?"

Her mouth tightens and she gives me a stiff look. "I didn't expect that, Chance. But yes, I did expect you to at least call and check up on me."

"I didn't know," I remind her. "If I did…" I run a hand through my hair in frustration because now I'm just repeating myself and it sounds less convincing every time.

"I think this thing… between you and I… I think might have been a little hasty," April says.

This thing? Suddenly, I can't breathe.

"A relationship is like a car. Some say the engine is the most important, but a car can't go anywhere if it doesn't have wheels, or brake pads, or a frame." She inhales deeply. "The engine gives it power to move, but it's not everything."

April licks her lips.

I clamp down on the fidget spinner.

"I know you care about me, Chance."

"I do," I say through a tightening throat.

"I care about you too but," April's voice breaks, "sometimes, you need more than that."

"No, you don't, April. Don't be like this. We'll find a way through."

"Chance, we have to consider that we might have an engine but no wheels here."

"April."

"Look at us, Chance. Like you said, I am *never* leaving Lucky Falls. And you will always be Chance McLanely, *the* hockey star. Your dreams will take you further and further away from this little town and I can't, no—I won't follow you there."

Everything inside me goes deathly still. I stare at the woman I love more than my next breath and speak the words I've never wanted to say.

"Are you breaking up with me?"

"I don't know," April says.

A little hope springs out of the rubble of my heart.

Until she adds:

"But I think we should consider if a car with no wheels is worth keeping."

CHAPTER
FIFTY

APRIL

May tiptoes into my bedroom the next morning, her eyes drowning in concern. She takes one look at me and abandons the medicine pack on the desk.

"April... your face! You look awful!"

"Thanks," I say wryly.

"I think we should go back to the hospital."

"There's no need for that. I'm okay," I croak.

"Your eyes are blood-shot. It looks like you didn't sleep a wink last night. And your face is puffy like you were crying..." She gasps. "Were you in pain and didn't tell me?"

"No." I sit up and draw my knees to my chest.

"Your face is telling me a completely different story," my sister accuses.

"I... I've been thinking about breaking up with Chance," I tell her.

May looks like she's short-circuiting. "You—what? Is this because of what Evan said?"

I look down at the comforter.

"April, you can't let Evan get into your head."

"It's not just that. Chance and I were too naïve when he was in Lucky Falls. He was so excited about returning to the league and I was so happy for him. We had all these grand ideas of what long distance dating would look like."

"This isn't your first time being apart. He's been gone before."

"Yeah, but this is different. His home base isn't Lucky Falls anymore. He's not coming home to…"

"To you?"

I chew on my bottom lip.

My sister sets a comforting hand on mine. "I'm sure he had a good reason for not answering our calls when you were in the hospital."

"Yeah," I mutter. "He said he didn't get the messages."

"That's weird, but… I mean, do you believe him?"

I nod slowly.

"So what's the problem? You guys are *good* together, April," my sister says. "This isn't enough to tear you apart, is it?"

I bob my head pitifully.

May leans forward. "Do you know how hard it is to find an upstanding guy like Chance. He takes care of and appreciates you, doesn't he?"

"He does," I whisper. "When he's here."

"Okay, but don't you think the distance is a small price to pay? And it's not like it's forever. He'll retire from hockey someday."

"And in the meantime, I just… wait?"

"I mean… do you not want to wait for him?"

"That's the thing, May." My voice trembles and I feel tears pressing in the back of my throat. "I… I don't recognize myself anymore. It's, like, I need him."

May inhales sharply.

"I've always been independent. I've always done my own thing. There has never been a time in my life where I felt discontent with being alone. But then I met Chance. He showed me what it feels like to be loved and then he left." The tear does slip down now. "And I went back to my life. I went back to the garage, my career, dad. And something felt missing. I wasn't content with just being alone anymore. I wanted someone beside me. I wanted *him*."

My sister's eyes shuffle between mine, shocked. "I've ever seen you like this."

"It's ridiculous. It's embarrassing. Even when I was dating my ex, I still loved being alone. I think that's one of the reasons Chance fell for me. He believed I could handle having only the crumbs of him."

"The crumbs? Is that what it feels like you're getting?"

"No. I mean, not exactly. Maybe this is the monoxide talking." I shake my head. "I know what I signed up for, May. I know hockey will always take him away from me. I just… it scares me that I feel so upset by that. It scares me that I want to be selfish, that I want to be greedy, that I want all of him."

The truth hits me and I double over.

"I don't want to share Chance with anyone. And I don't want to share Chance with hockey. I know that's unfair to him. It's so unfair, May. I want him to be happy." My heart twists painfully. "I want him to live his dreams so badly, and I want to be by his side through it all. But I'm not the woman that he thought I was. I've changed. Soon, that resentment for hockey is going to take over me. And that's not fair to him."

"Oh April." May wraps her arms around me and gives me a long hug.

"I'm the worst," I mumble over and over again. "I'm the worst, May."

"No, you're not. You're human. And you're in love."

I push my hair out of my face and look up at her pathetically. "What do I do now?"

"I have no idea, but I'm confident that you'll figure it out. I've seen you fix cars every other mechanic had given up on. When you hit a wall, you did your research, you thought it through, and you attacked the problem again. This will be no different. The answer might be to keep going, to give Chance an ultimatum or just to break up with him—I don't know. But whatever you decide will be the right choice."

"Thank you," I say, looking up at her with glassy eyes.

"That therapy session will cost you."

I laugh, glad that she broke the moment with a joke. "How much?"

"Let me think about it." May clears her throat and walks over to my desk. "Take your medicine. I'll warm up the soup."

I look at my sister's retreating back and feel a sense of pride. After June left and dad got sick, I took on a pseudo-motherly role with her. It wasn't easy either. Dad was forgetting things, and May was in her angsty teenager stage.

Despite all that, I think I did alright. After all, she turned out amazing.

"Evan?" May's voice shrieks from the front room. "Why are you here again?"

"May! May, put the broom down. May!" Evan shrieks.

Alarmed, I shoot out of bed and race into the living room. My ex is cowering at the door while my little sister is threatening him with a broom.

"May!" I grab the broom from her before she actually whacks him with the thing. It would be deserved, but I don't want Evan complaining to his sheriff uncle. My sister might spend an evening in jail for assault.

"I think you need a restraining order, April," May says fiercely. "This has to count as stalking."

Evan's mouth opens and shuts. "S-stalking? I'm not stalking! I brought over some food from The Tipsy Tuna."

"We don't need—"

I hold out an arm before May can advance. "I'll take it from here."

"Are you sure?"

I nod.

My sister gives Evan a dark glare and stomps back to the kitchen.

Moving gingerly, I step onto the porch and close the door behind me. Evan gestures at the flat bench where we sometimes set out our Christmas decorations.

"You should sit. You still look weak," he says awkwardly.

I wave a hand. "Why are you here, Evan?"

"You like burgers and—"

"I meant, why are you here acting all sweet?"

"I'm always this sweet, April."

"No, you weren't. Not to me. We dated each other because we both could spend hours talking about cars. But ultimately, that was where the attraction ended for you. Didn't you say I was too much like a 'buddy' and that's why you cheated?"

He hems and haws. "I didn't mean it like that, April. And why bring up the past?"

"Tell me why you're buying me food and showing up at the hospital, Evan. And don't lie to me. I can tell when you're being dishonest now."

He scrubs the back of his head, makes a disgruntled noise and then admits, "I heard you're going to sue the shop."

I blink slowly, wondering if he's pulling a really bad prank. "Me?"

"Yeah. You." He shows me a document on his phone. It's got a fancy lawyer crest at the top, and the message urges Evan to 'provide witness statements' for a 'workplace harassment incident' that occurred the day we broke up. There's a whole bunch of fancy lawyer lingo, but I get the gist.

"That wasn't me," I say, handing back the phone and feeling absolutely perplexed. "My name isn't anywhere on that document either."

"April, you don't understand." Evan shoves the phone back into his pocket. "You're stealing clients from my uncle."

I want to point out that it's not 'stealing' if the customers are coming willingly because Rebel and I do better work.

"Every time someone calls and tells him they're going to you instead, he gets angrier and angrier. For the sake of our past relationship, I've been trying to calm him down, but he's not going to hold back any longer if you sue his shop."

"Hold back from what? I'm running my business fair and square and if he thinks his loyal customers are leaving him and coming to me to get their car fixed, maybe he should look at improving his own place."

Evan grabs my hand. "My uncle isn't someone you want to play with. I understand if you want to get back at me. I really regret hurting you and I'd love nothing more than to have a second chance. But if you're doing all this to get back at me, I'm telling you now that you better stop. It's not worth starting a fight with a Kinsey."

"It's not worth starting a fight with a Brooks," I say firmly.

Evan's eyes widen. "April…"

"Goodbye, Evan. And if you ever show up in front of me like this again, I'll file a restraining order against you and give your uncle no choice but to haul your backside to jail."

CHAPTER
FIFTY-ONE

CHANCE

I USED TO THINK THE WORST THING ABOUT PLAYING PRO HOCKEY WAS the risk of concussions, which happens sometimes, even when you're wearing a helmet.

But I was wrong.

The worst thing about being a pro athlete is that I can't sit on the couch and drink away my sorrows after a break up—an almost break up. A potential breakup? Whatever it is April is upset. I'm the one who upset her, and it all hurts like crazy.

Sadly, my new coach doesn't care that my love life is in shambles.

My teammates don't care that April hasn't responded to any of my texts.

The physical therapist could care less that I don't feel like eating.

Forcing my body to move, follow the PT schedule, and focus on training is supposed to be a distraction. I throw myself one hundred percent into my routine.

But none of it helps.

Instead of being able to fall asleep, I end up staring at the ceiling, beating my head against the wall trying to understand where it all went wrong.

Why didn't I get those text messages from April?

I'm still pondering the question during lunch when my phone buzzes.

The moment I see the name on screen, I push away the food I didn't feel like eating anyway and answer eagerly. "Hello?"

"Mr. McLanely, I have an update for you," the lawyer's crisp tone fills my ears.

I straighten my shoulders. "Did you find any evidence?"

"No."

My shoulders tighten. "Crowley, we're running out of time here."

"Unfortunately, my hands are tied."

Those tied hands sure cost a fortune. I shake my head. "That's not good enough."

The lawyer sighs. "It is *extremely* difficult to find evidence without a witness statement."

"I don't want to involve April until we have something solid," I say firmly. "Dragging her back to that moment over and over again is not something I'm willing to do."

"I'm aware of your preferences, but there's a reason cases are built on victim statements. I informed you of this from the moment you hired me. If we can't find evidence, the statement is a must."

I squeeze the bridge of my nose. "Even if we submit one, the harassment and discrimination took place between April and her boss. No one else was in the room at the time. I'm no lawyer, but even I know we can't build a case on 'he-said, she-said'. It has to be more substantial than that if we're going to make this guy pay."

The lawyer remains quiet, which tells me I'm right.

I hunker over the table. My voice is low but heated. "This guy took April into his office, looked her right in the eyes, made unsolicited remarks about her appearance and then fired her. That wasn't a one-off incident. It's a habit. I *know* we can find other women to come forward if we keep searching."

"That's the other issue. This man seems very well-respected in the town. Our investigators haven't found anyone willing to say anything negative."

There's a hint of a question in there. As if I'm sending him and his team on a witch hunt after an innocent man.

I fold my fingers into fists. "Small town closets aren't any different than big city ones. Give it a shake and the skeletons will fall out."

"I'll keep working every angle, but don't get your hopes up, McLanely. Sometimes, shielding the victim and not letting them tell their story hurts more than helps in the end."

The lawyer hangs up and I massage the bridge of my nose. My temple is throbbing and I wish I could pop a Tylenol and go to sleep.

Unfortunately, I have afternoon training and a suit fitting for the conference tomorrow.

A few hours later, Derek picks me up from the rink and takes me to the fitting. My hair is still damp from the shower since training ran late and I didn't have much time to do anything with it.

Derek talks loudly on the phone beside me, "No, Sinclair. I don't want just any makeup artist. I want the world's best. Give me one of those guys who work on those K-pop idols. I want this guy's face plastered on the walls of teenaged girls. I want crazed fans lining up around the block, willing to jump into traffic for him."

I give Derek a squeamish look.

Derek waves away my concern like a common mosquito. He keeps negotiating on the phone and finally hangs up.

"That was the new PR company. I upgraded to a team that works with A-list Hollywood celebrities. Cost me an arm and a leg, but the results speak for themselves."

I give my fidget spinner a flick. "Why are you talking to Hollywood PR companies?"

"Chance, did that small town mess with your brain or your eyes?"

I scowl.

Derek doesn't seem to notice and prattles on. "You're not seeing the big picture. You're thinking too small."

"I'm thinking about hockey." *And April.* "I pay you to do the rest."

My agent hooks an arm around the back of his seat and swivels his body so he's facing me. Those eyes that only see dollar signs are beaming with excitement. He does a flick of his wrist so his Rolex catches the light. "You were all about hockey before and look where that got you?"

"I was suspended," I say flatly.

"Precisely." Derek delivers the word with a dramatic flair. "An athlete's true value isn't his stats. It's his *influence*. And you Chance McLanely have magnified *influence*."

"We've talked about this, Derek. I'd rather be known for my skill."

"It's too late for that. If I hadn't stepped in and saved your reputation, no one would have remembered your skill on the ice. You would have been known for that suspension."

I give the fidget spinner another tap, annoyed but unable to argue back when it's the truth.

"The thing is, Chance, your story is *exactly* the kind that people prefer. No one cares about a talented hockey player who exceeds at everything. But they do love an underdog. That's exactly what you are. You fell to the bottom and then rose to the top in such a spectacular fashion that the world took notice. More people know you *now* than in your best days pre-suspension."

"I wasn't happy with that suspension, Derek. And I'm not proud of having to lie to get it back."

He scoffs and faces ahead. "For someone who's not proud, I

don't see you complaining about getting exactly what you want out of it. Anyway, the league is a stepping stone, a tool in the hands of an expert artist, if you will." He taps his palm. "With *your* influence and my know-how, we'll be the Michael Jordan of the league."

"Michael Jordan?"

"I'm thinking your own skates. Your own sneakers. Your own arena."

"Derek, take a breath. Who said I wanted all that?"

"Whether you want it or not, it's coming."

I stare at my agent as he taps furiously on his phone. A thought filters through my mind. The day April got sent to the hospital, I'd been on set for a photoshoot and Derek had my phone. The device had been turned off at the time, so when April accused me of ignoring her message, I hadn't once suspected Derek.

But now…

"Do I still need to date April in this grand future of yours?" I ask cautiously.

"Of course not!" Derek rambles, still distracted by his phone. "The small-town, humble-pie thing worked for a season, but now you'd be better off with someone who matches your prestige. I'm thinking of someone more… aspirational."

"And April isn't aspirational?"

"April's too Plain Jane, Girl Next Door. She was great when you wanted sympathy. People related to her and so they related to you. But for this next stage," he keeps tapping, "it won't work. I'll get in contact with some B-list actresses who do intense humanitarian efforts. You still want to portray yourself as a good person. That's important."

As he speaks, the truth becomes clearer and clearer. The fidget spinner comes to an abrupt stop.

"Derek," I say gravely.

"Hm," he speaks without looking up.

"Did you delete April's texts the night of the photoshoot?"

Derek's eyes don't stray from his phone, but I see his jaw tightening. His grip on the cell gets much tighter.

"Why would you ask that?" he says uncertainly.

In that moment, I feel a distinct sense of sadness. For all his uncouth habits and lavish lifestyle, Derek is the one who saw something in me before anyone else did.

He scouted me in college and promised he'd get me into the league. He kept that promise and has been keeping all his promises since then, helping me go after bigger and bigger contracts and larger brand deals.

Thanks to Derek, I even got a chance to play with legends in an All-Star tournament, a pro-athlete's dream.

Too late, I'm realizing that Derek promised me we'd make history together, but he never actually promised that I'd be proud of that history.

"Derek?"

"Hm?"

"You're fired."

His eyebrows hike to the top of his forehead.

"Stop the car," I growl.

The driver rolls the car to a stop.

I pocket my fidget spinner, calmly open the door, and step into the black night.

CHAPTER
FIFTY-TWO

APRIL

Every television in town is turned to the sports channel. Lucky Falls is buzzing about Chance's press conference.

No official announcements have been made, but it's obvious to everyone—both inside and outside of the hockey world—what Chance is going to say when he gets behind that mike.

Since I've known this 'secret' for a while, all the excited chatter in The Tipsy Tuna just makes me feel sick.

"Honey, you don't look so well," Mauve comments, looking me over.

I force an unconvincing smile. "I'm probably still weak from the poisoning."

"Did you drink the soup I dropped off for you?"

"I did. It was delicious, thank you."

She sets a warm cup of tea in front of me. "Is something else going on?"

I duck my head sheepishly. "Nope. Everything is great. Really great."

"Mm-hm." She purses her lips and studies me.

Bobby's wife has always treated us like a second grandmother. I can't hide anything from her.

"Are you nervous for Chance?" She points to the television. "Today's a big day for him. A big day for both of ya'll."

"I guess so," I respond in a lackluster fashion.

"The moment he makes that announcement, his career goes turbo. It's gonna be a wild ride. You better strap in."

My smile wobbles and then putters out.

Mauve picks up on it right away and her brows knit together. "Sweetheart, what's wrong?"

I inhale shakily as my eyes dart from side to side. "I, uh, have a headache."

The lie burns my tongue. I revealed a few things to May, but I never told her that I had an actual 'we might need to break up' talk with Chance. I haven't told Rebel either. It's a secret I've kept close to my chest.

"Mm." Mauve makes another one of her noncommittal sounds. "You got some time, April?"

"I've got…" I glance at the running banner on the television screen, counting down to Chance's big press conference. "About an hour."

I plan to be far away from all televisions, radios and cell phones streaming his announcement. If I see Chance in front of me, I might start crying. Ridiculous. I turned into a cry-baby after meeting him and that's a habit I want to shake.

"Let me tell you a little story about when me and Bobby were dating."

I bring the tea to my lips, listening closely.

"My friends were the ones who told me that the boy down the street was sweet on me. Now, mind you, I wasn't paying no mind to him and had my sights set on Phineas Booker, a boy from church and my first love."

Mauve laughs and shakes her head, as if reliving a memory. "Bobby started coming to my church and hanging around me and my friends. I thought he was nice enough, but he wasn't

Phineas, you know? I had my mind set on being Phineas's wife. I did everything I could. Practically threw myself at the man." She rolls her eyes. "Finally, Phineas asked me to be his girl."

A customer walks up to the bar and Mauve moves away from me to tend to him. I nurse my tea, while trying not to look at the television countdown.

Mauve returns a few minutes later and continues, "The Phineas I thought I knew was a total fantasy. The real Phineas treated me horridly. Just wretchedly. When he cheated on me, that was the final straw and I broke up with him."

"Good for you, Mauve."

She checks my cup, sees that it's empty and pours me another. "I was crying non-stop and hurting so bad in my heart. One day, Bobby found me like that. He wiped my tears and told me that someday I'd find a good man. Someone who treasured me and treated me right."

"Did he ask you out right then?"

"Nope." Mauve laughs. "Took eight months before he asked me. Later on, Bobby said he didn't want to take advantage of my broken heart."

I nod, impressed.

"When he *did* ask me, I was smart enough to say yes." She grins. "I started dating Bobby and it was a total one-eighty from Phineas. I didn't realize men like Bobby, a *love* like Bobby's, existed. I kicked myself every day for taking so long to give that man my heart. I'd found the one and I knew he was fixin' to ask me to marry him any day now."

"Mauve!" A table waves.

I groan.

"I'll be right back, sweetheart." She winks.

I wait for what feels like an eternity. Why does everyone in The Tipsy Tuna suddenly need Mauve's attention?

When, at last, she rounds the bar again, I lunge forward. "Did he ask you to marry him?"

"Huh? Oh…" Mauve picks up a dirty glass and washes it in

the sink. "No, he didn't. Right at that point, Bobby joined the army."

I sink slowly into my seat. "I didn't know Bobby was a solider."

"Mm-hm." She bobs her head. "It hit me like a ton of bricks. One day, he was here. The next, he was gone and I didn't know if he'd come back alive or in a body bag."

Her comment resonates with me and I glance at the television screen.

Thirty minutes until the press conference.

"Funny enough, Bobby was more worried about me than about himself. So I put on a brave face and told him we'd get through it. We decided to keep dating through the war. I wrote him letters and I'd run to the mailbox every day to check if he'd written back. Most times, he had. But one day, the letters stopped coming."

I place my hand on Mauve's. "I'm sorry, Mauve. That must have been tough."

She pastes on a brave smile, but I can see her bottom lip trembling. "I thought he was dead. My heart was absolutely crushed and I couldn't even get out of bed."

"Mauve!" A customer bellows from a table.

I swerve around. "Could you give us a—"

Mauve yells over me. "Right there!" She slants me a scolding look and tuts, "April Elizabeth Brooks…"

Despite her scolding, I wait on pins and needles for Mauve to finish waiting on the table. At last, she comes back and I pounce on her.

"What happened next?"

"Why are you so excited? Bobby's with me today. You know what happens." She wipes a beer mug dry.

"Yes, but *how*," I stress.

She laughs, deepening the wrinkles around her eyes. "One day, I came home and saw a letter in my mailbox."

I heave a giant sigh of relief. "Thank goodness."

Mauve releases a belly-laugh. "Yes, I was very grateful."

"So did he come home right after that?"

"Nope. Took a lot more months until I saw him again." She gazes softly at the glass. "But this waiting period was different. This time, I wrote those letters with joy in my heart."

"Are you saying... you weren't happy before that scare?"

Mauve sets the glass on the shelf. "I never told Bobby outright, but I'd resented the fact that he joined the army. He'd always talked about doing it, but I just... I felt blindsided. How dare he make me love him so much, make him such a part of my daily life, and then just disappear?"

"Exactly." I sit up a little straighter. "It's so selfish."

"Very much so." Mauve's strong voice trembles with laughter.

I realize she's making fun of me and glance down at my tea.

"But," Mauve taps a dark finger on the bar counter, "after I stopped getting those letters, my entire perspective changed. I was the girlfriend of a soldier. There wasn't no changing that. Bobby wasn't with me, but he still made all that effort to write as much as he could. Those letters meant he was pulling through. Those letters meant he was thinking of me. Those letters meant he was coming back to me. And in the end, I'd rather have those letters and know he's alive than to not have Bobby at all."

Her words tangle in my mind. "It just... doesn't seem fair."

"Life isn't fair. We can't always get what we want when we want it. Now this isn't saying to put up with nonsense. At times, we do have to let people go if they aren't good for us. But when we find the people who..."

"Write love letters in war?" I supply.

"Yeah." Mauve laughs. Then she glances at the television and back at me with a knowing grin. "When you find your person, sometimes, you gotta let them love you from afar until they can come home."

At her words, the clouds in my heart start to clear. I look back over everything I've been through with Chance and determination wells within me.

We've fought to be together.

We've come this far.

Like Mauve said, I'd rather have his texts, calls and video chats until he can come home. And that might come with some adjustments, I'm sure… but I want this to work.

"Can you excuse me? I need to make a call," I say, slipping out of the bar stool.

Mauve just smiles knowingly.

As I'm about to dial Chance, my phone lights up with an incoming call instead.

It's the nursing home.

I put the phone to my ear, still looking at Mauve. "Hello, how can I help—"

"Miss Brooks, I'm sorry to inform you but your father…"

I explode out of my seat. "What happened to my dad?"

"He's… missing."

CHAPTER
FIFTY-THREE

APRIL

"April, baby. Take a deep breath." Mauve hurries around the bar, untying the apron at her waist.

"I need to find him. Dad... I need to find him." I stumble to the door like a drunk.

Mauve steps in front of me, blocking me with her hands on her hips. "We're gonna find your daddy. I doubt he would have wandered far, but there is no way you can get behind a wheel in this state."

"I have to go."

"Yes, you will go. Just give me a second." She wipes her hands against the sides of her pants and yells, "Earl!"

"Yeah!" A head pokes out from the kitchen window.

"Call Steph and the others. Anyone who isn't on duty right now. April's dad is missing. He's got dementia, so it's a potentially dangerous situation. The faster we can find him, the better. Text the group chat too. Tell 'em to keep an eye out."

"On it!"

Earl's head disappears.

One of the regulars, Tom—a retired pilot who offers flight trainings on his downtime—runs up to us.

"Did I hear that right, April? Your dad is missing?"

"That's right, Tom. I'm going to drive April to the nursing home."

"I'll be on standby, Mauve. If you need eyes in the sky, I can fire up the rig."

Tears fill my eyes at the offer. "Thank you."

"Thank you." Mauve dips her chin and leads me out into the sunshine.

Behind me, I hear a thunderous boom of footsteps. I look over my shoulder and spot half the patrons of The Tipsy Tuna pouring through the doors and heading for their cars.

As they pass me by, they call out encouraging words.

"We're gonna find him, April."

"Don't worry about a thing."

"It'll be alright."

My bottom lip trembles and I'm overwhelmed by gratitude. Seeing everyone rally around me and dad gives me courage.

I take a deep breath, settle my emotions and stop Mauve when she tries to slip in the driver's seat. "It's alright. I can drive there myself."

"Are you sure?" She eyes me up and down.

"Dad might wander over here."

"Earl and the rest will be here."

"Yeah, but he won't remember them like he'll remember you."

She nods slowly. "Call me if you find him."

"I will." I start the car and look out through the window. "Thank you again, Mauve."

"Go. Drive safe."

On the way to the nursing home, I call Rebel who immediately announces that she's locking up the shop and heading out to join the search.

Dad has no idea that I own a garage now and I doubt he'll show up there, so I reluctantly agree.

Next, I call Stewart Kinsey.

Although it kills me to have to ask that man for any favor, his garage is where dad spent most of his life. It wouldn't surprise me to hear that dad somehow found his way there.

"No, I haven't seen him," Kinsey says flatly. "But I'll keep an eye out."

"Thank..." The dial tone rings and I realize he hung up. "You," I finish lamely.

I guess I can't expect more than that given Kinsey thinks I'm suing him.

After a few moments of internal debate, I decide to alert May to what's going on. She's my little sister and I want to shield her from panicking, especially when she's on campus. However, if the shoe were on the other foot, I would be *furious* if dad was in danger and I wasn't informed.

"Where could he be?" May shrieks. "How could this happen? Why are we paying that crazy expensive fee and they can't take care of dad properly?"

"I have all these questions too. I'm heading to the nursing home right now. I'll get there in about..." I check my watch, "thirteen minutes."

"It'll take me an hour to get back to town." Her voice trembles.

"I didn't tell you so you could rush back."

"You can't *possibly* think I'll attend any lectures with dad missing, do you?"

"By the time you get back to town, he'll already have been found," I say as optimistically as I can.

"I wouldn't be able to concentrate anyway. I'm catching a bus now," she says resolutely.

There's no point in arguing with her.

May ends the call, and I dial all the places dad used to love.

The old cafe run by the Duncans.

Phil's Burgers.

The hockey rink.

No one has seen dad.

It's been almost thirty minutes since he wandered off and my brain keeps picturing the absolute worst.

Frantic and sick to my stomach, I call the nursing home again.

"Is dad back?" I ask in a harried voice. "Was there any update from the security guard? Did the security cameras reveal what direction he went?"

"Unfortunately, he's not back yet, but we do have everyone we could possibly spare on staff out looking for him."

My grip around the steering wheel tightens. Worry consumes me and I snap, "What about the security cameras?"

"We're still working on that, ma'am," she explains sheepishly. "Our security company had a system wide update yesterday and there were some bugs. We made an urgent request to their technicians. One arrived and is working on restoring the data now."

I can't believe this. I chew on my bottom lip. "Every second that passes by is a second my dad could walk into incoming traffic or fall down a ravine or…" My throat clogs with painful emotions. I refuse to let my mind wander down that frightening path. "I need *something*."

"We've already sent out an alert to the police with a description of what your father was wearing when he wandered out of the garden. We investigated all the landscapers at length. The one who left the back door open claimed your father had been hanging around the construction area an hour ago, so he must have left after that point."

I squeeze the bridge of my nose.

"This is unprecedented, Miss Brooks, but I assure you that we're doing everything we can to find him. We will return your father safe and sound."

"You can't promise me that," I grind out.

She goes quiet.

I know I'm taking out my anger unfairly on her and even my breathing. "I'm almost there. I want to talk to the worker who last saw my father myself."

"We can certainly arrange that, Ms. Brooks."

The indicator makes a ticking noise as I flick it and turn into the parking lot of the nursing home. Throwing open my door, I jump out and rush inside.

"This way, Miss Brooks," the receptionist says, personally escorting me to the manager's office.

On the way, my phone vibrates with more and more new texts.

MAUVE: *Your father hasn't shown up here. Any new update?*

REBEL: *I drove by the park. He's not there. I asked my embroidery group to be on the look out too.*

As I'm about to type a response, I hear the creak of a wheelchair spinning and narrowly jump out of the way before I'm mowed down by a senior citizen on a mission.

"Did I miss it?" The woman squawks.

My thoughts are totally occupied with finding my father, but something makes me stop and follow the woman's trajectory. She brings her wheelchair to rest next to the other residents in the great room.

They're flocked around a television that, like the rest of Lucky Falls, is turned to Chance's press conference. The red button on the left of the television says 'LIVE'. A ton of mikes are strapped to a podium decorated with Chance's team colors.

But the seat is empty.

There's no Chance.

"*Where is he?*" The crowd of residents murmur.

"*Why is no one saying anything?*"

"*What's going on?*"

"Miss Brooks?" The receptionist calls to me. She's several steps ahead at the mouth of the hallway. Her back is ramrod straight as she beckons to me.

I shake my head. Chance's delayed press conference is probably for dramatic effect. He would never miss such an important moment.

Hurrying along until I catch up with the receptionist, I walk into the manager's office. A man in a tattered grey cap, worn jeans and a black T-shirt shoots to his feet the moment I enter.

"Miss Brooks," the manager says solemnly from behind her desk.

"Miss Brooks, I'm so sorry." He approaches me, eyes wide. "I thought I locked the gate securely. I had no idea—oh, you probably don't want to hear this, but I'm so sorry."

I lift a hand, indicating that he should stop. "Was my dad upset the last time you saw him? Did he say anything?"

"No, he wasn't upset, but he did seem… how do I put this." The man scrubs his fingers over his hair. "Agitated, maybe? He kept saying that Chance McLanely was coming and he shouldn't be here."

"Chance? He talked about Chance?" I squeeze the bridge of my nose and turn to face the manager. "We need to tell the police to look everywhere on the route to the ice rink. Dad's been having delusions about talking to Chance for quite some time now. I should have paid more attention."

The manager gives me a confused stare. "Miss Brooks, rest assured, we did tell the police this and we have people out looking along that very route."

"Good. I'll join them." I reach for the doorknob.

"But," the manager continues firmly, "your father was not suffering any delusions about Chance McLanely."

My fingers freeze around the knob.

My back muscles stiffen.

Slowly, I turn to face the manager. "What do you mean?"

Her words and gaze remain frank. "Chance called your father frequently. They often spoke about hockey among other things. Your father's mood improved after every call." She pauses and studies my face. "Did you really not know?"

I didn't.

Not at all.

But suddenly, I have a memory of dad grumbling about how Chance would scold him if he didn't eat.

"Did Chance call recently?"

"I believe it was yesterday." She picks up a folder, slips her glasses on her nose and nods. "Yes, it was yesterday."

Yesterday.

Chance and I were fighting and our future as a couple was up in the air, but he still called to encourage my dad.

My heart picks up speed.

Without a word, I wrench the door open and take off down the hallway. Chance used to make off-hand comments about taking my dad for a drive in his Lambo and dad would threaten that all he wanted to do was get under the hood.

What if dad went looking for Chance's car?

I put the phone to my ear, ready to call Rebel and ask her to check the local car dealership, when the door of the nursing home bursts open.

My eyes trail from the dirty plastic slippers, loose pants, and soft cotton shirt to the green eyes I know so well. Relief collapses my heart and I stumble forward, gasping, "Dad."

Tears crowd my eyes and slip down my cheeks as I wrap my father in my arms. He gruffly tries to push me off, but I don't care. I hold tighter, violent sobs wracking my chest.

After a while, dad goes still and lets me cry on his shoulder.

"Thank you. Thank you for coming back safely," I cry in a hoarse voice.

Eventually, I notice that there's someone standing behind my father. I loosen my grip on dad and look at the man who escorted him here.

Surprise sends me skittering back a step.

The man has dark blue eyes, Prince Eric black hair, and he's supposed to be on TV right this minute.

Chance.

CHAPTER
FIFTY-FOUR

CHANCE

April looks quickly away, wraps an arm around her father and tries to steer him toward the hallway.

"Hey, stop pushing," he rasps. Glancing over his shoulder, he arches a wiry brow. "Chance, don't let them take me away."

"It's okay, sir."

"No, it's not. They'll lock me up again. They think I'm *senile*, son. You can't trust them."

"I do trust them." I stare at April for a long beat. "Especially this woman, sir. I trust her with my life."

April finally looks at me. Tears glisten in her eyes and wet her thick, dark lashes.

Whoa. My heart jackhammers wildly and then stops beating altogether. That look is brutally soft and vulnerable and all I want to do is wrap her in my arms.

"Thank you," she says in a quiet, broken voice.

"You're welcome."

Another nurse appears and takes April's dad a little to the side, inspecting him for injuries.

April eyes me uneasily. "What are you…" She shakes her head and then says instead, "Where did you find him?"

"There's a path outside the west gate that leads to a hidden grotto. It's close enough that he can walk without getting too tired and needing his wheelchair. He took me there when we visited him last time. He said no one knew where it was so they never bothered him."

April seems shocked. "He was on the property the entire time?"

"I checked that area first just in case, but I didn't think he'd actually be there. Did the cameras not pick it up?"

"The cameras were down and there were construction workers in the garden. One of them admitted to leaving the gate open so everyone assumed dad had gone in that direction."

I'm trying to listen, but only half of me is engaged. It takes patience not to step closer to her. To brush her hair away from her face. To hold her hand and give it a squeeze.

She looks as exhausted as I do. It grieves me to see her so torn up about her dad. Or maybe it's not just her dad. I bet there are other things on her mind.

"Miss Brooks, would you like to come with us?" Another nurse asks, gesturing to a long corridor. "The doctor is waiting."

April speaks to me without meeting my eyes. "I'll go with them."

"I'll wait for you," I assure her.

I watch as April and the nurses escort her dad away.

When they're gone, a thick and pressing silence fills my ears. I realize I'm being stared at by a large group of elderly men and women.

"Hey, aren't you supposed to be out there?" A gruff old man points to the television screen that's turned to the sports channel.

My lips quirk. "Yes."

"Then why are you *here*?" Another asks.

I contemplate how to answer that. "Because my future is here."

"What future?" An older woman croaks.

It feels like I'm being grilled by the most determined journalists in the world.

"That's a secret." I wink.

A woman waddles up to me and leans in. She smells of coffee and saltines. "Is April pregnant?"

I jerk back in shock. "No, she isn't."

The woman gives me a disbelieving look, but I'm spared from her questions when a shout goes up from the crowd.

"Someone's talking!"

"They're announcing it now!"

The sweet grandmother shuffles away from me on her walker. On the TV screen, a PR manager stands behind the mike and delivers a word salad of platitudes about the league and their hopes for the upcoming season.

I watch it with a wry grin.

Derek, Derek, Derek. I told my ex-agent I wouldn't be at the press conference and he insisted that he would wait.

'You'll change your mind about firing me. There's no way I'm cancelling the press conference.'

'I won't, Derek. You're still fired and I'm taking the first flight back to Lucky Falls.'

'You're not an idiot, Chance. You worked so hard to get back on top. Why would you give it all up for a woman?'

I guess he really believed that I wouldn't.

The PR manager refuses to answer questions after the conference ends. It's a smart move, and I follow suit, slipping out of the nursing home while the residents are occupied.

In my car, I text April and ask her to meet in the parking lot when she's finished with her dad.

Time ticks by, but I promised April I would wait and do so patiently.

Hours later, April jogs out of the nursing home's front doors. I watch the way her hair floats behind her in the evening breeze and my lips curl up in a smile. Everything about the woman makes me incredibly happy.

April climbs into my convertible and, though it's impolite, I can't stop staring. She's the only woman I know who can make a mechanic jumpsuit look stunning. The translucent glow of her skin, the thick fall of her silky brown hair, and the freckles that adorn her face is more than I can take.

I have to remind myself to breathe.

"Are you… not going to say anything?" April asks, reaching for one of my fidget spinners in the console.

She's nervous, I realize.

"How's your dad?"

The tenseness in her shoulders seeps away. "He's sleeping." There's a long pause. "The manager seems a little embarrassed about reporting him missing when he was so close by. To be honest, so am I." She folds her hands and sets them in her lap. "I had the entire town looking for dad."

"The entire town *chose* to look for him," I tell her.

She bobs her head. "I guess what matters is that he's safe. I already sent a text to the neighborhood group chat. They'll spread the word."

I nod.

"Thank you again, Chance."

"No need for that. I'm happy it ended the way it did."

April looks straight ahead. "I'm not just thanking you for today. The nurses said you checked in regularly for a long time, long before we… before you and I…"

"Got together for real?"

She smiles slightly and my world brightens.

To my surprise, April places a soft hand on top of mine. It's warm to the touch with a hint of callouses from all her years of working on cars. It's a beautiful, feminine hand and I immediately turn my palm over to capture her fingers.

"Chance," she says softly, "I'm sorry about that night."

"You don't have to apologize. I should have been there. This all started because I wasn't."

"Not necessarily." She draws in a steadying breath. "I think… I was waiting for a reason to run away from you. I let my fear take over at the first sign of trouble."

I lean forward, listening to every word.

"It's true that I've never been in a long-distance relationship and that part was a little difficult for me. It's also true that I felt like I was competing with hockey for your attention, but when I thought about it, you made every effort you could to keep in touch with me." She stops and squints. "Except for that time I was in the hospital."

"I can explain what happened."

She waves it away. "My point is… even a machine isn't perfect. Humans definitely aren't perfect, so, logically, relationships can't be either."

I frown a bit at her conclusion. As someone who aims to be the best at whatever he puts his mind to, I do want a perfect relationship. At least, as close to perfect as it can get. And I want that for April too.

"I know way more about cars than I do about love." She ducks her head sheepishly. "And as a mechanic, I warn people constantly about ignoring check engine lights or weird sounds. Still, most people *only* bring their vehicle to me after it completely breaks down. They ignore every warning sign because maintenance is expensive. It's a lot of work. Sometimes, it feels like a waste. But in every case, a car that's maintained well will outrun a car that's not."

I nod. At least this is a level of auto repair I can understand. What I don't understand is what that has to do with us.

"You, Chance," April's green eyes sparkle at me as if she can read my thoughts, "you take great care of the car."

Warmth rushes through me. I look at her, see the collision of sweetness and strength. Of beauty and intelligence. Of innocence and tenacity. And I know she's going to be the mother of my children.

"April…"

"I can't do it, Chance. I can't break up with you." Her voice is quiet but firm, like the strongest glass. "I support your dreams and I want you to live without regrets so…" She inhales deeply. "No matter how long it takes or how far you go, I'll be here. I'll wait for you."

My heart slams against my ribs.

The love I feel for April Elizabeth Brooks is bone-deep, encoded in my DNA and one hundred percent immoveable.

"Alright then." April sets the fidget spinner down and leans back like a great weight's been lifted off her.

"Alright then," I agree.

She peers at me. "Is that all you have to say?"

"Can anyone top that speech?"

A blush spreads over her face. She quickly changes the subject. "By the way, what are you doing here?"

"Here as in…?"

"In Lucky Falls. What happened to the press conference? Why didn't you announce you were back in the league today?"

"Because I'm not back in the league."

"What do you mean?"

"I made a choice."

She looks at me uneasily. "What choice?"

"I chose you."

CHAPTER
FIFTY-FIVE

APRIL

He's wrong.

Those three words topped my entire speech.

I chose you.

I can't believe he just said that.

My first thought is that Chance is joking, but no. He's way too serious and looks too intense.

My next thought is that I made a huge mistake.

Chance is about to throw his dreams, his goals, and his progress away because I had a moment of immaturity. Had I not broken down on the phone that night, had I not been so selfish, he wouldn't be talking like this.

"No, Chance."

"No?" His eyebrows fly up.

"I can't let you do that."

"April, you're not *letting* me—"

My phone buzzes.

It's May.

I updated her and Rebel on dad's state earlier. May was already on her way to the nursing home when I called. It took a ton of maneuvering, but I eventually convinced my sister to return to school. Her classes must have ended now.

"Are you with dad?" May asks, sounding breathless. "I called Rebel, but she said you weren't at the garage and the last time she drove by, you weren't home yet. Is everything okay?"

"Yeah."

"Is he still sleeping? Did the doctors say anything after his checkup?"

"Everything's fine."

"That's a relief. And what about Chance?"

"I'm with him right now," I answer, glaring at the stubborn hockey player who smiles back at me.

"Speaking of Chance, did you hear? Everyone is saying that he skipped out on his press conference because he's back in town for good."

"No, he's not."

"But there's already an article online."

"Don't listen to the gossip on the internet. Chance *is* going back to the league," I snap.

May goes quiet.

I sigh and squeeze my eyes shut. Regulating my breathing, I finish quietly. "Do you need a ride to the nursing home?"

"No, I just caught the bus. I'll be there soon."

"I'll wait for you."

I hang up with my sister and stare straight ahead. The sun is low in the sky, sending a burnt-orange halo over the treetops. The sky is so serene, but inside I'm restless.

Chance reaches for me. "Don't be angry, April."

"I'm not angry. I'm worried." I feel my eyebrows tightening. "You're an amazing hockey player, Chance. I know how much you love the sport. You faked a relationship with a stranger so you could play! Was that all for nothing?"

"Of course not," he says calmly. "That was all for *this* moment." He sticks his finger down. "So I could fall in love with you for real."

"*Don't.* Don't try to make this romantic."

"I'm not," he says frankly. "It's just a fact."

"The fact is you're being impulsive because things were rocky between us, but they're fine now. You don't have to do anything drastic."

"I've thought about it a lot, April. This isn't an impulse."

The calmer he is about it, the more unhinged I feel. "What if you look back in twenty years and regret this moment for the rest of your life?"

"I won't."

"What if you do?" I plead.

"What if I don't?" He counters.

"Everyone is going to blame me if you abandon hockey now. They'll say I ruined you right when you were at the top of your game."

"Who cares what everyone thinks? This is between you and me. And I'm not abandoning hockey. I've already talked to Max. He's thrilled to have me back with the Lucky Strikers."

"They're only in the minors. Who knows if they'll *ever* qualify for the league?"

"April…" He reaches for my other hand.

I shake my head and pull that hand to my chest. "No, *no*, Chance. You call Derek and tell him you'll reschedule the press conference."

"I fired Derek," he says nonchalantly.

My jaw drops. "You did *what?*"

"He's the reason I missed your text," Chance admits.

"What do you mean?"

"He had my phone when you called and he intentionally deleted your messages. He didn't think you were good for my image and had other plans for me that didn't involve you."

I frown severely. "That jerk."

"I couldn't continue to work with anyone who'd sabotage my relationship with you."

"How'd you find out it was him? Derek doesn't seem like a

guy who'd admit to anything," I mumble. The agent always struck me as sleazy.

"I figured it out on my own."

My eyes narrow when I think of Derek's manipulation. "Hand me your phone. In fact, forward Derek's number. I need to give him a piece of my mind."

"I think firing him was enough," Chance adds, offering his phone to me despite his advice. "Don't waste your time and energy on him."

He's right. I turn Chance's phone around and around in my palm before offering it back.

For a while, there's silence.

"Chance," I break the quiet first, "are you serious about quitting the league?"

"I am, April."

Struggling for a way to make him see my side of things, I stammer, "Imagine if you'd come to me, demanding that I give up on being a mechanic? Imagine you told me you were embarrassed by my dirty nails or my over-alls or my obsession with car repair videos?"

He seems horrified by the very thought. "I would never."

"Yes, but *imagine* it. Imagine you came to me and said I should choose my mechanic career or you?"

"This is different," Chance argues, a half-smile twitching on his lips. "I'm willing to give up hockey. I'll gladly give it up. I choose you over my career a hundred times over."

My heart pumps hard and fast. "Chance—"

"April." He frowns and I can tell that his next words will be very serious. "Years ago, when I was in high school, I got into a car accident. It was my junior year and I'd been drinking with some friends after a hockey game."

My eyes widen. I'd looked Chance up online several times and had heard nothing of this incident.

"One of us stupidly got behind the wheel and as we were driving, we hit a patch of ice on the road. My friend tried to get control of the vehicle, but the road was too slippery. We were heading straight for a steep ravine that could kill us all."

I hold my breath, feeling like I'm right there in that spinning car with him.

"For a moment, my life flashed before my eyes and I didn't like what I saw. Partying, getting caught up with girls, doing stupid dares, not having a purpose, I hated it. I decided right then and there that I'd dedicate myself to my family and to hockey. Just those two. Nothing else."

"I had no idea," I whisper.

"Underage drinking isn't something my parents could have on the news. Not at the time. So they took care of it." He shrugs. "But I remember that moment vividly." He pauses and waits for me to meet his eyes. "April, after talking with you that night on the phone, I had a similar experience."

"Our break up conversation was as violent as a car accident?"

His smile unfurls fully and I can't stare directly at it. It's like staring into the sun. Too brilliant. Too blinding.

"In the silence after you hung up, I saw my life play out like a movie," Chance says. "I saw me going all the way with hockey. I saw all the trophies, the accolades, the recognition. I saw the fame and the awards, and I didn't like what I saw." Distaste etches itself into his handsome face. "It all seemed meaningless… because you weren't there."

Emotions claw at my throat and I blink rapidly to keep them back.

I don't deserve this. I don't deserve him.

I plead one more time. "Let's work it out some other way. There has to be another way—"

"Hey, hey," he calls soothingly. "I respect your career choice. I respect your path. I one hundred percent support you in whatever future you want to have, whether it's with marriage, the garage, *our* future kids."

"*Our* kids? Really?" I sniff.

His eyes soften as he says, "All I ask is that you respect my choice too."

A mangled sob gets caught in my chest and I can't speak. Chance brackets my face with his hands. Slowly, tenderly, he plants a whisper-soft kiss on my forehead.

Tilting my face up so I'm looking at him, he breathes out, "I don't just love you, April Elizabeth Brooks. I'd sacrifice everything for you. I'd give my life for you. I *choose* you."

"I really hate…" I sniff harder this time, "how often I cry with you."

"At least you're still pretty when you cry."

I ball my fist and land a light punch against his chest. "I'll accept your decision, but please, *please* tell me if you ever want to leave and change your mind, okay?"

"I won't leave, April. And I'm not changing my mind."

"But if you ever—"

"If I ever cause you to think that I regret it, I want *you* to talk to *me*. Because whatever we face in the future, whatever challenges we'll go through, it won't be because of this moment."

A tear slips down my cheek. "You're so…"

"Charming?"

"Insane," I mumble.

Chance laughs and pulls me into his strong embrace. I hug him fiercely, wishing I could say something profound, wishing the English language had words that would accurately describe everything I'm feeling.

But all I can say is, "I love you."

And when he whispers 'I love you too', I know, without a shadow of a doubt, that he means it.

CHAPTER
FIFTY-SIX

CHANCE

May and Rebel show up at the same time to visit Mr. Brooks. I'm forced to let April go so she can escort her best friend and sister into the nursing home.

The moment the door shuts behind April and I'm left alone, my arms ache with longing.

I'm down bad for this woman.

There's no other explanation for the way everything in my life feels okay as long as April's beside me.

Since I came back to town without much of a plan, I decide to get dinner for everyone before checking into a hotel.

Phil's Burgers is my first stop.

The bell jangles cheerfully behind me when I step in. I nod to all the patrons who stop and smile at me.

"Chance! Heard you're back."

"Welcome home, son!"

"We missed you."

I wave and return all the greetings with a warm grin.

The teenager behind the counter beams when I walk up. "Hey, Chance."

"Shaina." I nod.

Shaina wipes her hands down the apron with my signature on the front. "Are you really back with the Lucky Strikers?" she asks, punching in my order.

"Yeah, I am."

She glances up with a barely suppressed smile. "Because of April?"

"Among other things."

She takes my card.

Mr. Mathews, the town plumber and a fan who's never missed a Lucky Strikers game, immediately pops up and offers his card instead. "It's on me."

"There's no need, Mr. Mathews."

"Consider it a welcome home meal," he says.

"Thank you."

"Go Strikers!" He pumps two fists and jogs out with his order.

Shaina taps away. "So you're *really, really* back?"

"I am."

"To stay? In this small town where nothing ever happens?"

"That's right."

Shaina rolls her eyes, though she doesn't stop smiling. "I guess Lucky Falls is more special than I thought."

I silently agree as I take a seat around a table to wait.

The air feels different tonight and I can't help comparing it to the day I first rolled into Phil's Burgers. This time, there are no cameras flashing behind my back. No excited whispers. No subtle pointing in my direction.

A few of the townsfolk wander by and ask me how I've been, but that's the extent of it.

Back then, when someone called my name, it was because they wanted pictures and autographs. Now, every time my name is called, it's someone who genuinely wants to know *me*.

It's startlingly refreshing.

My next stop after Phil's is The Tipsy Tuna for April's favorite drink. I'm half-hoping I'll see my teammates there and, when I recognize Gunner's truck in the parking lot, I take the stairs two at a time.

"There he is!" Theilan explodes from his seat.

"The prodigal son returns!" Watson is right behind him.

Another teammate bellows, "Chance, is it true! You're coming back?"

I grin at all the familiar faces. Renthrow isn't there, though he rarely goes out with the team and spends most of his free time with his daughter, so I'm not surprised by that.

For the next few seconds, I'm trapped in a maze of back-slaps, high-fives and one-armed hugs. When I step back, I realize Gunner isn't around the table. He's at the bar instead, accepting a bag of food from Mauve.

The moment the older woman catches my eye, she leaks a big grin.

"Welcome back, Chance," Mauve says.

Gunner walks toward me, somber as always. His eyes drill into mine. "Couldn't hack it in the big leagues?"

I laugh. When we first met, that statement would have started a brawl. Now, I slap him on the back.

"I couldn't let you take back the captain spot."

Gunner finally smiles a bit.

"Hey, Chance. Get over here and tell us what the heck happened! There are a thousand conspiracy theories online," Theilan invites, scooting down to make room.

"I can't stay long. I've got plans with April."

Groans and boos break out from my teammates and I snort at their reaction.

Gunner shakes his head. "Some things never change."

"Some things never will," I add confidently.

He takes a step back. "I'll catch you on the ice, McLanely. We'll have another discussion about that captain position."

"I'm always ready for you, Kinsey." I laugh.

After Gunner leaves, I hang out with my teammates. The guys welcome me back with open arms, and it feels like I never left.

Later, I tear myself away from the guys and drop off the food and drinks at April's.

"It's like you read my mind, Chance. Thanks so much," she says earnestly, wrapping her arms around my neck and giving me a hug.

I reluctantly let her go. "Don't stay up too late after you eat. Get some sleep. It's been a long day."

"Tell me about it." She tilts her face up with a mischievous smile. "You can still change your mind. I'll give you a thirty-day money back guarantee."

Laughing, I tap her nose twice. "What time are you heading to the garage tomorrow?"

"Why? You want to bring me breakfast too?"

"That and I want to drop you off. I need to catch up on all the mornings I missed with you."

She tilts her head, her hair falling over one shoulder. "You don't have practice?"

"Max is giving me time to sign a lease tomorrow."

"A lease, huh? You're not staying in a hotel this time?"

I loop my arms around her waist. "Don't get excited, Tink. I'm just renting a place while *our* house is being built."

"*Our* house?"

"You're the one who said we weren't going to find exactly what we wanted unless we built it. So I bought a few acres."

She pushes me away. "Chance McLanely, you better head home. You've made enough important life decisions for one day."

"It technically wasn't made in one day. I bought the property before I left for the league—"

"Good night," April says, pushing me down the stairs.

I whistle as I open my car. April's waiting on the stairs when I look over my shoulder. She gives me a wave.

I wave back.

Man, my heart is full.

As if by magic, mom calls as I'm leaving April's. It's funny how my mother always seems to know when I'm on an April-high.

"Chance, I saw all the speculations online and made a few calls. Is it true? Are you stepping away from hockey and finally joining the business?"

She sounds so excited that I almost hate to burst her bubble.

"No, mom," I say gently but firmly, "I'm still playing hockey. I'm moving to Lucky Falls permanently and sticking with the Lucky Strikers."

"What?" Mom explodes. "That backwater town? You can't be serious!"

"Lucky Falls is where April is, mom."

My mother says nothing for a few seconds.

"Are you sure about this, Chance? You've never, not once in your life, loved anything more than hockey."

She's not wrong. Hockey was my queen, my focus, my everything until I met April. Now, the number one slot in my life belongs to her.

"Final decision?" Mom asks one more time.

"It's April or nothing, mom."

She sighs heavily. "Then I suppose… I'll have to accept your choice. If you're determined to marry the girl, do it soon and give me grandbabies. Perhaps one of them will be business-minded and we can leave the estates in their name."

Rather than correcting mom for calling April 'the girl', I accept the heart behind her statement. "Thanks, mom. I love you. I'll call you later."

She hangs up and will, I'm sure, proceed to call her lawyers and immediately set up trust funds for my unborn children.

As I drive, I think of everyone's frantic responses compared to my own internal calm.

I hadn't felt nervous about firing Derek or officially withdrawing from my team. I hadn't cared about what people would say online or all the spectators who'll think I'm 'scared' to return to the league. I wasn't terrified of what mom would think of me leaving everything for April, and it didn't bother me even when April questioned my certainty.

Totally at ease, I crawl into bed that night and fall into a deep, peaceful sleep.

* * *

When I wake up the next day, there are hundreds of messages waiting to be read—mostly from journalists, a few agents who are itching to be Derek's replacement, and broken-hearted fans.

I ignore it all and get ready for the day.

April is waiting for me on her porch when I drive up. She skips down the stairs and automatically reaches for the door.

"Tink," I say in a warning voice.

She huffs out a breath, rolls her eyes, but waits for me to open her door. I do and watch as she scrambles inside.

"How'd you sleep?" I ask.

"Like a baby," she answers. "And you?"

I lean toward her. "I slept well, but I got up before dawn. I was too excited."

"About what? Finding an apartment?"

"About seeing you."

She rolls her eyes again but a pleased smile flirts with her lips.

I smirk and drive her to the garage, listening to her chat about her plans for the day and her intention to hire May as a marketing director when she graduates in a few weeks.

As I slow down in front of the garage, my eyes stray to the

vehicle parked on the curb. Someone steps out of the car and stares us down behind a pair of dark sunshades.

April stops talking.

I go stiff.

"Let me handle this," I growl, reaching for the door.

"Handle what?" April says, her firm tone making me turn to look at her.

She arches a brow.

I swallow hard. "April, there's something I haven't told you." Inhaling deeply, I admit, "I hired a lawyer before I left for the league. I want to sue Stewart Kinsey."

A frown stretches across her face. "It took you long enough to tell me."

"Wait, you knew?"

"It's a small town, Chance. Did you think you could send a bunch of suits sniffing around Lucky Falls and word wouldn't spread?"

I lean back in shock. "I... yeah, you're right. I should have thought of that."

"How could you sue someone on my behalf without even talking to me?" April folds her arms over her chest.

"I couldn't sleep knowing Stewart was living his life without consequences after hurting you."

"Yeah, but that's not your decision to make. It's mine."

"I just—"

"That was way out of line, Chance. And to make it worse, you kept it a secret from me. I thought you were going to put my name on a formal lawsuit and not actually inform me."

She's got me there. "You're right. That was a bad call. In my defense, I didn't want you to relive the trauma."

Her stare remains dark and unwavering.

I hang my head. "But I still should have told you."

Stewart sees us and takes a step toward our car.

My muscles tense and I reach for the door handle.

April stops me and points at the scowling man outside. "I got it."

I stare into her determined green eyes and though everything in me wants to protect her, I'm aware that she's right. She's got it.

"I've got *you*," I tell her. "And I'll be close by if you need back up. I'm not afraid to punch someone in the face, even if it means getting on the bad side of the Kinseys."

"Trust me. I know. I appreciate your intentions, Chance, but fist fights and secret lawsuits aren't going to fix this."

She undoes her seatbelt, reaches over the console to kiss my cheek and then steps out to meet with Stewart Kinsey.

CHAPTER
FIFTY-SEVEN

APRIL

I CAN FEEL CHANCE'S EYES BORING THROUGH THE WINDSHIELD AND into my back. He's one second away from springing out of the car and going full 'bodyguard boyfriend'.

I silently hope that he stays put.

Stewart Kinsey can't hurt me. At least, not emotionally.

Not anymore.

And if he tries to hurt me physically, well…

That's what wrenches are for.

"Mr. Kinsey," I say in a polite tone. "What an unexpected surprise."

"Let's not hide behind pleasantries, April. I've been patient with you long enough."

I arch a brow. Kinsey's tone is rubbing me the wrong way, but I refuse to be ruffled. My father taught me to keep a cool head even in the face of chaos.

'You know what hurts the most when someone's trying to get a rise out of you, April? When you don't give them the response they were looking for.'

I fold my arms over my chest, emanating calm.

Kinsey yanks his sunglasses off and sticks them on top of his head. "This talk is long overdue."

"I agree that it is." Courage snakes its way into my heart. It stems from a place deep within, a part of me that was untended for too long.

I'm ready.

Kinsey glares at me with his beady blue eyes bracketed by deep wrinkles. Those eyes look mighty old and tired, like perhaps he needs to sleep more than he needs to be making judgements on women's appearances.

"Lucky Falls is a family, April. A *family*. Families don't settle their disagreements in court and they don't muddy each other's reputations over nothing." He tacks a finger at Chance's Lamborghini. "City slickers do things a different way. They're all about backstabbing and stepping on each other to get ahead. You've let that man influence you in the wrong direction, April. This is unlike you. I'm highly disappointed and I'm here hoping that you end this madness."

I fold my arms over my chest, ignoring most of what he said and focusing on only one part.

"Who exactly is your family, Mr. Kinsey?"

His eyes widen in surprise. It's an involuntary reaction and he quickly shields his expression again.

I tap my chin. "If I remember correctly, when Evan and I broke up, you fired *me* precisely because you know who your *actual* family is."

"Are you still holding that against me? I was downsizing, April. It wasn't personal. You're a business owner now. You know how it goes."

"You're right, Mr. Kinsey. I'm a business owner now, which means I'm very aware that what you did as a boss to an employee that day was wrong. Please be prepared to face the consequences of your actions."

Now, Kinsey's face twists with bitterness. "I'm very hurt to hear you speaking this way, April. After everything I've done for you and your dad, I would think you'd be more grateful."

"Grateful?" I speak as calmly as I can because I know Mr. Kinsey will call me out as 'emotional' if there's even a hint of a tremble in my voice.

Eyes fixed and hands steady, I say, "Should I be grateful that you belittled me even though I fixed twice as many cars as the other men in the garage? Should I be grateful that you called me 'sensitive' because I spoke up when the other mechanics talked crudely about women? What about your parting 'advice' that I should 'show more skin' if I wanted a boyfriend?"

"You know I've only ever had good intentions for you, April. If you had all these issues with me, you should have spoken to me about it rather than let it build into this lawsuit nonsense."

If those were examples of Mr. Kinsey's 'good intentions', I'd hate to see what he does when he's got bad intentions.

I tilt my chin up. "I worked hard in your shop, hoping to be acknowledged for my skill and not my gender. This isn't about me being too sensitive. This is about respect. If you respected me, Mr. Kinsey, you would *not* have spoken to me the way you did in that office."

His jaw tightens and he straightens to his full height. "If that's how you feel, I guess there's no point in talking." His nostrils flare. "And to think, I came here hoping to make an offer for a joint garage. If you were a little less emotional, April, we could have worked together. Instead, I'll now be suing *you* for stealing my customers!"

There's that 'emotional' word again.

I step closer, my voice dropping to a harsh tone. "Let's be real here, Mr. Kinsey. You didn't come to see me today with an offer to join forces because you truly think so highly of me. You're scrambling for a solution because your shop has been declining ever since I left."

His eyes flash with ire. "Don't think any of your newfound

popularity will last, April. This business is hard. Very hard. All kinds of unexpected things can happen."

"Are you threatening me, Mr. Kinsey?"

"It's merely advice from someone who's been running an auto shop longer. This business can get very dirty. That's why most women steer clear of it."

I lift up my calloused hands. "As you can see, I'm not afraid of a little dirt nor am I afraid of you. But since you had the audacity to threaten me on my own property, I'll make a promise of my own." I step closer, my eyes blazing. "I will continue to repair every car that rolls into my shop, expand my garage and make a name for this place until no one remembers that your garage exists. And one day, you won't be scared that I'll take customers away because there will be no... customers... left."

Mr. Kinsey moves threateningly toward me. At once, a car door slams shut and we both look to the left where Chance is standing with his hands folded, his brawny arms tight against his T-shirt.

Mr. Kinsey rethinks whatever he was going to do or say. Instead, he huffs back to his car, slams the door and speeds out of the parking lot.

Chance jogs toward me. "Are you okay? That looked like it was getting heated."

I smile and the knots in my stomach loosen for good. "Chance?"

"Yes, Tink."

"You and I aren't finished with our earlier conversation. We're going revisit why you sued people on my behalf without even telling me. And I also want to know what your lawyers found on Stewart."

He nods slowly. "Yes, I guess... that's fair."

"I also need to talk to Rebel about putting up some security cameras just in case."

"I'll have it done by tomorrow," Chance says, tapping something on his phone.

"But first," I slide my arms around his waist, "I want to say… 'thank you'."

"For what?"

"Reminding me how strong I am." I rise on my tiptoes. "And showing me we're even stronger together."

Chance leans down and whispers over my lips. "Always, Tink. Always."

EPILOGUE

APRIL

My boyfriend is Chance McLanely.

The Chance McLanely.

He's the one on the ice that looks like Prince Eric in hockey gear.

A roar goes up from the crowd, and I quickly pull my attention away from Chance. That noise means someone did something with the puck. I try to find the little rubber thing sliding around the ice.

Where... where... ah. Finally, I find it in the Lucky Striker's net.

"Come on!" Rebel screams, throwing her hands up and getting to her feet. "Defense!"

"Defense!" I mimic her, feeling the crowd's excitement. I've learned that screaming is an important part of the game and I do try to participate. I take my girlfriend responsibilities seriously, although I still don't understand half of what happens on the ice.

Chance, bless his big, generous... heart has tried his best to explain. He really has.

But I'm a lost cause.

"Come on, Watson!" Rebel yells and points.

"That wasn't Watson's fault." Gordie, the little girl who lent me her blanket at my first hockey game, steps on top of her chair and plants her hands on her hips. She stares Rebel down. "McLanely totally missed that pass."

"Hey, hey, hey. Let's not jump on Chance here," I say.

Gordie shakes her head as if I'm an utter disappointment and returns to watching the game intently. "Let's go, daddy!" she screams.

"Go, Chance!" I yell. "Don't let them get you!" Leaning toward my best friend, I ask over the deafening roar of the crowd, "Which one is trying to get him?"

"Don't worry your pretty little head about it," she teases, patting my cheek.

I laugh.

Rebel trains her eyes on the rink. "Oh look, the coach is taking Gunner out of the game." My best friend puts her hands around her mouth and whoops in celebration.

I arch an eyebrow at her. "You're not supposed to be cheering *along* with the rival team, you know."

"Really? Whups."

I keep staring at her face.

Rebel tosses her hair casually over her shoulder. "What?"

"What's going on between you and Gunner? Why do you hate him so much?"

"Who says I hate him?" Rebel counters.

I consider how to answer that question. I've never noticed before because we don't really hang in the Kinsey's circles but, now that I'm dating Chance, Rebel and I spend a lot more time around the team.

Every time we run into Gunner at The Tipsy Tuna, Rebel feigns some kind of illness and immediately leaves. The rare times I can convince her to stick around, she smiles and chats with everyone *except* him.

My best friend is a social butterfly, so it's pretty obvious when she's giving someone the cold shoulder.

I shake my head because now is not the time for a discussion about Gunner and Rebel.

Chance has control of the puck and I'm, at once, entranced. He moves as fast as lightning and as graceful as a gazelle. It's incredible the poise he has on the ice. As someone who still has a hate-hate relationship with ice skating, it amazes me how he handles himself on those skates... while chasing down a puck the size of a beef patty.

Speaking of the puck, where did it go again?

I whip my head back and forth until I locate the center of the action. Chance passed the puck to one of his teammates, Theilan —I think his name was.

Theilan gets into position, passes back to Chance, and circles around. I watch as Chance moves his hockey stick like I do when I'm scrambling eggs. It's so fast that I don't even realize he's making a shot until he sends the puck skittering into the net.

"Yeeeeess!" I scream. Along with most of the arena.

Chance continues to play amazingly, along with Gunner who's soon put back on the ice. The Lucky Strikers win over their opponents who, I'll admit, fought valiantly. But not as valiantly as we did.

Chance's teammates huddle together, celebrating Gunner who delivered the winning shot. Finally, Chance breaks out of the huddle and finds me in the crowd. His eyes brighten and he grins hard enough that I can see his teeth flashing beneath his helmet.

I wave happily.

Beside me, Gordie is also waving enthusiastically to her dad. It's easy to tell Renthrow out of the pack, not only because of his massive size but because of the Hello Kitty sticker on his jersey. He's also staring in our direction and waving at his daughter.

To my surprise, I notice Gunner looking over at us too.

It's hard to tell for sure but... is he staring at Rebel?

I lose that train of thought when Chance skates off the ice. I know he'll be looking for me in a short while so I give Gordie a hug goodbye, grab Rebel's hand and drag her down the bleachers.

"Are you April?" A fan asks, waving to me. "Hi!"

"Hi!" I wave back. I'm slowly getting used to people recognizing me.

A young girl wearing a hockey jersey stops me. "Can I have a picture, April?"

I stop to take the picture and the little girl gives me a big hug. "I'm going to be a mechanic too when I grow up."

"Aw! That's so sweet!" Rebel coos.

"I think that's awesome." I wink at the girl.

She grins wide.

My heart full, I follow the flow of people until I get to the lobby that splits into two hallways—one leading to the exits and the other to the admin building.

Bobby is at the door, doing crowd control. He smiles warmly at me and nods from afar. Rebel and I wave back.

"This arena is getting a little small," Rebel muses. "Max really needs to think about expanding. Especially now that Chance is a permanent part of the Lucky Strikers."

"I heard he wants to use our architect, but he'll have to wait in line. We asked for them to design our new garage first."

Rebel snorts. "And you said you weren't competitive."

I laugh.

At that moment, I feel someone's arms slide around my waist. At first, I stiffen in surprise and then look back to find Chance. He's wearing a low baseball cap, a T-shirt and jeans.

"How are you here?" I hiss, glancing around at the crowds. Chance uses a separate exit after games or he'll be bombarded.

Sometimes, he'll host meet and greets with fans, but we have a date tonight.

"I couldn't wait to see you," he says low in my ear.

"That means you didn't shower," Rebel mumbles beside me. I chuckle.

My best friend rolls her eyes, but a grin tugs at her lips. "You love birds are obnoxious. I'm dumping you on your boyfriend, April."

"No, I'll still ride with you," I insist.

"So will I," Chance says.

"You want me to watch you two being insufferably cute and in love all the way to The Tuna? No thanks." Rebel wiggles her fingers at me.

"You're still coming to The Tuna though?" I clarify.

"I'm a little tired," Rebel says, her eyes darting to the side the way she does when she's lying.

"Oh. Okay... I'll text you," I tell her.

"Night, Rebel," Chance says without taking his eyes off me.

As we walk forward in the crowd, trying to blend in, I ask Chance, "Is Gunner coming to The Tuna tonight?"

"Yeah, I think so."

I wonder if that's why Rebel isn't going. "Have you noticed a weird tension between Rebel and Gunner?"

"Not particularly." He shrugs. "But it's not like I've been paying attention."

"Huh."

A fan bumps into us and Chance lowers his baseball cap, ducking his head into my neck to remain incognito. I giggle as he presses a little kiss at my pulse point and swat at him.

"Behave, we're in public," I grumble.

He laughs.

By some miracle, we make it to the car without being mobbed by his excited fans. Chance climbs into his convertible after opening the door for me.

Immediately, he reaches for my hand and brings it to his lips. "What do you say we skip The Tuna and head straight to the library for some... reading?"

I laugh at the way he wiggles his eyebrows. "So I can get bonked in the head by another book? No thanks."

The laugh lines around Chance's mouth deepen as he smiles. I love those little lines. But to be fair, I love everything about him.

"Then where would you like to go? I don't want to share you right now," Chance says.

"Mm." I run a finger down his arm. "How about you and I…"

"Yes?" He leans in.

"Go to the garage and you can help me fix the cruiser in the bay?"

Chance releases a long-suffering sigh. "Should have known. The only thought in your head is cars."

"Not true. Forty-nine point nine percent is cars."

"And the fifty-one point one percent?" Chance asks, a teasing smile on his lips.

"It's… the new garage plans."

Chance pouts. "So I don't even get one percent?"

"Don't be mad. There's something you own one hundred percent of."

"What?" He tilts his head, studying me in the moonlight.

I point to my chest, right above my heart. "Here."

A smile blooms on his handsome face. In a beat, Chance tangles his hand in my hair and pulls me in for a long, breathless kiss.

After we come up for air, he fastens my seatbelt for me and takes my hand as we drive off into the night.

* * *

Thank you for reading *Ice Mechanic*. Rebel's book is coming in 2025! Want more of Chance and April?

Read an exclusive deleted scene that was a little too hot to make the book. To access the scene, sign up to my newsletter www.liabevans.com

Enjoy!
Love and blessings,
Lia

THE COWBOY'S ACCIDENTAL WIFE

SNEAK PEEK! THE COWBOY'S ACCIDENTAL WIFE CHAPTER ONE

NATE WIPED the sweat on his brow with his forearms. The heat pressed against him like a physical presence and he longed to take a dip in the Belize River to cool off. He glanced at the hay pile before him. Unfortunately, a swim was not in the cards today.

His cousin, Jared, approached him and offered a drink of water. "Really appreciate you coming out to our homestead to help today."

"Of course. You're trying to get your cattle business up and running. Mom and dad understand."

"I'm glad they could spare you." Jared smiled.

Nate swung the cap off the bottle and took a big swig. The water went down his throat, cool and refreshing. He turned the rest over and poured it on his head, swinging his hair around and sighing as the cool liquid slipped down his neck to his back.

He'd taken off his shirt long ago. The day was getting progressively hotter. He was probably going to crash into bed the moment he got home.

"Have you thought about getting your own land?" Jared asked, looking to be in a mood to talk. "Your wife is supposed to be coming next month, right?"

"Anissa's not my wife yet," Nate grunted, digging his fingers into the bottle.

"Semantics." Jared waved his hand. "Your engagement was arranged. Your marriage is basically a done deal anyway."

Nate slanted him a look from the corner of his eye. "If you have enough energy to talk, why don't you pick up a rake and help me out?"

Jared laughed and lifted both hands. "You don't have to tell me twice. I'll leave you alone, cousin."

As Jared walked away, Nate leaned against his shovel and let out a deep sigh. Since his betrothed wrote that she was moving to Belize, he'd had a perpetual headache. The trip would take about three weeks as Anissa was traveling all the way from his mother's home country.

Nate had nothing against the girl. They'd exchanged a few letters and she seemed smart and beautiful, but he didn't want to marry someone he didn't love.

He'd wrestled with what to do about his doubts. Nate understood exactly *why* his mother had fetched a wife from overseas. Most of the girls around his family's ranch were his cousins. The McCauleys were the first settlers in this rural area of Belize, traveling as a family a few years prior and building a nice little community.

Much to his mom's despair, Nate wasn't interested in marriage at all. The work on his parents' ranch was hard enough to deal with. But he did love his mom and wanted to make her happy.

Lately, the only thing that brought a smile to his parents' face was when they talked about his marriage to Anissa. It was one of the many reasons Nate told himself to just stuff his feelings deep inside, keep the peace and go along with it.

Besides, it would be right nice to have someone to come home to. Someone he could have good conversations with. Someone he could go on horseback rides with and laugh with. Someone with whom he could share a warm meal.

It was one thing to do so with his family and another entirely to do so with someone who 'belonged' to him.

Love wasn't that important an ingredient in marriage, was it? He could get along fine without it. And maybe, in time, love would grow.

With a shake of his head, Nate resumed shoveling when he heard a high-pitched scream rattle the air. He whirled around, his senses on high alert and adrenaline rushing through his veins.

In the distance, he saw a slender woman in a long skirt and a broad-brimmed hat staring in horror at the ground. His immediate thought was '*rattlesnake!*'.

"Ma'am, ma'am…" Nate approached her cautiously, his hand out and his eyes on the ground, searching for the dangerous creature. "You need to calm down and stay still."

The brim of the hat hid her face but, when the woman glanced up, he fell into the deepest brown eyes he'd ever seen in his life. Nate momentarily forgot about everything else as his gaze locked on her face.

She looked to be about his age or maybe younger. She had white skin, thick lashes, and a faint dash of freckles over her cheeks. He would probably have continued staring at her, slack-jawed, if she didn't let out another squeal.

"Is that *poop?*" She fluttered her slender hands and squeezed her eyes shut as if she could will the brown gunk on her foot away.

Nate's lips broke into an amused smile. "You've got to be careful around here. Jared lets his animals roam free while he's building the fences. They sometimes get close to the farmstead."

Her eyes dipped to his naked chest, and a flush spread over her face. She quickly averted her eyes. "I'm sorry. I'm just…" She straightened and gave him a polite nod, trying to look dainty. It was a hard feat though, with one leg lifted in the air like that. "My mother sent me over with pie. It's a welcome gift for our neighbor. I'm Mercy."

Nate was about to answer with his name when Mercy started wobbling. He acted on instinct and snatched her hand, keeping her upright. Electricity bolted through his veins at the touch of her hand and Nate's breathing quickened.

Mercy regained her balance, but she did not remove her hand. Staring into his eyes, she whispered, "Who are you?"

"I'm..." Nate's mind went blank and all he could think was... *smitten*.

* * *

READ THE REST OF THIS COWBOY ROMANCE NOVELLA FOR FREE BY joining my newsletter here: www.liabevans.com

ALSO BY LIA BEVANS

<u>Lucky Strikers Hockey Series</u>
Ice Mechanic
Ice Princess

<u>Cool M Ranch Series</u>
The Cowboy's Fake Wife
The Cowboy's Temporary Marriage

NOTES